The Keepsake for 1829

With an introduction by Paula R. Feldman

Literary annuals played a major role in the popular
culture of nineteenth-century Britain and America, and
The Keepsake was the most distinguished, successful, and
enduring of them all. The 1829 edition was stellar, with
contributions by William Wordsworth, Mary Shelley,
Samuel Taylor Coleridge, Walter Scott, Letitia Landon,
Felicia Hemans, and Percy Bysshe Shelley.

The whole of *The Keepsake for 1829* is reproduced
here in facsimile, so readers can experience it as it was
first published, with the text adorned by the original
illustrations. An in-depth introduction by Paula R.
Feldman contextualizes the volume for modern readers.

Paula R. Feldman holds the C. Wallace Martin Chair
in English at the University of South Carolina.
Her many books and articles focus on
Romantic-era literature and Women's Studies.

broadview encore editions

THE KEEPSAKE

FOR

1829

edited by Frederic Mansel Reynolds

and

with an introduction by Paula R. Feldman

broadview encore editions

Library and Archives Canada Cataloguing in Publication

The keepsake for 1829 / edited by Frederic Mansel Reynolds; and with an introduction by Paula R. Feldman.

(Broadview encore editions)
Includes bibliographical references.
ISBN 1-55111-585-9

1. English literature—19th century. 2. Art—Great Britain—19th century. 3. Gift books—Great Britain. I. Reynolds, Frederic Mansel, d. 1850 II. Feldman, Paula R. III. Series.

PR1143.K44 2006   820.8'007   C2006-901671-2

Broadview Press is an independent, international publishing house, incorporated in 1985. Broadview believes in shared ownership, both with its employees and with the general public; since the year 2000 Broadview shares have traded publicly on the Toronto Venture Exchange under the symbol BDP.

We welcome comments and suggestions regarding any aspect of our publications—please feel free to contact us at the addresses below or at broadview@broadviewpress.com.

North America
PO Box 1243, Peterborough, Ontario, Canada K9J 7H5
PO Box 1015, 3576 California Road, Orchard Park, NY, USA 14127
Tel: (705) 743-8990; Fax: (705) 743-8353
email: customerservice@broadviewpress.com

UK, Ireland, and continental Europe
NBN International, Estover Road, Plymouth, UK PL6 7PY
Tel: 44 (0) 1752 202300; Fax: 44 (0) 1752 202330
email: enquiries@nbninternational.com

Australia and New Zealand
UNIREPS, University of New South Wales
Sydney, NSW, Australia 2052
Tel: 61 2 9664 0999; Fax: 61 2 9664 5420
email: info.press@unsw.edu.au

www.broadviewpress.com

PRINTED IN CANADA

Contents

Introduction

> An annual is an offering at the shrine of friendship—a token of hallowed reminiscences ...
>
> Rev. S.D. Burchard[1]

Among all of the British literary annuals, *The Keepsake* was the most distinguished, successful, and longest running, appearing each autumn for twenty-nine years, from 1827 to 1856.[2] As such, it played a major but still largely undocumented role in the culture of nineteenth-century Britain. According to its first editor, William Harrison Ainsworth, its "principal object ... [was] to render the union of literary merit with all the beauty and elegance of art as complete as possible."[3] Indeed, annuals such as *The Keepsake* circulated literature to mainly middle-class readers, and, on an unprecedented scale, allowed ordinary people to own high quality reproductions of significant works of art.[4] They carried engravings of paintings by the most highly respected artists,[5] and within their pages the short story blossomed as a genre. Many of these books were best sellers.[6] Like other literary annuals, *The Keepsake* is a

---

1 "Annuals," *Laurel Wreath* (Hartford: S. Andrus & Son, 1845) 9.

2 *The Keepsake* for 1828 was published in late 1827 and so forth, so the last appearance of this annual, *The Keepsake* for 1857, likewise, appeared in 1856. Rival publishers exploited *The Keepsake* name and reputation to gain readership for such works as *The Juvenile Keepsake* (1829-30, 35), the *Biographical Keepsake* (1830), *Le Keepsake Français* (1830-1840), *The Hibernian Keepsake* (1832), *The Midsummer Keepsake* (1834), *The Christian Keepsake, and Missionary Annual* (1825-1838), *The Biblical Keepsake* (1835), *The Historical Keepsake* (1836), *Fisher's Oriental Keepsake* (1837-39), and *The Protestant Christian Keepsake* (1840), among others. Some volumes capitalized on *The Keepsake's* distinctive appearance as well as its title. For example, in 1854, T. Nelson and Sons, of London and Edinburgh, published an anthology of prose and poetry entitled *The Keepsake: A Gift for All Seasons*, bound in red cloth, to resemble its namesake, with elaborate gilt embossing on the front cover and spine and elaborate blind stamping on the back cover.

3 "Preface" to *The Keepsake* for 1828, p. vi.

4 Original art was, for the most part, inaccessible to the general populace; it hung in the private homes of the wealthy.

5 Artists included Turner, Martin, Lawrence, Opie, Gainsborough, Reynolds, and Landseer.

6 According to Altick, in 1828 approximately 100,000 copies of various British annuals sold to the public at a retail cost of over seventy thousand pounds, an enormous sum in those days (*English Common Reader*, p. 362). At the height of the craze, Alaric A. Watts' *Literary Souvenir* sold ten thousand copies in 1830 alone.

remarkable index to the taste and popular culture of the 1820s, '30s, and '40s. It documents, too, the increasing economic importance of female readers and the influence they came to exert on the subject matter and style of literature.

Crafted as beautifully as it was possible to make books in their day, annuals came bound in silk, pictorial paper boards or tooled leather, and sported leaves edged in gilt. They typically contained poetry, short fiction, and non-fiction works by important literary figures, such as Edgar Allan Poe, Walter Scott, Mary Shelley, Harriet Beecher Stowe, and Alfred, Lord Tennyson.[7] Authors found publishing in the literary annuals lucrative. Their editors, too, including women such as Sarah J. Hale and Lydia Sigourney in America and Letitia Elizabeth Landon and Caroline Norton in England, often made remarkably good livings from these volumes.

By modern standards, these books were extraordinarily expensive and, thus, were generally gifts, given on special occasions and as Christmas and New Year's presents.[8] They were, therefore, published each October or November, expressly for the holiday season. But they were also given at other times of year—for marriages, anniversaries, and birthdays—by sweethearts, siblings, parents, and close friends. They were titled to suggest value and beauty: *The Gem, The Ruby, The Pearl, The Amethyst, The Opal, The Bijou, The Amulet, The Hyacinth*. Their names sometimes reflected their social function: *The Token of Friendship, The Gift of Love, Forget Me Not*, and *Friendship's Offering*. Most had an elaborately engraved or embossed presentation page, with space for a personalized inscription from purchaser to recipient.[9]

This gift had special cultural significance. An American, the Reverend S.D. Burchard, explained in 1845: "when we find [literary annuals] on the center and parlor tables of our kindred and friends,

---

7 Other important contributors to literary annuals included Elizabeth Barrett Browning, Samuel Taylor Coleridge, Ralph Waldo Emerson, Nathaniel Hawthorne, Henry Wadsworth Longfellow, and William Wordsworth.

8 In England, literary annuals sold for between eight shillings and four pounds (or eighty shillings), depending upon the binding and the quality and size of the paper. *Leaflets of Memory*, one of the most sumptuous of the American annuals, sold in 1852 for six dollars (data from publisher's advertisements).

9 Often the book continued to be valued long after the demise of the relationship. Many presentation plates found in surviving copies have the name of the giver erased or scratched out.

we know that in every such family are the loved and valued."[10] Conversely, those who did not receive one risked embarrassment. Savvy publishers, who created and then exploited this powerful psychological strategy, were some of the earliest practitioners of niche marketing in the history of the book trade. What might otherwise have been a discretionary purchase became for some young women an essential item for the drawing room table. An anonymous "Introduction: Addressed to the Ladies," published in *The Offering* for 1834, outlined the social meaning of an annual:

> And when from the husband, the lover, or friend,
> You receive, as a proof of affection,
> The Offering, oh, say what emotions must blend
> With the gift, and cement the connection!
>
> And how sweet, as you turn o'er its pages, to think
> Such love as you there see depicted,
> In large copious draughts, you, too, freely may drink,
> Nor by judgment nor conscience restricted. (p. 8)

Thus, annuals could be physical mementos of desire or intimacy. As a wry commentator for *Blackwood's Edinburgh Magazine* observed in a review of *The Literary Souvenir* for 1825:

> Do you wish to give a small earnest graceful gift to some dearly-beloved one, then thank us for the happy hint, and with a kiss, or, if that be not yet permissible, at least with a smile of severest suavity ... lay the Literary Souvenir upon her tender lap, with a very few words, which it would be impertinent in us to particularize; only be sure 'you breathe them not far from her delicate auricle;' and with a low, a deep, and pleading tone, like the knight who won the bright and beauteous Genevieve. It is a hundred to one that you are a married man in six weeks or two months; nay, if it be a 'large paper copy,' one flesh will ye be before the new moon.[11]

Annuals may have been too melodramatic or sentimental for some tastes, but their social utility was inescapable.

---

10 "Annuals" in the *Laurel Wreath* (Hartford: S. Andrus & Son, 1845) 13.
11 (January 1825): 94.

Literary annuals became treasured objects not only for the attachment they communicated but also as status symbols. Only individuals of a certain means and, therefore, of a certain social class could afford to give them. Because they were published *annually*, having the latest one was essential to reaffirming status. So the annuals became a concrete embodiment of social aspiration.[12]

These were the *Vogue* magazines of their day, within whose pages women could unabashedly study images of stylish, successful, and alluring women, closely examining their hair, clothing, and accessories. In short stories, images, and poems, readers could indulge transgressive fantasy while exploring strategies for resolving ethical dilemmas, attracting a suitor, and becoming more self-assured.[13]

Literary annuals functioned in ways similar to the modern-day Valentine's Day card and the coffee table book. As a predecessor, they have much to teach today's readers about nineteenth-century popular culture, or as Frank Weitenkampf points out, the spirit of an age, not only in literature and art, but in typography and book binding.[14]

The aesthetic of the literary annuals derived principally from two traditions: (1) The pocketbook and almanac, originating in France and Germany, to which Leigh Hunt called attention in an 1828 essay in *The Keepsake*.[15] (2) The manuscript and commonplace book. This tradition was an enormous influence, which has never been properly recognized. In the late eighteenth and early nineteenth centuries, men and women of the leisured class kept commonplace books, or albums, which usually began as blank leaves bound in fine leather. Their owners might copy out epigrams, sayings, poems, or short quotes from favorite authors. Flowers and leaves could be pressed alongside pencil or pen and ink sketches of places visited.

---

12 For more on this subject, see Richard Altick, *English Common Reader*, p. 362; Sonia Hofkosh, "Disfiguring Economies," p. 206; and Anne Mellor, *Romanticism and Gender*, p. 111.

13 For a discussion of transgressive fantasy in *The Keepsake*, see Kathryn Ledbetter, "A Woman's Book: *The Keepsake* Literary Annual," Ph.D. dissertation, University of South Carolina, 1995.

14 "The Keepsake in Nineteenth-Century Art" in *The Illustrated Book* (Cambridge: Harvard U. Press, 1938) 148.

15 The *Forget Me Not* for 1823 was a cross between a pocket diary, English almanac, and German *Das Tachenbuch. Das Tachenbuch* was a small almanac containing poems, stories, and engravings for each month opposite blank pages. For a discussion of the development of the English literary annual, see Anne Renier, *Friendship's Offering: An Essay on the Annuals and Gift Books of the 19th Century* (London: Private Libraries Association, 1964).

Guests might contribute a watercolor drawing or might set down a favorite passage of poetry as a memento of the visit. Sometimes they offered original compositions. Many poets, undoubtedly, had a repertoire of album poems to "compose" extemporaneously on such occasions. Thus, people who never wrote for publication had their writing preserved, and, to some extent, circulated, for everyone who subsequently wrote in a book might read it, and all those in the family or social circle might have access to it. This practice explains the titles of many published poems of the era that begin "Lines Written in an Album ... ," including William Roscoe's fairly sophisticated contribution to the 1829 *Keepsake*.[16]

Elizabeth Cobbold uses an apt metaphor to describe the concept of the manuscript album or commonplace book in her poem "The Mosaic Picture," composed as the introductory piece for the album of a Perthshire friend.[17] It begins:

> Near a Cathedral Altar placed,
> Where mind alone the sketch had traced,
> The genius-gifted Artist stood,
> In inspiration's musing mood;
> Before his thoughtful eye display'd
> A tablet thick with cement laid,
> And oft he turn'd to contemplate
> Rough bits of marble, stone and slate;
> Then, as his fitful fancy pleas'd,
> The fragments eagerly he seiz'd,
> Black, red, white, green, all strangely wedded,
> And in the cement deeply bedded.

A mason, observing his unconventional project, inquires,

> 'This mass of morsels, red, blue, green,
> So oddly mix'd, what can it mean?'
> 'This work is called Mosaic, friend,
> And polishing, the scraps will blend.'

16 Page 312. See also S. T. Coleridge's "Lines written in the Album at Elbingerode, in the Hartz Forest," William Wordsworth's "Lines Written in the Album of the Countess of Lonsdale. November 5, 1834," Anna Letitia Barbauld's "Lines Written in a Young Lady's Album of Different-Coloured Paper," Charles Lamb's "Verses for an Album," and Dorothy Wordsworth's "Lines Intended for My Niece's Album."

17 Although Cobbold composed the poem in 1817, it was not published until 1825 in *Poems* (Ipswich: J. Raw, 1825) 86–88.

The puzzled mason sees only incongruous, isolated portions and, thus, cannot understand why a marble slab requiring far less labor and expense would not serve just as well. But the artist invites him to return in a month to see the completed work. When he does, he finds that by standing back, the parts become a whole:

> The time arriv'd, the Mason's eyes
> Gaz'd on the tablet with surprise,
> A lovely picture fill'd its place,
> Complete in form and colours' grace,
> Where every charm of shade and light,
> Had so combin'd to cheat the sight,
> That touch and reason scarce can prove
> These figures do not breathe and move!

When asked by the artist what he thinks now, the mason replies,

> '... I'm lost in admiration!
> Is this the motley combination,
> The mass of morsels? sure I never
> Saw any painting half so clever,
> 'Tis all creation's pow'r surprises
> When order from confusion rises.
> And with unmix'd delight I view
> What art like nature's self can do,
> Combining scraps to form a whole
> Replete with genius, taste, and soul.'

As Cobbold recognizes, in a similar way, a commonplace book is filled with disparate pieces of writing and art, which form a cohesive whole—a picture of the book's owner. This person's sensibility, life experiences, and relationships are the unifying force that make what might otherwise seem a chaotic mélange of bits and pieces appear, instead, as a coherent portrait.[18]

This concept, in slightly modified form, was also the organizing principle of the literary annual, which physically resembled the commonplace book. Annuals, too, gathered seemingly disconnected

---

18 The crazy quilt and the art of *découpage* follow similar aesthetic principles.

works of visual and verbal art in a cultural artifact that articulates the sensibility or aspirations of both giver and recipient.

The Keepsake was not the first of the literary annuals, either in Britain or on the Continent. In late 1822, Rudolph Ackermann published the earliest of the British annuals—the *Forget Me Not* for 1823. The advertisement appearing in the front of this volume proclaims, "The British Public is here presented with the first attempt to rival the numerous and elegant publications of the Continent, expressly designed to serve as tokens of remembrance, friendship, or affection, at that season of the year which ancient custom has particularly consecrated to the interchange of such memorials" (v). Fine emblematic engravings representing each of the twelve months of the year accompanied poetical "illustrations" of the months and a series of prose tales. The book also included an historical chronicle for 1822, data from the 1821 census (with population numbers for towns throughout England, Wales, and Scotland), lists of the diplomatic agents of the principal courts of Europe, and the reigning sovereigns of Europe and their genealogies. The frontispiece was an engraving of a painting by Vincenzio de San Gimignano of the Madonna and child, and engraved on the presentation plate was a wreath of flowers. Ackermann said that he hoped the book united "the agreeable with the useful," but, as the variety of content suggests, the new genre had not yet developed a fully focused identity or character.

Even so, by the following year, an English-language publishing phenomenon was fully launched. For the 1825 *Forget Me Not*, Ackermann introduced steel-plate engraving, a process that had been recently invented by an American, Jacob Perkins. This engraving process allowed mass production of images on a far greater scale than had been previously possible using copper.[19] As Eleanor

---

19 John Heath, *The Heath Family Engravers 1779-1878*, 2 vols. (Hants, England: Scolar Press, 1993) 21, 24. The method was patented in 1819. The harder metal allowed finer lines and, thus, greater detail in the engraving. In addition, considerably more impressions could be made of a single engraving before it became worn. Still, according to Ian Bain, "The printing of an engraved plate was a relatively slow and laborious business: a single man at the press could take ten minutes or more to take off a single impression from a moderately sized book illustration." ("Gift Book and Annual Illustrations: Some Notes on their Production" in Frederick W. Faxon, *Literary Annuals and Gift Books: A Bibliography 1823-1903* [Ravelston: Private Libraries Association, 1973] 23.) See also Basil Hunnisett.

Jamieson points out, "Steel engraving meant that for the first time, the finest art of the country could be reproduced at a reasonable price, and when such reproductions were diffused through the huge circulation of the annuals, they fostered in the general public an appreciation of painting never hitherto known."[20] Annuals such as *The Literary Souvenir* (1825) and *The Amulet* (1826) met with similar success. Charles Heath, son of the engraver James Heath, helped pioneer use of the steel-plate engraving process in these volumes.[21]

Soon Heath made the historic decision to launch his own annual—*The Keepsake*—and asked twenty-two-year-old William Harrison Ainsworth to be its first editor. Ainsworth told a friend, "It is to cost a guinea, and contain twenty plates; the literary matter will be first rate.... The name is execrable—Heath baptizes it *The Keepsake*, which to my thinking savours of a gift from Tunbridge Wells."[22] Heath had approached the fashionable publisher John Murray about the project, explaining, "I have commenced a work similar to the 'Forget me Not' and the 'Literary Souvenir' and I flatter myself that in the Embellishments it will surpass every Book hitherto published ... I think so splendid a work as could be brought out by our *united exertions*, and with your influence, would take the Lead in this sort of publication and we should divide annually very considerable Profit."[23] Murray, publisher of Lord Byron and of a list dominated by travel books, was not interested. Eventually, Heath organized a cooperative venture with the publishing firm of Hurst and Chance and the print-seller, Robert Jennings. William Henry McQueen produced the engravings, which could also be purchased separately.[24] The book was sold before publication through subscription, a practice abandoned after this first year but one that allowed Heath to amass sufficient capital to defray initial expenses.

---

20 *English Embossed Bindings 1825–1850* (Cambridge: Cambridge U. Press, 1972) 5.

21 He also used the process in earlier books such as an 1820 edition of Thomas Campbell's *Pleasures of Hope*.

22 That is to say, the name suggested to Ainsworth a cheap tourist souvenir. Letter dated Feb. 1827, quoted in S.M. Ellis, *William Harrison Ainsworth and His Friends*. 2 vols. (London: John Lane, 1911) 160.

23 Letter of 24 Oct 1826, quoted in Heath, p. 24.

24 According to publisher's advertisements, proofs on large India paper cost five pounds five shillings; standard India proofs without text below the engraving were four pounds four shillings. With the text still remaining, they cost three pounds three shillings. Engravings on ordinary paper of standard size cost two pounds two shillings.

Publication of the volume was delayed so far past the date it had been promised to subscribers that Heath took out an advertisement in *The London Literary Gazette* to assure purchasers that the book would, in fact, be ready for delivery by 11 December 1827—in time for holiday gift giving.[25]

The first *Keepsake* contained nineteen engravings—more than in any of the other annuals. Among them was a delicate, hand-colored presentation plate with a design by Thomas Stothard and a frontispiece after a painting by Thomas Lawrence, the most noted portraitist of the day.[26] Critics considered these engravings to be *The Keepsake*'s finest feature.[27] Heath had Frederick Westley bind the volume in bright crimson watered silk, with pale yellow endpapers and leaves edged in gilt. This was one of the earliest trade bindings in the history of British publishing and would remain *The Keepsake*'s hallmark until 1847. According to John Heath, one of Charles Heath's descendants, the choice of silk for the binding was "probably inspired by the well-publicized plight of the Spitalfields silk industry, which faced ruin from foreign competition."[28] This depressed market would have made the fabric more affordable. At the same time, the fabric may have appealed to the social consciousness or patriotism of some purchasers. Although impractically fragile as a binding material, the silk lent an air of elegance and femininity to the volume and,

---

25 See also *The London Literary Gazette* for 8 Dec. 1827, p. 784. Here Heath claims that "The great delay has been caused by the anxious care taken that not a single bad impression shall go forth to the public."

26 The vignette title page was printed in November 1827 by McQueen and engraved by Charles Heath after a painting by Henry Corbould. The publishers of the volume were listed as Hurst, Chance & Company, St. Paul's Churchyard, and Robert Jennings, Poultry, but the engravings were listed as published by Thomas Hurst & Company (St. Paul's Churchyard), Robert Jennings (2 Poultry), and William H[arrison] Ainsworth [the volume's editor] (Old Bond St). The presentation plate does not appear in all copies.

27 The engravings in an annual were often its most expensive element. For example, Alaric A. Watts said of the *Literary Souvenir* for 1829: "If the copyright and copper-plate printing be taken into account, only two of the engravings in the present volume will have cost less than a hundred guineas,—and some from one hundred and fifty to one hundred and seventy guineas each" (vii). Heath's ability to do much of the engraving work himself saved this major expense. At the same time, his reputation as an engraver enhanced sales.

28 John Heath, p. 55. Charles Heath told Robert Southey that the 1829 *Keepsake* binding would require four thousand yards of silk (*New Letters of Robert Southey*, ed. Kenneth Curry [New York: Columbia U. Press, 1965] 2:324.)

as is true of today's Valentines, scarlet was an evocative color. *The Keepsake* was expensive—thirteen shillings—and could be ordered in a larger, royal octavo India proof format for two pounds, twelve shillings and six pence.[29]

But despite the cost, Heath's formula worked, and *The Keepsake* was an immediate best-seller—said to have sold 15,000 copies.[30] As Robert Southey complained, "The Annuals are now the only books bought for presents to young ladies, in which way poems formerly had their chief vent. People ask for what is new."[31] In his introductory essay to the debut volume, "Pocket–Books and Keepsakes," Leigh Hunt[32] traces the history of *The Keepsake*'s forerunners and notes:

> We remember a series of pocket-books ... [which] contained acrostics and rebuses, household receipts for various purposes, and a list of public events. There was love, politics, and eating.... Pocket-books, now-a-days, are all for compression and minuteness. They endeavour to contain the greatest quantity of matter in the smallest compass.... Here people read the names of dukes and marquises, till they fancy coronets on their own heads.

Declining to credit the rival publisher Rudolph Ackermann by name, Hunt observes:

> It struck somebody, who was acquainted with the literary annuals of Germany, and who reflected upon this bookseller's winter flower-bed,—these pocket-books, souvenirs, and Christmas presents, all in the lump,—that he would combine the spirit of all of them, as far as labour, season, and sizeability went; and omitting the barren or blank part,

---

29 To put these prices in perspective, a middle-class family could live comfortably outside of London for £100 a year. See Paula R. Feldman, "The Poet and the Profits: Felicia Hemans and the Literary Marketplace," *Keats-Shelley Journal* 46 (1997):156 n. 12.

30 See Robert Southey's letter of 24 February 1828 to Caroline Bowles in *New Letters of Robert Southey*, 2:324.

31 8 Dec. 1828 in *The Life and Correspondence of Robert Southey*, ed. Charles Cuthbert Southey (1849-50; rpt. 6 vols. St. Clair Shores, Michigan, 1969) 5:336.

32 Anne Renier makes this attribution, p. 8.

and being entirely original, produce such a pocket-book as had not been yet seen.... Hence arose the Forget-me-not, the Literary Souvenirs, the Amulets, and the Keepsakes, which combine the original contribution of the German annual with the splendid binding of the Christmas English present."[33]

The literary contributions to the 1828 *Keepsake* were anonymous, but some authors can now be identified. Felicia Hemans is the author of "The Spirit's Mysteries." She published it under her own name the following May in *Records of Woman, With Other Poems*. Ainsworth boasted of having obtained "some lively sketches, in the best *Indicator* style, by Leigh Hunt."[34] The dedicatory stanzas, "The Ghost Laid," "The Cook and the Doctor," and "Opera Reminiscences for 1827," were written by Ainsworth himself.[35] "Sadak the Wanderer" is said to be by Percy Bysshe Shelley and would have been supplied by his widow, Mary Shelley, who was to publish much of her short fiction in *The Keepsake*.[36]

Readers evidently proved unenthusiastic about having to guess the identities of contributors; the next year, *The Keepsake* trumpeted authors' names. Heath placed an advertisement for *The Keepsake* for 1829 in *The Literary Gazette* and *The Athenaeum*, announcing,

> The extraordinary success of 'The Keepsake' of last year has induced the Proprietor, in the hope of meriting the increased patronage he anticipates, to spare no exertion nor expenditure, however immense, in the formation of his present volume; and to secure for it the assistance of so many authors of the highest eminence, that he ventures to assert, such a List of Contributors has never before been presented to the Public.[37]

33 *The Keepsake* for 1828, pp. 7-8, 11.
34 Letter of 3 Feb 1827 from Ainsworth to James Crossley, quoted in S.M. Ellis, *William Harrison Ainsworth and His Friends*, 2 vols. (London: John Lane, 1911) 1:160.
35 Ellis, 1:166-67.
36 See Davidson Cook, "Sadak the Wanderer, an Unknown Shelley Poem," *Times Literary Supplement* (16 May 1936): 424. Possibly one or more of the prose pieces is by Mary Shelley, who, in 1828, was better known as a writer than her late husband.
37 *The Literary Gazette* for 25 October 1828, p. 672 and *The Athenaeum* for 22 October 1828, p. 830.

Heath had, in fact, gone to considerable trouble and expense to recruit his authors. He and his new editor, Frederic Mansel Reynolds, toured the country in 1828 soliciting contributions. In Edinburgh, he sought out Walter Scott. Scott recorded in his journal that Heath's initial object was

> to engage me to take charge as Editor of a yearly publication call[e]d the *Keepsake*, of which the plates are beyond comparison beautiful. But the Letterpress indifferent enough. He proposed £800 a year if I would become Editor, and £400 if I would contribute from 70 to 100 pages. I declined both but told him I might give him some trifling thing or other.... Each novel of three volumes brings £4000 and I remain proprietor of the mine when the first ore is cropd out.... Now to become a stipendiary Editor of a New year gift book is not to be thought of, nor could I agree to work for any quantity of supply to such a publication ... one hundred of their close printed pages, for which they offer £400, is not nearly equal to one volume of a novel for which I get £1300 and have the reversion of the copyright. No—I may give them a trifle for nothing or sell them an article for a round price but no permanent engagement will I make.[38]

Scott eventually agreed to accept £500 for his contributions, but he stipulated that the copyright revert to him within three years. The 1829 *Keepsake* used as its lead piece his forty-four-page tale "My Aunt Margaret's Mirror," a complex and engaging story of magical vision and marital infidelity. Although his publishers had rejected the tale for *Chronicles of the Canongate*, Scott revised it before sending it to Heath. He noted in his journal, "Cadell will not like this but I cannot afford to have my goods thrown back upon my hands. The tale is a good one."[39] The reviewer for *The Souvenir* agreed:

---

38 Walter Scott, *The Journal of Sir Walter Scott*, ed. W.E.K. Anderson (Oxford: Clarendon Press, 1972) 421.
39 Ibid., p. 457.

[T]o the great good fortune of Mr. Heath and his Editor, the most illustrious of cotemporary writers, and the largest contributor to the Keepsake, has given something more than his name. Sir Walter Scott's articles, though not by any means first rate, are exceedingly good of their kind, and would be sufficient in our estimation to confer a great and lasting value upon the volume. The best of his pieces, entitled 'My Aunt Margaret's Mirror,' will be read with pleasure by all lovers of fiction; though we suspect the author during the early part of his story, intended to give it a different conclusion.[40]

Scott's three other contributions included a twenty-page, rather formulaic, ghost story with Gothic trappings, "The Tapestried Chamber, or the Lady in the Sacque;" a clever seven-page fictional account, "Death of the Laird's Jock," with an accompanying engraving by Heath, which details why verbal narrative and painting have difficulty describing the same picture, and then, in sculptural prose, does just that; and "Description of the Engraving Entitled A Scene at Abbotsford" (with the plate published opposite), which describes the context of Edward Landseer's painting.

It is unclear how much Mary Shelley received for the first appearances of two major short stories from her own pen and several important works by her late husband, Percy Bysshe Shelley, including "On Love," a short but highly sophisticated philosophical treatise written in exquisite poetic prose, and three remarkable poetic "Fragments."[41] But it was enough to keep her as a reliable contributor to *The Keepsake* for more than a decade.

In early February 1828, Heath visited Robert Southey, the poet laureate, in the Lake District and promised him fifty guineas for any poem he might offer. Southey confided to Allan Cunningham, the Scottish author and editor of another literary annual, *The Anniversary*, "Money,—money you know, makes the mare go,—and what after all is Pegasus, but a piece of horse-flesh? I sold him at that price a

---

40 Vol. II, no. 31 (Jan. 28, 1829): 241.
41 These include "Summer and Winter," with its brilliant imagery and heightened social consciousness, "The Tower of Famine," a powerful description of the prison of Ugolino, and the delightful lyric "The Aziola."

pig in a poke; a roaster would have contented him:'perhaps it might prove a porker,' I said; improvident fellow as I was not to foresee that it would grow to the size of a bacon pig before it came into his hands."[42] Southey's "Lucy and her Bird" is an inconsequential and moralistic poem that illustrates a sentimental engraving of the same title by Finden. His "Stanzas, Addressed to R.M.W. Turner, Esq. R.A. on his View of the Lago Maggiore from the Town of Arona," which accompanies an engraving of this painting, is an undistinguished but competent poetic tribute. Despite Southey's protestations, both of these works appear to have been written to order as poetic illustrations of the engravings, in the manner of many of Letitia Landon's *Drawing-room Scrapbook* poems.

Several pieces of fiction by authors little known today are, in fact, more distinguished achievements in their genre than what the poet laureate had to offer. Thomas Haynes Bayly contributed a well-told tale, "A Legend of Killarney," which praises Lady Morgan's and Maria Edgeworth's depictions of Irish brogues. Theodore Hook's "The Old Gentleman" has a contrived ending but is a good story about obsession, clairvoyance, and the appropriate limits of human knowledge. "Clorinda, or the Necklace of Pearl" by Lord Normanby is an excellent example of the best pulp fiction of the period. What Reynolds paid for these works is unknown.

We do know that William Wordsworth accepted one hundred guineas for five poems, including "The Triad," an eight-page ode-like work that had earlier been entitled "The Promise"; two lyrics: "The Wishing-Gate" and "The Country Girl," later entitled "The Gleaner"; and two sonnets. Although Wordsworth worried that the large sums the public paid for literary annuals such as *The Keepsake* detracted from the sale of individual volumes of poetry like those he produced, he "could not feel himself justified in refusing so advantageous an offer."[43] "The Wishing-Gate" is a delightful lyric about our belief in the mystical and the power of

---

42 Letter dated 24 Feb. 1828 in *The Life and Correspondence of Robert Southey* 5:322. See also his letter of the same date to Caroline Bowles in *New Letters of Robert Southey*, 2:324.

43 According to Dora Wordsworth in a letter to Maria Jane Jewsbury, another frequent contributor to annuals, quoted in *The Letters of William and Dorothy Wordsworth: The Later Years, Part I, 1821-1828*, 2nd edition, ed. Alan G. Hill (Oxford: Clarendon Press, 1978) 3:580, n. 1. Dora thought it degrading to appear in such a mass market volume, but it was an economic necessity.

hope, written in Wordsworth's most appealing style. But his longer poem, "The Triad," is not as successful. Sara Coleridge aptly remarked about this celebration of female beauty, "It is just what he came into the poetical world to condemn, and both by practice and theory to supplant; it is, to my mind, *artificial and unreal*. There is no truth in it as a whole.... The poem always strikes me as a mongrel and amphibious thing, neither poetical nor ideal."[44] "The Country Girl," while more typically Wordsworthian, is not his best work.

Samuel Taylor Coleridge, who did not drive so hard a bargain as his friend Wordsworth, got only £50 for five contributions, including four sets of epigrams and his extraordinary 109-line poem, "The Garden of Boccacio." Still, Coleridge told his friend Charles Aders that this sum was "more than all, *I* ever made by all my Publications, my week's Salary of 5£ as Writer of the Leading Articles in the Morning Post during the Peace of Amiens excepted."[45] A condition that Reynolds set as editor of *The Keepsake* was that authors could not contribute to any other annual during the year. Coleridge had already promised a poem to Alaric A. Watts for his *Literary Souvenir*, so Reynolds made an exception. This condition, however, probably explains why Felicia Hemans, whose popularity was growing steadily but who could not afford to limit her income, stopped contributing to *The Keepsake* after 1829 but continued to publish in other literary annuals. Her 1829 *Keepsake* poem, "The Broken Chain," explores the possibilities for freedom in a patriarchal society; but she, herself, evidently resisted the chains of publishing exclusivity that Reynolds demanded. Letitia Landon, author in the 1829 *Keepsake* of the metaphorically powerful and metrically adept lyric "The Altered River" as well as the less distinguished poetic accompaniment to a portrait of Georgiana, Duchess of Bedford, somehow negotiated an exemption from this policy. Her work appears not only in subsequent volumes of *The Keepsake* but in many other literary annuals published during the same years.

---

44 Letter from Sara Coleridge to Henry Reed, May 19-21, 1851 in *Transactions of the Wordsworth Society*, no. 5 (Edinburgh: Thomas and Archibald Constable, 1883), reprinted (London: William Dawson and Sons, 1966) pp. 117-18.

45 Letter of 14 August 1828 in *Collected Letters of Samuel Taylor Coleridge*, ed. Earl Leslie Griggs. 6 vols. (Oxford: Clarendon Press, 1956–1971) 6:752.

Heath had offered Thomas Moore £500 to edit the 1829 *Keepsake* before he settled on Reynolds (who was to edit *The Keepsake* for the next decade, with the exception of the 1836 issue edited by Caroline Norton). When Moore refused Heath's proposal, Heath offered £700. Once again, Moore declined. In early February 1828, Reynolds asked Moore for a contribution of one hundred lines, for which he offered to pay £100. Moore confided in a journal entry of 25 February 1828, "The fact is, it is my *name* brings these offers, & my name would suffer by accepting them."[46] In June, Reynolds repeated his offer of £100, then £500, and finally the astonishing sum of £600 for a single contribution. Moore would not budge. Still, Reynolds was undeterred. Without the author's permission, he printed "Extempore, to ——, to whose interference I chiefly owe the very liberal price given for Lalla Rookh." Moore was understandably outraged. He recorded in his journal, "Having got hold of some lines which I wrote one day after dinner (about ten years since) in Perry's Copy of Lalla Rookh, he, without saying a single word to me, clips this doggerel into his book, and announces me brazenly on the List of his Contributors. Thus, not having been able to *buy* my name, he tricks me out of it, and gets gratis what I refused six hundred pounds for."[47] The fierce competition among annual editors spawned many ethical excesses of this sort.

But payments to notable contributors were not all that lavish, given the remarkable cost of the full production. In his preface to the volume, Reynolds proudly announced that "the enormous sum of *eleven thousand guineas*" had been spent to produce the 1829 *Keepsake*, which he hoped would become "a reputed and standard work in every well-selected library."[48] The reviewer for *La Belle Assemblée* was incredulous: "Previously to this official and pompous announcement, a report was sedulously circulated ... that the sum of *two thousand pounds* had been appropriated to the literature of the volume only; and that, of the said *two thousand pounds*, Sir Walter Scott had been complimented with *five hundred* for a tale!

46 *The Journal of Thomas Moore*, ed. Wildred S. Dowden. 6 vols. (Newark: U of Delaware P, 1983) 3:1125.
47 Entry of 12 Oct. 1828 in Moore, 3:1162.
48 pp. iii–iv.

Really this is too formidable a dose for the variest gull in existence to swallow."[49] Evidence suggests, however, that these figures were fairly accurate. Heath's biographer notes, "In total, the various financial inducements handed out in the course of this extraordinary promotion during 1828 amounted to some 1600 guineas."[50] Still, the investment paid off. By the standards of the day, the volume was a best seller. The 1828 *Keepsake* had sold between twelve and fifteen thousand copies. The 1829 *Keepsake* was even more in demand, for, according to *The Bookseller*, "nearly 20,000 copies were disposed of in less than a month."[51] As is the case with many popular works, the overall quality of the 1829 *Keepsake*'s literary content is uneven. Not all of the thirty contributors were writers of the highest order, and there are some misses among those who were. But in among the pedestrian and sophomoric appear examples of some of the finest writing of the period.

Heath employed some of the finest engravers in the business and signed ten of the nineteen illustrations himself, including the frontispiece portrait of Mrs. Peel, wife of the Prime Minister, after a painting by Sir Thomas Lawrence, President of the Royal Academy. However, the work of many artisans connected to the firm went into the production of a single plate such as this one. John Heath notes that the engraving of Mrs. Peel "bears the signature of Charles Heath, but a very early proof copy is lettered in manuscript: 'Lane reduced, Goodyear etchd figure, Webb etchd fur and feathers, J.H. Watt drapery and hat, Rhodes worked up hat feathers, D. Smith background, and C. Heath flesh.'"[52] *The New Monthly Magazine* remarked that with Heath and other "distinguished" engravers having contributed their work "The plates are excellent ... carrying to the highest point of perfection the art of book plate engraving."[53] The design of the elaborate presentation plate was commissioned from Corbould. Over the years, Heath had developed close collaborative relationships with both

49 Dec. 1828, p. 252.
50 Heath, 2:51.
51 "Annuals" in *The Bookseller* for 29 Nov. 1858, p. 498.
52 Heath, p. 58.
53 Vol. 23 (Nov. 1828): 466.

Lawrence and J.M.W. Turner.[54] Other Royal Academy painters whose work appeared in the 1829 *Keepsake* included A.E. Chalon, Edwin Landseer, and Thomas Stothard. Indeed, as Charles Heath understood, the plates were the centerpiece of an annual, and twice as much money typically went to pay engravers as went to pay authors and editors. An advertisement for engravings from *The Amulet* for 1830, available for separate purchase, claimed that the engraving work alone for one of its plates, a depiction of the crucifixion, cost the publisher 180 guineas. Another entitled "the Minstrel of Chamouni" cost 145 guineas.[55]

William Wordsworth disparaged annuals as "picture-books for grown Children," and, in fact, authors were often engaged to write poetry or short stories to accompany engravings.[56] But writers sometimes found a way around this requirement. For example, Mary Shelley's "The Sisters of Albano," one of her most accomplished short stories, like the somewhat less successful "Ferdinando Eboli," features Italian scenes and characters with only a contrived connection to the accompanying engraving.

The reviewer for *Fraser's* deemed *The Keepsake* "remarkable for having the best plates and the worst contributions of any annual of them all." He expressed the scorn of many in the literary world: "Mr. Heath and his Keepsake, and the others ... we would abolish at a blow. They are undoubtedly very injurious to art, and not favourable to literature ... they *supersede* works of less pretension, but of infinitely more importance."[57] Many suspected that poets did not give the annuals their best work. When *The Souvenir* of Philadelphia reviewed the 1829 *Keepsake*, the poetry was pronounced "inferior to the prose."[58] Still, this judgment was kinder than that of *The Monthly Review* for January 1831: "in no other work of the kind,

---

54 John Heath recounts that "Turner preferred Charles Heath to be his promoter, not only because of his reputation as an engraver, but because he had access to, and the confidence of, the finest engravers in Britain to do justice to his work; as evidenced by the friendly cooperation between the two men over 27 years" (p. 47). For the first decade of *The Keepsake*'s run, Turner's work was a conspicuous presence.

55 The advertisement, with the heading "Proofs of the Amulet Illustrations," was bound in at the back of the *Amulet* for 1830.

56 *Letters of William and Dorothy Wordsworth*, 1:352.

57 Dec. 1830, pp. 544-45.

58 Vol. II, no. 31 (Jan. 28, 1829): 241.

is this mixture of bad literary taste with high excellence in art, so uniformly to be found as in the 'Keepsake.' We do not recollect, in the four or five numbers of it which have been published, a single composition, in verse or prose, that would be worth preserving."[59] But not all agreed. *The New Monthly Magazine* remarked, "We know not more agreeable presents than these annuals.... They serve as receptacles for the fugitive poetry of the best writers of the day; they encourage artists, and bring every year into view the most exquisite specimens of book-engraving ever laid before the public; they direct the attention of the young to polite literature and the arts; and though they may contribute little or nothing to the stock of our national literature, they are useful as records, from year to year, of the changes in literary taste and style which are for ever taking place amongst us."[60]

This Broadview Press reprinting of the 1829 *Keepsake* permits a twenty-first century audience to experience and to judge for itself that popular literary taste and style, which was, in its own time, so immoderately reviled and adored.

PAULA R. FELDMAN

---

59 At the time this review was written, there had been four numbers of *The Keepsake* published, including the one for 1831; *Souvenir*, p. 48.

60 Vol. 26 (Oct 1829): 478.

Bibliography

Books and Articles

Adburgham, Alison. *Silver Fork Society: Fashionable Life and Literature from 1814 to 1840.* London: Constable, 1983.

Alexander, Christine. "'That Kingdom of Doom': Charlotte Bronte, the Annuals, and the Gothic." *Nineteenth-Century Literature.* 47.4 (March 1993): 409–36.

Altick, Richard. *The English Common Reader: A Social History of the Mass Reading Public 1800–1900.* Chicago: U of Chicago P, 1957.

"The Annuals of Former Days." *The Bookseller* 1 (29 November 1858): 493–99.

Bose, A. "The Verse of the English Annuals." *Review of English Studies* 4 (1953): 38– 51.

Boyle, Andrew. *An Index to the Annuals.* Vol. I. *The Authors 1820–1850.* Worcester: Andrew Boyle Booksellers, 1967.

Coleridge, Samuel Taylor. *Collected Letters of Samuel Taylor Coleridge,* ed. Earl Leslie Griggs. 6 vols. Oxford: Clarendon Press, 1956–1971.

Cook, Davidson. "Sadak the Wanderer, an Unknown Shelley Poem." *Times Literary Supplement* (16 May 1936): 424.

Dickinson, Cindy. "Creating a World of Books, Friends, and Flowers: Gift Books and Inscriptions, 1825–60." *Winterthur Portfolio: A Journal of American Material Culture* 31.1 (Spring 1996): 53–66.

Dyson, Anthony. *Pictures to Print: The Nineteenth-Century Engraving Trade.* London: Farrand, 1984.

Ellis, S.M. *William Harrison Ainsworth and His Friends.* 2 vols. London: John Lane, 1911.

Faxon, Frederick W. *Literary Annuals and Gift Books: A Bibliography 1823–1903.* 1912. Reprint, Middlesex: Private Libraries Association, 1973.

Feldman, Paula R. "The Poet and the Profits: Felicia Hemans and the Literary Marketplace." *Keats-Shelley Journal* 46 (1997): 148–76.

———. "How Their Audiences Knew Them: Forgotten Media and the Circulation of Poetry by Women." In *Approaches to Teaching the Women Romantic Poets,* ed. Stephen Behrendt and Harriet Linkin, 32–39. New York: Modern Language Association, 1997.

Ford, John. *Ackermann 1783–1983: The Business of Art.* London: Ackermann, 1983.

Hall, Samuel Carter. *Retrospect of a Long Life: From 1815 to 1883.* New York: Appleton, 1883.

Hawkins, Ann R. "'Delicate' Books for 'Delicate' Readers: The 1830s Giftbook Market, Ackermann and Co., and the Countess of Blessington." *Kentucky Philological Review* 16 (2002): 20–26.

_____." Marguerite, Countess of Blessington, and L.E.L: Evidence of a Friendship." *ANQ: A Quarterly Journal of Short Articles, Notes, and Reviews* 16:2 (2003 Spring): 27–32.

Heath, John. *The Heath Family Engravers 1779–1878.* 3 vols. Hants, England: Scolar Press, 1993.

Hofkosh, Sonia. "Disfiguring Economies: Mary Shelley's Short Stories." In *The Other Mary Shelley: Beyond Frankenstein,* ed. Audrey Fisch, Anne Mellor, and Esther Schor, 204–19. New York: Oxford UP, 1993.

Hootman, Harry Edward. "British Literary Annuals and Gift Books, 1823–1861." Ph.D. diss., University of South Carolina, 2004.

Hunnisett, Basil. *Steel-engraved Book Illustration in England.* Boston: Godine, 1980.

Hutchison, Earl R. "Giftbooks and Literary Annuals: Mass Communication Ornaments." *Journalism Quarterly* 44 (1967): 470–74.

Jack, Ian. *English Literature 1815–1832.* Oxford: Clarendon Press, 1963.

Jamieson, Eleanor. *English Embossed Bindings 1825–1850.* Cambridge: Cambridge UP, 1972.

Jump, Harriet Devine. "'The False Prudery of Public Taste': Scandalous Women and the Annuals, 1820–1850." In *Feminist Readings of Victorian Popular Texts: Divergent Femininities,* ed. Emma Liggins and Daniel Duffy, 1–17. Aldershot, England: Ashgate, 2001.

Kirkham, E. Bruce and John W. Fink. *Indices to American Literary Annuals and Gift Books, 1825–1865.* New Haven: Research Publications, 1975.

Kutchner, Matthew Lawrence. "Flowers of Friendship: Gift Books and Polite Culture in Early Nineteenth-Century Britain." Ph.D. diss., University of Michigan, 1999.

Lachèvre, Frédéric. *Bibliographie Sommaire des Keepsakes et Autres Recueils Collectifs de la Période Romantique, 1823–1848*. Paris: L. Giraud-Badin, 1929.

Lawford, Cynthia. "Bijoux Beyond Possession: The Prima Donnas of L.E.L.'s Album Poems." In *Women's Poetry, Late Romantic to Late Victorian: Gender and Genre, 1830–1900*, ed. Isobel Armstrong, Virginia Blain, and Cora Kaplan, 102–14. Houndmills, England: Macmillan, 1999.

Ledbetter, Kathryn. "'BeGemmed and beAmuletted': Tennyson and Those 'Vapid' Gift Books." *Victorian Poetry* 34 (1996): 235–45.

———. "'The Copper and Steel Manufactory' of Charles Heath." *Victorian Review: The Journal of the Victorian Studies Association of Ontario* 28.2 (2002): 21–30.

———. "Domesticity Betrayed: The Keepsake Literary Annual." *Victorian Newsletter* 99 (Spring 2001): 16–24.

———. "Lucrative Requests: British Authors and Gift Book Editors." *Papers of the Bibliographical Society of America* 88.2 (June 1994): 207–16.

———. "'White Vellum and Gilt Edges': Imaging the Keepsake." *Studies in the Literary Imagination* 30.1 (Spring 1997): 35–47.

———. "A Woman's Book: The Keepsake Literary Annual." Ph.D. diss., University of South Carolina, 1995.

Ledbetter, Kathryn and Terence Hoagwood. "Introduction." In *The Keepsake, 1829: A Facsimile Reproduction*. Delmar, NY: Scholars' Facsimiles & Reprints, 1999: 3–15.

Linley, Margaret. "A Centre that Would Not Hold: Annuals and Cultural Democracy." In *Nineteenth-Century Media and the Construction of Identities*, ed. Laurel Brake, Bill Bell, and David Finkelstein, 57–74. Houndmills, England: Macmillan, 2000.

Lockhart, J.G. *The Memoirs of the Life of Sir Walter Scott, Bart.* 7 vols. Edinburgh: R. Cadell, 1837–38.

Lodge, Sara. "Romantic Reliquaries: Memory and Irony in the Literary Annuals." *Romanticism* 10:1 (2004): 23–40.

Manning, Peter J. "Wordsworth in *The Keepsake*, 1829." In *Literature in the Marketplace: Nineteenth-Century British Publishing and Reading Practices*, ed. John O. Jordan, Robert L. Patten, and Gillian Beer, 44–73. Cambridge: Cambridge UP, 1995.

Mellor, Anne K. *Romanticism and Gender*. New York: Routledge, 1993.

Moore, Thomas. *The Journal of Thomas Moore*, ed. Wilfred S. Dowden. 6 vols. Newark: U of Delaware P, 1983.

Paley, Morton D. "Coleridge and the Annuals." *Huntington Library Quarterly* 57.1 (Winter 1994): 1–24.

Pascoe, Judith. "Poetry as Souvenir: Mary Shelley in the Annuals." In *Mary Shelley in Her Times*, ed. Betty T. Bennett and Stuart Curran, 173–84. Baltimore: Johns Hopkins UP, 2000.

Pulham, Patricia. "'Jewels-Delights-Perfect Loves': Victorian Women Poets and the Annuals." *Victorian Women Poets: Essays and Studies*. Woodbridge, England: Brewer, 2003.

Rappoport, Jill. "Buyer Beware: The Gift Poetics of Letitia Elizabeth Landon." *Nineteenth-Century Literature* (March 2004).

Renier, Anne. *Friendship's Offering: An Essay on the Annuals and Gift Books of the Nineteenth Century*. London: Private Libraries Association, 1964.

St. Clair, William. *The Reading Nation in the Romantic Period*. Cambridge: Cambridge UP, 2004.

Scott, Walter. *The Journal of Sir Walter Scott*, ed. W.E.K. Anderson. Oxford: Clarendon Press, 1972.

Southey, Robert. *The Life and Correspondence of Robert Southey*, ed. Charles Cuthbert Southey, 6 vols. London: Longman, Brown, Green and Longmans, 1849–50; rpt. St. Clair Shores, Michigan: Scholarly Press, 1969.

———. *New Letters of Robert Southey*, ed. Kenneth Curry. New York: Columbia UP, 1965.

Stephenson, Glennis. "'For Women of Taste and Refinement': The Use and Abuse of the Drawing Room Annual." In *Letitia Landon: The Woman Behind L.E.L.* New York: Manchester UP, 1995.

Tallent-Bateman, Chas. T. "The 'Forget-Me-Not.'" *Papers of the Manchester Literary Club* 28 (1902): 78–98.

Taylor, Beverly. "Elizabeth Barrett Browning's Subversion of the Gift Book Model." *Studies in Browning and His Circle* 20 (1992): 62–69.

Thompson, Ralph. *American Literary Annuals and Gift Books 1825–1865*. New York: H.W. Wilson, 1936. [The 1966 edition is available on microfilm, indexed by E. Bruce Kirkham.]

———. "The Liberty Bell and Other Anti-Slavery Gift-Books." *New England Quarterly: A Historical Review of New England Life and Letters* 7:1 (1934 Mar): 154–68.

Warne, Vanessa K. "'Purport and Design': Print Culture and Gender Politics in Early Victorian Literary Annuals." *Dissertation Abstracts* 62.10 (April 2002): 3407.

Watts, Alaric Alfred. *Alaric Watts: A Narrative of His Life.* 2 Vols. London: R. Bentley and Son, 1884.

Weitenkampf, Frank. "The Keepsake in Nineteenth-Century Art." In *The Illustrated Book.* Cambridge: Harvard UP, 1938.

Wordsworth, William and Dorothy Wordsworth. *The Letters of William and Dorothy Wordsworth: The Later Years, Part I, 1821–1828,* 2nd edition, ed. Alan G. Hill. Oxford: Clarendon Press, 1978.

Electronic Resources

Barnhill, George B. "Literary Annuals." American Antiquarian Society. <http://www.americanantiquarian.org/annuals.htm> (accessed 25 October 2005).

Dibert-Himes, Glenn. "Early Nineteenth-Century British Gift Books and Annuals." <http://www.shu.ac.uk/annuals/> (accessed 8 October 2005).

"Gift Books and Annuals." Harris Collection, Brown University Library. <http://www.brown.edu/Facilities/University_Library/collections/harris/Harris.GiftB.html> (accessed 8 October 2005).

"Gift Books and Annuals." American Women/American Memory. The Library of Congress. <http://memory.loc.gov/ammem/awhhtml/awgc1/gift.html> (accessed 25 October 2005).

Harris, Katherine D. "Forget Me Not: A Hypertextual Archive." <http://www.orgs.muohio.edu/anthologies/FMN/> (accessed 8 October 2005).

Hawkins, Ann R. "'Formed with Curious Skill': Blessington's Negotiation of the 'Poetess' in *Flowers of Loveliness.*" Romanticism on the Net 29–30 (Feb–May 2003), ed. Laura Mandell. <http://www.erudit.org/revue/ron/2003/v/n29/007721ar.html> (accessed 8 October 2005).

Hoagwood, Terence, Kathryn Ledbetter, and Martin M. Jacobsen. "L.E.L.'s 'Verses' and The Keepsake for 1829." <http://www.rc.umd.edu/editions/lel> (accessed 25 October 2005).

Hootman, Harry E. "British Annuals and Giftbooks: a comprehensive index to the literary and pictorial contents of 283 British annuals." <http://www.britannuals.com> (accessed 25 October 2005).

———. "British Literary Annuals and Gift Books." <http://www.geocities.com/britannualsinfo> (accessed 25 October 2005).

"Literary Annuals." Special Collections and Archive, University of Liverpool. 3 April 2004. <http://sca.lib.liv.ac.uk/collections/colldescs/litann.html> (accessed 8 October 2005).

Mandell, Laura. "The Bijou; or Annual of Literature and the Arts 1828." London: William Pickering, 1828. <http://www.orgs.muohio.edu/anthologies/bijou/> (accessed 25 October 2005).

———. "Hemans and the Gift-Book Aesthetic." *Cardiff Corvey: Reading the Romantic Text* 6 (June 2001). <http://www.cf.ac.uk/encap/corvey/articles/cc06_n01.html> (accessed 8 October 2005).

"Nineteenth-Century British & American Literary Annuals." Rare Books and Special Collections. University of South Carolina, Columbia. <http://www.sc.edu/library/spcoll/britlit/litann.html> (accessed 8 October 2005).

Tallent-Bateman, Chas. T. "The 'Forget-Me-Not.'" *Manchester Quarterly* 21 (1902). Electronic edition by Glenn Dibert-Himes. <http://www.shu.ac.uk/annuals/intro/Bateman.html> (accessed 25 October 2005).

Wertz-Orbaugh, Tonya. "19th Century Literary Annuals: A Brief History." <http://tonyawertzorbaugh.homestead.com> (accessed 8 October 2005).

A tribute of parting affection from James Brown to his sister Anne on her wedding day. Feb 10th 1829.

H. Corbould.

C. Heath.

Painted by Sir Thos Lawrence, P.R.A.   Engraved by Charles Heath.

MRS PEEL.

Printed by E.Brain.

Publd for the Proprietor by Hurst, Chance & Co. St. Paul's Church Yard & R. Jennings, 2, Poultry.

THE

KEEPSAKE,

FOR

1829.

Fancy descending among the Muses.

London:

PUBLISHED NOV. 1828, FOR THE PROPRIETOR, BY HURST, CHANCE, & Cº ST. PAUL'S CHURCH YARD,

AND ROBERT JENNINGS, 2, POULTRY.

Printed by McQueen.

THE

KEEPSAKE

FOR

MDCCCXXIX.

EDITED BY

FREDERIC MANSEL REYNOLDS.

LONDON:

PUBLISHED FOR THE PROPRIETOR,

BY HURST, CHANCE, AND CO., 65, ST. PAUL'S CHURCHYARD,

AND R. JENNINGS, 2, POULTRY.

LONDON:

PRINTED BY THOMAS DAVISON, WHITEFRIARS.

PREFACE.

In presenting another volume of the Keepsake to the public, it may, perhaps, be deemed necessary to make a few general observations.

The universal approbation which the embellishments of the previous number excited, and its unprecedented sale, have determined the Proprietor to make the most strenuous exertions to render the present, as perfect as possible, both in literary matter, and in pictorial illustration.

In prosecution of this design, and on the various departments of the Keepsake, the enormous sum of *eleven thousand guineas* has been expended.

" Necesse est facere sumptum, qui quærit lucrum."

In a speculation so extensive, the Proprietor is induced to hope that his book will not be a mere fleeting production, to *die* with the season of its birth, but *live*, a reputed and standard work in every well-selected library.

With this view, such a list of authors has been obtained as perhaps never before graced the pages of any one volume of *original* contributions: it is not however necessary to enumerate them here, as they will be found subjoined to the Table of Contents.

Neither is it necessary to particularize any of their contributions except two; one of which, as posthumous, and the other, as the gift of an individual, not its author: allusion is made to an Essay and Fragments by Percy Bysshe Shelley, for the possession of which, the Editor is indebted to the kindness of the Author of Frankenstein; and to a poem called Extempore by Thomas Moore.

So many, and such varied contents, could not, of course, be contained in the limits of the previous volume: in this present one, therefore, *three additional sheets* of letter-press have been inserted.

The Engravings have been considerably augmented in size, and, it is presumed, in value; no exertion having been spared to render them superior even to those of last year. The type, too, has been altered, and the binding and gilding materially improved; in fact, as before stated, every effort has been made to render the Keepsake *perfect* in all its departments.

To his Grace the Duke of Bedford, the Proprietor offers his grateful and respectful acknowledgments for the permission of engraving the Portrait of the Duchess of Bedford; similar acknowledgments he also returns to the Right Honourable Robert Peel, for a like permission with regard to the Portrait of Mrs. Peel; as well as to the Right Honourable William Adam, Lord Chief Commissioner of the Jury Court in Scotland, for the picture of "A Scene at Abbotsford;" and to Godfrey Windus, Esq., for the drawings of Lucy on the Rock, and of the Garden of Boccacio.

To the Artists, both painters and engravers, the Proprietor feels especially obliged for their exertions in maintaining the reputation of the work.

The Editor begs to return his sincere thanks to his contributors, generally; to specify any in particular, would be but an invidious act towards those omitted.

TABLE OF CONTENTS.

LIST OF CONTRIBUTORS.

SIR WALTER SCOTT, SIR JAMES MACKINTOSH, THOMAS MOORE,
LORD NORMANBY, LORD MORPETH, LORD PORCHESTER,
LORD HOLLAND, LORD F. L. GOWER, LORD NUGENT,
W. WORDSWORTH, R. SOUTHEY, S. T. COLERIDGE, WILLIAM ROSCOE,
PERCY BYSSHE SHELLEY, HENRY LUTTRELL,
THEODORE HOOK, J. G. LOCKHART, T. CROFTON CROKER,
R. BERNAL, M. P., THOMAS HAYNES BAYLY, W. JERDAN,
MRS. HEMANS, MISS LANDON, M. L.,
BARRY ST. LEGER, JAMES BOADEN, W. H. HARRISON,
F. MANSEL REYNOLDS, AND THE AUTHORS OF FRANKENSTEIN,
THE ROUÉ, AND THE O'HARA TALES.

LIST OF THE PLATES.

MY AUNT MARGARET'S MIRROR.

BY THE AUTHOR OF WAVERLEY.

" There are times
When Fancy plays her gambols, in despite
Even of our watchful senses, when in sooth
Substance seems shadow, shadow substance seems,
When the broad, palpable, and mark'd partition
'Twixt that which is and is not, seems dissolved,
As if the mental eye gain'd power to gaze
Beyond the limits of the existing world.
Such hours of shadowy dreams I better love
Than all the gross realities of life."

ANONYMOUS.

My Aunt Margaret was one of that respected sisterhood, upon whom devolve all the trouble and solicitude incidental to the possession of children, excepting only that which attends their entrance into the world. We were a large family, of very different dispositions and constitutions. Some were dull and peevish—they were sent to Aunt Margaret to be amused; some were rude, romping, and boisterous—they were sent to Aunt Margaret to be kept quiet, or rather, that their noise might be removed out of hearing: those who were indisposed were sent with the prospect of being nursed—those who were stubborn, with the hope of their being subdued by the kindness of Aunt Margaret's discipline: in short, she had all the various duties of a mother, without the credit and dignity of the maternal

B

character. The busy scene of her various cares is now over—of the invalids and the robust, the kind and the rough, the peevish and pleased children who thronged her little parlour from morning to night, not one now remains alive but myself; who, afflicted by early infirmity, was one of the most delicate of her nurselings, yet, nevertheless, have outlived them all.

It is still my custom, and shall be so while I have the use of my limbs, to visit my respected relation at least three times a week. Her abode is about half a mile from the suburbs of the town in which I reside; and is accessible, not only by the high road, from which it stands at some distance, but by means of a green-sward foot-path, leading through some pretty meadows. I have so little left to torment me in life, that it is one of my greatest vexations to know that several of these sequestered fields have been devoted as sites for building. In that which is nearest the town, wheel-barrows have been at work for several weeks in such numbers, that, I verily believe, its whole surface, to the depth of at least eighteen inches, was mounted in these monotrochs at the same moment, and in the act of being transported from one place to another. Huge triangular piles of planks are also reared in different parts of the devoted messuage; and a little group of trees, that still grace the eastern end, which rises in a gentle ascent, have just received warning to quit, expressed by a daub of white paint, and are to give place to a curious grove of chimneys.

It would, perhaps, hurt others in my situation to reflect that this little range of pasturage once belonged to my father (whose family was of some consideration in the world), and was sold by patches to remedy distresses in which he involved himself in an attempt by commercial adventure to redeem his diminished fortune. While the building scheme was in full operation, this circumstance was often pointed out to me by the class of friends who are anxious that no part of your misfortunes should escape your observation. " Such pasture ground!—lying at the very town's-end—in turnips and potatoes, the packs would bring £20 per acre, and if leased for building—O, it was a gold mine!—And all sold for an old song out of the ancient possessor's hands." My comforters cannot bring me to repine much on this subject. If I could be allowed to look back on the past without interruption, I could willingly give up the enjoyment of present income, and the hope of future profit, to those who have purchased what my father sold. I regret the alteration of the ground only because it destroys associations, and I would more willingly (I think) see the Earls' Closes in the hands of strangers, retaining their sylvan appearance, than know them for my own, if torn up by agriculture, or covered with buildings. Mine are the sensations of poor Logan:

" The horrid plough has razed the green
Where yet a child I stray'd;
The axe has fell'd the hawthorn screen,
The school-boy's summer shade."

I hope, however, the threatened devastation will not be consummated in my day. Although the adventurous spirit of times short while since passed gave rise to the undertaking, I have been encouraged to think, that the subsequent changes have so far damped the spirit of speculation, that the rest of the woodland foot-path leading to Aunt Margaret's retreat will be left undisturbed for her time and mine. I am interested in this, for every step of

the way, after I have passed through the green already
mentioned, has for me something of early remembrance:
—There is the stile at which I can recollect a cross child's
maid upbraiding me with my infirmity, as she lifted me
coarsely and carelessly over the flinty steps, which my
brothers traversed with shout and bound. I remember
the suppressed bitterness of the moment, and, conscious of
my own inferiority, the feeling of envy with which I regarded the easy movements and elastic steps of my more
happily formed brethren.   Alas! these goodly barks have
all perished on life's wide ocean, and only that which
seemed so little sea-worthy, as the naval phrase goes, has
reached the port when the tempest is over.   Then there
is the pool where, manœuvring our little navy, constructed
out of the broad water-flags, my elder brother fell in, and
was scarce saved from the watery element, to die under
Nelson's banner.   There is the hazel copse, also, in which
my brother Henry used to gather nuts; thinking little that
he was to die in an Indian jungle in quest of rupees.

There is so much more of remembrance about the little
walk, that,—as I stop, rest on my crutch-headed cane, and
look round with that species of comparison between the
thing I was and that which I now am,—it almost induces
me to doubt my own identity; until I find myself in face
of the honey-suckle porch of Aunt Margaret's dwelling,
with its irregularity of front, and its odd projecting
latticed windows; where the workmen seem to have made
a study that no one of them should resemble another, in
form, size, or in the old-fashioned stone entablature, and
labels, which adorn them. This tenement, once the
manor-house of Earl's Closes, we still retain a slight hold
upon; for, in some family arrangements, it had been

settled upon Aunt Margaret during the term of her life.
Upon this frail tenure depends, in a great measure, the last
shadow of the family of Bothwell of Earl's Closes, and their
last slight connexion with their paternal inheritance. The
only representative will then be an infirm old man, moving
not unwillingly to the grave, which has devoured all that
were dear to his affections.

When I have indulged such thoughts for a minute or
two, I enter the mansion, which is said to have been the
gatehouse only of the original building, and find one being
on whom time seems to have made little impression; for
the Aunt Margaret of to-day bears the same proportional
age to the Aunt Margaret of my early youth, that the boy
of ten years old does to the man of (by'r Lady!) some
fifty-six years. The old lady's invariable costume has
doubtless some share in confirming one in the opinion, that
time has stood still with Aunt Margaret.

The brown or chocolate-coloured silk gown, with ruffles
of the same stuff at the elbow, within which are others of
Mechlin lace—the black silk gloves, or mitts, the white hair
combed back upon a roll, and the cap of spotless cambric,
which closes around the venerable countenance, as they were
not the costume of 1780, so neither were they that of 1826;
they are altogether a style peculiar to the individual Aunt
Margaret. There she still sits, as she sate thirty years
since, with her wheel or the stocking, which she works by
the fire in winter, and by the window in summer; or,
perhaps, venturing as far as the porch in an unusually fine
summer evening. Her frame, like some well-constructed
piece of mechanics, still performs the operations for which
it had seemed destined; going its round with an activity

which is gradually diminished, yet indicating no probability that it will soon come to a period.

The solicitude and affection which had made Aunt
Margaret the willing slave to the inflictions of a whole
nursery have now for their object the health and comfort
of one old and infirm man; the last remaining relative of
her family, and the only one who can still find interest in
the traditional stores which she hoards; as some miser
hides the gold which he desires that no one should enjoy
after his death.

My conversation with Aunt Margaret generally relates
little either to the present or to the future: for the passing
day we possess as much as we require, and we neither of
us wish for more; and for that which is to follow we have
on this side of the grave neither hopes, nor fears, nor
anxiety. We therefore naturally look back to the past;
and forget the present fallen fortunes and declined importance of our family, in recalling the hours when it was
wealthy and prosperous.

With this slight introduction, the reader will know as
much of Aunt Margaret and her nephew as is necessary
to comprehend the following conversation and narrative.

Last week, when, late in a summer evening, I went to
call on the old lady to whom my reader is now introduced,
I was received by her with all her usual affection and
benignity; while, at the same time, she seemed abstracted
and disposed to silence. I asked her the reason. "They
have been clearing out the old chapel," she said; "John
Clayhudgeons having, it seems, discovered that the stuff
within,—being, I suppose, the remains of our ancestors,—
was excellent for top-dressing the meadows."

Here I started up with more alacrity than I have displayed for some years; but sate down while my aunt added, laying her hand upon my sleeve, " The chapel has been long considered as common ground, my dear, and used for a penfold, and what objection can we have to the man for employing what is his own, to his own profit? Besides, I did speak to him, and he very readily and civilly promised, that, if he found bones or monuments, they should be carefully respected and reinstated; and what more could I ask? So, the first stone they found bore the name of Margaret Bothwell, 1585, and I have caused it to be laid carefully aside, as I think it betokens death; and having served my namesake two hundred years, it has just been cast up in time to do me the same good turn. My house has been long put in order, as far as the small earthly concerns require it, but who shall say that their account with Heaven is sufficiently revised?"

"After what you have said, aunt," I replied, " perhaps I ought to take my hat and go away, and so I should, but that there is on this occasion a little alloy mingled with your devotion. To think of death at all times is a duty—to suppose it nearer from the finding an old gravestone is superstition; and you, with your strong useful common sense, which was so long the prop of a fallen family, are the last person whom I should have suspected of such weakness."

"Neither would I deserve your suspicions, kinsman," answered Aunt Margaret, " if we were speaking of any incident occurring in the actual business of human life. But for all this, I have a sense of superstition about me, which I do not wish to part with. It is a feeling which separates me from this age, and links me with that to which I am hastening; and even when it seems, as now, to lead me to the brink of the grave, and bids me gaze on it, I do not love that it should be dispelled. It soothes my imagination, without influencing my reason or conduct."

" I profess, my good lady," replied I, " that had any one but you made such a declaration, I should have thought it as capricious as that of the clergyman, who, without vindicating his false reading, preferred, from habit's sake, his old Mumpsimus to the modern Sumpsimus."

" Well," answered my aunt, " I must explain my inconsistency in this particular, by comparing it to another. I am, as you know, a piece of that old-fashioned thing called a Jacobite; but I am so in sentiment and feeling only; for a more loyal subject never joined in prayers for the health and wealth of George the Fourth, whom God long preserve! But I dare say that kind-hearted Sovereign would not deem that an old woman did him much injury, if she leaned back in her arm-chair, just in such a twilight as this, and thought of the high-mettled men, whose sense of duty called them to arms against his grandfather; and how, in a cause which they deemed that of their rightful prince and country—

' They fought till their hand to the broadsword was glued,
They fought against fortune with hearts unsubdued.'

Do not come at such a moment, when my head is full of plaids, pibrochs, and claymores, and ask my reason to admit what, I am afraid, it cannot deny,—I mean, that the public advantage peremptorily demanded that these things should cease to exist. I cannot, indeed, refuse to allow the justice of your reasoning; but yet, being convinced against my will, you will gain little by your motion. You might as well read to an infatuated lover the catalogue of his mistress's imperfections; for, when he has been compelled to listen to the summary, you will only get for answer, that, ' he lo'es her a' the better.' "

I was not sorry to have changed the gloomy train of Aunt Margaret's thoughts, and replied in the same tone, " Well, I can't help being persuaded that our good King is the more sure of Mrs. Bothwell's loyal affection, that he has the Stuart right of birth, as well as the Act of Succession, in his favour."

" Perhaps my attachment, were its source of consequence, might be found warmer for the union of the rights you mention," said Aunt Margaret; " but, upon my word, it would be as sincere if the King's right were founded only on the will of the nation, as declared at the Revolution. I am none of your *jure divino* folks."

" And a Jacobite notwithstanding."

" And a Jacobite notwithstanding; or rather, I will give you leave to call me one of the party, which, in Queen Anne's time, were called *Whimsicals;* because they were sometimes operated upon by feelings, sometimes by principle. After all, it is very hard that you will not allow an old woman to be as inconsistent in her political sentiments, as mankind in general show themselves in all the various courses of life; since you cannot point out one of them, in which the passions and prejudices of those who pursue it are not perpetually carrying us away from the path which our reason points out."

" True, aunt; but you are a wilful wanderer, who should be forced back into the right path."

" Spare me, I entreat you," replied Aunt Margaret.

" You remember the Gaelic song, though I dare say I mis-
pronounce the words—

> ' Hatil mohatil, na dowski mi.'
> ' I am asleep, do not waken me.'

I tell you, kinsman, that the sort of waking dreams which
my imagination spins out, in what your favourite Wordsworth calls ' moods of my own mind,' are worth all the
rest of my more active days.   Then, instead of looking
forwards, as I did in youth, and forming for myself fairy
palaces, upon the verge of the grave, I turn my eyes backward upon the days, and manners, of my better time; and
the sad, yet soothing recollections, come so close and interesting, that I almost think it sacrilege to be wiser or
more rational, or less prejudiced, than those to whom I
looked up in my younger years."

" I think I now understand what you mean," I answered, " and can comprehend why you should occasionally prefer the twilight of illusion to the steady light
of reason."

" Where there is no task," she rejoined, " to be performed, we may sit in the dark if we like it—if we go to
work, we must ring for candles."

" And amidst such shadowy and doubtful light," continued I, " imagination frames her enchanted and enchanting visions, and sometimes passes them upon the
senses for reality."

" Yes," said Aunt Margaret, who is a well-read woman,
" to those who resemble the translator of Tasso,

> ' Prevailing poet, whose undoubting mind
> Believed the magic wonders which he sung.'

It is not required for this purpose, that you should be

sensible of the painful horrors, which an actual belief in
such prodigies inflicts—such a belief, now-a-days, belongs
only to fools and children. It is not necessary, that your
ears should tingle, and your complexion change, like that
of Theodore, at the approach of the spectral huntsman.
All that is indispensable for the enjoyment of the milder
feeling of supernatural awe is, that you should be susceptible of the slight shuddering which creeps over you,
when you hear a tale of terror—that well-vouched tale
which the narrator, having first expressed his general disbelief of all such legendary lore, selects and produces, as
having something in it which he has been always obliged
to give up as inexplicable. Another symptom is, a momentary hesitation to look round you, when the interest of
the narrative is at the highest; and the third, a desire to
avoid looking into a mirror, when you are alone, in your
chamber, for the evening. I mean such are signs which
indicate the crisis, when a female imagination is in due
temperature to enjoy a ghost story. I do not pretend to
describe those which express the same disposition in a
gentleman."

"That last symptom, dear aunt, of shunning the mirror, seems likely to be a rare occurrence amongst the fair
sex."

"You are a novice in toilette fashions, my dear cousin.
All women consult the looking-glass with anxiety, before
they go into company; but when they return home, the
mirror has not the same charm. The die has been cast—
the party has been successful or unsuccessful, in the impression which she desired to make. But, without going
deeper into the mysteries of the dressing-table, I will tell

you that I, myself, like many other honest folks, do not like to see the blank black front of a large mirror in a room dimly lighted, and where the reflection of the candle seems rather to lose itself in the deep obscurity of the glass, than to be reflected back again into the apartment. That space of inky darkness seems to be a field for Fancy to play her revels in.   She may call up other features to meet us, instead of the reflection of our own; or, as in the spells of Hallowe'en, which we learned in childhood, some unknown form may be seen peeping over our shoulder. In short, when I am in a ghost-seeing humour, I make my hand-maiden draw the green curtains over the mirror, before I go into the room, so that she may have the first shock of the apparition, if there be any to be seen. But to tell you the truth, this dislike to look into a mirror in particular times and places has, I believe, its original foundation in a story, which came to me by tradition from my grandmother, who was a party concerned in the scene of which I will now tell you."

THE MIRROR.

CHAPTER I.

You are fond (said my aunt) of sketches of the society which has passed away.   I wish I could describe to you Sir Philip Forester, the 'Chartered Libertine' of Scottish good company, about the end of the last century.   I never saw him, indeed, but my mother's traditions were full of his wit, gallantry, and dissipation. This gay knight flourished about the end of the 17th and beginning of

the 18th century. He was the Sir Charles Easy and the
Lovelace of his day and country: renowned for the number of duels he had fought, and the successful intrigues
which he had carried on. The supremacy which he had
attained in the fashionable world was absolute; and when we
combine it with one or two anecdotes, for which, 'if laws
were made for every degree,' he ought certainly to have
been hanged, the popularity of such a person really serves
to show, either, that the present times are much more
decent, if not more virtuous, than they formerly were; or,
that high breeding then was of more difficult attainment
than that which is now so called; and, consequently, entitled the successful professor to a proportional degree of
plenary indulgences and privileges. No beau of this day
could have borne out so ugly a story as that of Pretty
Peggy Grindstone, the miller's daughter at Sillermills—it
had well nigh made work for the Lord Advocate. But it
hurt Sir Philip Forester no more than the hail hurts the
hearth-stone. He was as well received in society as ever,
and dined with the Duke of A—— the day the poor girl
was buried. She died of heart-break. But that has nothing
to do with my story.

Now, you must listen to a single word upon kith, kin,
and ally; I promise you I will not be prolix. But it is
necessary to the authenticity of my legend, that you should
know that Sir Philip Forester, with his handsome person,
elegant accomplishments, and fashionable manners, married the younger Miss Falconer, of King's-Copland. The
elder sister of this lady had previously become the wife of
my grandfather, Sir Geoffrey Bothwell, and brought into
our family a good fortune. Miss Jemima, or Miss Jemmie

Falconer, as she was usually called, had also about ten thousand pounds sterling; then thought a very handsome portion indeed.

The two sisters were extremely different, though each had their admirers while they remained single. Lady Bothwell had some touch of the old King's-Copland blood about her. She was bold, though not to the degree of audacity: ambitious, and desirous to raise her house and family; and was, as has been said, a considerable spur to my grandfather, who was otherwise an indolent man; but whom, unless he has been slandered, his lady's influence involved in some political matters which had been more wisely let alone. She was a woman of high principle, however, and masculine good sense, as some of her letters testify, which are still in my wainscot cabinet.

Jemmie Falconer was the reverse of her sister in every respect. Her understanding did not reach above the ordinary pitch, if, indeed, she could be said to have attained it. Her beauty, while it lasted, consisted, in a great measure, of delicacy of complexion and regularity of features, without any peculiar force of expression. Even these charms faded under the sufferings attendant on an ill-sorted match. She was passionately attached to her husband, by whom she was treated with a callous, yet polite, indifference; which, to one whose heart was as tender as her judgment was weak, was more painful perhaps than absolute ill-usage. Sir Philip was a voluptuary, that is, a completely selfish egotist: whose disposition and character resembled the rapier he wore, polished, keen, and brilliant, but inflexible and unpitying. As he observed carefully all the usual forms towards his lady, he had the art to deprive her

even of the compassion of the world; and useless and unavailing as that may be while actually possessed by the
sufferer, it is, to a mind like Lady Forester's, most painful
to know she has it not.

The tattle of society did its best to place the peccant
husband above the suffering wife. Some called her a poor
spiritless thing, and declared, that with a little of her sister's spirit, she might have brought to reason any Sir Philip
whatsoever, were it the termagant Falconbridge himself.
But the greater part of their acquaintance affected candour,
and saw faults on both sides; though, in fact, there only
existed the oppressor and the oppressed. The tone of such
critics was—"To be sure, no one will justify Sir Philip
Forester, but then we all know Sir Philip, and Jemmie
Falconer might have known what she had to expect from
the beginning.—What made her set her cap at Sir Philip?
—He would never have looked at her if she had not thrown
herself at his head, with her poor ten thousand pounds.
I am sure, if it is money he wanted, she spoiled his market.
I know where Sir Philip could have done much better.—
And then, if she *would* have the man, could not she try to
make him more comfortable at home, and have his friends
oftener, and not plague him with the squalling children,
and take care all was handsome and in good style about the
house? I declare I think Sir Philip would have made a
very domestic man, with a woman who knew how to
manage him."

Now these fair critics, in raising their profound edifice
of domestic felicity, did not recollect that the corner-stone
was wanting; and that to receive good company with good
cheer, the means of the banquet ought to have been furnished by Sir Philip; whose income (dilapidated as it was)

was not equal to the display of the hospitality required, and at the same time to the supply of the good knight's *menus plaisirs.* So, in spite of all that was so sagely suggested by female friends, Sir Philip carried his good humour every where abroad, and left at home a solitary mansion, and a pining spouse.

At length, inconvenienced in his money affairs, and tired even of the short time which he spent in his own dull house, Sir Philip Forester determined to take a trip to the continent, in the capacity of a volunteer. It was then common for men of fashion to do so; and our knight perhaps was of opinion that a touch of the military character, just enough to exalt, but not render pedantic, his qualities as a *beau garçon,* was necessary to maintain possession of the elevated situation which he held in the ranks of fashion.

Sir Philip's resolution threw his wife into agonies of terror; by which the worthy baronet was so much annoyed, that, contrary to his wont, he took some trouble to soothe her apprehensions; and once more brought her to shed tears, in which sorrow was not altogether unmingled with pleasure. Lady Bothwell asked, as a favour, Sir Philip's permission to receive her sister and her family into her own house during his absence on the continent. Sir Philip readily assented to a proposition which saved expense, silenced the foolish people who might have talked of a deserted wife and family, and gratified Lady Bothwell; for whom he felt some respect, as for one who often spoke to him, always with freedom, and sometimes with severity, without being deterred either by his raillery, or the *prestige* of his reputation.

A day or two before Sir Philip's departure, Lady Bothwell took the liberty of asking him, in her sister's presence, the direct question, which his timid wife had often desired, but never ventured, to put to him.

"Pray, Sir Philip, what route do you take when you reach the continent?"

"I go from Leith to Helvoet by a packet with advices."

"That I comprehend perfectly," said Lady Bothwell drily; "but you do not mean to remain long at Helvoet, I presume, and I should like to know what is your next object?"

"You ask me, my dear lady," answered Sir Philip, "a question which I have not dared to ask myself. The answer depends on the fate of war. I shall, of course, go to head-quarters, wherever they may happen to be for the time; deliver my letters of introduction; learn as much of the noble art of war as may suffice a poor interloping amateur; and then take a glance at the sort of thing of which we read so much in the Gazette."

"And I trust, Sir Philip," said Lady Bothwell, "that you will remember that you are a husband and a father; and that though you think fit to indulge this military fancy, you will not let it hurry you into dangers which it is certainly unnecessary for any save professional persons to encounter."

"Lady Bothwell does me too much honour," replied the adventurous knight, "in regarding such a circumstance with the slightest interest. But to soothe your flattering anxiety, I trust your ladyship will recollect, that I cannot expose to hazard the venerable and paternal character which you so obligingly recommend to my protection, without putting in some peril an honest fellow, called Philip Forester, with whom I have kept company for

c

thirty years, and with whom, though some folks consider him a coxcomb, I have not the least desire to part."

"Well, Sir Philip, you are the best judge of your own affairs; I have little right to interfere—you are not my husband."

"God forbid!"—said Sir Philip hastily; instantly adding, however, "God forbid that I should deprive my friend Sir Geoffrey of so inestimable a treasure."

"But you are my sister's husband," replied the lady; "and I suppose you are aware of her present distress of mind——"

"If hearing of nothing else from morning to night can make me aware of it," said Sir Philip, "I should know something of the matter."

"I do not pretend to reply to your wit, Sir Philip," answered Lady Bothwell; "but you must be sensible that all this distress is on account of apprehensions for your personal safety."

"In that case, I am surprised that Lady Bothwell, at least, should give herself so much trouble upon so insignificant a subject."

"My sister's interest may account for my being anxious to learn something of Sir Philip Forester's motions; about which otherwise, I know, he would not wish me to concern myself: I have a brother's safety too to be anxious for."

"You mean Major Falconer, your brother by the mother's side:—What can he possibly have to do with our present agreeable conversation?"

"You have had words together, Sir Philip," said Lady Bothwell.

"Naturally; we are connexions," replied Sir Philip, "and as such have always had the usual intercourse."

"That is an evasion of the subject," answered the lady. "By words, I mean angry words, on the subject of your usage of your wife."

"If," replied Sir Philip Forester, "you suppose Major Falconer simple enough to intrude his advice upon me, Lady Bothwell, in my domestic matters, you are indeed warranted in believing that I might possibly be so far displeased with the interference, as to request him to reserve his advice till it was asked."

"And being on these terms, you are going to join the very army in which my brother Falconer is now serving."

"No man knows the path of honour better than Major Falconer," said Sir Philip. "An aspirant after fame, like me, cannot choose a better guide than his footsteps."

Lady Bothwell rose and went to the window, the tears gushing from her eyes.

"And this heartless raillery," she said, "is all the consideration that is to be given to our apprehensions of a quarrel which may bring on the most terrible consequences? Good God! of what can men's hearts be made, who can thus dally with the agony of others?"

Sir Philip Forester was moved; he laid aside the mocking tone in which he had hitherto spoken.

"Dear Lady Bothwell," he said, taking her reluctant hand, "we are both wrong:—you are too deeply serious; I, perhaps, too little so. The dispute I had with Major Falconer was of no earthly consequence. Had any thing occurred betwixt us that ought to have been settled *par voie du fait*, as we say in France, neither of us are persons that are likely to postpone such a meeting. Permit me to say, that, were it generally known that you or my Lady Forester are apprehensive of such a catastrophe, it might be the very means of bringing about what would not otherwise be likely to happen. I know your good sense, Lady Bothwell, and that you will understand me when I say, that really my affairs require my absence for some months; —this Jemima cannot understand; it is a perpetual recurrence of questions, why can you not do this, or that, or the third thing; and when you have proved to her that her expedients are totally ineffectual, you have just to begin the whole round again. Now, do you tell her, dear Lady Bothwell, that *you* are satisfied. She is, you must confess, one of those persons with whom authority goes farther than reasoning. Do but repose a little confidence in me, and you shall see how amply I will repay it."

Lady Bothwell shook her head, as one but half satisfied. "How difficult it is to extend confidence, when the basis on which it ought to rest has been so much shaken! But I will do my best to make Jemima easy; and farther, I can only say, that for keeping your present purpose I hold you responsible both to God and man."

"Do not fear that I will deceive you," said Sir Philip; "the safest conveyance to me will be through the general post-office, Helvoetsluys, where I will take care to leave orders for forwarding my letters. As for Falconer, our only encounter will be over a bottle of Burgundy; so make yourself perfectly easy on his score."

Lady Bothwell could *not* make herself easy; yet she was sensible that her sister hurt her own cause by *taking on*, as the maid-servants call it, too vehemently; and by showing before every stranger, by manner, and sometimes by words also, a dissatisfaction with her husband's journey, that was sure to come to his ears, and equally certain to displease him. But there was no help for this domestic dissension, which ended only with the day of separation.

I am sorry I cannot tell, with precision, the year in which Sir Philip Forester went over to Flanders; but it was one of those in which the campaign opened with extraordinary fury; and many bloody, though indecisive, skirmishes were fought between the French on the one side, and the allies on the other. In all our modern improvements there are none, perhaps, greater than in the accuracy and speed with which intelligence is transmitted from any scene of action to those in this country whom it may concern. During Marlborough's campaigns, the sufferings of the many who had relations in, or along with, the army were greatly augmented by the suspense in which they were detained for weeks, after they had heard of bloody battles, in which, in all probability, those for whom their bosoms throbbed with anxiety had been personally engaged. Amongst those who were most agonized by this state of uncertainty was the, I had almost said deserted, wife of the gay Sir Philip Forester. A single letter had informed her of his arrival on the continent—no others were received. One notice occurred in the newspapers, in which Volunteer Sir Philip Forester was mentioned as having been intrusted with a dangerous reconnoissance, which he had executed with the greatest courage, dexterity, and intelligence, and received the thanks of the commanding officer. The sense of his having acquired distinction brought a momentary glow into the lady's pale cheek; but it was instantly lost in ashen whiteness at the recollection of his danger. After this they had no news whatever, neither from Sir Philip, nor even from their brother Falconer. The case of Lady Forester was not indeed different from that of hundreds in the same situation; but a feeble mind is necessarily an irritable one, and the suspense which some bear with constitutional indifference or philosophical resignation, and some with a disposition to believe and hope the best, was intolerable to Lady Forester, at once solitary and sensitive, low-spirited, and devoid of strength of mind, whether natural or acquired.

CHAPTER II.

As she received no further news of Sir Philip, whether directly or indirectly, his unfortunate lady began now to feel a sort of consolation, even in those careless habits which had so often given her pain. " He is so thoughtless," she repeated a hundred times a day to her sister, "he never writes when things are going on smoothly; it is his way: had any thing happened he would have informed us."

Lady Bothwell listened to her sister without attempting to console her. Probably she might be of opinion, that even the worst intelligence which could be received from Flanders might not be without some touch of consolation; and that the Dowager Lady Forester, if so she was doomed to be called, might have a source of happiness unknown to the wife of the gayest and finest gentleman in Scotland. This conviction became stronger as they learned from inquiries made at head-quarters, that Sir Philip was no longer with the army; though whether he had been taken or slain in some of those skirmishes which were perpetually occurring, and in which he loved to distinguish himself, or whether he had, for some unknown reason or capricious change of mind, voluntarily left the service, none of his countrymen in the camp of the allies could form even a conjecture. Meantime his creditors at home became clamorous, entered into possession of his property, and threatened his person, should he be rash enough to return to Scotland. These additional disadvantages aggravated Lady Bothwell's displeasure against the fugitive husband; while her sister saw nothing in any of them, save what tended to increase her grief for the absence of him whom her imagination now represented,—as it had before marriage,—gallant, gay, and affectionate.

About this period there appeared in Edinburgh a man of singular appearance and pretensions. He was commonly called the Paduan Doctor, from having received his education at that famous university. He was supposed to possess some rare receipts in medicine, with which, it was affirmed, he had wrought remarkable cures. But though, on the one hand, the physicians of Edinburgh termed him an empiric, there were many persons, and among them some of the clergy, who, while they admitted the truth of the cures and the force of his remedies, alleged that Doctor Baptista Damiotti made use of charms and unlawful arts in order to obtain success in his practice. The resorting to him was even solemnly preached against, as a seeking of health from idols, and a trusting to the help which was to come from Egypt. But the protection which the Paduan doctor received from some friends of interest and consequence enabled him to set these imputations at defiance, and to assume, even in the city of Edinburgh, famed as it was for abhorrence of witches and necromancers, the dangerous character of an expounder of futurity. It was at length rumoured, that, for a certain gratification, which of course was not an inconsiderable one, Doctor Baptista Damiotti could tell the fate of the absent, and even show his visitors the personal form of their absent friends, and the action in which they were engaged at the moment. This rumour came to the ears of Lady Forester, who had reached that pitch of mental agony in which the sufferer will do any thing, or endure any thing, that suspense may be converted into certainty.

Gentle and timid in most cases, her state of mind made her equally obstinate and reckless, and it was with no small surprise and alarm that her sister, Lady Bothwell, heard her express a resolution to visit this man of art, and learn from him the fate of her husband. Lady Bothwell remonstrated on the improbability that such pretensions as those of this foreigner could be founded in any thing but imposture.

" I care not," said the deserted wife, " what degree of ridicule I may incur: if there be any one chance out of a hundred that I may obtain some certainty of my husband's fate, I would not miss that chance for whatever else the world can offer me."

Lady Bothwell next urged the unlawfulness of resorting to such sources of forbidden knowledge.

" Sister," replied the sufferer, " he who is dying of thirst cannot refrain from drinking even poisoned water. She who suffers under suspense must seek information, even were the powers which offer it unhallowed and in-fernal. I go to learn my fate alone; and this very evening will I know it: the sun that rises to-morrow shall find me, if not more happy, at least more resigned."

" Sister," said Lady Bothwell, " if you are determined upon this wild step, you shall not go alone. If this man be an impostor, you may be too much agitated by your feelings to detect his villany. If, which I cannot believe, there be any truth in what he pretends, you shall not be exposed alone to a communication of so extraordinary a nature. I will go with you, if indeed you determine to go. But yet re-consider your project, and renounce inquiries which cannot be prosecuted without guilt, and perhaps without danger."

Lady Forester threw herself into her sister's arms, and, clasping her to her bosom, thanked her a hundred times for the offer of her company; while she declined with a melancholy gesture the friendly advice with which it was accompanied.

When the hour of twilight arrived,—which was the period when the Paduan doctor was understood to receive the visits of those who came to consult with him,—the two ladies left their apartments in the Canongate of Edinburgh, having their dress arranged like that of women of an inferior description, and their plaids disposed around their faces as they were worn by the same class; for, in those days of aristocracy, the quality of the wearer was generally indicated by the manner in which her plaid was disposed, as well as by the fineness of its texture. It was Lady Bothwell who had suggested this species of disguise, partly to avoid observation as they should go to the conjuror's house, and partly in order to make trial of his penetration by appearing before him in a feigned character. Lady Forester's servant, of tried fidelity, had been employed by her to propitiate the doctor by a suitable fee, and a story intimating that a soldier's wife desired to know the fate of her husband; a subject upon which, in all probability, the sage was very frequently consulted.

To the last moment, when the palace clock struck eight, Lady Bothwell earnestly watched her sister, in hopes that she might retreat from her rash undertaking; but as mildness, and even timidity, is capable at times of vehement and fixed purposes, she found Lady Forester resolutely unmoved and determined when the moment of departure arrived. Ill satisfied with the expedition, but determined not to leave her sister at such a crisis, Lady Bothwell accompanied Lady Forester through more than one obscure street and lane, the servant walking before, and acting as their guide. At length he suddenly turned into a narrow court, and knocked at an arched door, which seemed to belong to a building of some antiquity. It opened, though no one appeared to act as porter; and the servant stepping aside from the entrance, motioned the ladies to enter. They had no sooner done so, than it shut, and excluded their guide. The two ladies found themselves in a small vestibule, illuminated by a dim lamp, and having, when the door was closed, no communication with the external light or air. The door of an inner apartment, partly open, was at the further side of the vestibule.

" We must not hesitate now, Jemima," said Lady Bothwell, and walked forwards into the inner room, where, surrounded by books, maps, philosophical utensils, and other implements of peculiar shape and appearance, they found the man of art.

There was nothing very peculiar in the Italian's appearance. He had the dark complexion and marked features of his country, seemed about fifty years old, and was handsomely, but plainly, dressed in a full suit of black clothes, which was then the universal costume of the medical profession. Large wax-lights, in silver sconces, illuminated the apartment, which was reasonably furnished. He rose as the ladies entered; and, notwithstanding the inferiority of their dress, received them with the marked respect due to their quality, and which foreigners are usually punctilious in rendering to those to whom such honours are due.

Lady Bothwell endeavoured to maintain her proposed incognito; and as the doctor ushered them to the upper end of the room, made a motion declining his courtesy, as unfitted for their condition. " We are poor people, sir," she said; "only my sister's distress has brought us to consult your worship whether—"

He smiled as he interrupted her—" I am aware, madam, of your sister's distress, and its cause; I am aware, also, that I am honoured with a visit from two ladies of the highest consideration—Lady Bothwell and Lady Forester. If I could not distinguish them from the class of society which their present dress would indicate, there would be small possibility of my being able to gratify them by giving the information which they came to seek."

" I can easily understand," said Lady Bothwell——

" Pardon my boldness to interrupt you, mi-lady," cried the Italian; " your ladyship was about to say, that you could easily understand that I had got possession of your names by means of your domestic. But in thinking so, you do injustice to the fidelity of your servant, and I may add, to the skill of one who is also not less your humble servant—Baptista Damiotti."

" I have no intention to do either, sir," said Lady Bothwell, maintaining a tone of composure, though somewhat surprised, " but the situation is something new to me. If you know who we are, you also know, sir, what brought us here."

" Curiosity to know the fate of a Scottish gentleman of rank, now, or lately, upon the continent," answered the seer; "his name is Il Cavaliero Philippo Forester; a gentleman who has the honour to be husband to this lady, and, with your ladyship's permission for using plain language, the misfortune not to value as it deserves that inestimable advantage."

Lady Forester sighed deeply, and Lady Bothwell replied—

" Since you know our object without our telling it, the only question that remains is, whether you have the power to relieve my sister's anxiety."

" I have, madam," answered the Paduan scholar; " but there is still a previous inquiry. Have you the courage to behold with your own eyes what the Cavaliero Philippo Forester is now doing? or will you take it on my report?"

" That question my sister must answer for herself," said Lady Bothwell.

" With my own eyes will I endure to see whatever you have power to show me," said Lady Forester, with the same determined spirit which had stimulated her since her resolution was taken upon this subject.

" There may be danger in it."

" If gold can compensate the risk," said Lady Forester, taking out her purse.

" I do not such things for the purpose of gain," answered the foreigner. " I dare not turn my art to such a purpose. If I take the gold of the wealthy, it is but to bestow it on the poor; nor do I ever accept more than the sum I have already received from your servant. Put up your purse, madam; an adept needs not your gold."

Lady Bothwell, considering this rejection of her sister's offer as a mere trick of an empiric, to induce her to press a larger sum upon him, and willing that the scene should be commenced and ended, offered some gold in turn, observing that it was only to enlarge the sphere of his charity.

" Let Lady Bothwell enlarge the sphere of her own charity," said the Paduan, " not merely in giving of alms, in which I know she is not deficient, but in judging the character of others; and let her oblige Baptista Damiotti by believing him honest till she shall discover him to be a knave. Do not be surprised, madam, if I speak in answer to your thoughts rather than your expressions, and tell me once more whether you have courage to look on what I am prepared to show?"

" I own, sir," said Lady Bothwell, " that your words strike me with some sense of fear; but whatever my sister desires to witness I will not shrink from witnessing along with her."

" Nay, the danger only consists in the risk of your resolution failing you. The sight can only last for the space of seven minutes; and should you interrupt the vision by speaking a single word, not only would the charm be broken, but some danger might result to the spectators. But if you can remain steadily silent for the seven minutes, your curiosity will be gratified without the slightest risk; and for this I will engage my honour."

Internally Lady Bothwell thought the security was but an indifferent one; but she suppressed the suspicion, as if she had believed that the adept, whose dark features wore a half-formed smile, could in reality read even her most

secret reflections. A solemn pause then ensued, until Lady
Forester gathered courage enough to reply to the physician,
as he termed himself, that she would abide with firmness
and silence the sight which he had promised to exhibit to
them. Upon this, he made them a low obeisance, and
saying he went to prepare matters to meet their wish, left
the apartment. The two sisters, hand in hand, as if seeking by that close union to divert any danger which might
threaten them, sat down on two seats in immediate contact
with each other: Jemima seeking support in the manly and
habitual courage of Lady Bothwell; and she, on the other
hand, more agitated than she had expected, endeavouring
to fortify herself by the desperate resolution which circumstances had forced her sister to assume. The one
perhaps said to herself, that her sister never feared any
thing; and the other might reflect, that what so feeble a
minded woman as Jemima did not fear, could not properly
be a subject of apprehension to a person of firmness and
resolution like her own.

In a few moments the thoughts of both were diverted
from their own situation, by a strain of music so singularly
sweet and solemn, that, while it seemed calculated to avert
or dispel any feeling unconnected with its harmony, increased, at the same time, the solemn excitation which the
preceding interview was calculated to produce. The music
was that of some instrument with which they were unacquainted; but circumstances afterwards led my ancestress
to believe that it was that of the harmonica, which she
heard at a much later period in life.

When these heaven-born sounds had ceased, a door
opened in the upper end of the apartment, and they saw
Damiotti, standing at the head of two or three steps, sign

to them to advance. His dress was so different from that
which he had worn a few minutes before, that they could
hardly recognise him; and the deadly paleness of his
countenance, and a certain stern rigidity of muscles, like
that of one whose mind is made up to some strange and
daring action, had totally changed the somewhat sarcastic
expression with which he had previously regarded them
both, and particularly Lady Bothwell. He was barefooted,
excepting a species of sandals in the antique fashion; his
legs were naked beneath the knee; above them he wore
hose, and a doublet of dark crimson silk close to his body;
and over that a flowing loose robe, something resembling
a surplice, of snow-white linen: his throat and neck were
uncovered, and his long, straight, black hair was carefully
combed down at full length.

As the ladies approached at his bidding, he showed no
gesture of that ceremonious courtesy of which he had been
formerly lavish. On the contrary, he made the signal of
advance with an air of command; and when, arm in arm,
and with insecure steps, the sisters approached the spot
where he stood, it was with a warning frown that he
pressed his finger to his lips, as if reiterating his condition
of absolute silence, while, stalking before them, he led the
way into the next apartment.

This was a large room, hung with black, as if for a
funeral. At the upper end was a table, or rather a species
of altar, covered with the same lugubrious colour, on which
lay divers objects resembling the usual implements of
sorcery. These objects were not indeed visible as they advanced into the apartment; for the light which displayed
them, being only that of two expiring lamps, was extremely
faint.—The master—to use the Italian phrase for persons

of this description—approached the upper end of the room, with a genuflexion like that of a catholic to the crucifix, and at the same time crossed himself. The ladies followed in silence, and arm in arm. Two or three low broad steps led to a platform in front of the altar, or what resembled such. Here the sage took his stand, and placed the ladies beside him, once more earnestly repeating by signs his injunctions of silence. The Italian then, extending his bare arm from under his linen vestment, pointed with his forefinger to five large flambeaux, or torches, placed on each side of the altar. They took fire successively at the approach of his hand, or rather of his finger, and spread a strong light through the room. By this the visitors could discern that, on the seeming altar, were disposed two naked swords laid crosswise; a large open book, which they conceived to be a copy of the Holy Scriptures, but in a language to them unknown; and beside this mysterious volume was placed a human skull. But what struck the sisters most was a very tall and broad mirror, which occupied all the space behind the altar, and, illumined by the lighted torches, reflected the mysterious articles which were laid upon it.

The master then placed himself between the two ladies, and, pointing to the mirror, took each by the hand, but without speaking a syllable. They gazed intently on the polished and sable space to which he had directed their attention. Suddenly the surface assumed a new and singular appearance. It no longer simply reflected the objects placed before it, but, as if it had self-contained scenery of its own, objects began to appear within it, at first in a disorderly, indistinct, and miscellaneous manner, like form arranging itself out of chaos; at length, in distinct and

Drawn by J.M.Wright   Engraved by E.Portbury

THE MAGIC MIRROR.

Printed by McQueen.

Pub.^d for the Proprietor by Hurst, Chance, & Co St Paul's Churchyard,& R.Jennings,Poultry.

defined shape and symmetry. It was thus that, after some shifting of light and darkness over the face of the wonderful glass, a long perspective of arches and columns began to arrange itself on its sides, and a vaulted roof on the upper part of it; till, after many oscillations, the whole vision gained a fixed and stationary appearance, representing the interior of a foreign church. The pillars were stately, and hung with scutcheons; the arches were lofty and magnificent; the floor was lettered with funeral inscriptions. But there were no separate shrines, no images, no display of chalice or crucifix on the altar. It was, therefore, a Protestant church upon the continent. A clergyman dressed in the Geneva gown and band stood by the communion-table, and, with the Bible opened before him, and his clerk awaiting in the back ground, seemed prepared to perform some service of the church to which he belonged.

At length, there entered the middle aisle of the building a numerous party, which appeared to be a bridal one, as a lady and gentleman walked first, hand in hand, followed by a large concourse of persons of both sexes, gaily, nay richly, attired. The bride, whose features they could distinctly see, seemed not more than sixteen years old, and extremely beautiful. The bridegroom, for some seconds, moved rather with his shoulder towards them, and his face averted; but his elegance of form and step struck the sisters at once with the same apprehension. As he turned his face suddenly, it was frightfully realised, and they saw, in the gay bridegroom before them, Sir Philip Forester. His wife uttered an imperfect exclamation, at the sound of which the whole scene stirred and seemed to separate.

" I could compare it to nothing," said Lady Bothwell

while recounting the wonderful tale, " but to the dispersion of the reflection offered by a deep and calm pool, when a stone is suddenly cast into it, and the shadows become dissipated and broken." The master pressed both the ladies' hands severely, as if to remind them of their promise, and of the danger which they incurred. The exclamation died away on Lady Forester's tongue, without attaining perfect utterance, and the scene in the glass, after the fluctuation of a minute, again resumed to the eye its former appearance of a real scene, existing within the mirror, as if represented in a picture, save that the figures were moveable instead of being stationary.

The representation of Sir Philip Forester, now distinctly visible in form and feature, was seen to lead on towards the clergyman that beautiful girl, who advanced at once with diffidence and with a species of affectionate pride. In the meantime, and just as the clergyman had arranged the bridal company before him, and seemed about to commence the service, another group of persons, of whom two or three were officers, entered the church. They moved, at first, forward, as though they came to witness the bridal ceremony, but suddenly one of the officers, whose back was towards the spectators, detached himself from his companions, and rushed hastily towards the marriage party; when the whole of them turned towards him, as if attracted by some exclamation which had accompanied his advance. Suddenly the intruder drew his sword; the bridegroom unsheathed his own, and made towards him; swords were also drawn by other individuals, both of the marriage party, and of those who had last entered. They fell into a sort of confusion, the clergyman, and some elder and graver persons, labouring apparently to keep the peace, while the hotter spirits on both sides brandished their weapons. But now, the period of the brief space during which the soothsayer, as he pretended, was permitted to exhibit his art, was arrived. The fumes again mixed together, and dissolved gradually from observation; the vaults and columns of the church rolled asunder, and disappeared; and the front of the mirror reflected nothing save the blazing torches, and the melancholy apparatus placed on the altar or table before it.

The doctor led the ladies, who greatly required his support, into the apartment from whence they came; where wine, essences, and other means of restoring suspended animation, had been provided during his absence. He motioned them to chairs, which they occupied in silence; Lady Forester, in particular, wringing her hands, and casting her eyes up to heaven, but without speaking a word, as if the spell had been still before her eyes.

" And what we have seen is even now acting?" said Lady Bothwell, collecting herself with difficulty.

" That," answered Baptista Damiotti, " I cannot justly, or with certainty, say. But it is either now acting, or has been acted, during a short space before this. It is the last remarkable transaction in which the Cavalier Forester has been engaged."

Lady Bothwell then expressed anxiety concerning her sister, whose altered countenance, and apparent unconsciousness of what passed around her, excited her apprehensions how it might be possible to convey her home.

" I have prepared for that," answered the adept; " I have directed the servant to bring your equipage as near to this place as the narrowness of the street will permit. Fear not for your sister; but give her, when you return home, this composing draught, and she will be better to-morrow morning. Few," he added, in a melancholy tone, " leave this house as well in health as they entered it. Such being the consequence of seeking knowledge by mysterious means, I leave you to judge the condition of those who have the power of gratifying such irregular curiosity. Farewell, and forget not the potion."

" I will give her nothing that comes from you," said Lady Bothwell; " I have seen enough of your art already. Perhaps you would poison us both to conceal your own necromancy. But we are persons who want neither the means of making our wrongs known, nor the assistance of friends to right them."

" You have had no wrongs from me, madam," said the adept. " You sought one who is little grateful for such honour. He seeks no one, and only gives responses to those who invite and call upon him. After all, you have but learned a little sooner the evil which you must still be doomed to endure. I hear your servant's step at the door, and will detain your ladyship and Lady Forester no longer. The next packet from the continent will explain what you have already partly witnessed. Let it not, if I may advise, pass too suddenly into your sister's hands."

So saying, he bid Lady Bothwell good night. She went, lighted by the adept, to the vestibule, where he hastily threw a black cloak over his singular dress, and opening the door, entrusted his visitors to the care of the servant. It was with difficulty that Lady Bothwell sustained her sister to the carriage, though it was only twenty steps distant. When they arrived at home, Lady Forester required medical assistance. The physician of the family attended, and shook his head on feeling her pulse.

"Here has been," he said, "a violent and sudden shock on the nerves. I must know how it has happened." Lady Bothwell admitted they had visited the conjuror, and that Lady Forester had received some bad news respecting her husband, Sir Philip.

"That rascally quack would make my fortune were he to stay in Edinburgh," said the graduate; "this is the seventh nervous case I have heard of his making for me, and all by effect of terror." He next examined the composing draught which Lady Bothwell had unconsciously brought in her hand, tasted it, and pronounced it very germain to the matter, and what would save an application to the apothecary. He then paused, and looking at Lady Bothwell very significantly, at length added, "I suppose I must not ask your ladyship any thing about this Italian warlock's proceedings?"

"Indeed, doctor," answered Lady Bothwell, "I consider what passed as confidential; and though the man may be a rogue, yet, as we were fools enough to consult him, we should, I think, be honest enough to keep his counsel."

"May be a knave—come," said the doctor, "I am glad to hear your ladyship allows such a possibility in any thing that comes from Italy."

"What comes from Italy may be as good as what comes from Hanover, doctor. But you and I will remain good friends, and that it may be so, we will say nothing of whig and tory."

"Not I," said the doctor, receiving his fee; and taking his hat, "a Carolus serves my purpose as well as a Willielmus. But I should like to know why old Lady Saint Ringan's, and all that set, go about wasting their decayed lungs in puffing this foreign fellow."

" Ay—you had best set him down a Jesuit, as Scrub says." On these terms they parted.

The poor patient—whose nerves, from an extraordinary state of tension, had at length become relaxed in as extraordinary a degree—continued to struggle with a sort of imbecility, the growth of superstitious terror, when the shocking tidings were brought from Holland, which fulfilled even her worst expectations.

They were sent by the celebrated Earl of Stair, and contained the melancholy event of a duel betwixt Sir Philip Forester, and his wife's half-brother, Captain Falconer, of the Scotch-Dutch, as they were then called, in which the latter had been killed. The cause of quarrel rendered the incident still more shocking. It seemed that Sir Philip had left the army suddenly, in consequence of being unable to pay a very considerable sum, which he had lost to another volunteer at play. He had changed his name, and taken up his residence at Rotterdam, where he had insinuated himself into the good graces of an ancient and rich burgomaster, and by his handsome person and graceful manners captivated the affections of his only child, a very young person of great beauty, and the heiress of much wealth. Delighted with the specious attractions of his proposed son-in-law, the wealthy merchant—whose idea of the British character was too high to admit of his taking any precaution to acquire evidence of his condition and circumstances—gave his consent to the marriage. It was about to be celebrated in the principal church of the city, when it was interrupted by a singular occurrence.

Captain Falconer having been detached to Rotterdam to bring up a part of the brigade of Scottish auxiliaries, who were in quarters there, a person of consideration in the town, to whom he had been formerly known, proposed to him for amusement to go to the high church, to see a countryman of his own married to the daughter of a wealthy burgomaster. Captain Falconer went accordingly, accompanied by his Dutch acquaintance, with a party of his friends, and two or three officers of the Scotch brigade. His astonishment may be conceived when he saw his own brother-in-law, a married man, on the point of leading to the altar the innocent and beautiful creature, upon whom he was about to practise a base and unmanly deceit. He proclaimed his villany on the spot, and the marriage was interrupted of course. But against the opinion of more thinking men, who considered Sir Philip Forester as having thrown himself out of the rank of men of honour, Captain Falconer admitted him to the privileges of such, accepted a challenge from him, and in the rencounter received a mortal wound. Such are the ways of Heaven, mysterious in our eyes. Lady Forester never recovered the shock of this dismal intelligence.

" And did this tragedy," said I, " take place exactly at the time when the scene in the mirror was exhibited?"

" It is hard to be obliged to maim one's story," answered my aunt; " but to speak the truth, it happened some days sooner than the apparition was exhibited."

" And so there remained a possibility," said I, " that by some secret and speedy communication the artist might have received early intelligence of that incident."

" The incredulous pretended so," replied my aunt.

" What became of the adept?" demanded I.

" Why, a warrant came down shortly afterwards to arrest him for high-treason, as an agent of the Chevalier

St. George; and Lady Bothwell recollecting the hints which had escaped the doctor, an ardent friend of the Protestant succession, did then call to remembrance, that this man was chiefly *proné* among the ancient matrons of her own political persuasion. It certainly seemed probable that intelligence from the continent, which could easily have been transmitted by an active and powerful agent, might have enabled him to prepare such a scene of phantasmagoria as she had herself witnessed. Yet there were so many difficulties in assigning a natural explanation, that, to the day of her death, she remained in great doubt on the subject, and much disposed to cut the Gordian knot by admitting the existence of supernatural agency."

"But, my dear aunt," said I, "what became of the man of skill?"

"Oh, he was too good a fortune-teller not to be able to foresee that his own destiny would be tragical if he waited the arrival of the man with the silver greyhound upon his sleeve. He made, as we say, a moonlight flitting, and was nowhere to be seen or heard of. Some noise there was about papers or letters found in the house, but it died away, and Doctor Baptista Damiotti was soon as little talked of as Galen or Hippocrates."

"And Sir Philip Forester," said I, "did he too vanish for ever from the public scene?"

"No," replied my kind informer. "He was heard of once more, and it was upon a remarkable occasion. It is said that we Scots, when there was such a nation in existence, have, among our full peck of virtues, one or two little barleycorns of vice. In particular, it is alleged that we rarely forgive, and never forget, any injuries received; that we used to make an idol of our resentment, as poor Lady

Constance did of her grief; and are addicted, as Burns
says, to 'Nursing our wrath to keep it warm.' Lady Bothwell was not without this feeling; and, I believe, nothing
whatever, scarce the restoration of the Stuart line, could
have happened so delicious to her feelings as an opportunity of being revenged on Sir Philip Forester for the deep
and double injury which had deprived her of a sister and
of a brother. But nothing of him was heard or known
till many a year had passed away."

At length—it was on a Fastern's E'en (Shrovetide) assembly, at which the whole fashion of Edinburgh attended,
full and frequent, and when Lady Bothwell had a seat
amongst the lady patronesses, that one of the attendants on
the company whispered into her ear, that a gentleman
wished to speak with her in private.

"In private? and in an assembly-room?—he must be
mad—tell him to call upon me to-morrow morning."

"I said so, my lady," answered the man, "but he desired me to give you this paper."

She undid the billet, which was curiously folded and
sealed. It only bore the words, " *On business of life and
death,*" written in a hand which she had never seen before.
Suddenly it occurred to her that it might concern the safety
of some of her political friends; she therefore followed the
messenger to a small apartment where the refreshments
were prepared, and from which the general company was
excluded. She found an old man, who at her approach
rose up and bowed profoundly. His appearance indicated
a broken constitution, and his dress, though sedulously rendered conforming to the etiquette of a ball-room, was worn
and tarnished, and hung in folds about his emaciated person. Lady Bothwell was about to feel for her purse, ex-

pecting to get rid of the supplicant at the expense of a little money, but some fear of a mistake arrested her purpose. She therefore gave the man leisure to explain himself.

"I have the honour to speak with the Lady Bothwell?"

"I am Lady Bothwell; allow me to say that this is no time or place for long explanations.—What are your commands with me?"

"Your ladyship," said the old man, "had once a sister."

"True; whom I loved as my own soul."

"And a brother."

"The bravest, the kindest, the most affectionate," said Lady Bothwell.

"Both these beloved relatives you lost by the fault of an unfortunate man," continued the stranger.

"By the crime of an unnatural, bloody-minded murderer," said the lady.

"I am answered," replied the old man, bowing, as if to withdraw.

"Stop, sir, I command you," said Lady Bothwell.—"Who are you, that, at such a place and time, come to recal these horrible recollections? I insist upon knowing."

"I am one who means Lady Bothwell no injury; but, on the contrary, to offer her the means of doing a deed of Christian charity which the world would wonder at, and which Heaven would reward; but I find her in no temper for such a sacrifice as I was prepared to ask."

"Speak out, sir; what is your meaning?" said Lady Bothwell.

"The wretch that has wronged you so deeply," rejoined the stranger, "is now on his deathbed. His days have been days of misery, his nights have been sleepless hours of anguish—yet he cannot die without your forgiveness. His life has been an unremitting penance—yet he dares not part from his burthen while your curses load his soul."

"Tell him," said Lady Bothwell sternly, "to ask pardon of that Being whom he has so greatly offended; not of an erring mortal like himself. What could my forgiveness avail him?"

"Much," answered the old man. "It will be an earnest of that which he may then venture to ask from his Creator, lady, and from yours. Remember, Lady Bothwell, you too have a deathbed to look forward to; your soul may, all human souls must, feel the awe of facing the judgment-seat, with the wounds of an untented conscience, raw, and rankling—what thought would it be then that should whisper, 'I have given no mercy, how then shall I ask it?'"

"Man, whosoever thou mayst be," replied Lady Bothwell, "urge me not so cruelly. It would be but blasphemous hypocrisy to utter with my lips the words which every throb of my heart protests against. They would open the earth and give to light the wasted form of my sister—the bloody form of my murdered brother.—Forgive him?—Never, never!"

"Great God!" cried the old man, holding up his hands; "is it thus the worms which thou hast called out of dust obey the commands of their Maker? Farewell, proud and unforgiving woman. Exult that thou hast added to a death in want and pain the agonies of religious despair; but never again mock Heaven by petitioning for the pardon which thou hast refused to grant."

He was turning from her.

"Stop," she exclaimed; "I will try; yes, I will try to pardon him."

"Gracious lady," said the old man, "you will relieve the over-burdened soul which dare not sever itself from its sinful companion of earth without being at peace with you. What do I know—your forgiveness may perhaps preserve for penitence the dregs of a wretched life."

"Ha!" said the lady, as a sudden light broke on her, "it is the villain himself." And grasping Sir Philip Forester, for it was he, and no other, by the collar, she raised a cry of "Murder, murder! seize the murderer!"

At an exclamation so singular, in such a place, the company thronged into the apartment, but Sir Philip Forester was no longer there. He had forcibly extricated himself from Lady Bothwell's hold, and had run out of the apartment which opened on the landing-place of the stair. There seemed no escape in that direction, for there were several persons coming up the steps, and others descending. But the unfortunate man was desperate. He threw himself over the balustrade, and alighted safely in the lobby, though a leap of fifteen feet at least, then dashed into the street, and was lost in darkness. Some of the Bothwell family made pursuit, and had they come up with the fugitive they might have perhaps slain him; for in those days men's blood ran warm in their veins. But the police did not interfere; the matter most criminal having happened long since, and in a foreign land. Indeed it was always thought that this extraordinary scene originated in a hypocritical experiment, by which Sir Philip desired to ascertain whether he might return to his native country in safety from the resentment of a family which he had injured so deeply. As the result fell out so contrary to his wishes, he is believed to have returned to the continent, and there died in exile. So closed the tale of the MYSTERIOUS MIRROR.

STANZAS

BY LORD F. L. GOWER,

ON THE EXECUTION MILITAIRE,

A PRINT FROM A PICTURE BY VIGNERON.

It exhibits the moment when the condemned soldier kneels to receive the fire of the party appointed to be his executioners. His friend, and the priest, are seen retiring. His dog, whom he is endeavouring to shake off, still fawns upon him, and seems desirous to share his fate.

His doom has been decreed,
He has own'd the fatal deed,
    And its forfeit is here to abide:
No mercy now can save,
They have dug the soldier's grave,
And the hapless and the brave
    Kneels beside.

No bandage wraps his eye,
He is kneeling there to die,
    Unblinded, undaunted, alone.
His parting prayer has ceased,
And his comrade, and the priest,
From their gloomy task released,—
    Both are gone.

His kindred are not near
The fatal shot to hear,
    They can but weep the deed when 'tis done;

They would shriek, and wail, and pray,
It is good for him to-day
That his friends are far away,
   —All but one!

In mute, but wild despair,
The faithful hound is there;
   He has reach'd his master's side with a spring.
To the hand which rear'd and fed,
Till the ebbing pulse has fled,
Till that hand is cold and dead,
   He will cling.

What art, in lure or wile,
That one can now beguile
   From the side of his master and friend?
He has burst his cord in twain;
To the arm which strives in vain
To repel him, he will strain
   To the end.

The tear-drop who shall blame,
Though it dim the veteran's aim,
   Though each breast along the line heave the sigh?
Yet 't were cruel now to save,
And together in the grave,
The faithful and the brave,
   Let them lie.

ON LOVE.

BY PERCY BYSSHE SHELLEY.

WHAT is Love? Ask him who lives what is life; ask him who adores what is God.

I know not the internal constitution of other men, nor even of thine whom I now address. I see that in some external attributes they resemble me, but when, misled by that appearance, I have thought to appeal to something in common and unburthen my inmost soul to them, I have found my language misunderstood, like one in a distant and savage land. The more opportunities they have afforded me for experience, the wider has appeared the interval between us, and to a greater distance have the points of sympathy been withdrawn. With a spirit ill-fitted to sustain such proof, trembling and feeble through its tenderness, I have every where sought, and have found only repulse and disappointment.

Thou demandest what is Love. It is that powerful attraction towards all we conceive, or fear, or hope beyond ourselves, when we find within our own thoughts the chasm of an insufficient void, and seek to awaken in all things that are, a community with what we experience within ourselves. If we reason we would be understood; if we imagine we would that the airy children of our brain were born anew within another's; if we feel we would that another's nerves should vibrate to our own, that the beams of their eyes should kindle at once and mix and melt into our own; that lips of motionless ice should not reply to lips quivering and burning with the heart's best blood:—this is Love. This is the bond and the sanction which connects not only man with man, but with every thing which exists. We are born into the world, and there is something within us, which from the instant that we live, more and more thirsts after its likeness. It is probably in correspondence with this law that the infant drains milk from the bosom of its mother; this propensity develops itself with the development of our nature. We dimly see within our intellectual nature, a miniature as it were of our entire self, yet deprived of all that we condemn or despise, the ideal prototype of every thing excellent and lovely that we are capable of conceiving as belonging to the nature of man. Not only the portrait of our external being, but an assemblage of the minutest particles of which our nature is composed *: a mirror whose surface reflects only the forms of purity and brightness: a soul within our own soul that describes a circle around its proper Paradise, which pain and sorrow and evil dare not overleap. To this we eagerly refer all sensations, thirsting that they should resemble and correspond with it. The discovery of its antitype; the meeting with an understanding capable of clearly estimating our own; an imagination which should enter into and seize upon the subtle and delicate peculiarities which we have delighted to cherish and unfold in secret, with a frame, whose nerves, like the chords of two exquisite lyres, strung to the accompaniment of one delightful voice, vibrate with the vibrations of our own; and a combination of all these in such proportion as

---

* These words are ineffectual and metaphorical. Most words are so, —no help!

the type within demands: this is the invisible and unattainable point to which Love tends; and to attain which, it urges forth the powers of man to arrest the faintest shadow of that, without the possession of which, there is no rest nor respite to the heart over which it rules. Hence in solitude, or that deserted state when we are surrounded by human beings and yet they sympathize not with us, we love the flowers, the grass, the waters, and the sky. In the motion of the very leaves of spring, in the blue air, there is then found a secret correspondence with our heart. There is eloquence in the tongueless wind, and a melody in the flowing brooks and the rustling of the reeds beside them, which by their inconceivable relation to something within the soul awaken the spirits to dance of breathless rapture, and bring tears of mysterious tenderness to the eyes, like the enthusiasm of patriotic success, or the voice of one beloved singing to you alone. Sterne says that if he were in a desert he would love some cypress. So soon as this want or power is dead, man becomes a living sepulchre of himself, and what yet survives is the mere husk of what once he was.

TO ———

BY F. MANSEL REYNOLDS.

THAT e'er my visits will become
  Too frequent, much I doubt;
For though I 've found you oft at home,
  Too oft I 've *found you out!*

THE COUNTRY GIRL.

BY W. WORDSWORTH.

THAT happy gleam of vernal eyes,
Those locks from summer's golden skies,
   That o'er thy brow are shed;
That cheek—a kindling of the morn,
That lip—a rose-bud from the thorn,
   I saw; and Fancy sped
To scenes Arcadian, whispering, through soft air,
Of bliss that grows without a care;
Of happiness that never flies—
How can it where love never dies?
Of promise whispering, where no blight
Can reach the innocent delight;
Where Pity to the mind convey'd
In pleasure is the darkest shade,
That Time, unwrinkled grandsire, flings
From his smoothly-gliding wings.

   What mortal form, what earthly face,
Inspired the pencil, lines to trace,
And mingle colours that could breed
Such rapture, nor want power to feed?
For, had thy charge been idle flowers,
Fair Damsel, o'er my captive mind,
To truth and sober reason blind,

Painted by J. Holmes.   Engraved by C. Heath.

THE COUNTRY GIRL.

Printed by Mc Queen.

Published by T. Hurst & Co St Paul's Churchyard, and R. Jennings, 2, Poultry.

'Mid that soft air, those long-lost bowers,
The sweet illusion might have hung for hours!
—Thanks to this tell-tale sheaf of corn,
That touchingly bespeaks thee born
Life's daily tasks with them to share,
Who, whether from their lowly bed
They rise, or rest the weary head,
Do *weigh* the blessing they entreat
From heaven, and *feel* what they repeat,
While they give utterance to the prayer
That asks for daily bread.

ON TWO SISTERS.

BY F. M. REYNOLDS.

YOUNG Dora's gentle, pure, and kind,
With lofty, clear, and polish'd mind:
But Dora, rich in mental grace,
Alas! is somewhat poor in face;
Pity her noble soul don't warm,
A Grecian statue's perfect form!

But, Anne, in thee all charms combine;
Each gift of beauty, sweet, is thine!
Thy form surpasses e'en desire;
Thine eyes are rolling orbs of fire!
Enchanting, perfect, is the whole—
Pity the statue wants a soul!

THE HALF-BROTHERS.

BY THE AUTHORS OF THE O'HARA TALES.

LUCY HAWKINS, at sixteen, was the belle, if not the beauty, of her little sea-washed village on the coast of Kent. Other girls might boast a more perfect shape and handsomer features; but her effect, her expression, or—if a fashionable French word may, with allowances, be applied to a lowly maiden—her *tournure* eclipsed them all. She was also celebrated for a vivacity of manner and conversation unusual amongst young females of her class; nay, in the opinions of a numerous circle of good judges, who constantly enjoyed her company and discourse, Lucy Hawkins deserved to be termed witty.

Her mother kept the post-office of the village, together with a general huckster's shop, and a hotel in one of her out-houses for very humble wanderers or sojourners—beds threepence per night. Upon a large deal chest, the good dame's flour-store, which stood under her shop window, opposite to her counter, hard-worked labourers, employed in the neighbourhood, would sit and eat their four pennyworth of bread and cheese, and drink their half pint of small-beer, by way of the morning's or afternoon's meal; and Lucy generally served them, or else stood by while they were served, and, at the same time, her good humour materially helped to give zest to their meagre breakfast or dinner. At the upper end of the counter was a rush-bottomed, curiously-legged, old oak chair, a fixture, put forward for any chatty neighbour or visitor who might like an hour's gossiping; and since its establishment it had, indeed, seldom been left empty, as was indicated, even during its leisure moments, by a little round cavity worn in the tiled floor, just at the spot where its successive occupants necessarily rested their heels. And with the revellers on the chest, and the numerous patrons of this oak chair, to say nothing of ordinary customers and her own particular friends, Lucy became quite a public character, and, as has been hinted, quite a favourite. The poor people, who, towards night, crept through the shop to their straw beds over the hen-house in the yard, also shared her sparkling conversation, and acknowledged its cheery influence.

And there were other visitors who also admitted her attractions, though it would have been better for Lucy if we could limit her encomiastic friends to those already mentioned. Over one department of the manifold concern she had absolute sway; her mother did not know how to read hand-writing, and, considering the frequency of almost illegible superscriptions on the backs of letters, the de-putation of authority alluded to became a matter of pru-dence, if not of necessity. At the inquiry of every claimant for letters " to be left till called for," it was Lucy, therefore, who always unlocked the little rude deal box—about the size and much in the shape of a salt-box—which, clumsily nailed against the wooden pane with the slit in the shop window, formed the whole ma-terial of the post-office branch of the establishment.

Many officers of the preventive-service, although they had abundance of unemployed men to go to Mrs. Hawkins's shop in their stead, would call in every morning to ask for

their letters; and at different hours of their idle day return
to purchase a quarter of an ounce of Scotch snuff, or something else of which they could have less use, such as a row
of pins, a yard of tape, or a reel of thread. In fact, it
became evident that three of them were rivals for the
smiles of Lucy Hawkins.

Two of the three soon ensured to themselves however
any thing but her smiles. For offences separately received
at their hands, she invariably left the shop whenever they
entered it; and as Lucy's conduct was not a mere show of
female anger, they absented themselves, and gave up their
unmanly pursuit. The third, whose visits were still received, was more seriously in love with Lucy than either of
his friends; but, whether from a nicer sense of honour, or
that the fate of the others had taught him a lesson, Lieut.
Stone did not lightly or hastily tell her so. Much younger
than his rivals, perhaps he was more romantic, and, particularly since Lucy's late specimen of self-assertion, would
not indulge his admiration with a view to any mean indulgence of it. And, in fact, when, after sitting in the shop,
upon the flour-chest, or in the old chair, day after day for
more than six months, he at last whispered his sentiments
to Lucy, the declaration sounded seriously and respectfully
to her ear, and, she concluded, could be made only in one
hope—that of obtaining her hand, with the due consent of
father and mother.

The scene must now be very abruptly changed to the
reader, with a breach of the three unities of time, place,
and action.

Twelve years after Lucy Hawkins accepted the suit of
her chosen lover, we enter a small wooden house, indeed a
very poor shed, in another little sea-coast hamlet, many

miles distant from her native one. The walls of its only sitting-room, a kitchen, are bare; the floor is tiled; and the few articles of indispensable furniture are old, common, and crazy: and yet the poor apartment looks clean, or, to use an humble but expressive and very English word, tidy. A woman, as ill-clad as her house is ill-appointed, but, like it, tidy too, sits on a stool teaching a sturdy, sun-burnt boy of seven years to read out of a Reading Made Easy. She seems about forty, but may be much younger than she looks, for her composed features would suggest long acquaintance with misfortune—the often successful anticipator of time's utmost efforts to destroy. A half-finished female dress, of materials too costly, and of shape too fashionable to be destined to the use of the lowly occupant of the lowly abode, lies, together with the implements of woman's industry, upon a table at her side, hinting the mode of pursuit by which she earns scanty bread for her young pupil and herself.

The task is over, and Billy is kissed and called a good boy: and while his mother combs his yellow hair in smooth and equal portions towards either temple—" There, my king," she says; " and now, where is brother to take you out to play?"

" The naughty great boys were *quarrelling* Charley on the beach, mother, when he sent Billy home to his task to be rid of them."

" And what game did they quarrel over, Billy?"

" No ga-om, mother; but Dick Saunders called Charley a bad name."

" Tell mother the bad name, my man."

" Billy caunt—he doesn't know it now, mother."

Their conversation was interrupted by the quick entrance of Charley himself. The moment his mother saw him, she uttered an alarmed cry. His clenched hands were thrust into his trowsers' pockets; he frowned, for the first time in his life his mother had seen him do so; his lips quivered; tears glazed his eyes; his face, nay, his forehead and ears flamed scarlet, and blood trickled down his cheeks. Obviously, he had been fighting a hard battle, but, as obviously, was the victor. The boy was about twelve.

" Let Billy go play at the door, and I 'll tell you, mother," he said, after she had addressed many anxious inquiries to him.

She led the little fellow out, and shut the door upon herself and Charley. He dropt in a chair, flung his arms over the table, laid his face upon them, and burst into a furious fit of tears.

" Naughty Dick Saunders has hurt you, Charley, mother's darling!" she cried, approaching him.

" No—not as well as I have hurt *him*—the storyteller! the puppy!" sobbed Charles. " Mother, Dick Saunders spoke ill of me, and of you."

" What did he say, Charley?"

" I can't repeat it after him—I won't. But, mother, I be old enough to ask you what I 'm going to ask—Was Master Turner, who died last year, Billy's father?"

" To be sure he was, Charley."   She grew uneasy.

" And your husband?"

" Yes."

" And *my* father too?"

She changed colour, and dropt her eyes beneath the deep glance of her child.

" Now, Charley, I know what they said of you and me; and the time is indeed come for me to speak to you of what nearly concerns you."

" Did Dick Saunders tell no story, mother?" interrupted Charley, sitting upright, and again unconsciously scrutinizing her face. She raised her eyes, met his for an instant, and then sank back in her chair, covering her features with her hands, and weeping dolefully.

" I ask pardon, mother," said the generous and hitherto gentle boy, as he gained her side, and put his arms round her neck: " you always loved me, and I shall always love you, let them say what they will of us. Kiss Charley, mother, won't you?"

Fondly, almost wildly she embraced him, and resumed. " No, Charley—Master Turner, my husband, was *not* your father: stop a moment." She stept into her little bedroom; returned with a small, oval, red-leather case; placed it in his hand; sat down; averted her head; began to move the work on the table, and would vainly hide her continued tears, as she added, " Open that, and you will know more of your father."

While he obeyed her commands, Charley recollected that he had more than once detected his mother weeping over the little red-leather case. When the miniature met his eye, the boy started.

" My father was a ship's captain!" he cried.

" He was an officer in the king's navy," she answered.

" And a gentleman, mother?"

" His commission made him one, Charley; but he would have been a true gentleman without it."

" And he married you before Master Turner married you, mother?"

" Charley, your father and I never were married."

A pause ensued. Charley's features betrayed a bitter and a fierce inward combat, as his glance still fixed on the miniature.

" Is he dead?" he at length asked.

" I hope not, but I am not sure. Sometimes I think one thing, sometimes another. Listen, my king. I was very young when I met your father; and I wondered, and many others wondered what he could see in me to love. I was his inferior in every way. To be sure, my poor mother had managed to keep me at good schools till I was a great girl, and perhaps this made me something in his eyes. Then, when we began to keep company, with father's and mother's consent, he taught me, like a master, himself, a great many things that improved my mind and my manners, ay, and my heart too; but I am not going on with my story. We were to be married at the end of two years. Before the first year came round he was ordered from the blockade-service to a ship, at only a few hours' notice. He ran down to our shop, and showing the letter, prayed mother to let us be made man and wife that very evening. She would not hear of it, saying I was too young, and did not know my own mind, and would not know how to behave as his wife. He begged and prayed once again, and cried tears, and went on his knees; she held firm to her word. But, alas! Charley, it had been doing better if she had not held so firm to it, or else not have left us alone to take leave of each other that evening. Crying and sobbing, in sorrow and in love, we forgot ourselves, Charley; and next day, ay, before it was day, your father left our village, and I have never seen him since."

" But he has sent letters to you, mother?"

" I got none, if he did: though I believe he did, and that an enemy kept them from my hands. A very short time after he left us, my father died, my mother grew poor, and we were turned out of our comfortable little house, not being able to pay our rent. The shop was re-opened by a woman and her daughter who bore me no good will, and on your father's account too. He had paid some compliments to the daughter before he met me, and they blamed me for taking him from them. And—God forgive me if I wrong either mother or daughter—but I do fear that letters from your father to me, and from me to him, were stopt by the new keepers of our post-office. Well, Charley, you were born while my mother and I lived in a very poor way, trying to support ourselves with our needles, and keep out of the work-house. Your father's silence almost broke my heart. I did not suspect foul play about the letters then; 'tis only lately people gave me some hints, and all I could think was that he had forsaken us both, my king. Mother died too, and you and I were left quite alone, Charley. Years after, when, try as I would or could, we were getting worse and worse off, Master Turner came from his village to ours, on business, and knowing my whole story, asked me to marry him. He was a man well to do in the world at that time, and a kind man too; and so, after giving up all other hopes, I thought, Charley, that, even for your sake, I ought not to refuse a comfortable home and comfortable living. But it seemed as if every one was to have ill-luck with me. Good Master Turner began to grow poor from that very day, till last year, when he died, leaving us as badly off as he found us; and that's the whole story, Charley; only, here are you and I living alone again, with your little half-brother, Billy, to keep us company."

"Well; and I be glad of his company, mother," said Charley: "I always loved little Billy for his own sake, and because he loved me"—(the mutual affection of the boys was indeed very remarkable) "and now, though, as you say, he turns out to be only my half-brother, I'll love him better for his father's sake, who was a friend to you when you wanted a friend. But we must open the door and let him in."

Billy's voice had been heard calling on Charles to run down with him to the beach, and see the grand three-masted ship that was passing but a little way out, and, people said, seemed about to send a boat ashore. Ere Charles went to the door, he held out the miniature, and asked, "May I see it often again, mother?"

"Keep it,—'tis your own, Charley—here"—passing a riband through the loop at its top, "hang it round your neck."

As his mother secured it, he once more felt her tears dropping fast on his head, and looking up into her face, he stole his arms around her.

"Go, now, mother's darlings," as hand in hand they left her humble threshold; "but, Charley, do not stray out far on the sands: it will be a spring-tide, I fear, and the breeze comes fresh from the sea."

Still hand in hand they proceeded on their walk, Billy unusually communicative, and Charles unusually silent. Indeed the younger boy remarked his brother's taciturnity, and taxed him with it. They met groups of their former playmates in the village-street, whom the child wished to join; but Charles, chucking him closer to his side, passed them by, knitting his brow and holding up his head. On the shingles appeared other groups, and the young misanthrope would not descend to the water's edge until he had proceeded several hundred yards above their position.

It was a beautiful spring day. The breeze lashed the waves into a sportive fury. Sun and cloud, light and shade, alternated their effects over the wide bosom of the sea, streaking it with gold and pea-green, with dark purple or deep blue. Now a distant sail was a white speck on the horizon, now a spot of dark, dotting a clear sky. The three-master, of which little Billy had spoken, lay-to, about a mile from shore. Charles knew her to be an East-Indiaman. His brother urged him to approach her as closely as the sands permitted. Still wrapt up in his own thoughts and feelings, Charles silently stepped down the shingles, looking jealously around to note if they were alone.

Behind him, as he began to move towards the waves, was a low line of cliff, forming, at a particular point, a jutting platform, from the outward edge of which the continuation of the cliff swept, like a buttress, to the shingles. Before him stretched the strand, to nearly the distance of half a mile, where it was met by an irregular circle of black rocks, closely wedged together, and enclosing the last patch of sand visible even at low tide. Charles had not intended to approach this spot; but as he walked in an oblique direction from it, some straggling boys appeared coming against him, and he hastily led his little charge to the convenient screen of the tall rocks.

The tide had for some time been coming in. Often before, however, Charles had ventured farther out, when it was more advanced, and returned to shore with only wet

feet and a splashing. The rocks could not at any point
be easily scaled, so high and broad was their barrier;
nor did they admit of egress into the sandy area they
girded, save at a particular spot, sea-ward, where, some
feet from their base, appeared a narrow fissure, still difficult of access. Charles therefore walked round them
until he gained this opening; then, assisting his little
brother to climb up to it, the two boys soon stood upon a
projection inside the rocky belt, and turned their faces
towards the sea.

They could perceive, by a bustle on the deck of the In-
diaman, now so near to them, that a boat would soon be
lowered from her side. They looked out, much interested,
until the boat lightly touched the tossing waves near the
vessel's prow, and became strongly manned, as if to put off
for shore. Still, however, the men rested on their oars,
and seemed waiting for some other person to descend.
And, in a mood that sympathized with the scene, Charles
continued to watch the boat, dancing to and fro, and sometimes almost jumping out of the water; for the breeze
grew stiffer, and the waves rougher. Half an hour he
stood motionless, disregarding, for the first time in his life,
the prattle of the little boy at his side. At last the individual for whom the boat waited, clad in blue and white,
and gold lace, to Billy's great delight, jumped in amongst
his men, stood up, at their head, pointed to shore, and was
rapidly rowed towards it.

For some time the near roar of waters had been ring-
ing in Charles's ear, but he made light of the warning, for he confidently argued from experience, whenever his thoughts reverted to the matter, that there was
still sufficient time to return to the shingles with scarce

a wet shoe. But he did not reckon that the spot of sand, along with which he now stood enclosed, was much higher than the outer sands which stretched to the bases of the rocks. He did not reckon that the tide, at a certain period of its flow, after turning a near point of land, usually ran with almost the rapidity of a mill-stream, against the right-hand segment of the barrier, and then, directed by its curve, inundated in a trice the previously open space between it and the shingles. Above all, he did not remember what his mother had hinted at parting; for, indeed, her omen proved true; it was a spring-tide.

The ship's boat, still seen at a distance, glanced athwart the patch of sea revealed through the fissure at which the boys looked out. More alive, after its disappearance, to the unusual noise of the waters, Charley took his brother's hand to lead him home by the way they had come. To his consternation, a fiercely-crested wave leaped into their faces through the narrow opening, drenching both to the skin. He let go Billy's hand, and sprang up to the top of the circular wall of rocks. A foamy sea tossed all around him. His eye caught the gallant boat, about a quarter of a mile distant. He screamed to it; jumped down to his little brother; dragged him up to the spot he had just quitted, and screamed again. There was a little cavity, formed by the irregular junction, at their sharp extremities, of the rocks, and in this he placed the now bewildered and weeping child, to preserve him from being dashed inward by the quickly increasing sea; and clinging himself to the highest pinnacle he could grasp, once more he wildly hailed the boat.

Most probably he had now caught its notice. It put

round and pulled towards him; but soon seemed deterred from venturing too near the dangerous rocks.

"Oh God!—oh, mother, mother! your Billy! Mother's darling! *he* at least will be drowned, though I may swim till they pick me up—and all *my* fault!—but no, no!" He pulled off his jacket and vest, and tore his shirt into long strips.—"No! he shall not!—Come, Billy! I will tie you to my back; never fear, my king—and see if I don't swim like a fish for you!"

The child, having heard and noted all his words and actions, had stopped crying, and, as if struck with Charles's noble conduct and sentiments, and unconsciously sympathizing them, answered: "I won't, Charley, I won't;—I should sink you, and we should only be drowned together, then, and no one left with mother."

All this while breakers had been dashing from without nearly up to the summits of the rocks at the opposite sweep of the circle, and as Charles eagerly, indeed violently renewed his entreaties, they at last came leaping and plunging up to its very edge, like dark, white-maned warhorses, trying to rear and paw over some high and well-guarded embankment. Once again he hoarsely cried out to the boat. It was nearer to him, but still seemed cautious of actual approach. He turned for the last time to Billy, and seized him in his arms to compel him to do his bidding. The riband which held his father's miniature round his neck snapped in the exertion; the miniature itself was rolling outwardly into the surf; he snatched at it, and secured it, but lost his balance, and the next instant was kicking among the breakers.

The captain of the East-Indiaman had witnessed the

Painted by R. Westall R.A.

Engraved by C. Heath.

LUCY.

greater part of the scene between the young brothers, and, as he saw Charles tumble from the rocks, gallantly ordered his men to dare a good deal, and pull towards the spot where the boy had sunk. Presently Charley reappeared, swimming stoutly; not for the boat, however, but back again to the now almost invisible rocks. The captain and his men called to him, but he did not heed them. It has been mentioned that when the boys walked out to the sands, they directly turned their backs upon a platform formed in a low line of cliff. At that moment, not only the platform and its rugged buttress-base, but the shingles beneath, were perfectly dry. Now the raging surf of a spring-tide, excited by a stiff breeze, foamed up to the level of the former: and almost simultaneously with Charley's reappearance, a woman, screaming loudly, descended the difficult passage from the brow of the cliff, and gained the slippery shelf. Many people followed her to the top line of the precipice, but no one ventured to her side. Her cries reached the young swimmer, through all the roar of the sea, and he redoubled his vain efforts to reach his little brother. But very soon exertion became useless. At one enraged and reinforced charge of the breakers, the area enclosed by the rocky circle, hitherto little intruded on, was inundated, and no part of the black barrier-line remained visible, except that formed by the pinnacles amid which the child stood wedged: a curling chain of foam supplied its place. And now, his mother from the shore, his brother from the sea, and the captain and his men from their boat, witnessed the conduct of the little sufferer. He had been sitting; he stood up: a breaker struck him; he staggered: another came; he fell, disappeared: was still seen, however, upon a point of rock, raising his hands, and clapping them over his head, until at the third blow the little fellow became ingulfed in the whirling waters.

The boat was now very near to Charles; and, at last, seemingly attentive to the remonstrance of its crew, he turned, and languidly swam towards its side.

"What the deuce has the young grampus fished up between his teeth?" said the captain, as he assisted in reaching out an oar; "a boiled crab, I reckon; though, where they got a fire to boil it, at the bottom of this surf, is more than I can imagine."

Charles was dragged into the boat, and without a word or a cry fell stupified upon its bottom. The miniature dropped from his unclenched teeth; the captain took it up, opened it, and startled his men by uttering a loud exclamation. Then he stooped to Charley's face, and peered into it; then glanced to the cliff; and, finally, ordering every oar to pull for the shingles, he knelt on one knee, raised Charley's head to the other; and his crew were still more surprised to see their bluff captain embrace the almost senseless lad, kiss his cheeks and forehead, and weep over him profusely, though in silence.

The boat had not shot far, when little Billy floated ahead. The captain gently, though hastily, put Charles down, and with much energy assisted in picking up the child, who soon lay stretched beside his half-brother, rescued indeed from the sea, but, it seemed evident, quite dead. Still the captain cried, "Pull, men, pull!"

Vigorously and skilfully obeying his orders, they ran the lively boat upon the shingles, a good distance below the point at which the low cliff gradually dipped to their surface. The mother flew down to meet her children and their unknown friends. The anxious crowd followed her. She received Charley from the captain's arms; a sailor followed, holding Billy, wrapped in the captain's jacket, to his bosom. At her first word the elder boy opened his eyes; after straining him to her heart she flew to his brother. No word had effect upon him. The captain called out for a surgeon: the village practitioner and the blockade surgeon were both at hand. They caused the child to be conveyed into a neighbouring cottage, and there, in the presence of the mother and the captain, promptly engaged in all the usual measures for restoring animation: but all failed. They repeated their exertions, still without effect; and at length, pronouncing Billy to be a corse, left the cottage.

Charles had been stretched across the foot of the bed upon which, wrapped in blankets, lay his little half-brother. At first he did not comprehend his situation, or notice the occurrences around him. Now, however, he seemed to hear the departing words of the surgeons, for, raising himself upon his elbow, he gazed first into his mother's face, as she sat in silent anguish by the bedside, and then he tried to move upward towards Billy. While making this effort, the captain, gently laying his hand on the mother's shoulder, asked to speak aside with her. She arose, in the languid indifference of grief, and followed him into a corner of the room, out of view of the boat. "Lucy!" was the captain's only word, soothingly whispered at her ear. She drew back, looked up into his face, and was caught in his arms. A brief explanation proved that her suspicions of her revengeful rival at the village post-office were well-founded. While, from the suppression of the captain's letters to her, Lucy had believed him cruel and

F 2

faithless, the holding back, also, of her letters to him had caused her sincere lover to conclude that she was no better than a village-coquette, who, the moment he left her presence, forgot him, and insulted his memory and his devotion in the smiles of a new admirer; perhaps in the smiles of more than one. Hence, after her seeming silence of many years, he had proudly struggled to give up Lucy Hawkins for ever; and though, since their parting, he could often have returned to her village, he would not so far humiliate himself. Some inquiries, however, he condescended to make by a confidential person sent for the purpose, merely with the view of ascertaining if Lucy was alive or dead,—for death alone, he argued, could explain her supposed conduct. About the very time his emissary arrived in the village, she had become the envied wife of the rich Master Turner; and this intelligence necessarily confirmed his former angry resolutions.

The captain and Lucy yet spoke, when Charles's voice sounded shrill and joyfully from the bed; "Yes, Billy, yes!—'t is Charley! Billy!—mother's darling!" They stepped round to the bedside. He had crept under the blankets, and clasped the child close to his bosom; and now, indeed, the efforts of the surgeons, although despaired of by themselves, began to yield a good result.

" He would not die, to let you say I killed him, mother," said Charles, laughing through his tears.

"The child lives, by Heavens!" cried the captain.

That day Captain Stone was married to the woman of his early choice; and having despatched before evening the trifling business which first called him to shore, he conveyed his wife to his ship, together with her two sons, and pursued his voyage.

SCRAPS OF ITALY.

BY LORD MORPETH.

I.

ON SEEING A TREE IN THE ISOLA BELLA UPON WHICH
BUONAPARTE HAD CARVED SOME LETTERS TWO
DAYS BEFORE THE BATTLE OF MARENGO.

PERCHANCE as here, beside the crystal flood,
In pleased repose the hero-despot stood,
Where art and nature emulously smile
With all their charms on each enchanted isle,
The scene's own soft contagion gently stole
O'er each stern purpose of his toil-worn soul:
Perchance e'en here he griev'd awhile to mar
Such climes of beauty with the waste of war;
Wish'd that the tumult of his days might cease
In some bright vale, in some blest home of peace;
Sigh'd for the joys he ne'er was doom'd to gain;
Then rush'd to conquer on Marengo's plain.

II.

ON LEAVING BOLOGNA.

FAREWELL, Bologna!   Peace be on thy walls,
Thy long-drawn porticoes, thy marble halls!
I sing not, that thy broad and sunny plain
With plenty girds the Adriatic main;

That the pale olive and the purple vine
Love to ascend thy neighb'ring Apennine.
The Muse for thee would fondly seek to raise
At Painting's sister-shrine one note of praise.
With art unerring, since to nature true,
The bold design here each Caracci drew;
Here great Domenichino caught the flame,
Equall'd, but not obscur'd, his master's fame;
Here on the canvas Guido learn'd to trace
The might of passion, and the soul of grace;
With darker lineaments, and sterner shade,
Guercino's skill each manly form array'd;
While soft Albano from the Paphian grove
Stole every gentle form of infant love.

III.

ON VIRGIL'S TOMB.

And dost thou rest e'en here, thou mighty shade?
　　Can yon gray mound be so indeed divine?
Was all of thee that could remain here laid?
　　All—save thy deathless, save thy matchless line?

For none like thine, howe'er the creed be wrong,
　　E'er o'er my soul held such transcendent sway;
Not e'en blind Homer's universal song,
　　Not my own Shakspeare's wild and passion'd lay.

And oh! the vision to my view unfurl'd,
　　That makes thy tomb be worthy e'en of thee!
Earth, sea, and sky, the brightest of the world:
　　Beneath me is thy own Parthenope.

Still where the vine's young tendrils freshest creep,
Where all is lovely that is not sublime,
Honour'd thy grave, and peaceful be thy sleep,
Art's fav'rite son, mid nature's fairest clime.

IV.

ON LEAVING ITALY.

My steps are turn'd to England—yet I sigh
To leave Ausonia's blue and balmy sky;
I fain would linger mid her hills and plains,
Their living beauties, or their bright remains;
Still tread each ruin's haunted round, and still
Explore the windings of each storied rill,
The cypress grove, the vineyard's trellis'd shade,
The olive thicket, and the poplar glade.

My steps are turn'd to England—yet I grieve
That this should be my last Italian eve.
And ye eternal snows! whom now I hail
In twilight's rosy hues from Turin's vale,
Whom nature to the land a barrier gave,
Sublime to view, but impotent to save,
Thus the next sun shall o'er ye set, but I
Must gaze upon it in a colder sky.

My steps are turn'd to England—and oh shame
To son of hers who thrills not at that name!
Call'd by the inspiring sound, before my eyes
My home's loved scenes, my country's glories rise;

The free and mighty land that gave me birth,
Her moral beauty, and her public worth ;
All that can make the patriot bosom swell.—
Yet one more sigh—bright Italy, farewell!

THE TRIAD.

BY W. WORDSWORTH.

SHOW me the noblest Youth of present time,
Whose trembling fancy would to love give birth ;
Some God or Hero from the Olympian clime
Return'd, to seek a consort upon earth;
Or, in no doubtful prospect, let me see
The brightest Star of ages yet to be,
And I will " mate and match him" blissfully!

I will not fetch the Naiad from a flood
Pure as herself—(song lacks not mightier power),
Nor leaf-crown'd Dryad from a pathless wood,
Nor Sea-nymph glistening from her coral bower;—
Mere Mortals, bodied forth in vision still,
Shall with Mount Ida's triple lustre fill
The chaster coverts of a British hill.

" Appear!—obey my lyre's command!
Come, like the Graces, hand in hand!
For ye, though not by birth allied,
Are sisters in the bond of love ;
And not the boldest tongue of envious pride

In you those interweavings could reprove
Which they, the progeny of Jove,
Learnt from the tuneful spheres, that glide
In endless union earth and sea above."—
——I speak in vain,—the pines have hush'd their waving.
A peerless Youth expectant at my side,
Breathless as they, with unabated craving
Looks to the earth and to the vacant air;
And, with a wandering eye that seems to chide,
Asks of the clouds what occupants they hide.—
But why solicit more than sight could bear,
By casting on a moment all we dare?
Invoke we those bright beings one by one,
And what was boldly promised, truly shall be done.

" Fear not this constraining measure!
Drawn by a poetic spell,
LUCIDA! from domes of pleasure,
Or from cottage-sprinkled dell,
Come to regions solitary,
Where the eagle builds her aery,
Above the hermit's long-forsaken cell!"
——She comes!—behold
That figure, like a ship with silver sail!
Nearer she draws—a breeze uplifts her veil—
Upon her coming wait
As pure a sunshine and as soft a gale
As e'er, on herbage covering earthly mould,
Tempted the bird of Juno to unfold
His richest splendour, when his veering gait
And every motion of his starry train
Seem govern'd by a strain

Of music audible to him alone—
——O Lady! worthy of earth's proudest throne,
Nor less, by excellence of nature, fit
Beside an unambitious hearth to sit
Domestic queen, where grandeur is unknown;
What living man could fear
The worst of Fortune's malice, wert thou near,
Humbling that lily stem, thy sceptre meek,
That its fair flowers may brush from off his cheek
The too, too happy tear?
——Queen, and handmaid lowly!
Whose skill can speed the day with lively cares,
And banish melancholy
By all that mind invents or hand prepares;
O thou, against whose lip, without its smile
And in its silence even, no heart is proof;
Whose goodness, sinking deep, would reconcile
The softest nursling of a gorgeous palace
To the bare life beneath the hawthorn roof
Of Sherwood's archer, or in caves of Wallace—
Who that hath seen thy beauty could content
His soul with but a *glimpse* of heavenly day?
Who that hath loved thee but would lay
His strong hand on the wind, if it were bent
To take thee in thy majesty away?
——Pass onward (even the glancing deer
Till we depart intrude not here);
That mossy slope, o'er which the woodbine throws
A canopy, is smooth'd for thy repose!

Glad moment is it when the throng
Of warblers in full concert strong

Strive, and not vainly strive, to rout
The lagging shower, and force coy Phœbus out,
Met by the rainbow's form divine,
Issuing from her cloudy shrine;—
So may the thrillings of the lyre
Prevail to further our desire,
While to these shades a nymph I call,
The youngest of the lovely Three.—
" Come, if the notes thine ear may pierce,
Submissive to the might of verse,
By none more deeply felt than thee!"
—I sang; and lo! from pastimes virginal
She hastens to the tents
Of nature, and the lonely elements.
Air sparkles round her with a dazzling sheen:
But mark her glowing cheek, her vesture green!
And, as if wishful to disarm
Or to repay the potent charm,
She bears the stringed lute of old romance,
That cheer'd the trellis'd arbour's privacy,
And soothed war-wearied knights in rafter'd hall.
How light her air! how delicate her glee!
So tripp'd the Muse inventress of the dance;
So, truant in waste woods, the blithe Euphrosyne!

But the ringlets of that head,
Why are they ungarlanded?
Why bedeck her temples less
Than the simplest shepherdess?
Is it not a brow inviting
Choicest flower that ever breathed,

Which the myrtle would delight in,
With Idalian rose enwreathed?
But her humility is well content
With *one* wild floweret, (call it not forlorn!)
FLOWER OF THE WINDS, beneath her bosom worn;
Yet is it more for love than ornament.

Open, ye thickets! let her fly,
Swift as a Thracian nymph, o'er field and height!
For she, to all but those who love her, shy,
Would gladly vanish from a stranger's sight;
Though where she is beloved, and loves, as free
As bird that rifles blossoms on a tree,
" Turning them inside out" with arch audacity.

Alas! how little can a moment show
Of an eye where feeling plays
In ten thousand dewy rays;
A face o'er which a thousand shadows go!—
—She stops—is fasten'd to that rivulet's side;
And there, while, with sedater mien,
O'er timid waters, that have scarcely left
Their birthplace in the rocky cleft,
She bends, at leisure may be seen
Features to old ideal grace allied,
Amid their smiles and dimples dignified—
Fit countenance for the soul of primal truth,
The bland composure of eternal youth!

What more changeful than the sea?
But over his great tides

Fidelity presides,
And this light-hearted maiden constant is as he.—
High is her aim as heaven above,
And wide as ether her good-will,
And, like the lowliest reed, her love
Can drink its nurture from the scantiest rill;
Insight as keen as frosty star
Is to *her* charity no bar,
Nor interrupts her frolic graces
When she is, far from these wild places,
Encircled by familiar faces.

O the charm that manners draw,
Nature, from thy genuine law!
Through benign affections—pure,
In the slight of self—secure,
If, from what her hand would do,
Or tongue utter, there ensue
Aught untoward or unfit,
Transient mischief, vague mischance,
Shunn'd by guarded elegance,
Hers is not a cheek shame-stricken,
But her blushes are joy-flushes—
And the fault (if fault it be)
Only ministers to quicken
Laughter-loving gayety,
And kindle sportive wit—
Leaving this daughter of the mountains free,
As if she knew that Oberon the fairy
Had cross'd her purpose with some quaint vagary,
And heard his viewless bands
Over their mirthful triumph clapping hands!

" Last of the Three, though eldest born!
Reveal thyself, like pensive morn,
Touch'd by the skylark's earliest note,
Ere humbler gladness be afloat.
But whether in the semblance drest
Of dawn, or eve—fair vision of the west,
Come with each anxious hope subdued
By woman's gentle fortitude,
Each grief through meekness settling into rest!
——Or I would hail thee when some high-wrought page
Of a closed volume lingering in thy hand,
Has raised thy spirit to a fearless stand
Among the glories of a happier age."—
—Her brow hath open'd on me—see it there,
Brightening the umbrage of her hair;
So gleams the crescent moon, that loves
To be descried through shady groves.—
—Tenderest bloom is on her cheek;
Wish not for a richer streak,
Nor dread the depth of meditative eye;
But let thy love, upon that azure field
Of thoughtfulness and beauty, yield
Its homage offered up in purity.—
—What wouldst thou more? In sunny glade,
Or under leaves of thickest shade,
Was such a stillness e'er diffused
Since earth grew calm while angels mused?
Softly she treads, as if her foot were loth
To crush the mountain dew-drops, soon to melt
On the flowers' breast; as if she felt
That flowers themselves, whate'er their hue,

With all their fragrance, all their glistening,
Call to the heart for inward listening;
And though for bridal wreaths and tokens true
Welcomed wisely—though a growth
Which the careless shepherd sleeps on,
As fitly spring from turf the mourner weeps on,
And without wrong are cropp'd the marble tomb to strew.

The charm is over; the mute phantoms gone,
Nor will return—but droop not, favour'd Youth!
The apparition that before thee shone
Obey'd a summons covetous of truth.
From these wild rocks thy footsteps I will guide
To bowers in which thy fortune may be tried,
And one of the bright Three become thy happy bride!

TO ———.

F. M. REYNOLDS.

THEY told me, with their feelings bitter,
 That in your wealth your beauty lies;
And I believed them, for there glitter
 Ten thousand diamonds in your eyes.

THE SISTERS OF ALBANO.

BY THE AUTHOR OF FRANKENSTEIN.

And near Albano's scarce divided waves
Shine from a sister valley;—and afar
The Tiber winds, and the broad ocean laves
The Latian coast where sprang the Epic war,
" Arms and the Man," whose re-ascending star
Rose o'er an empire; but beneath thy right
Tully reposed from Rome; and where yon bar
Of girdling mountains intercepts the sight
The Sabine farm was till'd, the weary bard's delight.

IT was to see this beautiful lake that I made my last
excursion before quitting Rome. The spring had nearly
grown into summer, the trees were all in full but fresh
green foliage, the vine-dresser was singing, perched among
them, training his vines: the cicala had not yet begun her
song, the heats therefore had not commenced; but at
evening the fireflies gleamed among the hills, and the
cooing aziolo assured us of what in that country needs
no assurance, fine weather for the morrow. We set out
early in the morning to avoid the heats, breakfasted at
Albano, and till ten o'clock passed our time in visiting
the Mosaic, the villa of Cicero, and other curiosities of the
place. We reposed during the middle of the day in a
tent elevated for us at the hill top, whence we looked on
the hill-embosomed lake, and the distant eminence crowned
by a town with its church. Other villages and cottages

LAKE ALBANO.

Drawn by J.M.W. Turner, R.A.

Engraved by R. Wallis.

Published for the Proprietors by Hurst Chance & C: S.t Paul's Churchyard, & R. Jennings, 2. Poultry.

Printed by M.c Queen.

were scattered among the foldings of mountains, and beyond we saw the deep blue sea of the southern poets,
which received the swift and immortal Tiber, rocking it
to repose among its devouring waves. The Coliseum
falls and the Pantheon decays—the very hills of Rome are
perishing, but the Tiber lives for ever, flows for ever—and
for ever feeds the land-encircling Mediterranean with fresh
waters.

Our summer and pleasure-seeking party consisted of
many: to me the most interesting person was the Countess
Atanasia D——, who was as beautiful as an imagination
of Raphael, and good as the ideal of a poet. Two of
her children accompanied her, with animated looks and
gentle manners, quiet, yet enjoying. I sat near her,
watching the changing shadows of the landscape before
us. As the sun descended, it poured a tide of light into
the valley of the lake, deluging the deep bank formed by
the mountain with liquid gold. The domes and turrets of
the far town flashed and gleamed, the trees were dyed in
splendour; two or three slight clouds, which had drunk
the radiance till it became their essence, floated golden
islets in the lustrous empyrean. The waters, reflecting
the brilliancy of the sky and the fire-tinted banks, beamed
a second heaven, a second irradiated earth, at our feet.
The Mediterranean gazing on the sun—as the eyes of a
mortal bride fail and are dimmed when reflecting her
lover's glance—was lost, mixed in his light, till it had become one with him.—Long (our souls, like the sea, the
hills, and lake, drinking in the supreme loveliness) we
gazed, till the too full cup overflowed, and we turned away
with a sigh.

At our feet there was a knoll of ground, that formed

the foreground of our picture; two trees lay basking against the sky, glittering with the golden light, which like dew seemed to hang amid their branches—a rock closed the prospect on the other side, twined round by creepers, and redolent with blooming myrtle—a brook crossed by huge stones gushed through the turf, and on the fragments of rock that lay about, sat two or three persons, peasants, who attracted our attention. One was a hunter, as his gun, lying on a bank not far off, demonstrated, yet he was a tiller of the soil; his rough straw hat, and his picturesque but coarse dress, belonged to that class. The other was some contadina, in the costume of her country, returning, her basket on her arm, from the village to her cottage home. They were regarding the stores of a pedlar, who with doffed hat stood near: some of these consisted of pictures and prints—views of the country, and portraits of the Madonna. Our peasants regarded these with pleased attention.

" One might easily make out a story for that pair," I said: " his gun is a help to the imagination, and we may fancy him a bandit with his contadina love, the terror of all the neighbourhood, except of her, the most defenceless being in it."

" You speak lightly of such a combination," said the lovely countess at my side, " as if it must not in its nature be the cause of dreadful tragedies. The mingling of love with crime is a dread conjunction, and lawless pursuits are never followed without bringing on the criminal, and all allied to him, ineffable misery. I speak with emotion, for your observation reminds me of an unfortunate girl, now one of the Sisters of Charity in the convent of Santa Chiara at Rome, whose unhappy passion for a man, such as you mention, spread destruction and sorrow widely around her."

I entreated my lovely friend to relate the history of the nun: for a long time she resisted my entreaties, as not willing to depress the spirit of a party of pleasure by a tale of sorrow. But I urged her, and she yielded. Her sweet Italian phraseology now rings in my ears, and her beautiful countenance is before me. As she spoke, the sun set, and the moon bent her silver horn in the ebbing tide of glory he had left. The lake changed from purple to silver, and the trees, before so splendid, now in dark masses, just reflected from their tops the mild moonlight. The fire-flies flashed among the rocks; the bats circled round us: meanwhile thus commenced the Countess Atanasia:

The nun of whom I speak had a sister older than herself; I can remember them when as children they brought eggs and fruit to my father's villa. Maria and Anina were constantly together. With their large straw hats to shield them from the scorching sun, they were at work in their father's *podere* all day, and in the evening, when Maria, who was the elder by four years, went to the fountain for water, Anina ran at her side. Their cot—the folding of the hill conceals it—is at the lake side opposite; and about a quarter of a mile up the hill is the rustic fountain of which I speak. Maria was serious, gentle, and considerate; Anina was a laughing, merry little creature, with the face of a cherub. When Maria was fifteen, their mother fell ill, and was nursed at the convent of Santa Chiara at Rome. Maria attended her, never leaving her bedside day or night. The nuns thought her an angel, she deemed them saints: her mother died, and they persuaded her to make one of them; her father could not but acquiesce in her holy intention, and she became one of the Sisters of Charity, the nun-nurses of Santa Chiara. Once or twice a year she visited her home, gave sage and kind advice to Anina, and sometimes wept to part from her; but her piety and her active employments for the sick reconciled her to her fate. Anina was more sorry to lose her sister's society. The other girls of the village did not please her: she was a good child, and worked hard for her father, and her sweetest recompense was the report he made of her to Maria, and the fond praises and caresses the latter bestowed on her when they met.

It was not until she was fifteen that Anina showed any diminution of affection for her sister. Yet I cannot call it diminution, for she loved her perhaps more than ever, though her holy calling and sage lectures prevented her from reposing confidence, and made her tremble lest the nun, devoted to heaven and good works, should read in her eyes, and disapprove of the earthly passion that occupied her. Perhaps a part of her reluctance arose from the reports that were current against her lover's character, and certainly from the disapprobation and even hatred of him that her father frequently expressed. Ill-fated Anina! I know not if in the north your peasants love as ours; but the passion of Anina was entwined with the roots of her being, it was herself: she could die, but not cease to love. The dislike of her father for Domenico made their intercourse clandestine. He was always at the fountain to fill her pitcher, and lift it on her head. He attended the same mass; and when her father went to Albano, Velletri, or Rome, he seemed to learn by instinct the exact moment of his departure, and joined her in the *podere*, labouring with her and for her, till the old man was seen descending

the mountain-path on his return. He said he worked for
a contadino near Nemi. Anina sometimes wondered that
he could spare so much time for her; but his excuses were
plausible, and the result too delightful not to blind the
innocent girl to its obvious cause.

Poor Domenico! the reports spread against him were
too well founded: his sole excuse was that his father had
been a robber before him, and he had spent his early years
among these lawless men. He had better things in his
nature, and yearned for the peace of the guiltless. Yet he
could hardly be called guilty, for no dread crime stained
him; nevertheless, he was an outlaw and a bandit, and
now that he loved Anina these names were the stings of
an adder to pierce his soul. He would have fled from his
comrades to a far country, but Anina dwelt amid their
very haunts. At this period also, the police established by
the French government, which then possessed Rome, made
these bands more alive to the conduct of their members,
and rumours of active measures to be taken against those
who occupied the hills near Albano, Nemi, and Velletri,
caused them to draw together in tighter bonds. Domenico
would not, if he could, desert his friends in the hour of
danger.

On a *festa* at this time—it was towards the end of
October—Anina strolled with her father among the villagers, who all over Italy make holiday, by congregating
and walking in one place. Their talk was entirely of the
laddri and the French, and many terrible stories were related
of the extirpation of banditti in the kingdom of Naples,
and the mode by which the French succeeded in their undertaking was minutely described. The troops scoured
the country, visiting one haunt of the robbers after the

other, and dislodging them, tracked them, as in those
countries they hunt the wild beasts of the forest, till
drawing the circle narrower, they enclosed them in one
spot. They then drew a cordon round the place, which
they guarded with the utmost vigilance, forbidding any to
enter it with provisions, on pain of instant death. And as
this menace was rigorously executed, in a short time the
besieged bandits were starved into a surrender. The
French troops were now daily expected, for they had been
seen at Velletri and Nemi; at the same time it was affirmed
that several outlaws had taken up their abode at Rocca
Giovane, a deserted village on the summit of one of these
hills, and it was supposed that they would make that place
the scene of their final retreat.

The next day, as Anina worked in the *podere*, a party
of French horse passed by along the road that separated her
garden from the lake. Curiosity made her look at them;
and her beauty was too great not to attract: their observations and address soon drove her away—for a woman in
love consecrates herself to her lover, and deems the admiration of others to be profanation. She spoke to her
father of the impertinence of these men, and he answered
by rejoicing at their arrival, and the destruction of the
lawless bands that would ensue. When, in the evening,
Anina went to the fountain, she looked timidly around,
and hoped that Domenico would be at his accustomed
post, for the arrival of the French destroyed her feeling of
security. She went rather later than usual, and a cloudy
evening made it seem already dark; the wind roared among
the trees, bending hither and thither even the stately
cypresses; the waters of the lake were agitated into high
waves, and dark masses of thunder-cloud lowered over the

hill tops, giving a lurid tinge to the landscape. Anina passed quickly up the mountain-path: when she came in sight of the fountain, which was rudely hewn in the living rock, she saw Domenico leaning against a projection of the hill, his hat drawn over his eyes, his *tabaro* fallen from his shoulders, his arms folded in an attitude of dejection. He started when he saw her; his voice and phrases were broken and unconnected; yet he never gazed on her with such ardent love, nor solicited her to delay her departure with such impassioned tenderness.

" How glad I am to find you here!" she said: " I was fearful of meeting one of the French soldiers: I dread them even more than the banditti."

Domenico cast a look of eager inquiry on her, and then turned away, saying, " Sorry am I that I shall not be here to protect you. I am obliged to go to Rome for a week or two. You will be faithful, Anina mia; you will love me, though I never see you more?"

The interview, under these circumstances, was longer than usual: he led her down the path till they nearly came in sight of her cottage; still they lingered: a low whistle was heard among the myrtle underwood at the lake side; he started; it was repeated, and he answered it by a similar note: Anina, terrified, was about to ask what this meant, when, for the first time, he pressed her to his heart, kissed her roseate lips, and, with a muttered " Carissima addio," left her, springing down the bank; and as she gazed in wonder, she thought she saw a boat cross a line of light made by the opening of a cloud. She stood long absorbed in reverie, wondering and remembering with thrilling pleasure the quick embrace and impassioned farewell of her lover. She delayed so long that her father came to seek her.

Each evening after this, Anina visited the fountain at the Ave Maria; he was not there; each day seemed an age; and incomprehensible fears occupied her heart. About a fortnight after, letters arrived from Maria. They came to say that she had been ill of the mal'aria fever, that she was now convalescent, but that change of air was necessary for her recovery, and that she had obtained leave to spend a month at home at Albano. She asked her father to come the next day to fetch her. These were pleasant tidings for Anina; she resolved to disclose every thing to her sister, and during her long visit she doubted not but that she would contrive her happiness. Old Andrea departed the following morning, and the whole day was spent by the sweet girl in dreams of future bliss. In the evening Maria arrived, weak and wan, with all the marks of that dread illness about her; yet, as she assured her sister, feeling quite well.

As they sat at their frugal supper, several villagers came in to inquire for Maria; but all their talk was of the French soldiers and the robbers, of whom a band of at least twenty was collected in Rocca Giovane, strictly watched by the military.

" We may be grateful to the French," said Andrea, "for this good deed: the country will be rid of these ruffians."

" True, friend," said another; " but it is horrible to think what these men suffer: they have, it appears, exhausted all the food they brought with them to the village, and are literally starving. They have not an ounce of maccaroni among them; and a poor fellow, who was taken and executed yesterday, was a mere anatomy; you could tell every bone in his skin."

"There was a sad story the other day," said another, "of an old man from Nemi, whose son, they say, is among them at Rocca Giovane: he was found within the lines with some *baccalà* under his *pastrano*, and shot on the spot."

"There is not a more desperate gang," observed the first speaker, " in the states and the regno put together. They have sworn never to yield but upon good terms: to secure these, their plan is to way-lay passengers and make prisoners, whom they keep as hostages for mild treatment from the government. But the French are merciless; they are better pleased that the bandits wreak their vengeance on these poor creatures than spare one of their lives."

" They have captured two persons already," said another; "and there is old Betta Tossi half frantic, for she is sure her son is taken: he has not been at home these ten days."

" I should rather guess," said an old man, " that he went there with good will: the young scape-grace kept company with Domenico Baldi of Nemi."

" No worse company could he have kept in the whole country," said Andrea: "Domenico is the bad son of a bad race. Is he in the village with the rest?"

" My own eyes assured me of that," replied the other. " When I was up the hill with eggs and fowls to the piquette there, I saw the branches of an ilex move; the poor fellow was weak perhaps, and could not keep his hold; presently he dropt to the ground; every musket was levelled at him; but he started up and was away like a hare among the rocks. Once he turned, and then I saw Domenico as plainly, though thinner, poor lad, by much than he was, as plainly as I now see——Santa Virgine! what is the matter with Nina?"

She had fainted; the company broke up, and she was left to her sister's care. When the poor child came to herself she was fully aware of her situation, and said nothing, except expressing a wish to retire to rest. Maria was in high spirits at the prospect of her long holiday at home, but the illness of her sister made her refrain from talking that night, and blessing her, as she said good night, she soon slept. Domenico starving!—Domenico trying to escape and dying through hunger, was the vision of horror that wholly possessed poor Anina. At another time, the discovery that her lover was a robber might have inflicted pangs as keen as those which she now felt; but this, at present, made a faint impression, obscured by worse wretchedness. Maria was in a deep and tranquil sleep. Anina rose, dressed herself silently, and crept down stairs. She stored her market basket with what food there was in the house, and, unlatching the cottage-door, issued forth, resolved to reach Rocca Giovane, and to administer to her lover's dreadful wants. The night was dark, but this was favourable, for she knew every path and turn of the hills; every bush and knoll of ground between her home and the deserted village which occupies the summit of that hill: you may see the dark outline of some of its houses about two hours' walk from her cottage. The night was dark, but still; the libeccio brought the clouds below the mountain-tops, and veiled the horizon in mist; not a leaf stirred; her footsteps sounded loud in her ears, but resolution overcame fear. She had entered yon ilex grove, her spirits rose with her success, when suddenly she was challenged by a sentinel;

no time for escape; fear chilled her blood; her basket dropped from her arm; its contents rolled out on the ground; the soldier fired his gun and brought several others round him; she was made prisoner.

In the morning, when Maria awoke, she missed her sister from her side. I have overslept myself, she thought, and Nina would not disturb me. But when she came down stairs and met her father, and Anina did not appear, they began to wonder. She was not in the *podere;* two hours passed, and then Andrea went to seek her. Entering the near village, he saw the contadini crowding together, and a stifled exclamation of "Ecco il padre!" told him that some evil had betided. His first impression was that his daughter was drowned; but the truth, that she had been taken by the French carrying provisions within the forbidden line, was still more terrible. He returned in frantic desperation to his cottage, first to acquaint Maria with what had happened, and then to ascend the hill to save his child from her impending fate. Maria heard his tale with horror; but an hospital is a school in which to learn self-possession and presence of mind. "Do you remain, my father," she said: "I will go. My holy character will awe these men, my tears move them: trust me; I swear that I will save my sister." Andrea yielded to her superior courage and energy.

The nuns of Santa Chiara when out of their convent do not usually wear their monastic habit, but dress simply in a black gown. Maria, however, had brought her nun's habiliments with her, and thinking thus to impress the soldiers with respect, she now put it on. She received her father's benediction, and asking that of the Virgin and the saints, she departed on her expedition. Ascending the hill, she was soon stopped by the sentinels. She asked to see their commanding officer, and being conducted to him, she announced herself as the sister of the unfortunate girl who had been captured the night before. The officer, who had received her with carelessness, now changed countenance: his serious look frightened Maria, who clasped her hands, exclaiming, "You have not injured the child! she is safe!"

"She is safe—now," he replied with hesitation; "but there is no hope of pardon."

"Holy Virgin, have mercy on her! what will be done to her?"

"I have received strict orders; in two hours she dies."

"No! no!" exclaimed Maria impetuously, "that cannot be! you cannot be so wicked as to murder a child like her."

"She is old enough, madame," said the officer, "to know that she ought not to disobey orders; mine are so strict, that were she but nine years old, she dies."

These terrible words stung Maria to fresh resolution: she entreated for mercy; she knelt; she vowed that she would not depart without her sister; she appealed to Heaven and the saints. The officer, though cold-hearted, was good-natured and courteous, and he assured her with the utmost gentleness that her supplications were of no avail; that were the criminal his own daughter he must enforce his orders. As a sole concession, he permitted her to see her sister. Despair inspired the nun with energy; she almost ran up the hill, out-speeding her guide: they crossed a folding of the hills to a little sheep-cot, where sentinels paraded before the door. There was no glass to the windows, so the shutters were shut, and when Maria first went in from the bright daylight she hardly saw the slight figure of her sister leaning against the wall, her dark hair fallen

below her waist, her head sunk on her bosom, over which
her arms were folded. She started wildly as the door
opened, saw her sister, and sprung with a piercing shriek
into her arms.

They were left alone together: Anina uttered a thousand
frantic exclamations, beseeching her sister to save her, and
shuddering at the near approach of her fate. Maria had felt
herself, since their mother's death, the natural protectress
and support of her sister, and she never deemed herself so
called on to fulfil this character as now that the trembling
girl clasped her neck; her tears falling on her cheeks, and
her choked voice entreating her to save her. The thought
—O could I suffer instead of you! was in her heart, and
she was about to express it, when it suggested another
idea, on which she was resolved to act. First she soothed
Anina by her promises, then glanced round the cot; they
were quite alone: she went to the window, and through a
crevice saw the soldiers conversing at some distance. "Yes,
dearest sister," she cried, "I will—I can save you—quick—
we must change dresses—there is no time to be lost!—you
must escape in my habit."

"And you remain to die?"

"They dare not murder the innocent, a nun! Fear not
for me—I am safe."

Anina easily yielded to her sister, but her fingers trembled; every string she touched she entangled. Maria was
perfectly self-possessed, pale, but calm. She tied up her
sister's long hair, and adjusted her veil over it so as to conceal it; she unlaced her bodice, and arranged the folds of
her own habit on her with the greatest care—then more
hastily she assumed the dress of her sister, putting on,
after a lapse of many years, her native contadina costume.

Anina stood by, weeping and helpless, hardly hearing her sister's injunctions to return speedily to their father, and under his guidance to seek sanctuary. The guard now opened the door. Anina clung to her sister in terror, while she, in soothing tones, entreated her to calm herself.

The soldier said, they must delay no longer, for the priest had arrived to confess the prisoner.

To Anina the idea of confession associated with death was terrible; to Maria it brought hope. She whispered, in a smothered voice, " The priest will protect me—fear not—hasten to our father!"

Anina almost mechanically obeyed: weeping, with her handkerchief placed unaffectedly before her face, she passed the soldiers; they closed the door on the prisoner, who hastened to the window, and saw her sister descend the hill with tottering steps, till she was lost behind some rising ground. The nun fell on her knees—cold dew bathed her brow, instinctively she feared: the French had shown small respect for the monastic character; they destroyed the convents and desecrated the churches. Would they be merciful to her, and spare the innocent! Alas! was not Anina innocent also? Her sole crime had been disobeying an arbitrary command, and she had done the same.

" Courage!" cried Maria; " perhaps I am fitter to die than my sister is. Gesu, pardon me my sins, but I do not believe that I shall out-live this day!"

In the meantime, Anina descended the hill slowly and tremblingly. She feared discovery—she feared for her sister— and above all at the present moment, she feared the reproaches and anger of her father. By dwelling on this last idea, it became exaggerated into excessive terror, and she determined, instead of returning to her home, to make a circuit among the hills, to find her way by herself to Albano, where she trusted to find protection from her pastor and confessor. She avoided the open paths, and following rather the direction she wished to pursue than any beaten road, she passed along nearer to Rocca Giovane than she anticipated. She looked up at its ruined houses and bell-less steeple, straining her eyes to catch a glimpse of him, the author of all her ills. A low but distinct whistle reached her ear, not far off; she started—she remembered that on the night when she last saw Domenico a note like that had called him from her side; the sound was echoed and re-echoed from other quarters; she stood aghast, her bosom heaving, her hands clasped. First she saw a dark and ragged head of hair, shadowing two fiercely gleaming eyes, rise from beneath a bush. She screamed, but before she could repeat her scream three men leapt from behind a rock, secured her arms, threw a cloth over her face, and hurried her up the acclivity. Their talk, as she went along, informed her of the horror and danger of her situation.

Pity, they said, that the holy father and some of his red stockings did not command the troops: with a nun in their hands, they might obtain any terms. Coarse jests passed as they dragged their victim towards their ruined village. The paving of the street told her when they arrived at Rocca Giovane, and the change of atmosphere that they entered a house. They unbandaged her eyes: the scene was squalid and miserable, the walls ragged and black with smoke, the floor strewn with offals and dirt; a rude table and broken bench was all the furniture; and the leaves of Indian corn, heaped high in one corner, served, it seemed, for a bed, for a man lay on it, his head buried in his folded arms. Anina looked round on her savage hosts: their countenances expressed every variety of brutal ferocity, now rendered more dreadful from gaunt famine and suffering.

"O there is none who will save me!" she cried. The voice startled the man who was lying on the floor; he leapt up—it was Domenico: Domenico, so changed, with sunk cheeks and eyes, matted hair, and looks whose wildness and desperation differed little from the dark countenances around him. Could this be her lover?

His recognition and surprise at her dress led to an explanation. When the robbers first heard that their prey was no prize, they were mortified and angry; but when she related the danger she had incurred by endeavouring to bring them food, they swore with horrid oaths that no harm should befall her, but that if she liked she might make one of them in all honour and equality. The innocent girl shuddered. "Let me go," she cried; "let me only escape and hide myself in a convent for ever!"

Domenico looked at her in agony. "Yes, poor child," he said; "go, save yourself: God grant no evil befall you; the ruin is too wide already." Then turning eagerly to his comrades, he continued—"You hear her story. She was to have been shot for bringing food to us: her sister has substituted herself in her place. We know the French; one victim is to them as good as another: Maria dies in their hands. Let us save her. Our time is up; we must fall like men, or starve like dogs: we have still ammunition, still some strength left. To arms! let us rush on the poltroons, free their prisoner, and escape or die!"

There needed but an impulse like this to urge the outlaws to desperate resolves. They prepared their arms with looks of ferocious determination. Domenico, meanwhile, led Anina out of the house, to the verge of the hill, inquiring whither she intended to go. On her saying, to Albano, he observed, " That were hardly safe; be guided by me, I entreat you: take these piastres, hire the first conveyance you find, hasten to Rome, to the convent of Santa Chiara: for pity's sake, do not linger in this neighbourhood."

" I will obey your injunctions, Domenico," she replied, " but I cannot take your money; it has cost you too dear: fear not, I shall arrive safely at Rome without that ill-fated silver."

Domenico's comrades now called loudly to him: he had no time to urge his request; he threw the despised dollars at her feet.

" Nina, adieu for ever," he said: " may you love again more happily!"

" Never!" she replied. " God has saved me in this dress; it were sacrilege to change it: I shall never quit Santa Chiara."

Domenico had led her a part of the way down the rock; his comrades appeared at the top, calling to him.

" Gesu save you!" cried he: " reach the convent—Maria shall join you there before night. Farewell!" He hastily kissed her hand, and sprang up the acclivity to rejoin his impatient friends.

The unfortunate Andrea had waited long for the return of his children. The leafless trees and bright clear atmosphere permitted every object to be visible, but he saw no trace of them on the hill side; the shadows of the dial showed noon to be passed, when, with uncontrollable impatience, he began to climb the hill, towards the spot where Anina had been taken. The path he pursued was in part the

H

same that this unhappy girl had taken on her way to Rome. The father and daughter met: the old man saw the nun's dress, and saw her unaccompanied: she covered her face with her hands in a transport of fear and shame; but when, mistaking her for Maria, he asked in a tone of anguish for his youngest darling, her arms fell; she dared not raise her eyes, which streamed with tears.

"Unhappy girl!" exclaimed Andrea, "where is your sister?"

She pointed to the cottage prison, now discernible near the summit of a steep acclivity. "She is safe," she replied: "she saved me; but they dare not murder her."

"Heaven bless her for this good deed!" exclaimed the old man, fervently; "but you hasten on your way, and I will go in search of her."

Each proceeded on an opposite path. The old man wound up the hill, now in view, and now losing sight of the hut where his child was captive: he was aged, and the way was steep. Once, when the closing of the hill hid the point towards which he for ever strained his eyes, a single shot was fired in that direction: his staff fell from his hands, his knees trembled and failed him; several minutes of dead silence elapsed before he recovered himself sufficiently to proceed: full of fears he went on, and at the next turn saw the cot again. A party of soldiers were on the open space before it, drawn up in a line as if expecting an attack. In a few moments from above them shots were fired, which they returned, and the whole was enveloped and veiled in smoke. Still Andrea climbed the hill, eager to discover what had become of his child: the firing continued quick and hot. Now and then, in the pauses of musquetry and the answering echoes of the mountains, he heard a funereal chant; presently, before he was aware, at a turning of the hill, he met a company of priests and contadini, carrying a large cross and a bier. The miserable father rushed forward with frantic impatience; the awe-struck peasants set down their load—the face was uncovered, and the wretched man fell lifeless on the corpse of his murdered child.

The countess Atanasia paused, overcome by the emotions inspired by the history she related. A long pause ensued: at length one of the party observed, " Maria, then, was the sacrifice to her goodness."

" The French," said the countess, " did not venerate her holy vocation ; one peasant girl to them was the same as another. The immolation of any victim suited their purpose of awe-striking the peasantry. Scarcely, however, had the shot entered her heart, and her blameless spirit been received by the saints in Paradise, when Domenico and his followers rushed down the hill to avenge her and themselves. The contest was furious and bloody; twenty French soldiers fell, and not one of the banditti escaped; Domenico, the foremost of the assailants, being the first to fall."

I asked, " And where are now Anina and her father?"

" You may see them, if you will," said the countess, " on your return to Rome. She is a nun of Santa Chiara. Constant acts of benevolence and piety have inspired her with calm and resignation. Her prayers are daily put up for Domenico's soul, and she hopes, through the intercession of the Virgin, to rejoin him in the other world.

" Andrea is very old; he has outlived the memory of his sufferings; but he derives comfort from the filial attentions of his surviving daughter. But when I look at

his cottage on this lake, and remember the happy laughing
face of Anina among the vines, I shudder at the recollection of the passion that has made her cheeks pale, her
thoughts for ever conversant with death, her only wish to
find repose in the grave."

INVITATION.

TO A BEAUTIFUL BUT VERY SMALL YOUNG LADY.

F. M. REYNOLDS.

You little, light-hearted, and gossamer thing,
You promised to visit us during the Spring;
We are gloomy, and sad, and are pining to see
One that's dear to us all, and dearest to me!
Have you grown any larger, or still are the same?
For Fame speaks of you oddly—but who credits Fame?
She declares, that you dread e'en the cracks in the floor,
And with putty and paste we must cover them o'er,
Or th' apartment beneath you may chance to explore!
And she says, if one holds up a pin to one's eye,
To discern you behind it, in vain we shall try—
But, I candidly tell you, I think this a lie.
Yet, I'll even do more—on these points I'll be dumb,
If you will, my sweet maiden, but promise to come;
You sha'n't be detain'd 'bove a month, at the most,
And then we'll return you, per—*twopenny post!*

Drawn by H. Richter.   Engraved by Chas Rolls.

ANNE PAGE AND SLENDER.

Printed by McQu.

Published for the Proprietor, by Hurst, Chance & Co. St Pauls Churchyard, & R. Jennings Poultry.

ILLUSTRATIONS OF THE CHARACTERS OF ANNE PAGE AND SLENDER.

BY THE AUTHOR OF THE LIFE OF KEMBLE.

Mr. Richter is an artist admirably qualified to illustrate Shakspeare. The point of time which he has chosen in the present subject is the following. The courteous, but playful, Anne Page is in the action which accompanied the last words she spoke to Master Slender, "I pray you, sir, walk in." The idiot has just sent in his man, Simple, to wait upon his cousin the Justice, and regardless of the trouble he is giving, assures his lovely monitress, that instead of walking *in*, "he had rather walk where he was." And with a fatuity that did not allow him to think that *she* might want her dinner, whether he did or not, he proceeds to assign reasons for conduct that admitted no excuse. The second finger of his awkward left hand is an index to the bruised shin, which he got in playing for *stewed prunes* with a master of fence, the exquisite reason why he cannot bear the smell of *roast meat* since. He accompanies this bald unjointed chat by a laugh of no meaning, and a glance of gloting fondness upon the. beautiful but alarming object before him.

But the artist has done more than this. In his portrait of the fair Mistress Anne he has shown that sparkling intelligence and enjoyment of Slender's confusion, that may be supposed to have won for her the affections of a good judge of character like Fenton; a man who had taken the full range of life, with the master spirits of his time, the wild Prince and Poins. Her eye anticipates what she afterwards, with shrove-tide pleasantry, says to her mo-ther—"I had rather be set quick i' the earth and bowl'd to death with turnips, than married to such a fool."

Slender too bears upon him, in the concrete, all the various indications of his character. This is the "gentle-man born," whose man Simple is to carry about with him a "book of songs and sonnets," which constitutes his mas-ter's only chance of amusing his associates; and being lent at present to "Alice Shortcake," reduces him to absolute and hopeless insignificance. This is he who lost his "shovel-boards" when he was drunk, and took for *Latin* the red-lattice phrases of Bardolph and Nym and Pistol. This is he, who "would not have the Postmaster's Boy for a *wife*, even if he had been married to him." To such an intellect he has a body fully corresponding;—all its mem-bers are slack, nerveless, without direction, and from mental fatuity awkward, though without deformity. The round tower in the distance shows the scene to be near Windsor Castle.

This very beautiful design recals to a lover of Shakspeare the peculiar character bestowed upon the oaf himself by the poet, and a reason for some of the features, which seem exaggerated. The clue to these may be found in the re-lation he bears to Justice Shallow, as to family, and to the Master Stephen of Jonson's comedy of Every Man in his Humour.

It had been a received notion, long undisturbed until the late Mr. Malone endeavoured to shake it, that, in the character of Justice Shallow, Shakspeare remembered his

Warwickshire persecutor, Sir Thomas Lucy. And accordingly a charge is brought against Falstaff by the Justice, which is thus specified in the first act of the Merry Wives of Windsor.

Shal. "Knight, you have beaten my men, kill'd my deer, and broke open my lodge."

The knight does not affect to deny a tittle of the accusation ; he rather boasts of the illegal offence : but, as if he classed *her* among the *feræ naturæ,* disclaims having "kissed the keeper's daughter." Now tradition having affirmed that Charlecote was the scene of Shakspeare's youthful offence, Mr. Malone set himself to work to discover whether that manor was actually parked or disparked in the poet's time ; that, if the latter should turn out to be the case, he might destroy the offence by the fact ; since such an enclosure was necessary to subject the deer-stealer to the penalty. That there might be deer in other situations is highly probable, and a trespass upon the grounds of any landholder was surely at all times punishable. In my opinion Mr. Malone's labour to shake the tradition only confirmed it, and he should have remembered that, as Charlecote had been a park, it was likely for a long time to be popularly called so ; and in support of this anecdote, I may remark, that Shakspeare's Shallow, though he mentions a lodge, says nothing whatever about a park.

However, that some lasting resentment had been excited in the poet's mind by Sir Thomas Lucy is too apparent to need a word beyond the sort of arms he has bestowed upon his Justice. He bears the "dozen white luces" in his coat. This is a cognizance derived from a family name; and, however old the coat may be, the Shallows have no *verbal* claim to it ; nor is this fresh water inhabitant at all significant of folly. It is bestowed alone to mark out the object whom he intended to be the victim of the satire.

Our admiration of exalted genius renders us often morally unjust. The truth is, that commentators see no faults in their authors. Sir Thomas Lucy anticipated no future *genius* when he sought satisfaction of a freebooter; and our great bard, in the high triumph of his talents, should have excused the *justice*, rather than himself. But I am afraid that even the simpleton Slender fares the worse under his hands, because he is the nephew of Shallow, the stage representative of Lucy; and this leads me to look into the real original of Slender. The royal, masculine taste of Elizabeth delighted in the character of Falstaff; and she wished to see him in love: her mind no doubt luxuriating in the hair-breadth scapes which the fertility of his creator's fancy, as she well knew, could contrive, to molest either his avarice or his lechery. Shakspeare is reported to have produced a first sketch of the subject within a fortnight. In such an emergency he would naturally call upon memory for some of his materials. Now, in the year 1598, Shakspeare himself acted Old Kno'well in Ben Jonson's Every Man in his Humour. There he found on the stage, in close personal connexion with himself, the character of *Master Stephen*, decidedly the ground-work of his own Master Slender. To obviate any doubt on the subject, I premise that, in its *Italian*, or its *English* fable and characters, Ben's play had been years on the stage, *before* Shakspeare was commanded to produce the Merry Wives of Windsor.

The simple gulls of the two friends have most qualities in common. They are very self-important, and very ignorant; eternally played on, cheated, and laughed at. Fatuity,

like the chameleon, catches all the colouring it has from
the objects about it. Master Stephen has his *hawk and his
bells*, and wants a book to keep it by. Slender is fond of
bear-baiting, and takes the mighty Sackerson by his chain,
while the women shriek at his daring. He is quarrelsome,
and is reported to have once fought with a warrener.
Master Stephen is also sudden and quick in quarrel, and
finding an opportunity to decorate himself cheaply with a
sword of Spain, a blade from Toledo (which the fighting
gallants knew they could *trust*), he buys a Fleming instead,
and loses his own temper with that of his weapon. He
is bullied too like Slender, and affects to quarrel with a
serving-man, and way-lay him, to try to win a reputation
for courage from the poor man's humility or endurance.
But I come now to the discrimination between them, and
it is an affair only of words. Such dolts commonly speak
the language of their associates, without care, without
thought, and always as it comes to their ear; its literal
form they neither conceive nor inquire. But taking only
the words in vulgar use, and their application along with
the words, they are commonly right and intelligible. And
this is always the case with Master Stephen, who, however
mean his diction, never once, if I recollect, falsifies the
terms he employs. But as to Slender, Shakspeare, either
to extort laughter, or to degrade him below humanity,
does not allow him the power of declaring his mind about
any thing, without having his words run exactly *counter*
to his ideas. As far as association goes too, Slender is of
higher rank than Stephen; he is a gentleman born, has
" three hundred pounds a year," though " he keeps but
three men and a boy till his mother be dead;" and he can
afford to make his intended wife a jointure of one hundred

and fifty pounds a year*. But we must look a little into his language. Of his uncle he thus tries to express the gentility, by his adding *armigero* to his signature.

> " All his successors (gone *before* him) hath don't;
> And all his ancestors (that come *after* him) may."

Of his mistress, Anne Page, who "has browne haire, and speaks small *like a woman*," in which Master Stephen would have agreed with him, he thus opens his mind, after full consideration of the premises.

" I will marry her, sir, at your request; but if there be no great love at the beginning, yet Heaven may *decrease* it upon better acquaintance, when we are married, and have more occasion to know one another: I hope upon familiarity will grow more *content :* but if you say marry her, I will marry her, that I am freely *dissolved,* and *dissolutely.*"

But however little inviting either the gallantry or the phraseology of Slender may be, Shallow reminds him that " he had a *father*" who would not have trifled with opportunity, and whose undaunted nature seems to reproach his less adventurous son. He was guilty of many an *excellent jest,* which are numbered among 'the choice " modern instances" of his brother the justice, and no doubt had often set the quorum in a roar; and Slender calls upon him to repeat one of them, I suppose the *crown* of his achievements, " how he stole *two geese* out of a pen," to impress Mrs. Anne with a suitable respect for the blood

---

* Stephen has a little property at Hogsden, and his name has been inserted among the soldier aspirant of the Artillery Ground. He is but just clear of the company of such as came " a ducking to the ponds at Islington."

that flowed in his veins, simple as he might seem to stand
before her.

It will readily be acknowledged that even gentry were
often shamefully illiterate in the time of our poet; and
Mr. John Shakspeare, his father, though mayor of Strat-
ford, if he could annex *armigero* to his signature, was incapable of *writing* the word; but this circumstance, as I
have shown, did not affect the propriety of their language,
upon any subject with which they were acquainted. I
therefore think that the slip-slop of Slender is dropt gra-
tuitously upon his tongue, from his connexion with Shallow,
the stage echo of Sir Thomas Lucy.

I have already noticed the eagerness of our poet's admirers to vindicate or excuse in him any trace of undue
resentment: but it is extraordinary that they did not find
a high probability of Lucy's being obnoxious to Shakspeare
on several accounts, besides the old affair at Charlecote.
There were many local interests in agitation about the
time that he was incited to the production of the Merry
Wives. His townsmen were besieging Sir Thomas Lucy
with complaints against the maltsters, and they wanted to
be exempted from subsidy; they had applied to Shakspeare for his interest at court, and he may reasonably be
presumed to have had a great deal: it is therefore not only
possible, but very likely, that he did not take the liberty of
bestowing Sir Thomas Lucy's arms upon Shallow, merely
out of revenge for a chastisement received in his youth,
though he remembered it, as the *first* of a series of offences,
which he thought justified a little wholesome ridicule on a
weak, a petulant, and, perhaps, oppressive man of fortune
in his native county.

THE WISHING-GATE.

BY W. WORDSWORTH.

In the vale of Grasmere, by the side of the highway leading to Ambleside, is a Gate which, time out of mind, has been called the Wishing-gate, from a belief that wishes formed or indulged there have a favourable issue.

Hope rules a land for ever green.
All powers that serve the bright-eyed queen
   Are confident and gay;
Clouds at her bidding disappear:
Points she to aught?—the bliss draws near,
   And Fancy smooths the way.

Not such the land of Wishes—there
Dwell fruitless day-dreams, lawless prayer,
   And Thoughts with Things at strife;
Yet how forlorn, should *ye* depart,
Ye superstitions of the *heart*,
   How poor, were human life!

When magic lore abjured its might,
Ye did not forfeit one dear right,
   One tender claim abate;
Witness this symbol of your sway,
Surviving near the public way,
   The rustic Wishing-gate.

Inquire not if the fairy race
Shed kindly influence on the place,
   Ere northward they retired;
If here a warrior left a spell,
Panting for glory as he fell;
   Or here a saint expired.

Enough that all around is fair,
Composed with Nature's finest care,
   And in her fondest love;
Peace to embosom and content,
To overawe the turbulent,
   The selfish to reprove.

Yes! even the stranger from afar,
Reclining on this moss-grown bar,
   Unknowing and unknown,
The infection of the ground partakes,
Longing for his Belov'd—who makes
   All happiness her own.

Then why should conscious spirits fear
The mystic stirrings that are here,
   The ancient faith disclaim?
The local Genius ne'er befriends
Desires whose course in folly ends,
   Whose just reward is shame.

Smile if thou wilt, but not in scorn,
If some by ceaseless pains outworn,
   Here crave an easier lot;
If some have thirsted to renew
A broken vow, or bind a true,
   With firmer, holier knot.

And not in vain, when thoughts are cast
Upon the irrevocable past,
  Some penitent sincere
May for a worthier future sigh,
While trickles from his downcast eye,
  No unavailing tear.

The worldling, pining to be freed
From turmoil, who would turn or speed
  The current of his fate,
Might stop before this favour'd scene,
At Nature's call, nor blush to lean
  Upon the Wishing-gate.

The sage, who feels how blind, how weak
Is man, though loth such help to *seek*,
  Yet, passing, here might pause,
And yearn for insight to allay
Misgiving, while the crimson day
  In quietness withdraws;

Or when the church-clock's knell profound
To Time's first step across the bound
  Of midnight, makes reply;
Time pressing on, with starry crest,
To filial sleep upon the breast
  Of dread eternity!

APROPOS OF BREAD.

BY LORD NUGENT.

Dans cet antre
Je vois fort bien comme l'on entre,
Mais je ne vois pas comme on en sort.

LA FONTAINE.

YOUR apropos is a most faithless figure of speech. What is he but an insinuating rogue of a Frenchman, who, give him an inch will take an ell, slides himself into company where he is the least expected, obtaining his welcome by never appearing to doubt it, and then leads forward the confiding ear under false pretences heaven knows whither, until, too late, we find the word of promise broken both to it and to the hope.

Not long ago the following story was told me apropos of a remark I happened, without calculating consequences, to make on bread. " What deleterious' stuff they *do* put into their white bread," said I to a fresh-looking elderly man, with whom I had left London in the eight o'clock Gloucester night-coach; for it was not easy to hit upon any other subject in common between us, who were total strangers to each other, but bread, which is common to all who have it to eat. Not a word had passed since we started from Hatchett's, and we had now cleared the stones of Hammersmith. "I do wish the parliament men would do something to stop the bakers," quoth I, scholarly and wisely; " it's my belief that oyster shells and dead men's bones are the wholesomest ingredients in it."

" Sir," said my new acquaintance, putting into the side-pocket of the coach the fur cap, in which, despairing of a topic, he had disposed himself for sleep,—" Sir," said he, sitting bolt upright, and addressing himself to me for serious discourse, " the bakers have other ingredients; and if you are as little inclined to sleep as I am, sir, I will tell you, apropos of that, what happened to me several years ago. It is an awful story;—it sounds like a ghost story; but I have been brought up better than to believe in ghosts; I am not superstitious, sir, and am a serious member of the church of England, but some things *do* happen to people in the course of their lives, which it is very difficult to account for.

" I travel for the wholesale house of M. and Co. in the city. My name is Stephen Tudway. Towards the end of March, 1814, I had some patterns of articles in the cotton line to take orders upon from some respectable retail dealers at Derby. My business detained me in that town full four hours later than I had intended; for I had a longish journey to make that day, and several small retail houses to call at in my way to Matlock. Make what haste I could, the night had set in gloomy and wet, before I came upon the wild country that borders on that town. I had but lately undertaken to do business on that road, and was quite unacquainted with that part of England. It was so dark, and the country so wild, and I so much fatigued, that I was very well contented to put up for the night at the Peacock inn, on the edge of Matlock Heath. I must say the accommodations were all that a man need wish; for the people were civil, the refreshments good of their kind, and there was nothing remarkable in the appearance of any one, excepting a young woman at the bar, who had a cast in her eye that was unpleasant. With that I went to bed. The window of my chamber gave upon the inn-yard, which opened on one side to the heath. I closed the shutters and drew the curtains myself. Well, I lay sleepless for many hours, listening to the storm, which abated gradually, and I was in great hopes it was near morning, as I fancied I could hear the small birds twittering at my window; but still no light appeared, and all was so remarkably silent, that (I being accustomed to sleep in towns) some dread came over me. I quite longed to hear the cock crow. I began to draw my breath with difficulty, by reason of a strange feeling of weight on my chest. Suddenly I thought I heard a distant shriek; it was repeated, and seemed to approach from the heath till it was right under my window and very piercing; and I thought I could catch the words ' For God's sake, help !'

" Now, sir, I am a man who never cares to push myself forward into other people's concerns; and I guessed that the folks of the inn would be about in an hour or two at most, and might help the poor body. So I lay quiet, not knowing whether it was day or night; but I soon found that it was still night. Being in the habit of travelling with property, I had, as usual, fastened the door by double locking it: the key was,—begging your pardon,—in the pocket of my smalls,—and my smalls were,—saving your presence,—under my pillow. Notwithstanding all these precautions, the door was thrown open with violence, and by the light of the lamp on the stair-head I saw a tall figure of a woman, in an article of white cotton drapery, rush to my bed's head. ' For God's sake, help !' again it cried. I asked a few hurried questions, and felt much distressed; but the only answer I could obtain from her was, that I could save her life, perhaps more; for that she meditated a crime which I might prevent. ' For God's sake, help!' again she cried, ' I am on the point of committing suicide! I left my father's house on purpose to throw myself from the rock where *he*, the deceiver, last met me. But Heaven is kind. An impulse, which I could not resist, led me off my path to this inn. Something told me that I should here find one who has the power to help and save me. Follow me directly: I am distracted. Be witness to my crime, or prevent it!' So saying, the poor creature burst into a flood of tears, and rushed out of the door; and I could hear her hurrying down the stairs. What could I do, sir, but follow her? I had luckily my horseman's cloak within reach, which I threw round me, and it is my habit to sleep in my worsted stockings—I like to be particular. As I followed her out of the door of the house, the moon was shining bright and clear; I tracked her by her white cotton drapery, and, during the intervals when I could not see her, by the sound of her voice, which still cried ' For God's sake, help!'

" The scenery around the inn, which I now for the first time saw clearly by the light of the moon, was wild and terrific: rock and tangled brakes, with here and there a birch or an alder shooting up against the bright sky. The road which I had travelled the night before was left far to our right. After, as near as I can guess, three quarters of an hour's rapid pursuit (during which my feelings of wonder and fear were so strong, I could neither call nor speak to her, I could only follow,) we came to the foot of a tall rock, not very unlike some of those which I had passed on the skirts of Dove-dale the day before. To this rock she clung, and began to climb the side of it which was the least abrupt, till she reached the top. ' For God's sake, help!' again she cried; ' this is the spot where last *he* left me! I am going over—*you* may save me—make haste! make haste! For God's sake, help!'

" Now, sir, from my earliest youth I have had a strange dislike of clambering heights; I never was bred to it, nor made it a practice. I do not know whether it is peculiar to me—I dare say it is—but I feel in those situations a sort of sickness and dizziness-like come over me, and I lose all power of my limbs; and I never felt this peculiarity so strongly as on this occasion. I thought it would be a great risk, and I am a family man, and I was alone with the young woman, and nobody to help me; yet I wished to save her, and was just turning in my own mind what to do, when the poor soul flung herself off the rock on the contrary side to that on which I was standing: I just saw the white flare of her gown, streaming in the wind and the moonlight, as she fell; and in a moment after I heard a heavy sound, as if her head had come first to the ground and was crushed by the fall; a low moaning followed. But fancy, sir, my terror when I certainly heard these words, muttered indistinctly, but in a tone of voice I shall never forget; ' Mr. Tudway, I know you; you might have saved me; I am gone—gone—gone! but we shall meet again. This night twelvemonth such a cloud as is now sailing towards the moon will be in the sky, and you then *must* meet me at the foot of this rock:—remember—remember!' At this moment the cloud passed over the moon; it was quite dark, and I cannot tell how I got back, the young woman's end had so bewildered me—I had witnessed suicide!

" The next year seemed to pass strangely. I was with my family, and I plied my business as usual; but I never could banish this strange occurrence from my mind for a single moment; and never could I assume the courage to impart it even to Mrs. Tudway, before whom I never had a secret in my life. But I remember the newspapers were full of the tale of the young woman, and I lived in fear; for I thought I should be taken up as having consented to what my nature recoiled from. Time, which I wished to lag, seemed to fly rapidly; for I knew that next spring would take me again to a part of the country which I now so much wished to avoid.

" The March following, as I expected, I was again obliged to travel into Derbyshire with patterns. These journeys are regular in our business. On the 31st of March following I was again at Derby. Again I was detained, and till a still later hour than the year before. I was thoroughly benighted on the edge of Matlock Heath. I searched in vain for the Peacock inn; and lost myself among the wilds. The moon shone brightly, but the way was so rough that I was fain to dismount from my horse, who was sinking under me with fatigue. I led him with great trouble among the brakes and stones, until, pursuing a sheep path up a bank, I found myself stopped at the top by a precipice. It all at once occurred to me that this was the very rock from which the year before, on exactly such a night, the unhappy young woman had flung herself. Her last words suddenly came across me. I cannot tell how it was, sir, but I felt as if I had been brought there again by Providence to meet her, as she had promised me I *must* do. I lay down amid the brush-wood in utter despair, and looked over into the hollow, and, although

I am far from being superstitious, I really did expect to see something. A winding path led to a little glade surrounded by stones at the foot of the rock, which might be about one hundred yards from the place where I lay. Judge, sir, of my feelings, when I plainly saw the figure of a woman in white come slowly along the path into the glade. It seemed to walk with difficulty, and as if in pain; and it kept its hands to its head, round which an article of handkerchief, such as the country women wear, was closely folded. It stopped in the middle of the glade and looked round, as if expecting to find some one; and I thought it uttered a sound as if of disappointment. My blood curdled within me.—I felt that no wealth would tempt me to present myself before her, for I more than believed it was the same figure that had thrown itself from the rock. If I stirred among the brush-wood to make my escape she would surely have seen me, and, I warrant, done me a mischief. I could only lie still, gasping with fear; listening to my own heart beating, (as the song has it, 'the bounding hart amid the rocks'), and gazing stedfastly upon her as she paced to and fro, and I felt myself thoroughly powerless. At length the figure dropped its hands from its head, and I could see marks of blood and clay upon the handkerchief that bound her forehead. With another expression of discontent, the figure left the glade by the same path by which she had entered it. I cannot express how much I was relieved at being rid of the sight of this phantom,—for now I really believed it such. It was angered at not finding me where it had made the strange appointment to meet me. I lay, however, shuddering, and afraid to move, lest it should have only retired to some ambush, from whence, the moment I stirred, it might cross me.

"The moon had risen high behind my back as I lay looking stedfastly on the glade upon which it shone; gradually the light was dimmed, as if a cloud was passing across. I turned my head to look round and see what was the matter with the moon,—when, sir,—gracious heavens! —there stood the figure erect, the eyes bent down upon me, and it overshadowed me. The precipice was before me; what I feared worse was behind me. I started on my feet; and I felt myself on the edge of the rock and falling. Sir, a despairing man will cling to any thing; I caught by the white drapery of the ghastly figure itself. In *my* turn I cried, ' for God's sake, help!'—but the figure, which was stately as a corpse, laughed as we fell together!—

"A power of curious things may happen in a man's lifetime. I had fallen out of bed on the floor of my chamber at the Peacock inn on Matlock Heath, (though, thank God, not much hurt), and the clean white-striped Manchester head-curtain of the bed was in my hand; and the cock was crowing under my window like a Christian calling for help. In riding from the inn I was astonished to find that it stands in a remarkable flat country for two or three miles round; so that where could I have been for the precipice of the night before? Time, too, sir, had stood still: I had come to that inn on the night of the 31st of March, 1814; it was now but the 1st of April of the same year, and my bill mentioned but ' one night's lodging.' I have sometimes thought it might be all a dream;—but then, again, I cannot justly recollect going to sleep. Besides, I am no great dreamer at any time, and my supper that night had been nothing particular. If you will believe me, sir, it was but one blood pudding, a trifle of pickled salmon, some of their mild Derbyshire cheese toasted, (which I relished exceedingly); and not one drop did I drink that whole night, but one jug of egg flip!

" But sir, now I come to what we were talking of, apropos of bread. If it *was* a dream, it must have been all owing to the bread, in which, I am told, the Derbyshire bakers put a power of pounded Derbyshire spar.—But, sir, you seem sleepy——"

AN ANTICIPATION FOR A CERTAIN COQUETTE.

BY F. M. REYNOLDS.

SHE died—and behold, with her lures and her leers,
In a month she contrived to set hell by the ears,
  All its inmates with rancour and rivalry sought her;
This one, with her figure, and that, with her foot;
And this, with her spencer, and that, with her boot;
Not a devil so staid, but with baits she would suit;—
  Through hell there was nothing but duels and slaughter.

But the devils at last, simultaneously rose,
And appearing 'fore Satan proclaim'd all their woes,
  And affirm'd that with her, they no longer could dwell.
"Turn her out!" thunder'd Satan, and straight, with a shout,
All the youngsters and blackguards of hell turn'd her out,
While the bettermost classes re-echoed about,
  " Turn her out! turn her out! she's too wicked for hell!"

EXTEMPORE.

TO ————, TO WHOSE INTERFERENCE I CHIEFLY OWE
THE VERY LIBERAL PRICE GIVEN FOR
LALLA ROOKH.

WHEN they shall tell, in future times,
Of thousands giv'n for idle rhymes
  Like these—the pastime of an hour,
They'll wonder at the lavish taste
That could, like tulip-fanciers, waste
  A little fortune on a flower!

Yet wilt not thou, whose friendship set
  Such value on the bard's renown;
Yet wilt not thou, my friend, regret
  The golden shower thy spell brought down;

For thou dost love the free-born Muse,
Whose flight no curbing chain pursues;
  And thou dost think the song, that shrines
That image,—so ador'd by thee,
And spirits like thee,—Liberty,
  Of price beyond all India's mines!

THOMAS MOORE.

Painted by Edwin Landseer A.R.A.

Engraved by Chas. Heath.

GEORGIANA.

DUCHESS OF BEDFORD.

Printed by McQueen.

Published for the Proprietor by T. Hurst & Cº. Sᵗ Pauls Churchyard. and R. Jennings, 2. Poultry.

Lady, thy face is very beautiful,
A calm and stately beauty: thy dark hair
Hangs as the passing winds paid homage there;
And gems, such gems as only princes cull
From earth's rich veins, are round thy neck and arm;
Ivory, with just one touch of colour warm;
And thy white robe floats queen-like, suiting well
A shape such as in ancient pictures dwell!
If thou hadst lived in that old haunted time,
When sovereign Beauty was a thing sublime,
For which knights went to battle, and her glove
Had even more of glory than of love;—
Hadst thou lived in those days, how chivalrie,
With brand and banner, would have honour'd thee!
Then had this picture been a chronicle,
Of whose contents might only poets tell
What king had worn thy chains, what heroes sigh'd,
What thousands nameless, hopeless, for thee died.
But thou art of the Present—there is nought
About thee for the dreaming minstrel's thought,
Save vague imagination, which still lives
Upon the charmed light all beauty gives.
What hath romancing lute, or fancied line,
Or colour'd words to do with thee or thine?
No, the chords sleep in silence at thy feet,
They have no measures for thy music meet;
The poet hath no part in it, his dream
Would too much idleness of flattery seem;
And to that lovely picture only pays
The wordless homage of a lingering gaze.

L. E. L.

EPIGRAMS.

BY S. T. COLERIDGE.

HOARSE Mævius reads his hobbling verse
  To all, and at all times;
And finds them both divinely smooth,
  His voice as well as rhymes.
But folks say Mævius is no ass;
  But Mævius makes it clear
That he's a monster of an ass—
  An ass without an ear!

———

THERE comes from old Avaro's grave
A deadly stench—why, sure, they have
Immured his *soul* within his grave?

———

LAST Monday all the papers said,
That Mr. ——— was dead;
  Why, then, what said the city?
The tenth part sadly shook their head,
And shaking sigh'd, and sighing said,
  "Pity, indeed, 'tis pity!"

But when the said report was found
A rumour wholly without ground,
  Why, then, what said the city?
The other *nine* parts shook their head,
Repeating what the tenth had said,
  "Pity, indeed, 'tis pity!"

THE TAPESTRIED CHAMBER,

OR

THE LADY IN THE SACQUE.

BY THE AUTHOR OF WAVERLEY.

THE following narrative is given from the pen, so far as memory permits, in the same character in which it was presented to the author's ear; nor has he claim to further praise, or to be more deeply censured, than in proportion to the good or bad judgment which he has employed in selecting his materials, as he has studiously avoided any attempt at ornament which might interfere with the simplicity of the tale.

At the same time it must be admitted, that the particular class of stories which turns on the marvellous, possesses a stronger influence when told, than when committed to print. The volume taken up at noonday, though rehearsing the same incidents, conveys a much more feeble impression, than is achieved by the voice of the speaker on a circle of fire-side auditors, who hang upon the narrative as the narrator details the minute incidents which serve to give it authenticity, and lowers his voice with an affectation of mystery while he approaches the fearful and wonderful part. It was with such advantages that the present writer heard the following events related, more than twenty years since, by the celebrated Miss Seward, of Lichfield, who, to her numerous accomplishments, added, in a remarkable degree, the power of narrative in private conversation. In its present form the tale must necessarily lose all the interest which was attached to it, by the flexible voice and intelligent features of the gifted narrator. Yet still, read aloud, to an undoubting audience by the doubtful light of the closing evening, or, in silence, by a decaying taper, and amidst the solitude of a half-lighted apartment, it may redeem its character as a good ghost-story. Miss Seward always affirmed that she had derived her information from an authentic source, although she suppressed the names of the two persons chiefly concerned. I will not avail myself of any particulars I may have since received concerning the localities of the detail, but suffer them to rest under the same general description in which they were first related to me; and, for the same reason, I will not add to, or diminish the narrative, by any circumstance, whether more or less material, but simply rehearse, as I heard it, a story of supernatural terror.

About the end of the American war, when the officers of Lord Cornwallis's army, which surrendered at York-town, and others, who had been made prisoners during the impolitic and ill-fated controversy, were returning to their own country, to relate their adventures, and repose themselves, after their fatigues; there was amongst them a general officer, to whom Miss S. gave the name of Browne, but merely, as I understood, to save the inconvenience of introducing a nameless agent in the narrative. He was an officer of merit, as well as a gentleman of high consideration for family and attainments.

Some business had carried General Browne upon a tour

through the western counties, when, in the conclusion of a morning stage, he found himself in the vicinity of a small country town, which presented a scene of uncommon beauty, and of a character peculiarly English.

The little town, with its stately old church, whose tower bore testimony to the devotion of ages long past, lay amidst pastures and corn-fields of small extent, but bounded and divided with hedge-row timber of great age and size. There were few marks of modern improvement. The environs of the place intimated neither the solitude of decay, nor the bustle of novelty; the houses were old, but in good repair; and the beautiful little river murmured freely on its way to the left of the town, neither restrained by a dam, nor bordered by a towing-path.

Upon a gentle eminence, nearly a mile to the southward of the town, were seen, amongst many venerable oaks and tangled thickets, the turrets of a castle, as old as the wars of York and Lancaster, but which seemed to have received important alterations during the age of Elizabeth and her successor. It had not been a place of great size; but whatever accommodation it formerly afforded, was, it must be supposed, still to be obtained within its walls; at least, such was the inference which General Browne drew from observing the smoke arise merrily from several of the ancient wreathed and carved chimney-stalks. The wall of the park ran alongside of the highway for two or three hundred yards; and through the different points by which the eye found glimpses into the woodland scenery, it seemed to be well stocked. Other points of view opened in succession; now a full one, of the front of the old castle, and now a side glimpse at its particular towers; the former rich in all the bizarrerie of the Elizabethan school, while the simple and solid strength of other parts of the building seemed to show that they had been raised more for defence than ostentation.

Delighted with the partial glimpses which he obtained of the castle through the woods and glades by which this ancient feudal fortress was surrounded, our military traveller was determined to inquire whether it might not deserve a nearer view, and whether it contained family pictures or other objects of curiosity worthy of a stranger's visit; when, leaving the vicinity of the park, he rolled through a clean and well-paved street, and stopped at the door of a well-frequented inn.

Before ordering horses to proceed on his journey, General Browne made inquiries concerning the proprietor of the chateau which had so attracted his admiration; and was equally surprised and pleased at hearing in reply a nobleman named, whom we shall call Lord Woodville. How fortunate! Much of Browne's early recollections both at school, and at college, had been connected with young Woodville, whom, by a few questions, he now ascertained to be the same with the owner of this fair domain. He had been raised to the peerage by the decease of his father a few months before, and, as the general learned from the landlord, the term of mourning being ended, was now taking possession of his paternal estate, in the jovial season of merry autumn, accompanied by a select party of friends to enjoy the sports of a country famous for game.

This was delightful news to our traveller. Frank Woodville had been Richard Browne's fag at Eton, and his chosen intimate at Christ Church; their pleasures and their tasks had been the same; and the honest soldier's

heart warmed to find his early friend in possession of so
delightful a residence, and of an estate, as the landlord
assured him with a nod and a wink, fully adequate to
maintain and add to his dignity. Nothing was more natural than that the traveller should suspend a journey,
which there was nothing to render hurried, to pay a visit
to an old friend under such agreeable circumstances.

The fresh horses, therefore, had only the brief task of
conveying the general's travelling carriage to Woodville
Castle. A porter admitted them at a modern gothic lodge,
built in that style to correspond with the castle itself, and at
the same time rang a bell to give warning of the approach
of visitors. Apparently the sound of the bell had suspended the separation of the company, bent on the various
amusements of the morning; for, on entering the court
of the chateau, several young men were lounging about in
their sporting dresses, looking at, and criticising, the dogs
which the keepers held in readiness to attend their pastime.
As General Browne alighted, the young lord came to the
gate of the hall, and for an instant gazed, as at a stranger,
upon the countenance of his friend, on which, war, with
its fatigues and its wounds, had made a great alteration.
But the uncertainty lasted no longer than till the visitor
had spoken, and the hearty greeting which followed was
such as can only be exchanged betwixt those, who have
passed together the merry days of careless boyhood or
early youth.

"If I could have formed a wish, my dear Browne,"
said Lord Woodville, "it would have been to have you
here, of all men, upon this occasion, which my friends are
good enough to hold as a sort of holiday. Do not think you
have been unwatched during the years you have been ab-

sent from us. I have traced you through your dangers, your triumphs, your misfortunes, and was delighted to see that, whether in victory or defeat, the name of my old friend was always distinguished with applause."

The general made a suitable reply, and congratulated his friend on his new dignities, and the possession of a place and domain so beautiful.

"Nay, you have seen nothing of it as yet," said Lord Woodville, "and I trust you do not mean to leave us till you are better acquainted with it. It is true, I confess, that my present party is pretty large, and the old house, like other places of the kind, does not possess so much accommodation as the extent of the outward walls appears to promise. But we can give you a comfortable old-fashioned room, and I venture to suppose that your campaigns have taught you to be glad of worse quarters."

The general shrugged his shoulders, and laughed. "I presume," he said, "the worst apartment in your chateau is considerably superior to the old tobacco-cask, in which I was fain to take up my night's lodging when I was in the Bush, as the Virginians call it, with the light corps. There I lay, like Diogenes himself, so delighted with my covering from the element, that I made a vain attempt to have it rolled on to my next quarters; but my commander for the time would give way to no such luxurious provision, and I took farewell of my beloved cask with tears in my eyes."

"Well, then, since you do not fear your quarters," said Lord Woodville, "you will stay with me a week at least. Of guns, dogs, fishing-rods, flies, and means of sport by sea and land, we have enough and to spare: you cannot pitch on an amusement but we will find the means of pursuing

it. But if you prefer the gun and pointers, I will go with
you myself, and see whether you have mended your shooting since you have been amongst the Indians of the back
settlements."

The general gladly accepted his friendly host's proposal
in all its points. After a morning of manly exercise, the
company met at dinner, where it was the delight of Lord
Woodville to conduce to the display of the high properties of
his recovered friend, so as to recommend him to his guests,
most of whom were persons of distinction. He led General
Browne to speak of the scenes he had witnessed; and as
every word marked alike the brave officer and the sensible
man, who retained possession of his cool judgment under
the most imminent dangers, the company looked upon
the soldier with general respect, as on one who had proved
himself possessed of an uncommon portion of personal
courage; that attribute of all others, of which every body
desires to be thought possessed.

The day at Woodville Castle ended as usual in such
mansions. The hospitality stopped within the limits of
good order: music, in which the young lord was a proficient,
succeeded to the circulation of the bottle: cards and bil-
liards, for those who preferred such amusements, were in
readiness: but the exercise of the morning required early
hours, and not long after eleven o'clock the guests began
to retire to their several apartments.

The young lord himself conducted his friend, General
Browne, to the chamber destined for him, which answered the description he had given of it, being comfortable, but old-fashioned. The bed was of the massive
form used in the end of the seventeenth century, and the
curtains of faded silk, heavily trimmed with tarnished

gold. But then the sheets, pillows, and blankets looked delightful to the campaigner, when he thought of his "mansion, the cask." There was an air of gloom in the tapestry hangings, which, with their worn-out graces, curtained the walls of the little chamber, and gently undulated as the autumnal breeze found its way through the ancient lattice-window, which pattered and whistled as the air gained entrance. The toilette, too, with its mirror, turbaned, after the manner of the beginning of the century, with a coiffure of murrey-coloured silk, and its hundred strange-shaped boxes, providing for arrangements which had been obsolete for more than fifty years, had an antique, and in so far a melancholy, aspect. But nothing could blaze more brightly and cheerfully than the two large wax candles; or if aught could rival them, it was the flaming bickering faggots in the chimney, that sent at once their gleam and their warmth, through the snug apartment; which, notwithstanding the general antiquity of its appearance, was not wanting in the least convenience, that modern habits rendered either necessary or desirable.

"This is an old-fashioned sleeping apartment, general," said the young lord, "but I hope you find nothing that makes you envy your old tobacco-cask."

"I am not particular respecting my lodgings," replied the general; "yet were I to make any choice, I would prefer this chamber by many degrees, to the gayer and more modern rooms of your family mansion. Believe me, that when I unite its modern air of comfort with its venerable antiquity, and recollect that it is your lordship's property, I shall feel in better quarters here, than if I were in the best hotel London could afford."

"I trust—I have no doubt—that you will find yourself as comfortable as I wish you, my dear general," said the young nobleman; and once more bidding his guest good night, he shook him by the hand, and withdrew.

The general once more looked round him, and internally congratulating himself on his return to peaceful life, the comforts of which were endeared by the recollection of the hardships and dangers he had lately sustained, undressed himself, and prepared for a luxurious night's rest.

Here, contrary to the custom of this species of tale, we leave the general in possession of his apartment until the next morning.

The company assembled for breakfast at an early hour, but without the appearance of General Browne, who seemed the guest that Lord Woodville was desirous of honouring above all whom his hospitality had assembled around him. He more than once expressed surprise at the general's absence, and at length sent a servant to make inquiry after him. The man brought back information that General Browne had been walking abroad since an early hour of the morning, in defiance of the weather, which was misty and ungenial.

"The custom of a soldier,"—said the young nobleman to his friends; "many of them acquire habitual vigilance, and cannot sleep after the early hour at which their duty usually commands them to be alert."

Yet the explanation which Lord Woodville then offered to the company seemed hardly satisfactory to his own mind, and it was in a fit of silence and abstraction that he awaited the return of the general. It took place near an hour after the breakfast bell had rung. He looked fatigued

and feverish. His hair, the powdering and arrangement
of which was at this time one of the most important occupations of a man's whole day, and marked his fashion as
much as, in the present time, the tying of a cravat, or the
want of one, was dishevelled, uncurled, void of powder,
and dank with dew. His clothes were huddled on with
a careless negligence, remarkable in a military man, whose
real or supposed duties are usually held to include some
attention to the toilette; and his looks were haggered and
ghastly in a peculiar degree.

"So you have stolen a march upon us this morning, my
dear general," said Lord Woodville; "or you have not
found your bed so much to your mind as I had hoped and
you seemed to expect. How did you rest last night?"

"Oh, excellently well! remarkably well! never better in
my life"—said General Browne rapidly, and yet with an
air of embarrassment which was obvious to his friend.
He then hastily swallowed a cup of tea, and, neglecting or
refusing whatever else was offered, seemed to fall into a
fit of abstraction.

"You will take the gun to-day, general?" said his friend
and host, but had to repeat the question twice ere he received the abrupt answer, "No, my lord; I am sorry I
cannot have the honour of spending another day with your
lordship: my post horses are ordered, and will be here
directly."

All who were present showed surprise, and Lord Woodville immediately replied, "Post horses, my good friend!
what can you possibly want with them, when you promised
to stay with me quietly for at least a week?"

"I believe," said the general, obviously much embarrassed,

"that I might, in the pleasure of my first meeting with your lordship, have said something about stopping here a few days; but I have since found it altogether impossible."

"That is very extraordinary," answered the young nobleman. "You seemed quite disengaged yesterday, and you cannot have had a summons to-day; for our post has not come up from the town, and therefore you cannot have received any letters."

General Browne, without giving any further explanation, muttered something of indispensable business, and insisted on the absolute necessity of his departure in a manner which silenced all opposition on the part of his host, who saw that his resolution was taken, and forbore all further importunity.

"At least, however," he said, "permit me, my dear Browne, since go you will or must, to show you the view from the terrace, which the mist, that is now rising, will soon display."

He threw open a sash-window, and stepped down upon the terrace as he spoke. The general followed him mechanically, but seemed little to attend to what his host was saying, as, looking across an extended and rich prospect, he pointed out the different objects worthy of observation. Thus they moved on till Lord Woodville had attained his purpose of drawing his guest entirely apart from the rest of the company, when, turning round upon him with an air of great solemnity, he addressed him thus:

"Richard Browne, my old and very dear friend, we are now alone. Let me conjure you to answer me upon the word of a friend, and the honour of a soldier. How did you in reality rest during last night?"

"Most wretchedly indeed, my lord," answered the

general, in the same tone of solemnity;—"so miserably, that I would not run the risk of such a second night, not only for all the lands belonging to this castle, but for all the country which I see from this elevated point of view."

"This is most extraordinary," said the young lord, as if speaking to himself; "then there must be something in the reports concerning that apartment." Again turning to the general, he said, "For God's sake, my dear friend, be candid with me, and let me know the disagreeable particulars which have befallen you under a roof where, with consent of the owner, you should have met nothing save comfort."

The general seemed distressed by this appeal, and paused a moment before he replied. "My dear lord," he at length said, "what happened to me last night is of a nature so peculiar and so unpleasant, that I could hardly bring myself to detail it even to your lordship, were it not that, independent of my wish to gratify any request of yours, I think that sincerity on my part may lead to some explanation about a circumstance equally painful and mysterious. To others, the communication I am about to make, might place me in the light of a weak-minded, superstitious fool, who suffered his own imagination to delude and bewilder him; but you have known me in childhood and youth, and will not suspect me of having adopted in manhood, the feelings and frailties from which my early years were free." Here he paused, and his friend replied:

"Do not doubt my perfect confidence in the truth of your communication, however strange it may be," replied Lord Woodville; "I know your firmness of disposition too well, to suspect you could be made the object of im-

position, and am aware that your honour and your friendship will equally deter you from exaggerating whatever
you may have witnessed."

"Well then," said the general, "I will proceed with
my story as well as I can, relying upon your candour;
and yet distinctly feeling that I would rather face a battery
than recall to my mind the odious recollections of last
night."

He paused a second time, and then perceiving that Lord
Woodville remained silent and in an attitude of attention,
he commenced, though not without obvious reluctance, the
history of his night adventures in the Tapestried Chamber.

"I undressed and went to bed, so soon as your lordship
left me yesterday evening; but the wood in the chimney,
which nearly fronted my bed, blazed brightly and cheerfully,
and, aided by a hundred exciting recollections of my child-.
hood and youth, which had been recalled by the unexpected pleasure of meeting your lordship, prevented me
from falling immediately asleep. I ought, however, to
say, that these reflections were all of a pleasant and agreeable kind, grounded on a sense of having for a time exchanged the labour, fatigues, and dangers of my profession, for the enjoyments of a peaceful life, and the
reunion of those friendly and affectionate ties, which I had
torn asunder at the rude summons of war.

"While such pleasing reflections were stealing over my
mind, and gradually lulling me to slumber, I was suddenly
aroused by a sound like that of the rustling of a silken
gown, and the tapping of a pair of high-heeled shoes, as if
a woman were walking in the apartment. Ere I could
draw the curtain to see what the matter was, the figure
of a little woman passed between the bed and the fire.
The back of this form was turned to me, and I could

observe, from the shoulders and neck, it was that of an old woman, whose dress was an old-fashioned gown, which, I think, ladies call a sacque; that is, a sort of robe completely loose in the body, but gathered into broad plaits upon the neck and shoulders, which fall down to the ground, and terminate in a species of train.

" I thought the intrusion singular enough, but never harboured for a moment the idea that what I saw was any thing more than the mortal form of some old woman about the establishment, who had a fancy to dress like her grandmother, and who, having perhaps (as your lordship mentioned that you were rather straitened for room) been dislodged from her chamber for my accommodation, had forgotten the circumstance, and returned by twelve, to her old haunt. Under this persuasion I moved myself in bed and coughed a little, to make the intruder sensible of my being in possession of the premises.—She turned slowly round, but, gracious heaven! my lord, what a countenance did she display to me! There was no longer any question what she was, or any thought of her being a living being. Upon a face which wore the fixed features of a corpse were imprinted the traces of the vilest and most hideous passions which had animated her while she lived. The body of some atrocious criminal seemed to have been given up from the grave, and the soul restored from the penal fire, in order to form, for a space, an union with the ancient accomplice of its guilt. I started up in bed, and sat upright, supporting myself on my palms, as I gazed on this horrible spectre. The hag made, as it seemed, a single and swift stride to the bed where I lay, and squatted herself down upon it, in precisely the same attitude which I had assumed in the extremity of my horror, advancing her diabolical countenance within half a yard of mine,

Drawn by F. P. Stephanoff.

Engraved by J. Goodyear.

THE TAPESTRIED CHAMBER.

Pub.^d for the Proprietor by Hurst, Chance, & C.º St Paul's Churchyard & R. Jennings, 2, Poultry.

Printed by Edruin.

with a grin which seemed to intimate the malice and the derision of an incarnate fiend."

Here General Browne stopped, and wiped from his brow the cold perspiration with which the recollection of his horrible vision had covered it.

" My lord," he said, " I am no coward. I have been in all the mortal dangers incidental to my profession, and I may truly boast, that no man ever saw Richard Browne dishonour the sword he wears; but in these horrible circumstances, under the eyes, and, as it seemed, almost in the grasp of an incarnation of an evil spirit, all firmness forsook me, all manhood melted from me like wax in the furnace, and I felt my hair individually bristle. The current of my life-blood ceased to flow, and I sank back in a swoon, as very a victim to panic terror as ever was a village girl, or a child of ten years old. How long I lay in this condition I cannot pretend to guess.

" But I was roused by the castle clock striking one, so loud that it seemed as if it were in the very room. It was some time before I dared open my eyes, lest they should again encounter the horrible spectacle. When, however, I summoned courage to look up, she was no longer visible. My first idea was to pull my bell, wake the servants, and remove to a garret or a hay-loft, to be ensured against a second visitation. Nay, I will confess the truth, that my resolution was altered, not by the shame of exposing myself, but by the fear that, as the bell-cord hung by the chimney, I might, in making my way to it, be again crossed by the fiendish hag, who, I figured to myself, might be still lurking about some corner of the apartment.

" I will not pretend to describe what hot and cold fever-fits tormented me for the rest of the night, through broken sleep,

weary vigils, and that dubious state which forms the neutral
ground between them. An hundred terrible objects appeared to haunt me; but there was the great difference
betwixt the vision which I have described, and those which
followed, that I knew the last to be deceptions of my own
fancy and over-excited nerves.

"Day at last appeared, and I rose from my bed ill in health,
and humiliated in mind. I was ashamed of myself as a
man and a soldier, and still more so, at feeling my own extreme desire to escape from the haunted apartment, which,
however, conquered all other considerations; so that, hud-
dling on my clothes with the most careless haste, I made my
escape from your lordship's mansion, to seek in the open
air some relief to my nervous system, shaken as it was by
this horrible rencounter with a visitant, for such I must
believe her, from the other world. Your lordship has now
heard the cause of my discomposure, and of my sudden
desire to leave your hospitable castle. In other places I
trust we may often meet; but God protect me from ever
spending a second night under that roof!"

Strange as the general's tale was, he spoke with such a
deep air of conviction, that it cut short all the usual com-
mentaries which are made on such stories. Lord Woodville never once asked him if he was sure he did not dream
of the apparition, or suggested any of the possibilities by
which it is fashionable to explain apparitions,—wild vagaries
of the fancy, or deception of the optic nerves. On the
contrary, he seemed deeply impressed with the truth and
reality of what he had heard; and, after a considerable
pause, regretted, with much appearance of sincerity, that
his early friend should in his house have suffered so
severely.

" I am the more sorry for your pain, my dear Browne,"
he continued, " that it is the unhappy, though most unexpected, result of an experiment of my own. You must
know, that for my father and grandfather's time, at least,
the apartment which was assigned to you last night, had
been shut on account of reports that it was disturbed by
supernatural sights and noises. When I came, a few weeks
since, into possession of the estate, I thought the accommodation, which the castle afforded for my friends, was not
extensive enough to permit the inhabitants of the invisible
world to retain possession of a comfortable sleeping apartment. I therefore caused the Tapestried Chamber, as we
call it, to be opened; and, without destroying its air of
antiquity, I had such new articles of furniture placed in it
as became the more modern times. Yet as the opinion
that the room was haunted very strongly prevailed among
the domestics, and was also known in the neighbourhood
and to many of my friends, I feared some prejudice might be
entertained by the first occupant of the Tapestried Chamber,
which might tend to revive the evil report which it had
laboured under, and so disappoint my purpose of rendering it an useful part of the house. I must confess, my dear
Browne, that your arrival yesterday, agreeable to me for
a thousand reasons besides, seemed the most favourable
opportunity of removing the unpleasant rumours which
attached to the room, since your courage was indubitable,
and your mind free of any pre-occupation on the subject.
I could not, therefore, have chosen a more fitting subject
for my experiment."

" Upon my life," said General Browne, somewhat hastily,
" I am infinitely obliged to your lordship—very particularly indebted indeed. I am likely to remember for

some time the consequences of the experiment, as your lordship is pleased to call it."

" Nay, now you are unjust, my dear friend," said Lord Woodville.   " You have only to reflect for a single moment, in order to be convinced that I could not augur the possibility of the pain to which you have been so unhappily exposed.   I was yesterday morning a complete sceptic on the subject of supernatural appearances.   Nay, I am sure that had I told you what was said about that room, those very reports would have induced you, by your own choice, to select it for your accommodation.   It was my misfortune, perhaps my error, but really cannot be termed my fault, that you have been afflicted so strangely."

" Strangely indeed!" said the general, resuming his good temper; " and I acknowledge that I have no right to be offended with your lordship for treating me like what I used to think myself—a man of some firmness and courage. —But I see my post horses are arrived, and I must not detain your lordship from your amusement."

" Nay, my old friend," said Lord Woodville, " since you cannot stay with us another day, which, indeed, I can no longer urge, give me at least half an hour more. You used to love pictures, and I have a gallery of portraits, some of them by Vandyke, representing ancestry to whom this property and castle formerly belonged. I think that several of them will strike you as possessing merit."

General Browne accepted the invitation, though somewhat unwillingly.   It was evident he was not to breathe freely or at ease, till he left Woodville Castle far behind him.   He could not refuse his friend's invitation, however; and the less so, that he was a little ashamed of the peevishness which he had displayed towards his well-meaning entertainer.

The general, therefore, followed Lord Woodville through several rooms, into a long gallery hung with pictures, which the latter pointed out to his guest, telling the names, and giving some account of the personages whose portraits presented themselves in progression. General Browne was but little interested in the details which these accounts conveyed to him. They were, indeed, of the kind which are usually found in an old family gallery. Here, was a cavalier who had ruined the estate in the royal cause; there, a fine lady who had reinstated it by contracting a match with a wealthy round-head. There, hung a gallant who had been in danger for corresponding with the exiled court at Saint Germain's; here, one who had taken arms for William at the revolution; and there, a third that had thrown his weight alternately into the scale of whig and tory.

While Lord Woodville was cramming these words into his guest's ear, " against the stomach of his sense," they gained the middle of the gallery, when he beheld General Browne suddenly start, and assume an attitude of the utmost surprise, not unmixed with fear, as his eyes were caught and suddenly riveted by a portrait of an old lady in a sacque, the fashionable dress of the end of the seventeenth century.

" There she is!" he exclaimed, " there she is, in form and features, though inferior in demoniac expression to, the accursed hag who visited me last night."

" If that be the case," said the young nobleman, "there can remain no longer any doubt of the horrible reality of your apparition. That is the picture of a wretched ancestress of mine, of whose crimes a black and fearful catalogue

is recorded in a family history in my charter-chest.
The recital of them would be too horrible: it is enough to
say, that in yon fatal apartment incest, and unnatural
murder, were committed.   I will restore it to the solitude
to which the better judgment of those who preceded me
had consigned it; and never shall any one, so long as I can
prevent it, be exposed to a repetition of the supernatural
horrors which could shake such courage as yours."

Thus the friends, who had met with such glee, parted
in a very different mood; Lord Woodville to command
the tapstried chamber to be unmantled, and the door built
up; and General Browne to seek in some less beautiful
country, and with some less dignified friend, forgetfulness
of the painful night which he had passed in Woodville
Castle.

TO A SPINSTER.

LOVE'S CALENDAR.

BY F. M. REYNOLDS.

THAT courtship gay is *Lady Day*,
My pretty maid, you teach your lover;
But marry not, or you'll discover,
That Lady Day, most strange to say,
Will then become *no Quarter* day.

AN ATTEMPT AT A TOUR.

BY THE AUTHOR OF THE ROUE.

" When London's quicksilver's down at Zero, lo!
    Coach, chariot, luggage, baggage, equipage,
    Wheels whirl from Carlton-Palace to Soho,
    And happiest they who horses can engage."

BYRON.

HAVING no wife to control me, no daughter to marry, and no business to detain me in town after the opera is closed and Almacks finished, I am never one of the remanets in London when the season is over.

Nothing to me is so miserable as to walk up St. James's-street and find it a desert; nothing so disagreeable as to see the windows of Fenton's and Stevens' closed; or those of White's, Boodle's, and Brooks' without the usual quantity of heads reading newspapers, or eye-glasses looking out for nods of recognition.

The moment therefore that Pasta has chanted her last aria, Brocard danced her last pirouette, in short,

" When London's quicksilver's down at Zero,"

I throw off the trammels of society, start into the country in pursuit of adventure and of nature, and bid adieu to quadrilles, cards, and ceremony till the first blossoming beauties of spring proclaim that it is time to quit the country for London, and change my plush shooting-jacket and gaiters for velvet waistcoats and silk stockings. I am not one of those, however, who are content with a mere tour *à-la-mode;* with a journey to Paris, or a visit to a country-house or a watering-place. I go into the country for liberty; to wander where I have no chance of seeing any thing that can put me in mind of Piccadilly, or of hearing any thing that can bring to my remembrance a London party; and this I find it impossible to do within any moderate distance of the bills of mortality.

Surrey may be very beautiful, Middlesex may be very picturesque, and the shores of Brighton may be very expansive; but it requires the distance of, at least, two hundred miles to get out of the sound of those eternal and perpetual six sets of quadrilles, to which young men and women in town dance and flirt from March till August, and which ring in one's ears for weeks after the season is over.

The last time I left London, it seemed as though even this distance was not to relieve me; for at the very first inn at which I made any stay (and it was full two hundred miles from Hyde Park Corner), I was compelled to eat my dinner to Hart's seventeenth set from the eternal Frieschutz, which the landlady's daughter was practising on a piano, or rather a forte, for it was any thing but piano, in the bar.

Every experienced bachelor, and perhaps married man, knows the dear delight of quitting London alone and independent; with no horses, dogs, ladies, or bandboxes to claim those attentions, which are always troublesome, and never requited; with no ladies' maids grumbling at mounting the dicky before, or at being squeezed into a rumble-tumble behind; no coachman swearing that his horses will be knocked up; no young lady pouting in the corner, because she is hurried from London before Mrs. So-and-so's quadrille, or before Captain —————— can get leave of absence to follow her; no old gentleman cursing the wines and the waiters, because they are not so good as those of his own cellar and at his own sideboard; and no elderly lady fretting at every stage at the extortions of the landlords and postboys, and wondering what the world will come to at last.

The only way to travel with enjoyment, and to take adventures, like a knight-errant of old, as they come, is to travel alone, without even the prying eyes of your servant; since, though we may stop his tongue in the drawing-room, we cannot obliterate his memory in the servants'-hall, from which tales are often carried to the toilette of the ladies that are very detrimental to the characters of private gentlemen about town; and under these circumstances I think it a great defect in the creation, that a certain number of beings were not formed with precisely that quantity of memory, and tongue, necessary for the purposes of their masters and mistresses, and no more.

My fellow-passengers were too uninteresting to form themes for discussion; I shall not therefore trouble my readers with those who troubled me, nor with any description of two or three cottage scenes which have come under my observation, because I hate the rusticity of a country life; at least, that kind of splishy-splashy, draggle-tail, get-over-stile, wet through and dry again, sort of country life, which poets recommend, and some people pretend to enjoy. My country life must be associated with Italian colonnades and verandas; with geraniums, hydrangeas, and conservatories; with large oak dining-parlours, and well-stored larders and libraries; with your independent breakfasts from 10 till 2;

L

with hounds, and hunters, and whippers-in, and partridges, and pheasants, who philanthropically give their destroyers appetites to eat them with, as our punning friend P—— would have said, with pointers before dinner and *setters* after dinner, his orthography never standing in the way of a pun ; with dressing-bells and dinner-bells, and claret and conversation. Then, indeed, your blue sky and green meadow, your liquid lake and running stream, your gravel walk and puzzling labyrinth, may be delightful.

With these sentiments, it may be wondered at, that, on my arrival at Kendal, I should form the sudden determination to send on my luggage, and, with a wallet over my shoulder, to start upon a pedestrian tour round the lakes of Westmoreland and Cumberland, in the faint hope that my temporary vicinity to Southey and Wordsworth might inspire me with some particle of the genius of lake poetry.

Imagine me, then, doing the " pastorale," not as the celebrated dancing general does, when he puts his legs in a passion in a quadrille, nor as Peter Pastoral did it in the comedy, with a bouquet in his buttonhole, and a waistcoat embroidered with parsley and butter; but with a fishing-rod in one hand, by way of a pedestrian apology, and an umbrella in the other, poking my way through puddles and cart-ruts, through mud and mire, and hedges and ditches, on one of the wettest days with which our blessed climate has ever entertained us. I might, perhaps, here indulge you with a descriptive passage of the scenery, but that I hate any thing but the real picturesque, excepting it should be delineated with the masterly pencil of a Williams, a Glover, or a Robson; or worked up in pen and ink by the genius of the " great unknown," the only person who can create any *typical* representation of trees and flowers, and skies, and mountains, and forests, upon the pages of an octavo. Were I possessed of this genius it would have been useless on the present occasion, since from the direction of the wind and rain my umbrella was obliged to be placed directly between my eyes and the prospects which I came to enjoy. Once, indeed, at the head of the lake, did I attempt to get a peep at Windermere; but a sudden gust of the blustering railer, rude Boreas, turning my umbrella inside out, I had to run a quarter of a mile before the wind ere I could induce its whalebone ribs (which seemed quite as obstinate as other *ribs*) to resume their original position; and thus exhibited a figure in search of the picturesque that might have furnished a Rowlandson or a Cruikshank with a representative of a Syntax. At the fifth milestone, my right boot burst, and called down an anathema upon Hoby; in punishment for which, if there was one puddle deeper than another, the dilapidated boot was sure to go into it. Two miles before my arrival at the inn I was overtaken, and taken up, by a coach licensed to carry six in, and thirteen out, for the accommodation of tourists; five of which species of pleasure-hunters I found stowed in the vehicle, and packed them a little tighter by making a sixth, being quite as great a nuisance as a "middle man" as any that we read of in the sister kingdom. My five companions were all in search of the picturesque; all lamenting the weather; all looking out for particular points of view designated in their books and maps; so that the moment any turn in the road presented a new aspect to the scenery all their heads simultaneously rushed to the window on either side, at the expense of collisions of pericraniums, the effects of which

might have roused the genius of Gall, and puzzled Spurz-
heim himself.

Among these tourists was a dandy, who seemed amazingly
careful of his portmanteau. Every time the coach stopped
he exclaimed, " Pray, coachman, take care of my trunk. I
hope my trunk is safe. Pray don't let my trunk get wet."
At length, in thrusting his head out of the window to catch
a glimpse of the picturesque, he struck his head so violently
against the branch of a tree, that he fell back into his seat
nearly senseless. Recovering himself, however, " Bless me!"
said he, " it nearly knocked my head off; almost stunned
me. What *would* you have done if it had killed me?"

" We should have sent your *trunk* home," observed a
quiet traveller in the further corner of the coach.

I quitted the vehicle at Low-Wood Inn. My fellow-
passengers being " tied to time," as one of them expressed
it, pursued their way with the full determination, as another said, to " get through the lakes, at any rate;" and,
indeed, they could not have been much wetter if this had
actually been the case. So off they went, making their
observations on, and enjoying, the pleasure of the scenery
through apertures about twelve inches square; to the present great delight of themselves, and no doubt to the future
edification of those who are to be indulged with the description on their return.

At Low-Wood, I found a number of weather-bound
ladies and gentlemen, running every moment to a large
barometer in the hall, or watching with anxiety for the little
patches of blue sky which now and then appeared among
the watery clouds, that still scudded on in endless succession, to tantalize them with a hope which the pattering

rain against the windows perpetually disappointed. It is from the little public room of this inn, that, in a pair of dry slippers and a coat and pantaloons belonging to the landlord, I am penning these reminiscences of my attempt at a tour, having ordered a chaise and pair to carry me back to the delights of the high northern road the moment my clothes are dry. In the meantime my companions furnish me food for observation. One lady, rather impatient, has just given the barometer a shake, in the hope that the mercury may receive an impetus from her fair hand, more powerful than that of nature. Two young Irishmen, who have been upon an aquatic excursion, are wringing their neckcloths and wiping themselves dry with their wet pocket-handkerchiefs, at present quite uncertain whether they are drowned or not. Another is striving, might and main, until he is black in the face, to get a wet shoe up at heel; which, no doubt, fitted him tolerably well before his foot had been swollen, and the shoe shrunk from the consequences of the wet, but which now resists all the efforts of himself and the shoe-horn, united to the reiterated thumbing and fingering and coaxing of the "boots." He has given up the attempt with a hearty curse on the shoemaker, the shoe-horn, boots, and the weather, and has seated himself sulkily, with his feet buried in a pair of slippers that seem to have been imported from Brobdignag for the benefit of the *Titans*.

The sound of carriage-wheels has attracted every body to the window, where we can see an enormous coach, drawn by only a pair of horses, which appear as though they would have arrived at the last stage of their existence, if they had not got to the last stage of their journey. Out of the carriage-window are hung the heads of two or three gaping children, and one puppy-dog, by far the most saga-cious looking of the group, in spite of about half a yard of tongue which he hangs out to cool in the summer-shower. On the dicky before is seated a heap of great coats, with a straw hat on the top of them; while the rumble-tumble behind exhibits a male and female shrouding themselves under the coverture of the same cloak, from which their wet and cold hands are vainly trying to extricate them-selves. They are at length helped down, bringing with them a certain portion of mud from the wheels. The door of the carriage is opened, and out pour some half-dozen boys and girls, from the size of infants up to that of "hobble-de-hoys," dressed in nankeen spencers and white shirts, with the usual accompaniment of beaver hats, and feathers in profusion. This group is followed by a young lady about eighteen, whose languishing eyes and listless movements are strongly contrasted by the appearance of rude health on her cheeks, which resemble a red cabbage rather than a damask-rose. In one hand she holds a novel, with which she appears to have relieved the tedium of her journey, while the other displays a white pocket-handker-chief ready prepared to dry up the effects of her sensibility. As she alights from the carriage, a coarse but kind voice from behind exclaims, "Take care Lizzy, dear!" which is immediately followed by the appearance of the speaker, in the person of a short, round woman, clad in a light blue riding-habit, fitting her figure so closely as to show all its various rotundities both before and behind. Her head, bosom, and body, bear a striking resemblance to three hard dumplings of Lent placed pyramidally on a plum-pudding of Christmas; while a small beaver hat and fea-thers sits perched like a cockatoo upon the upper dumpling.

Just as she had reached the lower step of the carriage the hinder part of her blue riding-habit was caught by the upper one, and, being rather scanty in its dimensions, would not permit her to put her foot to the ground; so that one half of her short thick leg was exposed in the attempt, while the tail of the petticoat was still detained in the carriage. This was at length released so suddenly by the ostler, who could not resist the grin which extended his mouth as he performed the operation, that she fell forward, and nearly overturned the waiter in her descent. The carriage having thus discharged its contents, and all the books, maps, and fragments of pigeon-pies, and bottles of wine, being duly taken care of, the lady directed her attention to the heap of great coats and the straw hat on the front dicky, which covered up no less a person than the master of the carriage, the husband of the lady, and, to the best of his belief, the father of the children. The envelopes, being withdrawn, discovered a short pot-bellied man, buttoned up in a pea-green jacket covered with sugarloaf buttons, designed, as I afterwards understood, by his eldest daughter, as a specimen of the picturesque. His leather inexpressibles, which were met by a pair of short top-boots, were scarcely visible from the projection of that part of his body which has been called by citizens the corporation; while his apoplectic-looking head and neck were almost hid by the monstrous straw hat with which they were covered. In spite of his great coats, the poor gentleman was wet through and through. The water streamed out at both ends of his boat-hat, and seemed to run in and out of every aperture about him, from his ears, nose, and mouth, down to the knees of his breeches. In short, what with his dripping hat, eye-lashes, nose, and chin, he looked like a male "Niobe all tears." Every step he took, his feet went squash in his boots; and when he seated himself, you saw by his shrinking movement the unpleasant contact between his skin and the wet clothes. "I am afraid you are a *little* wet, my dear," exclaimed his dumpling wife; "but one mustn't mind trifles when one goes a pleasuring." "A pleasuring!" muttered the dripping sposo, but was prevented from a farther reply by a glance from his rib. The young gentlefolks amused themselves with various little amiable coloquies, consisting of such assertions and contradictions as 'tis—t'aint—t'was—t'wasn't—you did—I didn't—I will, and I wont. On which the elder miss cried out, with a languishing air, "Tezzy vous donck, mounseer mon frere;" but was stopped in her look at the surrounding company, to ascertain the extent of their admiration at her proficiency in the French language, by the eldest boy exclaiming, "I shan't tuzzy vous—tuzzy vous yourself, sister Liz."

Our attention was again drawn to the window by the rattling of other wheels and the arrival of another party. A hack chaise, drawn by four horses, made its appearance, and drove, with all the remaining vigour of the jaded cattle, which two or three smart lashes had elicited, up to the door.

The first person who presented himself to our view was a man apparently between thirty and forty. A frock coat, with Wellington pantaloons, covered with lace and frogs, together with a stiff black stock, gave outward intimation of a military man. He was what the world generally terms handsome, but with a sinister expression about the eyes, a supercilious curl of the lip, that greatly deteriorated from the effect which his features might otherwise have produced. He had all the external appearance of a gentleman, but wanted the ease which is the indispensable requisite of a true one. For this he had substituted assurance, depending upon his face and figure; and perhaps feeling the want of the last polish which he had observed in others, he determined to supply its place by *dash*, which, in his case, had partly degenerated into slang. A loose kind of strut in his walk announced the wish to convince spectators that he was somebody; while a fierce expression of the eye seemed to threaten those who should venture to dispute it even by a look.

He was altogether that kind of man whose person makes an impression which his manners efface. Behind him came a young lady, rather pretty than interesting, to whom he offered his arm with the air of one who says, " I have no longer any occasion to be more attentive than suits my inclination and convenience." She had an evident air of fashion about her, which ill accorded with the dress in which she was travelling; though that was fashionable too, but it was more fit for the ball-room than the carriage; nor could the large shawl in which she was enveloped prevent one seeing that she wore long kid, instead of habit, gloves, and short sleeves instead of long ones. She was followed by a dark-eyed female, with an exceedingly disagreeable, though handsome, face. The different style of her dress, and the parcel which she carried in her hand, announced her to be the waiting-woman. This parcel appeared to be the whole of the luggage belonging to the party; and being so inadequate to the length of the journey which the horses seemed to have performed, and the direction in which the carriage had come, first gave me the suspicion that they were a run-away couple returning from a matrimonial expedition to the north. This suspicion was afterwards confirmed. They had been actually married at Gretna on the night before, and had come across the country from Carlisle, either to avoid meeting any person who might have pursued them, or for the purpose of spending the first days of the honeymoon amidst the romantic scenery of the lakes. Alas! to judge from appearances, the honeymoon had already ceased, and the visions of romance already been dispelled by sad reality. The bridegroom's air proclaimed that he was the husband, and not the lover; while one could read, in his countenance and carelessness, that her fortune more than her person had been the object of his ambition. By the satisfied glances exchanged between him and the waiting-maid, I half suspect that she had been the means through which he had carried his point; and I believe that, in nine times out of ten, young ladies are more swayed by the insidious hints of their female attendant at the toilette than they are persuaded either by the strength of their own affection, or by the rhetoric of their lovers.

The young lady in question appeared to be one of those persuadeable beings who may be talked, or perhaps frightened, into any thing against their own judgments. Timidity and the absence of energy were strongly depicted on her countenance, as she was dragged shrinking into the presence of so many strangers ; and she sank, almost overpowered, into a chair in the remotest corner of the room. The almost authoritative encouragement of her waitingwoman, who assumed a certain ascendancy over her, seemed incapable of inspiring her with sufficient boldness to meet the glances of the company, or to prevent her muffling up her left hand in her shawl, as though she feared the fatal ring, which had sealed her destiny, was discoverable through her glove. That kindness which might and ought to have supported her was withheld, apparently more from carelessness than anger, until an infantine appeal to him for assistance in some trivial matter for her accommodation called from him so sharp a reply as to make her start in her chair, and she is now looking him tremblingly in the face. How truly that look exclaims, " Is this the man who at my feet two days ago swore he would be my slave for ever?" She sinks back into her seat, and draws her hand across her eyes, as though she would ascertain the reality of her being awake. She begins to doubt whether a few cabalistic words, uttered by a tradesman within the realm of Scotland, can have wrought such a change in a man who professed to adore her; or have bound her to a hypocrite by a knot which the sword of Alexander could not divide, unless it killed her husband, and by ties which nothing but death or crime can dissolve.

Poor thing! nursed perhaps in the lap of luxury, the uncontradicted idol of imprudent but indulgent parents, what a path hast thou chalked out for thyself! One little day, and your hopes of happiness are ended. All the blooming prospects of mutual affection, of domestic bliss, all blighted ere the title of wife has been thine for four-and-twenty hours. The waiting-maid appears to have persuaded the surly bridegroom to approach and speak to her; but he does it with an angry "pshaw!" which seems to say, "let her get pleased again." A little conscious, however, of his unkindness, he attempts to soothe her, but it is in vain; he cannot chase the gloom from her brow, or restore the colour to her cheek. The blow was too rude—too sudden—

> "And, once awake, she cannot dream again."

I would draw a moral from this runaway couple for the benefit of young ladies, but for two reasons—the first is, that they would not profit by it; and the second, that the chaise is at the door which is to carry me back to the north road and my portmanteau; and so ends my "Attempt at a Tour."

SONNET.

W. WORDSWORTH.

A GRAVESTONE UPON THE FLOOR IN THE CLOISTERS OF WORCESTER CATHEDRAL.

"Miserrimus!" and neither name nor date,
  Prayer, text, or symbol, grav'n upon the stone;
  Nought but that word assign'd to the unknown,
  That solitary word—to separate
  From all, and cast a cloud around the fate
  Of him who lies beneath. Most wretched One,
  Who chose his epitaph? Himself alone
  Could thus have dared the grave to agitate,
  And claim, among the dead, this awful crown.
  Nor doubt that he mark'd also for his own,
  Close to these cloistral steps, a burial-place,
  That every foot might fall with heavier tread,
  Trampling upon his vileness. Stranger, pass
  Softly!—to save the contrite, Jesus bled.

Drawn by J.M.Wright.   Engraved by W. Finden.

LUCY AND HER BIRD.

Printed by M. Queen.

Pub.d for the Proprietor by Hurst.Chance,& C.o S.t Pauls Churchyard,& R.Jennings.2,Poultry.

LUCY AND HER BIRD.

ROBERT SOUTHEY.

I.

THE Sky-Lark hath perceived his prison-door
Unclosed; for liberty the captive tries:
Puss eagerly hath watch'd him from the floor,
And in her grasp he flutters, pants, and dies.

II.

Lucy's own Puss, and Lucy's own dear Bird,
Her foster'd favourites both for many a day,
That which the tender-hearted girl preferr'd,
She in her fondness knew not sooth to say.

III.

For if the Sky-Lark's pipe were shrill and strong,
And its rich tones the thrilling ear might please,
Yet Pussybel could breathe a fireside song
As winning, when she lay on Lucy's knees.

IV.

Both knew her voice, and each alike would seek
Her eye, her smile, her fondling touch to gain:
How faintly then may words her sorrow speak,
When by the one she sees the other slain.

V.

The flowers fall scatter'd from her lifted hands;
A cry of grief she utters in affright;
And self-condemn'd for negligence she stands
Aghast and helpless at the cruel sight.

VI.

Come, Lucy, let me dry those tearful eyes;
    Take thou, dear child, a lesson not unholy,
From one whom Nature taught to moralise
    Both in his mirth and in his melancholy.

VII.

I will not warn thee not to set thy heart
    Too fondly upon perishable things;
In vain the earnest preacher spends his art
    Upon that theme; in vain the poet sings.

VIII.

It is our nature's strong necessity,
    And this the soul's unerring instincts tell:
Therefore, I say, let us love worthily,
    Dear child, and then we cannot love too well.

IX.

Better it is all losses to deplore,
    Which dutiful affection can sustain,
Than that the heart should, to its inmost core,
    Harden without it, and have lived in vain.

X.

This love which thou hast lavish'd, and the woe
    Which makes thy lip now quiver with distress,
Are but a vent, an innocent overflow,
    From the deep springs of female tenderness.

XI.

And something I would teach thee from the grief
    That thus hath fill'd those gentle eyes with tears,
The which may be thy sober, sure relief
    When sorrow visits thee in after years.

XII.

I ask not whither is the spirit flown
That lit the eye which there in death is seal'd;
Our Father hath not made that mystery known;
Needless the knowledge, therefore not reveal'd.

XIII.

But didst thou know, in sure and sacred truth,
It had a place assign'd in yonder skies;
There, through an endless life of joyous youth,
To warble in the bowers of Paradise:

XIV.

Lucy, if then the power to thee were given
In that cold clay its life to re-engage,
Wouldst thou call back the warbler from its heaven,
To be again the tenant of a cage?

XV.

Only that thou might'st cherish it again,
Wouldst thou the object of thy love recall
To mortal life, and chance, and change, and pain,
And death, which must be suffer'd once by all?

XVI.

Oh, no, thou say'st: oh, surely not, not so!
I read the answer which those looks express:
For pure and true affection well I know
Leaves in the heart no room for selfishness.

XVII.

Such love of all our virtues is the gem;
We bring with us the immortal seed at birth:
Of Heaven it is, and heavenly: woe to them
Who make it wholly earthly and of earth!

XVIII.

What we love perfectly, for its own sake
  We love and not our own; being ready thus
Whate'er self-sacrifice is asked, to make,
  That which is best for it, is best for us.

XIX.

O, Lucy! treasure up that pious thought;
  It hath a balm for sorrow's deadliest darts,
And with true comfort thou wilt find it fraught,
  If grief should reach thee in thy heart of hearts.

FRAGMENTS,

BY PERCY BYSSHE SHELLEY.

I.

SUMMER AND WINTER.

It was a bright and cheerful afternoon,
Towards the end of the sunny month of June,
When the north wind congregates in crowds
The floating mountains of the silver clouds
From the horizon—and the stainless sky
Opens beyond them like eternity.
All things rejoiced beneath the sun; the weeds,
The river, and the corn-fields, and the reeds;
The willow leaves that glanced in the light breeze,
And the firm foliage of the larger trees.

It was a winter, such as when birds do die
In the deep forests; and the fishes lie

Stiffen'd in the translucent ice, which makes
Even the mud and slime of the warm lakes
A wrinkled clod, as hard as brick; and when,
Among their children, comfortable men
Gather about great fires, and yet feel cold,
Alas! then for the homeless beggar old!

II.

THE TOWER OF FAMINE *.

AMID the desolation of a city,
Which was the cradle, and is now the grave
Of an extinguish'd people; so that pity

Weeps o'er the shipwrecks of oblivion's wave,
There stands the Tower of Famine. It is built
Upon some prison homes, whose dwellers rave

With bread, and gold, and blood: pain, link'd to guilt,
Agitates the light flame of their hours,
Until its vital oil is spent or spilt:

There stands the pile, a tower amid the towers
And sacred domes; each marble-ribbed roof,
The brazen-gated temples, and the bowers

Of solitary wealth; the tempest-proof
Pavilions of the dark Italian air,
Are by its presence dimm'd—they stand aloof,

---

* At Pisa there still exists the prison of Ugolino, which goes by the
name of " La Torre della Fame:" in the adjoining building the galley
slaves are confined. It is situated near the Ponte al Mare on the Arno.

M

And are withdrawn—so that the world is bare,
As if a spectre wrapt in shapeless terror
Amid a company of ladies fair

Should glide and glow, till it became a mirror
Of all their beauty, and their hair and hue,
The life of their sweet eyes, with all its error,
Should be absorb'd, till they to marble grew.

III.

THE AZIOLA.

" Do you not hear the Aziola cry?
Methinks she must be nigh,"
      Said Mary, as we sate
In dusk, ere stars were lit, or candles brought;
      And I, who thought
This Aziola was some tedious woman,
Asked, "Who is Aziola?" how elate
I felt to know that it was nothing human,
No mockery of myself to fear or hate:
      And Mary saw my soul,
And laugh'd, and said, " Disquiet yourself not;
      'Tis nothing but a little downy owl."

Sad Aziola! many an eventide
      Thy music I had heard
By wood and stream, meadow and mountain side,
      And fields and marshes wide,
Such as nor voice, nor lute, nor wind, nor bird,
      The soul ever stirr'd;
Unlike, and far sweeter than them all.
Sad Aziola! from that moment I
Loved thee and thy sad cry.

THE LADY AND HER LOVERS.

BY THE AUTHOR OF GILBERT EARLE.

" ———— In some auspicious hour,
In some sweet solitude, in some green bower,
Whither my fate should lead me, there, unseen,
I should behold my fancy's gracious queen,
Singing sweet song! that I should hear awhile,
Then catch the transient glory of a smile!"   CRABBE.

Seville, April, 1630.

OH! Carlos, such an adventure! If fortune favours the brave, it is certain that the other blind deity of the mythology is no less benignant to those whom he knows to be his true votaries. Is it wonderful, then, that he should have shown an especial kindness to *me*, who have studied and illustrated his code all my life; and who not only have ever been myself his ardent and active devotee, but have brought so many other worshippers to his shrine?

And what is it, think you, that has put me into this rapture of spirit? An adventure, which begins like that of a prince in romance, who always loses his way out hunting, and falls in with a fairy who is in love with him, or an enchanted lady whom he is fated to restore. Yet the parallel fails somewhat, for I had not absolutely lost my way, inasmuch as I was quite aware of the direction I had to pursue; but the chase had undoubtedly carried me beyond *pays de connoissance;* and, though I knew my way homeward, I did not exactly know where I was. *Au reste,* the fair creature whom you must perceive I am

M 2

going to meet, however like she may be to a fairy in other respects, certainly had not the particular quality in question, of being already in love with me; and as for enchantment, that is yet to come. Without the assistance of minerals, herbs, or hieroglyphics, I have been esteemed to have some skill in certain spells before now.

The chase ended, as I have told you, at a long distance from home; and leaving huntsmen and dogs to make their way as best they might, I pricked on before them as fast as Durandarte, who was somewhat less fresh than in the morning, could carry me. I knew my road lay to the south-eastward, and the brilliant sunset, that was fast approaching, served sufficiently to show me in which direction that was. At length I found myself in a small and picturesque wood, through the interstices of which I could perceive that there lay to my right an ornamented garden, fenced only by a slight paling, which was almost hidden by the hedge of flowering shrubs that was planted along it.

The garden seemed to be very beautiful and very extensive. Flowers of every kind that are yet in bloom were there in profusion; the wood, in which I was, continued to skirt it, and give it shade on one side; and in the distance stretched a lovely sheet of water, on which the setting sun was now shedding the reflection of its beams in every gradation of soft, and brilliant, and gorgeous beauty. I pulled up my horse to gaze upon this scene; when, as I looked, there came the only addition which can still embellish such specimens as this was of inanimate nature, viz. a specimen, equally admirable in its way, of animated nature. Two female figures advanced along the path which I concluded led from the house, and that at no

great distance; for they were bare-headed, and had scarcely
any out-of-door addition to their dress. At the distance
at which I was I could not see them with great distinct-
ness; but I could see quite enough to make me entertain
a very lively desire to see more; and, notwithstanding
that philosophic habit which you must so often have observed in me of repressing and controlling the more earthly
desires of humanity, I confess I yielded to this, with infinite promptitude; and getting off my horse, and fasten-
ing him to a tree, I advanced cautiously towards the
garden hedge.

Certainly that blind divinity, to whom I alluded at
the beginning of my letter, must for once have slipped his
bandage, and directed the whole of this proceeding in
person; for nothing could be more felicitous than every
incident from first to last. It so happened that the fair
Eves (if I may speak in the plural) of this Eden had come
out for the purpose of gathering some of its flowers; and
they chose a spot close to that on which I was, to begin
their task. They had with them a China vase, and a
basket, both of which they proceeded to fill. Figure to
yourself, Carlos, a scene like this: sunset, in all the varied
richness and sweetness of this season of many colours; a
garden, beautiful equally in situation and in culture, and
two of the most enchanting creatures that the handiwork of
God hath given to adorn and gladden the earth, namely,
lovely and youthful women; imagine *this*, Carlos, and you
will have no difficulty in conceiving the almost painful
state of cautious, hushed, and nearly *unbreathing* admiration with which, concealed by some intervening trees, I
watched them. One of them knelt, and plucking the
flowers, passed them to her companion who stood close to

her, and formed them into bouquets as she received them, ere she placed them in the vase.   I was so situated that I could discern minutely the features and the expression of both faces, and, of course, the contour of both forms.   She who knelt was beautifully and delicately shaped, and her face bespoke mingled sweet humour and animation.   Liveliness sparkled in her eyes as she tossed back the fine clustering hair which fell over her face as she stooped; and the smile of gay and fond affection beamed upon her beautiful lips as she looked up to her companion when she raised herself to give her the flowers.   ' What a charming Anna soror!' I said to myself; for it scarcely required a second glance to show me that the other was to be the Dido of my hunting adventure.   And truly she mingled the queenlike air of commanding beauty with the soft, and sweet, and somewhat melancholy character of the more subdued order of loveliness, to an extent such as I had never before beheld. The attitude in which she stood tended to give to her figure, at once, full display, and an added degree of what it would scarcely be exaggeration to denominate majesty; but majesty almost softened away from being strictly such, by the youthful and delicate nature of its gracefulness. She stood with the left arm partially extended and raised from the elbow; in this hand were the flowers which formed the nucleus of her bouquet; and, as she stretched the other to receive those which the fair gatherer handed to her, her head was slightly inclined to look upon them in a manner which gave to full view, that which is one of the greatest beauties of a beautiful woman, the line, namely, of inexpressible grace which sweeps from the point where the cheek and the neck unite, to the edge of the shoulder.

I continued to gaze at them from behind my tree till

Painted by F.P.Stephanoff.

Engraved by Cha. Heath.

L O V E.

Published for the Proprietor by T. Hurst & Cᵒ Sᵗ Pauls Churchyard, and R. Jennings, 2. Poultry.

their task seemed to be completed, and they were about to move away. I then felt that the moment was come, and that, unless I wished to lose my labour, I must advance at once. I am not usually, as you pretty well know, very backward upon such occasions; but on this, I by no means felt my usual alacrity. I had been contemplating the fine countenance of her, whom I had singled out as the heroine of the adventure—interpreting every ordinary glance and gesture as the indications of all manner of rare and lofty qualities; till at last I almost began to venerate that which might be, after all, like Pygmalion's animated figure, in great measure my own creation. But these feelings lasted only an instant: I recollected myself at once, and passed forward without tarrying longer. I took care to make some noise among the bushes, that my appearance at a little wicket-gate, which was close at hand, might not be startlingly unexpected. Still, when I did lift the latch of that gate, and approached the fair Floras of the garden, strong surprise, a little alarm, and considerable maidenly reserve and bashfulness, were depicted on the countenances of both as I advanced towards them. "Ladies," I said— but, pshaw! what matters it what I said? It must be quite clear, indeed, to you what I should say upon such an occasion. My dialogue, even if I remembered the words of it as well as I do the purport, I should not repeat to you: suffice it, that it terminated in an announcement of papa's name, an invitation to rest and refreshment at the house, and the offer of a guide home.

Now you are not to take it into your anticipating head— which always jumps to a conclusion, leaving out half the premises—that all this was the work of three minutes. On the contrary, I occupied nearly that period in what I said at first; partly, to give the fair damsel (I speak of one only, for the Dido manifestly, and yet indescribably, indicated that *she* was the person to be addressed) full time thoroughly to recover herself; and partly, that I might make her distinctly understand who I was, what I was, and what I did there. By this latter phrase, you will please to comprehend that I thought fit to be supposed to have been completely bewildered, and induced by the sound of voices to leave my horse in the wood, and seek the speakers for information.

In reply, the Dido, with diffidence and even some bashfulness, but without any thing approaching to embarrassment, said that she had often heard her father mention my family, and that she was certain he would be happy in showing me any courtesy in his power. With this, she made the communication and the offer aforesaid, and we proceeded slowly towards the house. Sister Anne, whom I have since discovered to be a cousin, only smiled, looked pretty, and said nothing.

It was evidently my business to *fournir les frais* of the conversation during our transit, and I did so; being most especially cautious as to what key I pitched my tone in, studiously avoiding any thing approaching to overmarked homage or admiration, yet taking equal care that my voice and manner (whatever my words were) should not be such as I might have used towards any indifferent person whom chance might have thus thrown in my way. Her father, old Don Diego de Lesma, I knew well by name, and I was aware that my father had known him formerly. I was glad of this, for I felt it would help me to make my way with the old man; with his daughter, I surmised that my father's son could make his own way.

I soon saw what must be my course. This was no village-maiden, with roses in her hair and on her cheeks, with bashfulness amounting to awkwardness, and a want of education almost approaching absolute ignorance; this was a person whom my walk to the house of half-a-mile (for so long, to my surprise, it proved) discovered to me to be cultivated in mind, even courtly in manners, and yet with an occasional dash of almost girlish simplicity, strongly in contra-distinction to both. I saw, too, that her feelings had been, to some extent certainly, developed. There was a shade of pain and melancholy that settled itself upon her brow at every pause in the conversation, as though it were its usual occupant, which proved this fact to me; and it was one which I was by no means gratified to learn. 'Is there an attachment there already?' thought I: ' she is apparently scarcely above eighteen—*that* says nothing;—it may be, or it may not be: if it be, I have only to mount Durandarte, and whistle a saraband as I canter home; if it be not, why, then, *le roi s'avisera*.'

When we reached the house, Donna Inez, for such I found to be her name, in a dozen words, made her father acquainted with how I came thither. Don Diego, old, gouty, and good-humoured, received me very graciously; and began some merciless mingled inquiries and reminiscences about an uncle of mine, with whom he had served in Holland, and who was killed the year I was born; and before he had half come to the end of his questions, or of his own answers to them, Inez and her cousin (whose name, absurdly enough, turned out really to be Anna) had vanished. My stay, you may be sure, was not unnecessarily prolonged; and the moment Durandarte was fed, off I set homeward under the most magnificent of all possible moons;

on my arrival supped ravenously, drank a flask of Malaga to Inez' health, and have ever since been writing this, till my fingers ache; though, thank Heaven! neither head nor heart has a twinge. On the contrary, both animal and mental spirits are on tip-toe; I must walk in the moonlight for at least an hour before I shall be able to sleep. Good night. Don't you envy me the dreams I shall have by and by?

Your friend,

ALONZO DE GAMEZ.

Seville, April.

Sweet, gentle, undoubting, accommodating, easily-led, and easily-trusting ' sister Anne,' I thank thee heartily! So! that is the history, is it? Again do I make to thee mine homage, erotic god! for these thy favours! Truly the hand of that adorable urchin is visible here: this is manifestly his own, immediate, and personal work. Such fortune could not be else.

Of course, it was not only allowable, but requisite that I should pay a visit of courtesy at Don Diego's. I did not wish, however, for many reasons, to be singularly soon in going thither, and yet my impatience spurred me much. At last I determined to go yesterday, six days after my first visit, and I went accordingly. I had gathered that the parterre, at which I had first seen the fair cousins culling flowers, was a favourite haunt; and, therefore, hoping to find them there, and thus gain some conversation with Inez before I encountered the old blunderbuss her father, I directed my steps in the first instance to the little wicket through which I had entered the garden on the former day. My heart fluttered;—ay, Carlos, even *my* heart

fluttered, which I thought it had given up long ago, as
I caught a glimpse through the trees of white drapery
rustling in the wind. I sprang from my horse, and reached
the gate in an instant. There was only one person there,
and that was Donna Anna.

At the moment I was exceedingly disappointed; but I
recollected the information I wished to gather, and rather
rejoiced that I had found an opportunity so soon. Donna
Anna was very bashful at first; but, like many bashful
people, when they are light-hearted also, she soon became,
under proper management, not only at her ease, but far
more frank and communicative than persons more used to
society. Her uncle and cousin, she told me, were gone
into Seville, but would be back at night. I felt that I
had full time to extract from her all that I wanted to know,
and I began leisurely to lead the conversation in the direction which was my object.

Do you know, Carlos, the devil came across me for a
moment? The creature looked so young, and so fresh,
and so handsome, and she smiled so animatedly in my
face, and, in a word, looked so tempting in every way,
that I caught myself upon the very point of making love
to her in her own proper person! I pulled short up, as I
would check my horse on the edge of a precipice; and,
conquering myself by a violent effort, continued the conversation in the same tone in which I had begun it. Santa
Maria! what a blunder I should have made! I should
have transformed a kind, lively, active, good-humoured
tiers into a slighted and jealous woman. As matters are,
I had even observed on my first visit, and her conversation
yesterday fully confirmed it, that Donna Anna was so accustomed to look up to her cousin as the noblest of created

beings (and, truly, she is not far wrong), that any idea of being thought of in her presence seems never to have crossed her mind. But not to gain a lover is one thing, and to lose him, having gained him, is quite another. If I had played the fool yesterday, and acted as I was on the very verge of acting, Donna Anna, instead of being, as I intend she shall be, of the greatest use to her cousin and me, would have become the implacable and irreconcilable enemy of us both; for as to my thinking of her when Inez was present, that is preposterous: and it will never do, either on the stage or real life, to sink into *confidante* after having played the heroine herself.

We had a long conversation; and I gathered from her all the information I desired. In the first place, I learned that Donna Inez had been only partially brought up at home, having been in the habit since her mother's death, which happened when she was six years old, of passing several months of the year at Madrid, with an aunt who has a place about the court. But her father (and I don't wonder at it) never would consent permanently to lose sight of her, but insisted on her passing the winter months with him here in Andalusia. Next, my informant communicated what had this year delayed Donna Inez' return so long beyond the usual period. "Alas! Don Alonzo," said the poor girl, the tears springing into her eyes as she spoke, "matters are sadly altered now. My uncle insists that Inez shall marry; and he has chosen her a husband from whom her soul shrinks in abhorrence!" Donna Anna pronounced these words with an energy of look and manner, of which I did not think her possessed. But women feel keenly, and speak strongly on such subjects as these: they come home at once to the bosoms of the whole sex.

The full truth was clear to me in a moment; but I sifted it more closely nevertheless. The *pretender* I found to be a person we both knew, Don Guzman de Mendez; a man certainly not calculated exactly to find favour in a lady's sight; and still less, I should think, in that of one of talents and education such as those of Inez. Poor, poor creature, I pity her most sincerely.

Yet, why should I grieve? Would I have her intended husband 'an angel in green and gold!'—a *preux chevalier*, fit theme for poets, fit model for painters, fit object for lady's love? Does it not suit my purpose better that he should be as he is, ungainly in person, savage in mind? My purpose!—what *is* my purpose? Faith! it is an ugly question; one, to speak the very truth, which I could not answer if I would; and, perhaps, if I could, I would not. *Le roi s'avisera.*

Seville, July.

By heavens! Carlos! I scarcely know where I am, or what I am doing! I am allowing my passions to hurry me away into all manner of follies; for such they are, unless I crown them with the grand folly of all, and *that* I cannot do. *Would* I?—Would I marry this creature who, while I thought I was toying gently with her feelings and my own, has twined herself round my very heart-strings; the noble and uncompromising intensity of whose affection has driven mine, in very shame, to an equal pitch. *Would* I marry her? Thank Heaven, I have not the question to resolve! or, pauper as my follies have left me, I think I should. But this is beyond my reach were I to wish it: little did I once think I should ever wish it! Her father's word is plighted to Don Guzman, and if it were pledged to the arch-fiend himself, old Diego's word would never be broken!

He knows not of my love for Inez; he would scarcely believe, 'though one should come from the dead' to tell it him, her love for me.   No one knows it but our own hearts, which it is consuming; and Anna, who pities and weeps over it, but cannot aid it,—and Guzman suspects it! Ay, Carlos! last night I stung him to the soul!—'twas folly, —twas madness;—but if my life had been staked upon it at the instant, I could not have forborne taking her from him as I did.   What may come of it I know not, I scarcely care.   It happened thus.

Don Diego gave last night a splendid fête.   Not the house only, but the whole of his beautiful gardens were thrown open.   Indeed the season caused them to be pre-ferred, and, besides the promenades, the dancing chiefly took place there.   You know that, during the summer, these gardens have been our chief haunt.   To the spot where we first met we have since constantly repaired; and not only there, but for a considerable distance around, there is scarcely a tree, a shrub, or even a flower, that is not en-deared to us by some of those recollections which, trivial in themselves, are perhaps among the deepest, as they are indisputably among the sweetest, of the thoughts which we enjoy in love.   There is one seat in particular, placed beneath a magnificent and overspreading acacia, on which we had often sat for hours; where, indeed, she first spoke to me in the language of unconcealed, unrepressed affection, and where my lips had been passionately pressed to hers while the avowal yet glowed upon them.   Here we have constantly passed hour after hour since, recalling all the reminiscences of the few last months; comparing our pro-

gressive feelings from their dawn to their blessed maturity.
The enthralling charm of *this* I need not, dear Carlos,
paint to you—you know it; and, therefore, you can well
conceive how dear the scene of such interviews must have
become. Well, yesterday evening, when I arrived at Don
Diego's, I at first could not see Inez. I sought her in the
house, and in the adjacent parts of the garden; and not
finding her, I bethought me she might be at one of our
usual places of tryst, in expectation of my seeking her there.
I did so, and went straight to the acacia seat. She was
there;—but, fiends and furies!—Guzman was with her.
She saw the fire of rage flash from my eyes, and gave me
a beseeching, imploring look, which calmed me in a
moment. Yes, Carlos! such is the mastery this adorable
woman has obtained over my soul, that one look from her
can check me, even when my anger is roused and burning
against the man I hate!

I learned afterwards, what I imagined at the time, that
my conjecture had been right, and that, having gone to
the seat to await me, Guzman had found her there, and
joined her. Now, although I have known so long the en-
gagements which Don Diego had entered into with Don
Guzman, yet as they never have been publicly announced,
nay, as they have never been by either party spoken of in
my presence, it was perfectly allowable, according to the
etiquettes of society, for me to join Donna Inez. As I sat
down, she again entreated me by her looks to curb my
feelings against Guzman; and, with a strong gulp, I determined to do so thoroughly. The best way was not to
talk with him: therefore, after a formally courteous saluta-
tion, I proceeded to converse with Inez. Of our conversation Guzman certainly could not understand eight words
out of twenty; for, while seeming to talk on the most

indifferent subjects, the crowd of allusions that were comprehended only by each other, and which lovers always possess in such abundance, and know so well how to use, rendered what we said barely intelligible to a third person. Guzman, I conceive, scarcely saw this; but was bewildered between surprise, at the extremely common-place stuff we seemed to be talking, and a sort of uneasy doubt that all was not right between us. He several times strove to join in the conversation, but was always somehow imperceptibly excluded, while we continued to talk composedly and continuously. He seemed fretted and galled, but knew not either how to prevent or to indulge his vexation.

At length, for this tone of masquerade suited neither my feelings at the time, nor, as I could plainly distinguish, those of Inez, I determined to get rid of the brute Guzman at once; and, seeing a party dancing in the distance, I proposed to Inez to join them. This, it seems, which I did not know, Guzman had done before I came up, and had, of course, been refused. He blustered out his prior claim in a moment; but, giving Inez a look of reassurance, that she need not doubt my temper, I said to him, "In these matters, sir, there is but one appeal, and that is immediate and final. When there are two rivals for the honour of dancing with a lady, it is for her to decide which has the preferable claim: Madam," I added, turning to Inez, "is Don Guzman, or am I, to have the honour of leading you to the dance?"

"Why," she answered, smiling—(ah! Carlos, she *can* smile)—"I think it must be you, Don Alonzo, for you have had the skill to ask me when I am in the mood; and, with a woman, they say, *that* is every thing."—And she gave me her hand, and I led her forth.

Carlos, you have never seen the full expression of the

Painted by F. P. Stephanoff.

Engraved by Cha.ˢ Heath.

JEALOUSY.

more sullen and savage passions of our nature; for you did not see Guzman's countenance then! Anger, jealousy, revenge, in a noble nature, borrow a portion of that nobleness; but in the bosom of a morose, selfish, and ferocious man, they almost sink into the animal fury of a brute. Could you but have seen the scowl of his small grey eye, the writhing of his thin lip, and the *grin* of hideous hatred which pervaded his whole visage as he, by instinct, grasped his dagger, you would know to what the human countenance *can* sink. I saw it; and I did so, because, knowing the man's ferocity, I almost expected some ebullition of violence; and I held myself prepared, therefore, to evade and repel his attack. But it went no farther: a dark flush came over his face, which had before been pale as that of a corpse, his hand fell from the haft of the dagger, and he sank back and threw himself upon the bench.

That, in an instant, there came over his mind the conviction of our mutual affection, even though he should never before have had even a glimmering suspicion of it, I cannot doubt. But I am rather inclined to believe that he previously did entertain some vague slight fumes of jealousy with regard to me. At all events, the die is cast; and how he will act I cannot guess. Alas! how I myself shall act is almost as little known to me. Ah, Carlos! I began, like the moth, to flutter round the flame for pleasure, and it has scorched my heart to the core! And here, alas! it is not the moth alone that suffers, but the very pyre from which the flame springs is itself consumed.

Seville, August.

Inez, the reality of life has arisen suddenly to dissipate this dear, enthralling—this dreadful dream. My regiment is ordered to the Low Countries, and I must leave Seville in four and twenty hours. Inez, I will not, I cannot see you! my heart would burst. I doubt even whether I should have force to leave you; whether I should not turn traitor and deserter, and leave my standard now it is called to the field. But these are words which must never be coupled with the name of Gamez. *I must go.*

How I have loved you, Inez; how my whole soul has fed for months upon your words, your looks, your smiles, your very presence, you know full well. Our hearts have been but one; they have felt, they have loved in common. Oh! what this agony of parting is, it is needless for me to speak; *you* feel it! Inez, I scarcely know what I write; the one fearful, damning thought that we are *to part* pervades my whole being. Our loves have not *been* happy; we thought yesterday that nothing could add to our wretchedness, and now!—

Dear, dear beloved, adored Inez, may the Almighty bless you! Farewell! I have never deserved you, but I have loved you as I did not know the human heart could love; and shall continue to love you as long as mine throbs! Farewell!

Seville, October, 1632.

Anna, they tell me he is returned. Oh heaven! his sight would kill me! He has always loved me; I feel I know he has! and I!—yes, I have loved him, have adored him as woman never loved man: and how have I acted? Another's wife!—the mother of another man's children! My soul sickens at the thought!

How *could* I act? Would you have had me incur my father's curse?—his dying curse? He lay on his deathbed, the blessings or the curses of his last breath hung upon whether I said Ay, or No, to Guzman! Oh God! I became his wife!

His wife!—ay for two long years have I sat at the board, and shared the bed of the man whom my soul loathes; for two years have I shrunk from his touch, and checked the imprecation that has risen to my lips as I have looked upon him. And he knows this, he feels this; and his treatment accords with the suggestions of his brutal spirit. Yet I would it were always thus: his ferocity I can bear; it affects only my physical frame, it passes almost harmless over my numbed heart. But his hideous fondness, his mingled sneer and caress, his *touch!*——

And I am the mother of that man's children, Anna; I feel it as an unheard-of sin; the very beasts of the field are more human than I; but I cannot love my children—cannot caress them; they are *his!*

I was last night at the acacia-seat. I go almost every night to weep there. But last night my tears were dry; I had heard of his return; I almost thought I saw him as when first we used to meet there, with his beaming eyes and gallant brow, and sweet, sweet smile of love! And then again he seemed changed; haggard and pale, and savage-looking—as he never looked; and, as I started forward to meet him, I thought he pushed me from him, and groaned forth, 'Go, thou art Guzman's wife!' I felt—I feel these things to be visions; but they will turn my brain.

Alas! alas! dear, dearest Anna, I am sick at heart. To your fond, unvarying friendship I turn, not for consolation, there is none for *me*, but for succour and support, that my heart may not burst in these bitter agonies; that

I may feel there is yet one on earth who loves me!—Alas!
and is there *only* one?

It was about a month after the date of this letter, that,
an hour after midnight, two persons were seated upon the
acacia-seat, of which so much mention has been made in
the course of these letters. I need scarcely say that these
were Alonzo and Donna Inez.

Alonzo had undoubtedly loved her to an extent which
he himself, of all men, would not have believed possible
at the date of the first letter the reader has seen. But he
had been, as indeed it must be almost needless to state, a
systematic libertine; and his heart was no longer in a
condition to feel a passion worthy of such an object as
Donna Inez, still less to excite an affection such as she
could feel. It had been, however, with perfect sincerity
that he had written the note to her on his departure.
His heart and mind had both been thoroughly excited
and devoted to her, for some months before, and the
pang of parting, suddenly and unexpectedly as it came,
was severe to the last degree. But time and absence, and
change of scene, and the stir and excitation of an active
campaign, soon swept away these more intense feelings;
and when the news of the marriage of Inez with Guzman
reached him, he received it with first a curse, and then
a sigh; and then reverted to his usual philosophy, of
which the spirit is expressed in the Scottish phrase, that
it is better to ' let bygones be bygones.' A tender recollection of the beautiful creature, whom he had loved so
fervently, occasionally crossed his mind, and clouded his
brow for a moment, but that was all. And thus it was
that *he* felt, while half her sufferings were from the thought

of what he must suffer!—Oh man, man! how little do you deserve—how scurvily do you repay the full fervour and intensity of woman's love!

But when Alonzo returned to Seville, the remembrance of his attachment to Inez arose most vividly amid the scenes that had witnessed it. " I will see that garden again," he exclaimed. " Alas! I may meet its lovely owner too; I will pledge my existence she still waters the flowers which Alonzo loved, and frequents the seat where he so often sat with her!"

He went—he did see her; not as she first crossed his eyes on that very spot, brilliant in youth and commanding beauty; but, though less than three years had passed, broken, and pale, and bent; her form dried up and shrunken, her eye dim, her voice decayed, her step weak and faltering.

They met again and again. The night of which I have spoken was their fourth meeting. Don Guzman was at Seville; and Inez had stolen forth to the acacia-bower, to meet that lover whose vows had been so often breathed beneath it. Their interviews were always sad; the recollection of the past, and the sense of the present, always rendered them scenes of gloom and distress.

" Alas! Alonzo," Donna Inez said, " had our first meeting been but of a few months' earlier date, how different had our fortunes been! My father respected your family, and loved you; and, had not his word been pledged to another, would, I know, gladly have chosen you for his son! Ah! how well I remember that first meeting!—my surprise at your appearance, and my determination to seem composed while my heart was fluttering with agitation. Well too do I remember my flight when we got into the house, although I longed to remain to listen to your voice, and to gaze upon your beaming face." She paused, and a deep sad sigh broke from her lips.

" Yes, dear Inez," he answered, " well do I, well shall I, ever remember that day! It is to me the era of a second existence; from that date every thing has been coloured by my love for you,—a love that has formed my existence itself." And at this moment, Alonzo believed himself to speak the truth!

" It almost drives me mad," she resumed, " to think upon what might have been, and what is; to think how I have been sacrificed to ————; but we will not speak—we will not, if it be possible, even think of *him* now. Your return, Alonzo, has given me renewed life; but even that I feel again beginning to decay: my heart is broken, and my happiness is gone beyond recall."

" Dearest Inez, speak not so—wound not so, the feelings of one who adores you! The consciousness of our mutual love shall give you fresh strength; you will struggle against your malady, for my sake, and wear again the bloom which your cheek displayed the day I first saw you."

" Alas! no; the germ of death is within me. But when I die, will you not come and strew some of my favourite flowers on my grave—will you not, Alonzo?—I know, I feel, you will."

" Thou liest, strumpet! that shall he never!" exclaimed a fierce voice, as Guzman, springing from behind the tree, struck a dagger into Alonzo's breast: it was but one blow, but it was home, it was to the heart. Alonzo sprang forward, and fell dead without a word.

The shriek which Inez uttered, as she threw herself upon Alonzo's corpse, would have appalled any nerves but those of Guzman. But he, unshaken, with his eyes glaring fire, his mouth dashed with foam, stretched out his hand, red with his victim's blood, and grasping Inez as with a vice, exclaimed, " Accursed cockatrice, thou shalt die with thy detested paramour!" But, as he lifted his hand to strike, he perceived that her head had fallen upon her shoulder, and that she was passive in his grasp. He suspended his blow. There needed none: she was already dead.

SONNET.

W. WORDSWORTH.

A TRADITION OF DARLEY-DALE, DERBYSHIRE.

'Tis said that to the brow of yon fair hill
Two brothers clomb, and, turning face from face,
Nor one look more exchanging, grief to still
Or feed, each planted on that lofty place
A chosen tree; then, eager to fulfil
Their courses, like two newborn rivers, they
In opposite directions urged their way
Down from the far-seen mount. No blast might kill
Or blight that fond memorial—the trees grew,
And now entwine their arms, but ne'er again
Embraced those brothers upon earth's wide plain,
Nor aught of mutual joy or sorrow knew,
Until their spirits mingled in the sea
That to itself takes all—Eternity.

OVER A COVERED SEAT

FLOWER-GARDEN AT HOLLAND-HOUSE, WHERE THE AUTHOR OF
THE " PLEASURES OF MEMORY" HAS BEEN ACCUSTOMED
TO SIT, APPEAR THE FOLLOWING LINES.

> HERE ROGERS sat, and here for ever dwell,
> To me, those pleasures that he sings so well.
>
> VASSALL HOLLAND.

How happily sheltered is he who reposes
In this haunt of the poet, o'ershadowed with roses,
While the sun is rejoicing, unclouded, on high,
And summer's full majesty reigns in the sky!
　Let me in, and be seated.—I'll try if, thus placed,
I can catch but one spark of his feeling and taste,
Can steal a sweet note from his musical strain,
Or a ray of his genius to kindle my brain.
　Well—now I am fairly installed in the bower.
How lovely the scene! How propitious the hour!
The breeze is perfumed by the hawthorn it stirs;
All is beauty around me;—but nothing occurs;
Not a thought, I protest, though I'm *here* and alone,
Not a line can I hit on, that ROGERS would own,
Though my senses are ravished, my feelings in tune,
And HOLLAND's my host, and the season is June.
　The trial is ended.　Nor garden nor grove,
Though poets amid them may linger or rove,

Nor a seat e'en so hallowed as *this* can impart
The fancy and fire that must spring from the heart.
So I rise, since the Muses continue to frown,
No more of a poet than when I sat down;
While ROGERS, on whom they look kindly, can strike
Their lyre, at all times, in all places, alike.

HENRY LUTTRELL.

THE THIEF DETECTED.

BY F. M. REYNOLDS.

As lovely Nature once explored
    Her cave of treasures, rich and rare,
She miss'd of female charms a hoard,
    Enough to form a thousand fair.

To Love the goddess quickly flew,
    And plainly told him her belief,
Indeed, conviction, that he knew
    The person who had been the thief.

Scarce ended was her tale of wo,
    Ere roguish Love the goddess left,
And speeding straight to one I know,
    Abruptly charged her with the theft.

The trembling maid denied, with grief;
    But Cupid has a judgment sound:
" 'Tis plain," he cried, " that you 're the thief,
    For *on you all the goods are found.*"

DEATH OF THE LAIRD'S JOCK.

TO THE EDITOR OF THE KEEPSAKE.

You have asked me, sir, to point out a subject for the pencil, and I feel the difficulty of complying with your request; although I am not certainly unaccustomed to literary composition, or a total stranger to the stores of history and tradition, which afford the best copies for the painter's art. But although *sicut pictura poesis* is an ancient and undisputed axiom—although poetry and painting both address themselves to the same object of exciting the human imagination, by presenting to it pleasing or sublime images of ideal scenes; yet the one conveying itself through the ears to the understanding, and the other applying itself only to the eyes, the subjects which are best suited to the bard or tale-teller are often totally unfit for painting, where the artist must present in a single glance all that his art has power to tell us. The artist can neither recapitulate the past nor intimate the future. The single *now* is all which he can present; and hence, unquestionably, many subjects which delight us in poetry or in narrative, whether real or fictitious, cannot with advantage be transferred to the canvas.

Being in some degree aware of these difficulties, though doubtless unacquainted both with their extent, and the means by which they may be modified or surmounted, I have, nevertheless, ventured to draw up the following tra-

ditional narrative as a story in which, when the general
details are known, the interest is so much concentrated
in one strong moment of agonizing passion, that it can be
understood, and sympathized with, at a single glance. I
therefore presume that it may be acceptable as a hint to
some one among the numerous artists, who have of late
years distinguished themselves as rearing up and supporting the British school.

Enough has been said and sung about

> The well contested ground,
> The warlike border-land—

to render the habits of the tribes who inhabited them before the union of England and Scotland familiar to most
of your readers. The rougher and sterner features of their
character were softened by their attachment to the fine arts,
from which has arisen the saying that, on the frontiers,
every dale had its battle, and every river its song. A rude
species of chivalry was in constant use, and single combats
were practised as the amusement of the few intervals of
truce which suspended the exercise of war. The invete-
racy of this custom may be inferred from the following
incident.

Bernard Gilpin, the apostle of the north, the first who
undertook to preach the protestant doctrines to the Border
dalesmen, was surprised, on entering one of their churches,
to see a gauntlet or mail-glove hanging above the altar.
Upon inquiring the meaning of a symbol so indecorous
being displayed in that sacred place, he was informed by
the clerk that the glove was that of a famous swordsman,
who hung it there as an emblem of a general challenge and
gage of battle, to any who should dare to take the fatal
token down. "Reach it to me," said the reverend church-

man. The clerk and sexton equally declined the perilous
office, and the good Bernard Gilpin was obliged to remove
the glove with his own hands, desiring those who were
present to inform the champion that he, and no other, had
possessed himself of the gage of defiance. But the champion was as much ashamed to face Bernard Gilpin as the
officials of the church had been to displace his pledge of
combat.

The date of the following story is about the latter years
of Queen Elizabeth's reign; and the events took place in
Liddesdale, a hilly and pastoral district of Roxburghshire,
which, on a part of its boundary, is divided from England
only by a small river.

During the good old times of *rugging and riving* (that
is, tugging and tearing), under which term the disorderly
doings of the warlike age are affectionately remembered,
this valley was principally cultivated by the sept or clan of
the Armstrongs. The chief of this warlike race was the
Laird of Mangerton. At the period of which I speak, the
estate of Mangerton, with the power and dignity of chief,
was possessed by John Armstrong, a man of great size,
strength, and courage. While his father was alive, he
was distinguished from others of his clan who bore the
same name, by the epithet of the *Laird's Jock*, that is to
say, the Laird's son Jock or Jack. This name he distinguished by so many bold and desperate achievements,
that he retained it even after his father's death, and is
mentioned under it both in authentic records and in tradition. Some of his feats are recorded in the Minstrelsy
of the Scottish Border, and others mentioned in contemporary chronicles.

At the species of singular combat which we have described the Laird's Jock was unrivalled, and no champion of Cumberland, Westmoreland, or Northumberland could endure the sway of the huge two-handed sword which he wielded, and which few others could even lift. This " awful sword," as the common people term it, was as dear to him as Durindana or Fushberta to their respective masters, and was near as formidable to his enemies as those renowned falchions proved to the foes of Christendom. The weapon had been bequeathed to him by a celebrated English outlaw named Hobbie Noble, who, having committed some deed for which he was in danger from justice, fled to Liddesdale, and became a follower, or rather a brother-in-arms to the renowned Laird's Jock; till venturing into England with a small escort, a faithless guide, and with a light single-handed sword instead of his ponderous brand, Hobbie Noble, attacked by superior numbers, was made prisoner and executed.

With this weapon, and by means of his own strength and address, the Laird's Jock maintained the reputation of the best swordsman on the border-side, and defeated or slew many who ventured to dispute with him the formidable title.

But years pass on with the strong and the brave as with the feeble and the timid. In process of time, the Laird's Jock grew incapable of wielding his weapons, and finally of all active exertion, even of the most ordinary kind. The disabled champion became at length totally bed-ridden, and entirely dependent for his comfort on the pious duties of an only daughter, his perpetual attendant and companion.

Besides this dutiful child, the Laird's Jock had an only son, upon whom devolved the perilous task of leading the clan to battle, and maintaining the warlike renown of his

native country, which was now disputed by the English
upon many occasions. The young Armstrong was active,
brave, and strong, and brought home from dangerous adventures many tokens of decided success. Still the ancient
chief conceived, as it would seem, that his son was scarce
yet entitled by age and experience to be intrusted with
the two-handed sword, by the use of which he had himself
been so dreadfully distinguished.

   At length, an English champion, one of the name of
Foster (if I rightly recollect), had the audacity to send a
challenge to the best swordsman in Liddesdale; and young
Armstrong, burning for chivalrous distinction, accepted
the challenge.

   The heart of the disabled old man swelled with joy,
when he heard that the challenge was passed and accepted,
and the meeting fixed at a neutral spot, used as the place
of rencontre upon such occasions, and which he himself
had distinguished by several victories. He exulted so
much in the conquest which he anticipated, that, to nerve
his son to still bolder exertions, he conferred upon him, as
champion of his clan and province, the celebrated weapon
which he had hitherto retained in his own custody.

   This was not all. When the day of combat arrived,
the Laird's Jock, in spite of his daughter's affectionate
remonstrances, determined, though he had not left his bed
for two years, to be a personal witness of the duel. His
will was still a law to his people; who bore him on their
shoulders, wrapt in plaids and blankets, to the spot where
the combat was to take place, and seated him on a
fragment of rock, which is still called the Laird Jock's
stone. There he remained with eyes fixed on the lists or
barrier, within which the champions were about to meet.

Drawn by H. Corbould.   Engraved by Charles Heath.

THE LAIRDS JOCK.

Printed by E. Brain.

Published for the Proprietor by T. Hurst & Cº Sᵗ Paul's Churchyard and R. Jennings, 2, Poultry.

His daughter, having done all she could for his accommodation, stood motionless beside him, divided between anxiety for his health, and for the event of the combat to her beloved brother. Ere yet the fight began, the old men gazed on their chief, now seen for the first time after several years, and sadly compared his altered features and wasted frame, with the paragon of strength and manly beauty which they had once remembered. The young gazed on his large form and powerful make, as upon some antediluvian giant who had survived the destruction of the deluge.

But the sound of the trumpets on both sides recalled the attention of every one to the lists, surrounded as they were by numbers of both nations, eager to witness the event of the day. The combatants met in the lists. It is needless to describe the struggle: the Scottish champion fell. Foster, placing his foot on his antagonist, seized on the redoubted sword, so precious in the eyes of its aged owner, and brandished it over his head as a trophy of his conquest. The English shouted in triumph. But the despairing cry of the aged champion, who saw his country dishonoured, and his sword, long the terror of their race, in possession of an Englishman, was heard high above the acclamations of victory. He seemed, for an instant, animated by all his wonted power; for he started from the rock on which he sate, and while the garments with which he had been invested fell from his wasted frame, and showed the ruins of his strength, he tossed his arms wildly to heaven, and uttered a cry of indignation, horror, and despair, which, tradition says, was heard to a preternatural distance, and resembled the cry of a dying lion more than a human sound.

His friends received him in their arms as he sank utterly exhausted by the effort, and bore him back to his castle in mute sorrow; while his daughter at once wept for her brother, and endeavoured to mitigate and soothe the despair of her father. But this was impossible; the old man's only tie to life was rent rudely asunder, and his heart had broken with it. The death of his son had no part in his sorrow: if he thought of him at all, it was as the degenerate boy, through whom the honour of his country and clan had been lost, and he died in the course of three days, never even mentioning his name, but pouring out unintermitted lamentations for the loss of his noble sword.

I conceive, that the moment when the disabled chief was roused into a last exertion by the agony of the moment is favourable to the object of a painter. He might obtain the full advantage of contrasting the form of the rugged old man, in the extremity of furious despair, with the softness and beauty of the female form. The fatal field might be thrown into perspective, so as to give full effect to these two principal figures, and with the single explanation, that the piece represented a soldier beholding his son slain, and the honour of his country lost, the picture would be sufficiently intelligible at the first glance. If it was thought necessary to show more clearly the nature of the conflict, it might be indicated by the pennon of Saint George being displayed at one end of the lists, and that of Saint Andrew at the other.

I remain, sir,

Your obedient servant,

THE AUTHOR OF WAVERLEY.

STANZAS.

BY R. BERNAL, M. P.

Oh Life! in thy confused, mysterious dream
Of bliss, some fleeting visions fondly rise,
Faint as those lights thrown o'er the brawling stream,
By fading sunbeams and by western skies.

What can thy ever-changing scenes convey,
But grief, repentance, frequent sighs and tears?
What in thy length'ning course can man survey,
But disappointment, endless doubts, and fears?

Oh, why are friendships form'd? Can they impart
A sure contentment, an enduring joy?
Ah no! too soon the mournful words, " We part,"
The fabric of our promised hopes destroy!

Hard, then, our lot! Alas! congenial minds,
At Friendship's shrine, will weave the sacred tie.
Doubt, Absence, Death, each in its turn unbinds
The silken bonds that sway man's destiny.

Vain mortal, cease! Behold that Heav'n above!
Where countless saints one boundless Pow'r adore;
There, in the realms of Mercy, Truth, and Love,
Shall Friendship's votaries meet to part no more!

o

REASONS FOR ABSENCE.

BY F. M. REYNOLDS.

Since you, fair lady, deign to ask
  The reason why I stay from you,
I'll e'en discard my wonted mask,
  And give for once, my motives true.
Then learn, despite what now I seem,
  That I have known the thrilling touch
Of passion in its wildest dream,
  Have known, and felt it, far too much.

I've been a slave beneath its thrall,
  Its doubts, its raptures, and vexations;
And I have run the round of all
  Its dear, delightful, d——d sensations!
I've borne as much as could be borne;
  I've felt the keenest throb of pain;
And I have deeply, deeply sworn
  To never feel the like again!

O were you but less kind and tender,
  Or were you less serene and fair,
O had your radiant eye less splendor,
  And less of gloss your silken hair;
Or were you but more lightly gay,
  Or were you e'en but more severe,
I then had never staid away,
  For nought I then had had to fear!

FERDINANDO EBOLI.

A TALE.

BY THE AUTHOR OF FRANKENSTEIN.

DURING this quiet time of peace, we are fast forgetting the excitements and astonishing events of the last war; and the very names of Europe's conquerors are becoming antiquated to the ears of our children. Those were more romantic days than these; for the revulsions occasioned by revolution or invasion were full of romance; and travellers in those countries in which these scenes had place hear strange and wonderful stories, whose truth so much resembles fiction, that, while interested in the narration, we never give implicit credence to the narrator. Of this kind is a tale I heard at Naples. The fortunes of war perhaps did not influence its actors; yet it appears improbable that any circumstances so out of the usual routine could have had place under the garish daylight that peace sheds upon the world.

When Murat, then called Gioacchino, king of Naples, raised his Italian regiments, several young nobles, who had before been scarcely more than vine-dressers on the soil, were inspired with a love of arms, and presented themselves as candidates for military honours. Among these was the young Count Eboli. The father of this youthful noble had followed Ferdinand to Sicily; but his estates lay principally near Salerno, and he was naturally desirous of preserving them; while the hopes that the French government held out of glory and prosperity to his country made him often regret that he had followed his legitimate but imbecile king to exile. When he died, therefore, he recommended his son to return to Naples, to present himself to his old and tried friend, the Marchese Spina, who held a high office in Murat's government, and through his means to reconcile himself to the new king. All this was easily achieved. The young and gallant Count was permitted to possess his patrimony; and, as a further pledge of good fortune, he was betrothed to the only child of the Marchese Spina. The nuptials were deferred till the end of the ensuing campaign.

Meanwhile the army was put in motion, and Count Eboli only obtained such short leave of absence as permitted him to visit for a few hours the villa of his future father-in-law, there to take leave of him and his affianced bride. The villa was situated on one of the Apennines to the north of Salerno, and looked down, over the plain of Calabria, in which Pæstum is situated, on to the blue Mediterranean. A precipice on one side, a brawling mountain torrent, and a thick grove of ilex, added beauty to the sublimity of its site. Count Eboli ascended the mountain path in all the joy of youth and hope. His stay was brief. An exhortation and a blessing from the Marchese, a tender farewell, graced by gentle tears, from the fair Adalinda, were the recollections he was to bear with him, to inspire him with courage and hope in danger and absence. The sun had just sunk behind the distant isle of Istria, when, kissing his lady's hand, he said a last "Addio," and with slower steps, and more melancholy mien, rode down the mountain on his road to Naples.

That same night Adalinda retired early to her apartment, dismissing her attendants; and then, restless from mingled fear and hope, she threw open the glass door that led to a balcony looking over the edge of the hill upon the torrent, whose loud rushing often lulled her to sleep; but whose waters were concealed from sight by the ilex trees, which lifted their topmost branches above the guarding parapet of the balcony.

Leaning her cheek upon her hand, she thought of the dangers her lover would encounter, of her loneliness the while, of his letters, and of his return. A rustling sound now caught her ear: was it the breeze among the ilex trees? her own veil was unwaved by every wind, her tresses even, heavy in their own rich beauty only, were not lifted from her cheek. Again those sounds. Her blood retreated to her heart, and her limbs trembled. What could it mean? Suddenly the upper branches of the nearest tree were disturbed; they opened, and the faint starlight showed a man's figure among them. He prepared to spring from his hold, on to the wall. It was a feat of peril. First the soft voice of her lover bade her "Fear not," and on the next instant he was at her side, calming her terrors, and recalling her spirits, that almost left her gentle frame, from mingled surprise, dread, and joy. He encircled her waist with his arm, and pouring forth a thousand passionate expressions of love, she leant on his shoulder, and wept from agitation; while he covered her hands with kisses, and gazed on her with ardent adoration.

Then in calmer mood they sat together; triumph and joy lighted up his eyes, and a modest blush glowed on her cheek; for never before had she sat alone with him, nor heard unrestrained his impassioned assurances of affection.

It was indeed Love's own hour. The stars trembled on the roof of his eternal temple; the dashing of the torrent, the mild summer atmosphere, and the mysterious aspect of the darkened scenery, were all in unison, to inspire security and voluptuous hope. They talked of how their hearts, through the medium of divine nature, might hold commune during absence; of the joys of re-union, and of their prospect of perfect happiness.

The moment at last arrived when he must depart. "One tress of this silken hair," said he, raising one of the many curls that clustered on her neck. "I will place it on my heart, a shield to protect me against the swords and balls of the enemy." He drew his keen-edged dagger from its sheath. "Ill weapon for so gentle a deed," he said, severing the lock, and at the same moment many drops of blood fell fast on the fair arm of the lady. He answered her fearful inquiries by showing a gash he had awkwardly inflicted on his left hand. First he insisted on securing his prize, and then he permitted her to bind his wound, which she did half laughing, half in sorrow, winding round his hand a riband loosened from her own arm. "Now farewell," he cried; "I must ride twenty miles ere dawn, and the descending Bear shows that midnight is past." His descent was difficult, but he achieved it happily, and the stave of a song, whose soft sounds rose like the smoke of incense from an altar, from the dell below, to her impatient ear, assured her of his safety.

As is always the case when an account is gathered from eye-witnesses, I never could ascertain the exact date of these events. They occurred however while Murat was king of Naples, and when he raised his Italian regiments, Count Eboli, as aforesaid, became a junior officer in them, and served with much distinction; though I cannot name either the country, or the battle in which he acted so conspicuous a part, that he was on the spot promoted to a troop. Not long after this event, and while he was stationed in the north of Italy, Gioacchino, sending for him to head-quarters late one evening, intrusted him with a confidential mission, across a country occupied by the enemy's troops, to a town possessed by the French. It was necessary to undertake the expedition during the night, and he was expected to return on that, succeeding the following, day, The king himself gave him his despatches and the word; and the noble youth, with modest firmness, protested that he would succeed, or die, in the fulfilment of his trust.

It was already night, and the crescent moon was low in the west, when Count Ferdinando Eboli mounting his favourite horse, at a quick gallop, cleared the streets of the town; and then, following the directions given him, crossed the country among the fields planted with vines, carefully avoiding the main road. It was a beauteous and still night; calm, and sleep, occupied the earth; war, the bloodhound, slumbered; the spirit of love alone had life at that silent hour. Exulting in the hope of glory, our young hero commenced his journey, and visions of aggrandizement and love formed his reveries. A distant sound roused him; he checked his horse and listened; voices approached; when recognising the speech of a German, he turned from the path he was following, to a still straighter way. But again the tone of an enemy was heard, and the trampling of horses. Eboli did not hesitate; he dismounted, tied his steed to a tree, and, skirting along the enclosure of the field, trusted to escape thus unobserved. He succeeded after an hour's painful progress, and arrived on the borders of a stream, which, as the boundary between two states, was the mark of his having finally escaped danger. Descending the steep bank of the river, which, with his horse, he might perhaps have forded, he now prepared to swim. He held his despatch in one hand, threw away his cloak, and was about to plunge into the water, when from under the dark shade of the *argine*, which had concealed them, he was suddenly arrested by unseen hands, cast on the ground, bound, gagged and blinded, and then placed in a little boat, which was sculled with infinite rapidity down the stream.

There seemed so much of premeditation in the act that it baffled conjecture, yet he must believe himself a prisoner to the Austrian. While, however, he still vainly reflected, the boat was moored, he was lifted out, and the change of atmosphere made him aware that they entered some house. With extreme care and celerity, yet in the utmost silence, he was stripped of his clothes, and two rings he wore, drawn from his fingers; other habiliments were thrown over him; and then no departing footstep was audible: but soon he heard the splash of a single oar, and he felt himself alone. He lay perfectly unable to move; the only relief his captor or captors had afforded him being the exchange of the gag for a tightly bound handkerchief. For hours he thus remained, with a tortured mind, bursting with rage, impatience, and disappointment; now writhing, as well as he could, in his endeavours to free himself, now still, in despair. His despatches were taken away, and the period was swiftly passing when he could by his presence have remedied in some degree this evil. The morning dawned; and though the full glare of the sun could not visit his eyes, he felt it play upon his limbs. As the day advanced, hunger preyed on him, and though amidst the visitation of mightier, he at first disdained this minor, evil; towards evening, it became, in spite of himself, the predominant sensation. Night approached, and the fear that he should remain, and even starve, in this unvisited solitude had more than once thrilled through his frame, when feminine voices and a child's gay laugh met his ear. He heard persons enter the apartment, and he was asked in his native language, while the ligature was taken from his mouth, the cause of his present situation. He attributed it to banditti: his bonds were quickly cut, and his banded eyes restored to sight. It was long before he recovered himself. Water brought from the stream, however, was some refreshment, and by degrees he resumed the use of his senses, and saw that he was in a dilapidated shepherd's cot; with no one near him save the peasant girl and a child who had liberated him. They rubbed his ankles and wrists, and the little fellow offered him some bread, and eggs; after which refreshment, and an hour's repose, Ferdinando felt himself sufficiently restored to revolve his adventure in his mind, and to determine on the conduct he was to pursue.

He looked at the dress which had been given him in exchange for that which he had worn. It was of the plainest and meanest description. Still no time was to be lost; and he felt assured that the only step he could take was to return with all speed to the head-quarters of the Neapolitan army, and inform the king of his disasters and his loss.

It were long to follow his backward steps, and to tell all of indignation and disappointment that swelled his heart. He walked painfully but resolutely all night, and by three in the morning entered the town where Gioacchino then was. He was challenged by the sentinels;

he gave the word confided to him by Murat, and was
instantly made prisoner by the soldiers. He declared to
them his name and rank, and the necessity he was under
of immediately seeing the king. He was taken to the
guard-house, and the officer on duty there listened with
contempt to his representations, telling him that Count
Ferdinando Eboli had returned three hours before, ordering him to be confined for further examination as a spy.
Eboli loudly insisted that some impostor had taken his
name; and while he related the story of his capture,
another officer came in, who recognised his person; other
individuals acquainted with him joined the party; and as
the impostor had been seen by none but the officer of the
night, his tale gained ground.

A young Frenchman of superior rank, who had orders
to attend the king early in the morning, carried a report
of what was going forward to Murat himself. The tale
was so strange that the king sent for the young Count;
and then, in spite of having seen and believed in his
counterfeit a few hours before, and having received from
him an account of his mission, which had been faithfully
executed, the appearance of the youth staggered him, and
he commanded the presence of him who, as Count Eboli,
had appeared before him a few hours previously. As Ferdinand stood beside the king, his eye glanced at a large
and splendid mirror. His matted hair, his blood-shot eyes,
his haggard looks, and torn and mean dress, derogated
from the nobility of his appearance; and still less did he
appear like the magnificent Count Eboli, when, to his utter
confusion and astonishment, his counterfeit stood beside
him.

He was perfect in all the outward signs that denoted

high birth; and so like him whom he represented, that it would have been impossible to discern one from the other apart. The same chestnut hair clustered on his brow; the sweet and animated hazel eyes were the same; the one voice was the echo of the other. The composure and dignity of the pretender gained the suffrages of those around. When he was told of the strange appearance of another Count Eboli, he laughed in a frank good humoured manner, and turning to Ferdinand, said, " You honour me much, in selecting me for your personation; but there are two or three things I like about myself so well, that you must excuse my unwillingness to exchange myself for you." Ferdinand would have answered, but the false Count, with greater haughtiness, turning to the king, said, " Will your majesty decide between us? I cannot bandy words with a fellow of this sort." Irritated by scorn, Ferdinand demanded leave to challenge the pretender; who said, that if the king and his brother officers did not think that he should degrade himself and disgrace the army by going out with a common vagabond, he was willing to chastise him, even at the peril of his own life. But the king, after a few more questions, feeling assured that the unhappy noble was an impostor, in severe and menacing terms reprehended him for his insolence, telling him that he owed it to his mercy alone that he was not executed as a spy, ordering him instantly to be conducted without the walls of the town, with threats of weighty punishment if he ever dared to subject his impostures to further trial.

It requires a strong imagination, and the experience of much misery, fully to enter into Ferdinand's feelings. From high rank, glory, hope, and love, he was hurled to utter beggary and disgrace. The insulting words of his triumphant rival, and the degrading menaces of his so lately gracious sovereign, rang in his ears; every nerve in his frame writhed with agony. But, fortunately for the endurance of human life, the worst misery in early youth is often but a painful dream, which we cast off when slumber quits our eyes. After a struggle with intolerable anguish, hope and courage revived in his heart. His resolution was quickly made. He would return to Naples, relate his story to the Marchese Spina, and through his influence obtain at least an impartial hearing from the king. It was not, however, in his peculiar situation, an easy task to put his determination into effect. He was pennyless; his dress bespoke poverty; he had neither friend nor kinsman near, but such as would behold in him the most impudent of swindlers. Still his courage did not fail him. The kind Italian soil, in the autumnal season now advanced, furnished him with chestnuts, arbutus berries, and grapes. He took the most direct road over the hills, avoiding towns, and indeed every habitation; travelling principally in the night, when, except in cities, the officers of government had retired from their stations. How he succeeded in getting from one end of Italy to the other it is difficult to say; but certain it is, that, after the interval of a few weeks, he presented himself at the Villa Spina.

With considerable difficulty he obtained admission to the presence of the Marchese, who received him standing, with an inquiring look, not at all recognising the noble youth. Ferdinand requested a private interview, for there were several visitors present. His voice startled the Marchese, who complied, taking him into another apartment. Here Ferdinand disclosed himself, and, with rapid and agitated utterance, was relating the history of his misfortunes, when the tramp of horses was heard, the great bell rang, and a domestic announced " Count Ferdinando Eboli." " It is himself," cried the youth, turning pale. The words were strange, and they appeared still more so, when the person announced entered; the perfect semblance of the young noble, whose name he assumed, as he had appeared, when last, at his departure, he trod the pavement of the hall. He inclined his head gracefully to the baron, turning with a glance of some surprise, but more disdain, towards Ferdinand, exclaiming, " Thou here!"

Ferdinand drew himself up to his full height. In spite of fatigue, ill fare, and coarse garments, his manner was full of dignity. The Marchese looked at him fixedly, and started as he marked his proud mien, and saw in his expressive features the very face of Eboli. But again he was perplexed when he turned and discerned, as in a mirror, the same countenance reflected by the new comer, who underwent this scrutiny somewhat impatiently. In brief and scornful words, he told the Marchese that this was a second attempt in the intruder to impose himself as Count Eboli; that the trick had failed before, and would again; adding, laughing, that it was hard to be brought to prove himself to be himself, against the assertion of a *briccone*, whose likeness to him, and matchless impudence, were his whole stock in trade.

" Why, my good fellow," continued he, sneeringly, " you put me out of conceit with myself, to think that one, apparently so like me, should get on no better in the world."

The blood mounted into Ferdinand's cheeks on his enemy's bitter taunts; with difficulty he restrained himself from closing with his foe, while the words " traitorous impostor!" burst from his lips. The baron commanded the fierce youth to be silent, and, moved by a look that he remembered to be Ferdinand's, he said, gently, "By your respect for me, I adjure you to be patient; fear not but that I will deal impartially." Then turning to the pretended Eboli, he added that he could not doubt but that he was the true Count, and asked excuse for his previous indecision. At first the latter appeared angry, but at length he burst into a laugh, and then, apologizing for his ill breeding, continued laughing heartily at the perplexity of the Marchese. It is certain, his gayety gained more credit with his auditor than the indignant glances of poor Ferdinand. The false Count then said that, after the king's menaces, he had entertained no expectation that the farce was to be played over again. He had obtained leave of absence, of which he profited to visit his future father-in-law, after having spent a few days in his own palazzo at Naples. Until now, Ferdinand had listened silently with a feeling of curiosity, anxious to learn all he could of the actions and motives of his rival; but at these last words he could no longer contain himself. "What!" cried he, "hast thou usurped my place in my own father's house, and dared assume my power in my ancestral halls?" A gush of tears overpowered the youth; he hid his face in his hands. Fierceness and pride lit up the countenance of the pretender. "By the eternal God and the sacred cross, I swear," he exclaimed, "that palace is my father's palace; those halls the halls of my ancestors!" Ferdinand looked up with surprise; "And the earth opens not," he said, "to swallow the perjured man." He then, at the call of the Marchese, related his adventures, while scorn mantled on the features of his rival. The Marchese, looking at both, could not free himself from doubt. He turned from one to the other: in spite of the wild and disordered appearance of poor Ferdinand, there was something in him that forbade his friend to condemn him as the impostor; but then it was utterly impossible to pronounce such the gallant and noble-looking youth, who could only be acknowledged as the real Count by the disbelief of the other's tale. The Marchese, calling an attendant, sent for his fair daughter. " This decision," said he, " shall be made over to the subtle judgment of a woman, and the keen penetration of one who loves." Both the youths now smiled—the same smile; the same expression—that, of anticipated triumph. The baron was more perplexed than ever.

Adalinda had heard of the arrival of Count Eboli, and entered, resplendent in youth and happiness. She turned quickly towards him who resembled most the person she expected to see; when a well-known voice pronounced her name, and she gazed aghast on the double appearance of the lover. Her father, taking her hand, briefly explained the mystery, and bade her assure herself which was her affianced husband.

" Signorina," said Ferdinand, " disdain me not because I appear before you thus in disgrace and misery. Your love, your goodness will restore me to prosperity and happiness."

" I know not by what means," said the wondering girl, " but surely you are Count Eboli."

" Adalinda," said the rival youth, " waste not your words on a villain. Lovely and deceived one, I trust, trembling I say it, that I can with one word assure you that I am Eboli."

"Adalinda," said Ferdinand, "I placed the nuptial ring on your finger; before God your vows were given to me."

The false Count approached the lady, and bending one knee, took from his heart a locket, enclosing hair tied with a green riband, which she recognised to have worn, and pointed to a slight scar on his left hand.

Adalinda blushed deeply, and turning to her father, said, motioning towards the kneeling youth,

"He is Ferdinand."

All protestations now from the unhappy Eboli were vain. The Marchese would have cast him into a dungeon; but, at the earnest request of his rival, he was not detained, but thrust ignominiously from the villa. The rage of a wild beast newly chained was less than the tempest of indignation that now filled the heart of Ferdinand. Physical suffering, from fatigue and fasting, was added to his internal anguish; for some hours madness, if that were madness which never forgets its ill, possessed him. In a tumult of feelings there was one predominant idea: it was, to take possession of his father's house, and to try, by ameliorating the fortuitous circumstances of his lot, to gain the upper hand of his adversary. He expended his remaining strength in reaching Naples, entered his family palace, and was received and acknowledged by his astonished domestics.

One of his first acts was to take from a cabinet a miniature of his father encircled with jewels, and to invoke the aid of the paternal spirit. Refreshment and a bath restored him to some of his usual strength; and he looked forward with almost childish delight to one night to be spent in peace under the roof of his father's house. This was not permitted. Ere midnight the great bell sounded: his rival entered as master, with the Marchese Spina.

The result may be divined. The Marchese appeared more indignant than the false Eboli. He insisted that the unfortunate youth should be imprisoned. The portrait, whose setting was costly, found on him, proved him guilty of robbery. He was given into the hands of the police, and thrown into a dungeon. I will not dwell on the subsequent scenes. He was tried by the tribunal, condemned as guilty, and sentenced to the galleys for life.

On the eve of the day when he was to be removed from the Neapolitan prison to work on the roads in Calabria, his rival visited him in his dungeon. For some moments both looked at the other in silence. The impostor gazed on the prisoner with mingled pride and compassion: there was evidently a struggle in his heart. The answering glance of Ferdinand was calm, free, and dignified. He was not resigned to his hard fate, but he disdained to make any exhibition of despair to his cruel and successful foe. A spasm of pain seemed to wrench the bosom of the false one; and he turned aside, striving to recover the hardness of heart which had hitherto supported him in the prosecution of his guilty enterprise. Ferdinand spoke first.

" What would the triumphant criminal with his innocent victim?"

His visitant replied haughtily, " Do not address such epithets to me, or I leave you to your fate: I am that which I say I am."

" To me this boast," cried Ferdinand, scornfully; " but perhaps these walls have ears."

" Heaven, at least, is not deaf," said the deceiver; " favouring Heaven, which knows and admits my claim. But a truce to this idle discussion. Compassion—a distaste to see one so very like myself in such ill condition—a foolish whim, perhaps, on which you may congratulate yourself—has led me hither. The bolts of your dungeon are drawn; here is a purse of gold; fulfil one easy condition, and you are free."

" And that condition?"

" Sign this paper."

He gave to Ferdinand a writing, containing a confession of his imputed crimes. The hand of the guilty youth trembled as he gave it; there was confusion in his mien, and a restless uneasy rolling of his eye. Ferdinand wished in one mighty word, potent as lightning, loud as thunder, to convey his burning disdain of this proposal: but expression is weak, and calm is more full of power than storm. Without a word, he tore the paper in two pieces, and threw them at the feet of his enemy.

With a sudden change of manner, his visitant conjured him, in voluble and impetuous terms, to comply. Ferdinand answered only by requesting to be left alone. Now and then a half word broke uncontrollably from his lips; but he curbed himself. Yet he could not hide his agitation when, as an argument to make him yield, the false Count assured him that he was already married to Adalinda. Bitter agony thrilled poor Ferdinand's frame; but he preserved a calm mien, and an unaltered resolution. Having exhausted every menace and every persuasion, his rival left him, the purpose for which he came unaccomplished. On the morrow, with many others, the refuse of mankind, Count Ferdinando Eboli was led in chains to the unwholesome plains of Calabria, to work there at the roads.

I must hurry over some of the subsequent events; for a detailed account of them would fill volumes. The assertion of the usurper of Ferdinand's right, that he was already married to Adalina, was, like all else he said, false. The day was, however, fixed for their union, when the illness and the subsequent death of the Marchese Spina delayed its celebration. Adalinda retired, during the first months of mourning, to a castle belonging to her father not far from Arpino, a town of the kingdom of Naples, in the midst of the Apennines, about fifty miles from the capital. Before she went, the deceiver tried to persuade her to consent to a private marriage. He was probably afraid that, in the long interval that was about to ensue before he could secure her, she would discover his imposture. Besides, a rumour had gone abroad that one of the fellow-prisoners of Ferdinand, a noted bandit, had escaped, and that the young Count was his companion in flight. Adalinda, however, refused to comply with her lover's entreaties, and retired to her seclusion with an old aunt, who was blind and deaf, but an excellent duenna.

The false Eboli seldom visited his mistress; but he was a master in his art, and subsequent events showed that he must have spent all his time disguised in the vicinity of the castle. He contrived by various means, unsuspected at the moment, to have all Adalinda's servants changed for creatures of his own; so that, without her being aware of the restraint, she was, in fact, a prisoner in her own house. It is impossible to say what first awakened her suspicions concerning the deception put upon her. She was an Italian, with all the habitual quiescence and lassitude of her countrywomen in the ordinary routine of life, and with all their energy and passion when roused. The moment the doubt darted into her mind, she resolved to be assured; a few questions relative to scenes that had passed between poor Ferdinand and herself sufficed for this. They were asked so suddenly and pointedly that the pretender was thrown off his guard; he looked confused, and stammered in his replies. Their eyes met, he felt that he was detected, and she saw that he perceived her now confirmed suspicions. A look such as is peculiar to an impostor, a glance that deformed his beauty, and filled his usually noble countenance with the hideous lines of cunning and cruel triumph, completed her faith in her own discernment. "How," she thought, "could I have mistaken this man for my own gentle Eboli?" Again their eyes met: the peculiar expression of his terrified her, and she hastily quitted the apartment.

Her resolution was quickly formed. It was of no use to attempt to explain her situation to her old aunt. She determined to depart immediately for Naples, throw herself at the feet of Gioacchino, and to relate and obtain credit for her strange history. But the time was already lost when she could have executed this design. The contrivances of the deceiver were complete—she found herself a prisoner. Excess of fear gave her boldness, if not courage. She sought her jailor. A few minutes before, she had been a young and thoughtless girl, docile as a child, and as unsuspecting. Now she felt as if she had suddenly grown old in wisdom, and that the experience of years had been gained in that of a few seconds.

During their interview, she was wary and firm; while the instinctive power of innocence over guilt gave majesty to her demeanour. The contriver of her ills for a moment cowered beneath her eye. At first he would by no means allow that he was not the person he pretended to be: but the energy and eloquence of truth bore down his

artifice, so that, at length driven into a corner, he turned—
a stag at bay. Then it was her turn to quail; for the
superior energy of a man gave him the mastery. He declared the truth. He was the elder brother of Ferdinand,
a natural son of the old Count Eboli. His mother, who
had been wronged, never forgave her injurer, and bred
her son in deadly hate for his parent, and a belief that the
advantages enjoyed by his more fortunate brother were
rightfully his own. His education was rude; but he had
an Italian's subtle talents, swiftness of perception, and
guileful arts.

"It would blanch your cheek," he said to his trembling
auditress, " could I describe all that I have suffered to
achieve my purpose. I would trust to none—I executed
all myself. It was a glorious triumph, but due to my
perseverance and my fortitude, when I and my usurping
brother stood, I, the noble, he, the degraded outcast, before
our sovereign."

Having rapidly detailed his history, he now sought to
win the favourable ear of Adalinda, who stood with averted
and angry looks. He tried by the varied shows of passion
and tenderness to move her heart. Was he not, in truth,
the object of her love? Was it not he who scaled her
balcony at Villa Spina? He recalled scenes of mutual
overflow of feeling to her mind, thus urging arguments
the most potent with a delicate woman: pure blushes
tinged her cheek, but horror of the deceiver predominated
over every other sentiment. He swore that as soon as
they should be united he would free Ferdinand, and bestow
competency, nay, if so she willed it, half his possessions,
on him. She coldly replied, that she would rather share
the chains of the innocent and misery, than link herself

with imposture and crime. She demanded her liberty, but the untamed and even ferocious nature that had borne the deceiver through his career of crime now broke forth, and he invoked fearful imprecations on his head, if she ever quitted the castle except as his wife. His look of conscious power and unbridled wickedness terrified her; her flashing eyes spoke abhorrence: it would have been far easier for her to have died than have yielded the smallest point to a man who made her feel for one moment his irresistible power, arising from her being an unprotected woman, wholly in his hands. She left him, feeling as if she had just escaped from the impending sword of an assassin.

One hour's deliberation suggested to her a method of escape from her terrible situation. In a wardrobe at the castle lay in their pristine gloss the habiliments of a page of her mother, who had died suddenly, leaving these unworn relics of his station. Dressing herself in these, she tied up her dark shining hair, and even, with a somewhat bitter feeling, girded on the slight sword that appertained to the costume. Then, through a private passage leading from her own apartment to the chapel of the castle, she glided with noiseless steps, long after the Ave Maria sounded at twenty-four o'clock, had, on a November night, given token that half an hour had passed since the setting of the sun. She possessed the key of the chapel door—it opened at her touch; she closed it behind her, and she was free. The pathless hills were around her, the starry heavens above, and a cold wintry breeze murmured around the castle walls; but fear of her enemy conquered every other fear, and she tripped lightly on, in a kind of ecstasy, for many a long hour over the stony mountain-

Drawn by A.E. Chalon, R.A.

Engraved by C. Heath.

ADELINDA.

Published for the Proprietor by T. Hurst, & Co. St. Paul's Churchyard, and R. Jennings, 2, Poultry.

path—she, who had never before walked more than a mile or two at any time in her life,—till her feet were blistered, her slight shoes cut through, her way utterly lost. At morning's dawn she found herself in the midst of the wild ilex-covered Apennines, and neither habitation nor human being apparent.

She was hungry and weary. She had brought gold and jewels with her; but here were no means of exhanging these for food. She remembered stories of banditti; but none could be so ruffian-like and cruel as him from whom she fled. This thought, a little rest, and a draught of water from a pure mountain-spring, restored her to some portion of courage, and she continued her journey. Noonday approached; and, in the south of Italy, the noonday sun, when unclouded, even in November, is oppressively warm, especially to an Italian woman, who never exposes herself to its beams. Faintness came over her. There appeared recesses in the mountain-side along which she was travelling, grown over with bay and arbutus: she entered one of these, there to repose. It was deep, and led to another that opened into a spacious cavern lighted from above: there were cates, grapes, and a flagon of wine, on a rough hewn table. She looked fearfully around, but no inhabitant appeared. She placed herself at the table, and, half in dread, ate of the food presented to her, and then sat, her elbow on the table, her head resting on her little snow-white hand; her dark hair shading her brow and clustering round her throat. An appearance of languor and fatigue diffused through her attitude, while her soft black eyes filled at intervals with large tears, as pitying herself, she recurred to the cruel circumstances of her lot. Her fanciful but elegant dress, her feminine form, her beauty and her grace, as she sat pensive and alone in the rough unhewn cavern, formed a picture a poet would describe with delight, an artist love to paint.

"She seemed a being of another world; a seraph, all light and beauty; a Ganymede, escaped from his thrall above to his natal Ida. It was long before I recognised, looking down on her from the opening hill, my lost Adalinda." Thus spoke the young Count Eboli, when he related this story; for its end was as romantic as its commencement.

When Ferdinando had arrived a galley-slave in Calabria, he found himself coupled with a bandit, a brave fellow, who abhorred his chains, from love of freedom, as much as his fellow-prisoner did, from all the combination of disgrace and misery they brought upon him. Together they devised a plan of escape, and succeeded in effecting it. On their road, Ferdinand related his story to the outlaw, who encouraged him to hope a favourable turn of fate; and meanwhile invited and persuaded the desperate man to share his fortunes as a robber among the wild hills of Calabria.

The cavern where Adalinda had taken refuge was one of their fastnesses, whither they betook themselves at periods of imminent danger for safety only, as no booty could be collected in that unpeopled solitude; and there, one afternoon, returning from the chase, they found the wandering, fearful, solitary, fugitive girl; and never was lighthouse more welcome to tempest-tost sailor than was her own Ferdinand to his lady-love.

Fortune, now tired of persecuting the young noble, favoured him still further. The story of the lovers interested the bandit chief, and promise of reward secured him. Ferdinand persuaded Adalinda to remain one night in the cave, and on the following morning they prepared to proceed to Naples; but at the moment of their departure they were surprised by an unexpected visitant: the robbers brought in a prisoner—it was the impostor. Missing on the morrow her who was the pledge of his safety and success, but assured that she could not have wandered far, he despatched emissaries in all directions to seek her; and himself, joining in the pursuit, followed the road she had taken, and was captured by these lawless men, who expected rich ransom from one whose appearance denoted rank and wealth. When they discovered who their prisoner was, they generously delivered him up into his brother's hands.

Ferdinand and Adalinda proceeded to Naples. On their arrival, she presented herself to Queen Caroline; and, through her, Murat heard with astonishment the device that had been practised on him. The young Count was restored to his honours and possessions, and within a few months afterwards was united to his betrothed bride.

The compassionate nature of the Count and Countess led them to interest themselves warmly in the fate of Ludovico, whose subsequent career was more honourable but less fortunate. At the intercession of his relative, Gioacchino permitted him to enter the army, where he distinguished himself, and obtained promotion. The brothers were at Moscow together, and mutually assisted each other during the horrors of the retreat. At one time overcome by drowsiness, the mortal symptom resulting from excessive cold, Ferdinand lingered behind his comrades; but Ludovico refusing to leave him, dragged him on in spite of himself, till, entering a village, food and fire restored him,

and his life was saved. On another evening, when wind
and sleet added to the horror of their situation, Ludovico,
after many ineffective struggles, slid from his horse lifeless; Ferdinand was at his side, and, dismounting, endeavoured by every means in his power to bring back
pulsation to his stagnant blood. His comrades went forward, and the young Count was left alone with his dying
brother in the white boundless waste. Once Ludovico
opened his eyes and recognised him; he pressed his hand,
and his lips moved to utter a blessing as he died. At that
moment the welcome sounds of the enemy's approach
roused Ferdinand from the despair into which his dreadful
situation plunged him. He was taken prisoner, and his
life was thus saved. When Napoleon went to Elba, he,
with many others of his countrymen, was liberated, and
returned to Naples.

QUATRAIN

ADDRESSED TO A LADY, AND WRITTEN ON THE ENVE-
LOPE IN WHICH WAS RETURNED HER OWN LETTER.

BY M. R.

Fair maid, we now are quits,
So be not melancholy;
Your beauty *turn'd* my wits,
My sense *returns* your folly.

THE TEST OF LOVE.

BY F. M. REYNOLDS.

Would you, lady fair, discover,
    If your heart be truly gain'd;
And if passion of your lover
    Be a real, or a feign'd.

With the test I will supply you:—
    If unhappy, when away,
If unhappy, when he's nigh you,
    If unhappy, night and day;

If perplex'd, abstracted, fretting,
    If pursued by causeless care,
If some trifle e'er regretting,
    Know you love him, lady fair!—

If by women loath'd, detested,
    If by you enchanting, thought,
If of ev'ry friend divested,
    Though by friends he once was sought;

If unto himself tormenting,
    If tormenting e'en to you,
If tormenting, though repenting,
    Then believe his love is *true!*—

Lady, thus, you may discover
    If your heart be truly gain'd,
And if passion of your lover
    Be a real, or a feign'd.

THE BOY AND THE BUTTERFLY.

BY T. CROFTON CROKER.

FAIR lady, see—yon butterfly,
  That freely roves from rose to rose,
Inhales their sweets; then wanders by,
  Now here, now there, to seek repose.

Thus had I hoped, in sunny hour,
  To sip of sweets from all around;
And only linger where a bower
  Of bloom and beauty I had found.

But, lady, see yon idle boy,
  Whose eye hath caught its painted wing,
Quick follows with an eager joy,
  And tries to seize the wretched thing.

'Tis thus that wicked urchin, Love,
  Pursues my soul's unfetter'd flight;
Thus follows quickly where I rove;
  Thus tries to snare me when I 'light.

Still, though my soul can gaily spring
  From flower to flower, in flight as wild
The tarnish'd hue, the ruffled wing,
  Mark many a struggle with the child.

AN INCIDENT.

BY F. M. REYNOLDS.

"Honour, wit, genius, wealth, and glory,
Good lack, good lack, are transitory;
Nothing is sure, and stable found;
The very earth itself turns round;
Monarchs, nay ministers must die;
Must moulder, rot, ah me! ah why?
Ah woful me, ah woful man,
Ah woful all, do all we can!"

CHURCHILL.

IN London, deaths, accidents, suicides, or the loss of a few thousands of fellow-creatures by war, conflagrations, shipwrecks, plagues, and so forth, are regarded with all the highminded philosophy of indifference; while a waist longer, or shorter, than the prescribed *ex cathedrâ* limits; a bad picture, or a bad actor; a hump behind a gown, or a hump before one, are the important causes that daily call into action the thousand bad and good feelings of this vast metropolis.

It was on this principle, I suppose, that, some ten or twelve years ago, we were all excited by the wonderful accounts of a then forthcoming ball and supper to be given by Lady d'Elmont. It was assiduously promulgated by the *attachés* of fashion, that three months had been expended in preparations; though those who wished to be thought on a particularly intimate footing with its fair donor, with inflated faces, and important air, mysteriously implied that they *knew* that *four* months and as many days was the precise time the preparations had occupied. Which party, however, was correct, cannot, I fear, be now determined: suffice it therefore to say, that when the long desired evening arrived, half the fashion, character, and eccentricity of the metropolis was present; some, in gratitude for their invitation,' ready to render themselves disagreeable to any body, or every body; some panting with envy, and some panting for the supper; hundreds wishing the absence of their neighbours, and a few that of themselves; two-thirds, in fact, in ill-humour with others, and *selon la regle*, on these occasions, all discontented with their hostess.

The majority of the ladies, however, were of the real bon ton; and lounged, limped, languished, and fiddled-faddled, with the exact mixture of vanity, levity, and affectation, prescribed by the highest breeding at that time.

The men too were especially fashionable; they stared with pertinacity, wore mustachios, talked of races, and paid particular attention to themselves.

However, in an assembly of four or five hundred people, it is scarcely possible that all should be equally select: consequently, there was to be seen a strange jumble of peers and plebeians; countesses, and citizens' wives, introduced by their husbands' influence in the lower house; barons and retainers; old ladies and young; professors of all the liberal arts; opulent men, and pennyless gentlemen.

Among this heterogeneous mass were two friends, young men of fortune. The one was called Mortimer, and the other Bryant: the first was the son of a rich Yorkshire landholder, a wild, good-natured, handsome, scatter-

brained fellow of about three and twenty, whose leading
trait was a mad penchant for chemistry, which he had
acquired when a boy, during his education at one of the
principal schools in the neighbourhood of London. The
other was a mild, gentlemanly young man, a few years
older than his companion; less handsome in his appearance,
but evidently more under the control of his reason.

At the period of the introduction of this pair to the
reader, Bryant was talking most energetically to his companion, when the eye of the latter was attracted by the
figure of Lady d'Elmont, the donor of the fête, who, exhausted by the heat and confusion, half reclined on a sofa,
unnoticed and neglected.

She appeared about five and twenty; her eyes were
black and sparkling; her foot was small, and her ankle
beautiful; her ebon-coloured hair hung in rich clusters of
curls over her forehead, and formed a striking contrast
with its brilliant white; her nose was Grecian, her mouth
small, her teeth polished and regular, and her lips were
naturally fragrant, pouting, and red; but when they were
not, she mumbled and bit them till they became so: an
admirable recipe, and infinitely preferable to painted salve.

"Now, you do not mean, with all your hyper-caution,"
cried Mortimer, as though replying to some expostulation
on the part of his friend, "that any evil can accrue from
my being civil to a beautiful but forsaken woman?" and,
so saying, Mortimer, advancing up to Lady d'Elmont,
addressed her in his most conciliating tone.

"If you are not engaged, may I have the honour of
dancing the next dance with you, madam?"

The baroness raised her eyes, and admired the fine
manly figure before her.

" Sir, I thank you, but I do not dance."

" You are fatigued then, madam?"

"Yes, sir;" and she agitated her fan with becoming languor.

" I must confess that the room is certainly most intensely warm.   Will you allow me to procure you an ice?"

" I thank you—no."

" You are right, I believe, madam; in this heated state of the atmosphere it might not be prudent:"—then, after a pause, "the Lady d'Elmont acts very foolishly in thus overfilling her rooms?"

Her ladyship looked at him for a moment with surprise, and then replied:

"Yes, sir."

"But it all results, madam, from the love of notoriety; from, in fact, the love of shining in the newspapers!"

"Yes, sir."

" And for this paltry, reprehensible vanity, many a charming cheek is deprived of its roses, and many a lovely creature oppressed;" glancing at the baroness with a most significant and tender expression.

" Yes, sir."

" But Lady d'Elmont, I understand from good authority, is a weak—a very weak woman indeed, madam."

The baroness arose, and walked away.

" Do you know, sir, to whom you have been speaking all this while?" cried a listener to Mortimer, with agony in his countenance.

" No, sir."

" It was Lady d'Elmont."

Mortimer was paralysed for an instant; but looking round and finding that his friend was not a witness to his *etourderie,* he speedily recovered himself, and walked away, muttering, " It is her own fault; public characters in parties, like decanters on tables, should be labelled, to warn us whom to pass and whom to taste; or ticketed like pictures in an exhibition room, so that as one looks for the name of the artist, to ascertain the merits of the painting, one might have the advantage of seeing the personal charms of the lady through the medium of her reputation."

In the mean time, the baroness walked away, apparently as calm and unruffled as though no *contre-temps* had occurred; for what woman of fashion ever allows herself to be ill-humoured with any body but her husband? As to the baroness, whether she had one or no, was a subject of indecision even with her intimates; for, if she had one, her grandeur threw so vast a shadow around her, that he was lost in it.

But her ladyship was really not disconcerted; for though her reputation as a woman of understanding had been, perhaps, a little mangled by Mortimer's remarks, yet too many compliments had been implied to her person not to render the set-off perfectly satisfactory. For the baroness was entirely of the opinion of Stratonice,

* * * * * *

" That princess with a thousand charms,
Whom some malignant painter drew,
As lying in a soldier's arms;
And yet this painter from the dame
Received reward, instead of rigour,
Because, though he belied her name,
He did full justice to—*her figure.*"

Shortly afterwards Bryant rejoined Mortimer, and was, no doubt, in the act of inculcating prudence, when the eye of the latter was again attracted by a very pretty girl; whom he immediately accosted, and engaged to dance the next quadrille with him.

Thus passed the evening, until supper was announced; and then, alas, it appeared more than probable, inferring at least from the rush of the ladies to the head of the stairs, and their active exertions in the struggle for precedency, that *gourmandise* formed no inconsiderable organ in the structure of the pericraniums of even the most lovely.

Great, however, must have been the disappointment of all those possessing a due development of the culinary propensity, when, after all their well-fought efforts, they reached their goal, to find that the supper was not of that vulgar sort, where chickens, hams, patisseries, and things meant to be eaten, are offered to the guests: no! this was a decidedly fashionable supper, for there was nothing to eat. When I say this, however, I am wrong; for there was a profusion of silver and gold plate, plateaux, candelabras, and cut glass; things that, though not usually recommended for the diet of dyspeptic patients, have yet been eaten, and, no doubt, digested: besides too, there were temples, pagodas, and pyramids in barley sugar; statues in the most beautiful and delicate Parian and Italian marbles; tables of mosaic; various coloured confectionaries; ices; pine-apples; blanc-mange; jellies, froths, syllabubs, and abundance of flowers and shrubs, the admiration of all botanists, particularly of those who had previously supped.

There was Rivesaltes too, and delicious Lunel; Champagne cremant and mousseux; St. Peray; Constantia; Chambertin, that the connoisseurs, with sapient countenances, pronounced full of body and genuine aroma: besides Maraschino, Crême de Thé, Dantzig, Eau d'Or and d'Argent, Petit Lait de Henri Quartre, and a thousand other of those nefarious beverages, that the fiend has circulated among us, for the ruin of digestive organs, and the curse of valetudinarians.

Every part of the whole arrangement was, in fact, perfect. The footmen were all of a size; fine tall men, of that species technically called " Ladies' Footmen." They were somewhat narrow-shouldered, it is true; but for this the tasteful uniformity of their livery was an ample compensation; they were lamed by the tightness of their shoes, but then their feet looked small; and they had no calves to their legs, but their faces were considered very pale and interesting.

Two much shorter than the rest attracted attention: their faces were black instead of white, and their hair white instead of black; their calves, though, were very ample; and their heads inclined towards the earth, while their toes and their noses turned towards the sky. Malice whispered them to be sheriff's officers, but the report was only believed by her ladyship's most particular friends.

At this faultless banquet, Fortune arranged that Mortimer should be seated next to the fair Lady d'Elmont. Not as well aware, however, as the reader, of the real effect his *bevue* had made on her ladyship's mind, he felt at first rather shy of addressing her; and he attempted to ply his conversation with his fair neighbour on the other side. But it was hopeless; not a word could he extract from her, till at last, abandoning his fruitless efforts, he sat in resigned silence.

In the mean time, at other parts of the table, the conversation proceeded more freely. It was, generally speaking, most excessively learned; indeed it was worse, it was most horribly blue, for *blueism* was the rage of the day.

Craniology was the first most prevailing topic: then ladies descanted on organs of destructiveness, amativeness, and half a dozen other organs with equally discordant terminations: and then gentlemen might have been seen expressing their desires to feel ladies' bumps, for the sake of theory, and for the general promotion of philosophical knowledge. This laudable investigation was superseded by a mineralogical discussion; and here the ladies were again of service, illustrating the subject by a loan of their jewels. Then, when it had been sufficiently debated whether diamond was carbon, or carbon was diamond; whether iron was the colouring matter of amethyst, and what was the base of topaz, the different necklaces and bracelets were returned to the lovely necks and wrists of their respective owners, by the practical philosophers nearest to them.

With all this scientific conversation and practical illustration, Mortimer was delighted: and the elation of the moment inspired him with sufficient courage to address Lady d'Elmont.

" Pray, is your ladyship fond of chemistry?"

" Dotingly; I am a regular attendant at Mr. Brande's lectures."

Quemque sua trahit voluptas: Mortimer was now on his hobby-horse, and most gallantly did he prance away.

" He is a delightful lecturer; clear, scientific, and elegant."

" I perfectly agree with you."

" What branch of chemistry does your ladyship peculiarly like to study? The salts, the metals, the gases, the earths, the alkalies, or what?"

" I think I am particularly partial to the experiments on oxygen and carbon."

" Do you believe diamond to be the real base of carbon?"

"I do not know; I sometimes think it is. You may easily, however, resolve your doubts by consuming a diamond under a burning-glass; you will then get at the fact synthetically."

"I am sorry to say that I do not possess so many diamonds, that I am inclined to waste any of them."

"Pardon me, your ladyship has an inexhaustible mine of them—in your eyes."

"Sir, you are a flatterer."

"I only speak what I feel, madam."

"And sometimes, perhaps, *look* even more than you *speak*."

"*Perhaps*—I wish, like old Fontenelle and his fair marchioness, you would allow me to take you under my tuition, and give you lectures in chemistry. I have made the science my especial study; and if you would engage to be as tractable as the marchioness, I would endeavour to be as instructive as the old philosopher."

"And possibly as gallant, too?—However, to save you your compliments, I will tell you that they would be all wasted. When I was young, and perhaps pretty, I was, doubtlessly, as prone to vanity as others of my age; but *now*"—pausing on the now, with an affected sigh, a radiant glance at Mortimer, and then a half arch and half complacent one at her own fine person—"but now, I have grown mistrustful of praise, and hard of heart. As Schiller says, ' The perjuries of men are innumerable; an angel would grow gray ere he could write them down.' Besides, too, I consider love an odious, enervating passion."

"O! say not so, madam: love to a woman is like varnish to a picture; it modifies all her indifferent qualities, and enhances all her good. A woman really, truly in love, is a thousand times more amiable in the eyes of——"

"Her lover than in those of any body else. I agree with you perfectly. My ideas of a lovesick damsel are always connected with something *sonneteering*, *pale-faced*, and *affected;* and with all my heart, I pity those natures inflammable——"

"Now that's just what I say, my lady," cried a stentorian voice opposite to them; "its nature *must* be inflammable; for if the oxygen do not burn——"

"Her ladyship, I am sure," eagerly interrupted his opponent, "sees the utter fallacy of your argument."

"Sir, I have never argued at all—you won't let me——"

"I say," continued his inflexible adversary, "the oxygen, my lady——"

"I say," vociferated the other, "the *nitrogen*, my lady——"

"And I say," exclaimed an old fat gentleman, who had been talking incessantly for the previous two hours, "that nobody will let me speak! I say, that the most beautiful specimen of combustion I ever witnessed was at the French opera the other night."

"Do you mean the red flame that——"

"To be sure I do!" cried the fat gentleman; and then grumbled sotto voce, "how people do love talking—I say that you have no idea of the effect of this red flame—the Parisians are all quite wild about it, and introduce it in every spectacle piece."

"I saw it!" exclaimed a little red-skinned man, whose tiny nose was the centre of a circle described by the outline of his forehead, cheeks, and chin; and whose whole face, in fact, would have served as an excellent substitute for Gibbon's, in engendering Madame du Deffand's extraordinary idea. " I saw it! and I candidly own, that my evidence is completely confirmatory of the prolocutor's; the red flame is wonderful."

" O," cried the Lady d'Elmont, " pray tell me where I can get some of this miraculous flame, for I intend, when I return to ——, to get up Don Giovanni at my theatre there; and how excellently and delightfully such a magnificent light as you describe would aid the effect of his descent with the ghost. I declare, it will be so charming, I think we must make him, if we can, go to the—you know where—*twice* in the same evening."

" I am sorry that I cannot gratify your ladyship's curiosity," replied the " prolocutor," as the circular-faced gentleman termed him, " but the composition of the powder that produces the flame is a profound secret; one for which the inventor asks an almost incredible sum."

" O," exclaimed the baroness, her desires particularly excited by this unexpected opposition to their gratification, " I would give the world to get some of it."

" Would you?" cried Mortimer, eagerly; " then you shall have some within a few minutes, and as much as you can desire in a few days; that is, if you will be kind enough to allow me to send one of your servants to my hotel, which is only a score of yards from hence."

Of course, the permission was readily accorded, and in a few minutes the servant returned, bearing a small piece of folded paper, which he delivered to Mortimer; who opened, and displayed to her ladyship about three or four ounces of a grey-coloured powder.

" This," cried he, " is the source of the ' red flame'

that these gentlemen have been describing to you. The moment I heard of its wonderful effects, I set strenuously to work to discover its composition; and knowing, of course, that hyper-oxy-muriate of potash must form a principal portion, after a fortnight's incessant labour, I at length discovered the secret. Now, should your ladyship like to see a small portion of it burnt, which I can easily effect on the back of one of these plates?"

" I should be delighted," replied Lady d'Elmont.

" And so should I!"—" And so should I!" echoed some score of half-starved wanderers, whom the emptiness of their stomachs rendered locomotive.

" Well, then," replied Mortimer, " I will immediately have the pleasure of gratifying your ladyship;" and he inverted a plate on a table in the centre of the room, and proceeded to arrange his materials; his friend, Bryant, at his elbow, vainly counselling him to desist.

In the mean time there circulated among the company enough reports of ' red flame,' ' handsome young man,' ' only son,' and ' ten thousand per annum,' to bring more than half of them round the spot where our hero was stationed: for such, at any rate, in his present situation, he may with propriety be designated.

Immediately over Mortimer's head hung an immense chandelier; all the lights of which, with the exception of some half dozen or so, he, with the consent of Lady d'Elmont, and in order to enhance the effect and splendor of his flame, desired to be extinguished. All the candles too were then removed.

Mortimer having distributed a certain portion of the powder on the plate, and deposited the rest in the paper on the table, rested for a moment over his labours, the great object of attraction, scrutiny, scandal, quizzing, and admiration to all of that immense assemblage, who were conscious of what was proceeding. Then lighting his paper, he slowly applied it to the powder, when, alas! alas! instead of red flames and beautiful coruscations, the powder violently exploded, and communicating with the large residue in the paper, ascended in a huge volume of brilliant flame to the ceiling; totally extinguishing the lights in the chandelier, and leaving the room in utter darkness.

The first impulse of each was, of course, to stand motionless and aghast with astonishment; the second, to rush towards the door as rapidly as possible; which all doing simultaneously, the pressure upon it closed it as effectually as though it had been barred with hooks of steel. In vain those near it struggled and struggled to open it; they could scarcely move a hand, much more the door.

Conceive, then, if you can, tender-hearted reader, the uncomfortable situation of three or four hundred people thus caged together in utter darkness. Conceive, if you can, the feelings, the ideas, the sensations, the fears, the distresses, and apprehensions of the many virtuous and delicate females present. Conceive, too, the sudden alteration of character; the instantaneous exchange of all the fashion of inertness and listlessness for all the vulgarity of activity and excitement; the squeezing of the *élégantes*, and the elbowing of the transcendents; in fact, imagine that, like a fiat from Heaven, the extinction of a few candles tore from each the mask of factitiousness, and laid her bare in all her native beauty, or deformity.

As to the sensations of the gentlemen, I will not attempt

to describe them; they are too acute, too susceptible, too sensitive, and too delicate to be communicable to an unknown, who might not duly appreciate the candour of my exposition.

However, to increase, if possible, this general scene of confusion and misfortune, a spark remaining in the ashes of the powder lighted an unconsumed portion of it, which, slightly exploding, brilliantly flamed, and then disappeared; after having illuminated the room for a few seconds, and set fire to some drapery about the table, to two or three gowns, and to a most ample, frizzy, oily, and inflammable wig of the gentleman like Mr. Gibbon, the celebrated historian of the Decline and Fall of the Roman Empire.

The moment this unhappy gentleman felt the fire at his head, with all his might he beat it, and another might have assisted him without injury to its contents; but as this did not succeed in extinguishing the flame, like a maniac, he forced his headlong way through the crowd, kindly imparting in his progress a portion of his superfluous warmth to all the inflammable materials within his reach, until he attained one of the windows, which being open at the top, in the phrensied hope of escape, he began to climb, setting instantaneously the whole of the light curtain drapery in one universal blaze. Finding matters, therefore, rather hotter in that quarter even than below, he turned his mind towards a descent; when, alas! and again alas! he became at that moment a beacon to a passing fire-engine without, the conductors of which seeing flames and smoke issuing from a window, began to pump with the utmost promptitude against the body of the unfortunate circular-faced gentleman, who, after a due quantity of soaking, burning, kicking, and screaming, was at length washed headlong into the room, a miserable addition to the comforts of his companions, leaving at the window a convenient vacancy for the triumphant entrance of a magnificent stream of water, of more than one inch in diameter, and three in circumference!

The moment the splashings from the body of the unfortunate circular-faced gentleman touched the ladies and their clothes, those theorists who were not thoroughly acquainted with the capabilities of the female voice internally pronounced the noise to be at its climax, conceiving that neither human nor mechanical means could increase it; but when the water in torrents, and a man into the bargain, were rained into the room, the aforesaid theorists penitently confessed themselves to be totally mistaken in their conjectures, and frankly and ingenuously added that they did not think all hell itself could make such an uproar.

Thanks to the discriminate selection of the firemen, the window broken was in the very centre of the room, and thus commanded a perfect range of the whole crowd within. Some of them sought refuge beneath the tables, and thus partly escaped; some got under the window itself, and allowed the torrent to pass over them, and some forcibly endeavoured to shelter themselves behind others. Vain were threats, tears, and supplications to stop the horrid spouting; the more they cried, the more the men pumped; for though the flames had disappeared from the window, the inconceivable noise within convinced the inveterate pumpers without that the fire must still rage somewhere. So they continued with the most obstinate diligence, till every one of their unfortunate victims was literally drenched to the bone.

It is hardly possible, indeed, to convey to the mind by description the confusion and disasters of that unparalleled scene. The fine statues and jellies, the diamond necklaces and blanc-manges, the bruised shins and bleeding noses, the bottles, slippers, turbans, wine, and false hair; the legs of women and legs of tables, arms of men and arms of chairs, all blended together in one inextricable combination. Add to this, the struggling, quarrelling, weeping, reproaching, regretting, and the soaking to boot, and yet, even then, the picture will fall far short of the reality.

At last, by the time the floor of this once magnificent room was ankle deep in water, the servants and people without managed to force an entry into it with lights; when forth rushed the victims in every variety of plight, from that of tolerable misery down to the extremity of desolation and despair.

Changed, indeed, was their appearance, as wildly they rushed down the grand stairs, from that which they had made when they last stood on them. One lady, who, when she ascended them, had been particularly noticed for her auburn silken locks, *mirabile dictu*, descended them without any hair at all. Another, who had all the evening acted Thalia, to show a beautiful row of pearly teeth, stalked down them Melpomene, in the vain hope of hiding her toothless gums. In fact, she that had gone in fair, walked out brown; and she that had been straight, limped out crooked. Like the alchymist's crucible, the events of the evening had transmuted fair into foul, and bad into worse; and I doubt whether husband, brother, or father could have recognised his property as she made her luckless exit from Lady d'Elmont's famous party.

Thus ended this eventful night, which, strange to say, made little noise at the time, and less since. All the papers spoke of the splendor of Lady d'Elmont's party, but not a word about the red flame. How the secret was so well kept has often been matter of surprise to me; but perhaps the disgrace was too universal, and too equal, for any to desire to promulgate it. Curious, however, as is the circumstance, it is a positive fact, that few knew the particulars of the occurrence in *that* day; and in *this*, I 'll venture to say, that scarcely one of my readers has ever even heard of it at all.

WHAT IS LOVE?

BY M. L.

Love is the passion which endureth,
Which neither time nor absence cureth;
Which nought of earthly change can sever:
Love is the light which shines for ever.

What cold and selfish breasts deem madness
Lives in its depths of joy and sadness:
In hearts, on lips, of flame it burneth;
One is its world—to *one* it turneth.

Its chain of gold—what hand can break it?
Its deathless hold—what force can shake it?
Mere passion aught of earth may sever,
But *souls* that love—love on for ever.

STANZAS,

ADDRESSED TO R. M.W. TURNER, ESQ. R.A. ON HIS VIEW OF
THE LAGO MAGGIORE FROM THE TOWN OF ARONA.

BY ROBERT SOUTHEY.

TURNER, thy pencil brings to mind a day
   When from Laveno and the Beuscer hill
I over Lake Verbanus held my way
   In pleasant fellowship, with wind at will;
Smooth were the waters wide, the sky serene,
And our hearts gladden'd with the joyful scene.

Joyful,—for all things minister'd delight,—
   The lake and land, the mountains and the vales:
The Alps their snowy summits rear'd in light,
   Tempering with gelid breath the summer gales;
And verdant shores and woods refresh'd the eye
That else had ached beneath that brilliant sky.

To that elaborate island were we bound
   Of yore the scene of Borromean pride,—
Folly's prodigious work; where all around,
   Under its coronet and self-belied,
Look where you will you cannot choose but see
The obtrusive motto's proud "HUMILITY!"

Far off the Borromean saint was seen,
   Distinct though distant, o'er his native town,
Where his Colossus with benignant mien
   Looks from its station on Arona down:
To it the inland sailor lifts his eyes,
From the wide lake, when perilous storms arise.

Drawn by J.M.W. Turner. R.A.

Engraved by W.R. Smith.

LAGO MAGGIORE.

Published for the Proprietor by Hurst, Chance, & Cº Stª Paul's Churchyard & R. Jennings. Poultry.

Printed by Mª Queen.

But no storm threaten'd on that summer-day;
　The whole rich scene appear'd for joyance made;
With many a gliding bark the mere was gay—
　The fields and groves in all their wealth array'd:
I could have thought the sun beheld with smiles
Those towns and palaces and populous isles.

From fair Arona, even on such a day,
　When gladness was descending like a shower,
Great painter, did thy gifted eye survey
　The splendid scene; and, conscious of its power,
Well hath thine hand inimitable given
The glories of the lake, and land, and heaven.

IMPROMPTU,

ON A POET WHO WAS COMPELLED BY POVERTY TO LODGE WITH A TAILOR.

BY F. M. REYNOLDS.

O, how cruelly fortune the poet misuses;
　He labours, and writes, and does all that he can,
Till, rejected and scorn'd by a Ninth of the Muses,
　He's forced to put up with the *Ninth of a Man!*

SKETCH OF A FRAGMENT OF THE HISTORY OF THE NINETEENTH CENTURY.

BY J. M.

[In the following sketch an attempt has been made to adopt the temper with which the writer believes that some events and persons of our time may be considered by a future historian; though with a conviction that it is impossible for him to reach that temper, and with a deep consciousness of the want of other qualification for the task which he thus ventures to undertake.]

THE wars of religious opinion continued to agitate Europe from the preaching of Luther in 1517 till the conclusion of the treaty of Westphalia in 1648, by which the security of both the catholic and protestant religions in Germany became a part of the European system. Perhaps indeed the religious contest may rather be said to close with the establishment of catholic intolerance in France, by the revocation of the edict of Nantz in 1685, and with that of protestant supremacy in the British islands by the reduction of Ireland in 1691; two events which prolonged for more than a century, in the former case the proscription, and in the latter the prostration of an obnoxious and vanquished communion.

The wars of political opinion which first disturbed British America in 1775, and in fourteen years afterwards broke out with more violence in France, of all countries subject to absolute power that where reason was most active and knowledge most diffused, raged with little remission for twenty-five years in the successive forms of a struggle to spread democracy over Europe, and of an attempt to impose on it a revolutionary dictatorship. They paused in 1814, when the restoration of the Bourbons to a limited authority, under a legal constitution, laid the foundation of peace between royalists and constitutionalists. Their source, however, lay so deep, that in ten years afterwards they shook the most distant regions where there was any fellow-feeling with the European spirit; severed Spanish America from Spain, and consumed the Turkish fetters, which for three centuries had galled the unhappy Greeks. The shocks of the same commotion, repeatedly felt in the Italian and Spanish peninsulas, being either weaker or counteracted by other intestine agents, were for the time compressed from without.

Mr. Canning was the first English minister who attempted to compose the general disorder by mediation between the contending parties. Probably the tempest must have so far spent its force before it was reasonable to entertain serious thoughts of such an arduous attempt... the fullness of time had not perhaps even then come: for a mediator is odious to all combatants till their strength be exhausted, and their pride and hatred subdued by necessity.

The coincidence of some particulars of Mr. Canning's public life with the history of an eminent contemporary in France, is not unworthy of observation, as an instance of the power of the general movements of mankind to dispose men in different countries, without concert, with unequal abilities, with little resemblance of character or fortune, to shape some remarkable parts of their political course alike. A coincidence of this sort may be offered as an example of the fainter and more obscure influence of such a series of revolutions on the temper and opinion of the majority of their contemporaries.

Both Mr. Canning and M. de Chateaubriant were enter-ing on man's estate when the states general of France were called together. They both partook, in unequal de-grees, the prevalent opinions from which the revolution sprung. In neither of them were these opinions embraced after such experience, or so much confirmed by habit, as to render subsequent modifications of them an indication of culpable levity; still less in themselves a ground for more grave reproach. The alienation from religion, which the alliance of church and state in despotic countries had blended with the reforming spirit, was soon thrown off by M. de Chateaubriant, and had never touched Mr. Canning. Both became rather the foremost champions than the leaders of the anti-revolutionary party in their respective countries; and they retained that station as long as any heavings of the original revolution were perceived by them. Their opposition was bold, and their language and measures were such as afterwards to supply their adversaries with charges of inconsistency, which might be explained, but could hardly be contradicted. M. de Chateaubriant con-curred in the invasion of Spain in 1823, at a moment when the unwise institutions but merciful measures of the Spanish leaders furnished no just ground of alarm and aggression. That invasion was loudly condemned by Mr. Canning, though he shrunk from so near an advance to the verge of war as might perhaps have prevented it. Soon after, when the reforming spirit was moderated, and its opponents struggled for the unreasonable retention or the oppressive exercise of power, both considered the grounds of difference to be so altered, that consistency allowed and reason required them to approach more and more near to the more cautious portion of the party then called liberal.

In conformity with this principle, when the general election of 1827 had manifested the unshaken adherence of France to a free government, M. de Chateaubriant contributed to form a moderate administration, in which he brought some royalists to take a share : as Mr. Canning some months before placed himself at the head of a government more liberal in its spirit, though less decisive in its domestic policy than that of France. For their unequal shares in these ministerial changes, both were assailed by their former associates with the bitterness of personal resentment rather than with the warmth of political opposition. Both were men of letters; though the compositions of Mr. Canning were all occasional, and it were presumption in a foreigner to question the justice of the admiration of the French nation for the larger and more elaborate writings of M. de Chateaubriant. Adverse, perhaps impartial criticism, considered the eloquence of both as too florid; though an English critic must add, that the adorned diction of Mr. Canning, if not exempted from profusion and display, is untainted with affectation.

Here the comparison, perhaps too long continued, must finally close. When Mr. Canning, in 1822, assumed the conduct of foreign affairs and of the House of Commons, he adopted measures and disclosed views which had no parallel among contemporary ministers. The wish, indeed, that England should retire into a more neutral station, and assume a more mediatorial attitude than perhaps her share in the alliance against France could before have easily allowed, had then become so prevalent, that even his predecessor, though entangled in another policy, showed no doubtful marks of a desire to change his course. Perhaps little could have been done to give it effect until all reasonable royalists were taught by experience that the passion for reformation was too deeply rooted to be torn up by force, and till the eagerness of inexperienced nations for sudden and violent changes had been chastised by defeat. In the five years which followed, the plan for re-establishing the tranquillity of Europe, by balancing the force and reconciling the pretensions of the parties then openly or secretly agitating every country, which probably arose by slow degrees in Mr. Canning's mind as circumstance became auspicious, and as his own power was more consolidated, began to be carried into execution by three measures, of which the spirit, object, and example were yet more important than the immediate effects; namely, the recognition of the Spanish republics in America, the aid to Portugal, with the countenance thereby afforded to limited monarchy in that country, and the treaty concluded with Russia and France for the rescue and preservation of Greece. The last of these transactions will now be considered as the most memorable, and as that which best illustrates the comprehensive policy towards which he at length approached. It was a measure eminently pacific, which aimed at the lasting establishment of amity between states, and peace between parties, and which, if executed with spirit, was likely to avoid the inconvenience even of a slight and short rupture with the Ottoman Porte itself. It engaged royalists and liberals in an enterprise on which the majority of both concurred; it tended to knit more closely the ties of friendship between the most powerful governments, and to fasten more firmly the bands between rulers and nations, by uniting the former for an object generally acceptable to the latter. It combined the lustre of a generous enterprise with the greatest probability of preventing the unsafe aggrandizement of any state. In the midst of these high designs, and before that pacific alliance, of which the liberation of Greece was to be the cement, had acquired consistence, Mr. Canning was cut off. He left his system, and much of his fame, at the mercy of his successors.

Without invidious comparison, it may be safely said that from the circumstances in which he died, his death was more generally interesting among civilized nations, than that, of any other English statesman had ever been. It was an event in the internal history of every country. From Lima to Athens, every nation struggling for independence or existence was filled by it with sorrow and dismay. The Miguelites of Portugal, the apostolicals of Spain, the Jesuitical faction in France, and the Divan of Constantinople, raised a shout of joy at the fall of their dreaded enemy. He was regretted by all who, heated by no personal or party resentment, felt for genius struck down in the act of attempting to heal the revolutionary distemper, and to render future improvements pacific:—on the principle since successfully adopted by more fortunate, though not more deserving, ministers; that of a deep and thorough compromise between the interests and the opinions, the prejudices and the demands of the supporters of establishment, and the followers of reformation.

* * * * * * * *

The family of Mr. Canning, which for more than a century had filled honourable stations in Ireland, was a younger branch of an ancient family among the English gentry. His father, a man of letters, was disinherited for an imprudent marriage, and the inheritance went to a younger brother, whose son was afterwards created Lord Garvagh. Mr. Canning was educated at Eton and Oxford, according to that exclusively classical system, which, whatever may have been its defects, must be owned, when taken with its constant appendages, to be eminently favourable to the cultivation of sense and taste, as well as to the developement of wit and spirit. From his boyhood he was the foremost among very distinguished contemporaries, and continued to be regarded as the best specimen, and the most brilliant representative of that eminently national education. His youthful eye sparkled with quickness and arch pleasantry, and his countenance early betrayed that jealousy of his own dignity, and sensibility to suspected disregard, which were afterwards softened, but never quite subdued. Neither the habits of a great school, nor those of a popular assembly, were calculated to weaken his love of praise and passion for distinction. But, as he advanced in years, his fine countenance was ennobled by the expression of thought and feeling; he more pursued that lasting praise, which is not to be earned without praiseworthiness; and, if he continued to be a lover of fame, he also passionately loved the glory of his country. Even He who almost alone was entitled to look down on fame as " That last infirmity of noble mind," had not forgotten that it was

> " The spur that the clear spirit doth raise,
> To scorn delights, and live laborious days *."

The natural bent of character is perhaps better ascertained from the undisturbed and unconscious play of the mind in the common intercourse of society, than from its movements under the power of strong interest or warm passions in public life. In social intercourse Mr. Canning was delightful. Happily for the true charm of his conversation, he was too busy otherwise, not to treat society as more

* Lycidas.

fitted for relaxation than display. It is but little to say, that he was neither disputatious, declamatory, nor sententious; neither a dictator, nor a jester. His manner was simple and unobtrusive, his language always quite familiar. If a higher thought stole from his mind, it came in its conversational undress. From this plain ground his pleasantry sprung with the happiest effect, and it was nearly exempt from that alloy of taunt and banter, which he sometimes mixed with more precious materials in public contest. He may be added to the list of those eminent persons who pleased most in their friendly circle. He had the agreeable quality of being more easily pleased in society, than might have been expected from the keenness of his discernment, and the sensibility of his temper. He was liable to be discomposed, or even silenced, by the presence of any one whom he did not like. His manner in society betrayed the political vexations or anxieties which preyed on his mind, nor could he conceal that sensitiveness to public attacks which their frequent recurrence wears out in most English politicians. These last foibles may be thought interesting as the remains of natural character, not destroyed by refined society and political affairs. He was assailed by some adversaries so ignoble as to wound him through his filial affection, which preserved its respectful character through the whole course of his advancement. The ardent zeal for his memory, which appeared immediately after his death, attests the warmth of those domestic affections which seldom prevail where they are not mutual. To his touching epitaph on his son parental love has given a charm which is wanting in his other verses. It was said of him at one time, that no man had so little popularity and such affectionate friends, and the truth was certainly more sacrificed to point in the former than in the latter member of the contrast. Some of his friendships continued in spite of political differences, which, by rendering intercourse less unconstrained, often undermine friendship; and others were remarkable for a warmth, constancy, and disinterestedness, which, though chiefly honourable to those who were capable of so pure a kindness, yet redound to the credit of him who was the object of it. No man is so beloved who is not himself formed for friendship.

Notwithstanding his disregard for money, he was not tempted in youth by the example or the kindness of affluent friends much to overstep his little patrimony. He never afterwards sacrificed to parade or personal indulgence; though his occupations scarcely allowed him to think enough of his private affairs. Even from his moderate fortune, his bounty was often liberal to suitors to whom official relief could not be granted. By a sort of generosity still harder for him to practise, he endeavoured, in cases where the suffering was great, though the suit could not be granted, to satisfy the feelings of the suitor by full explanation in writing of the causes which rendered compliance impracticable. Wherever he took an interest, he showed it as much by delicacy to the feelings of those whom he served or relieved, as by substantial consideration for their claims: a rare and most praiseworthy merit among men in power.

In proportion as the opinion of a people acquires influence over public affairs, the faculty of persuading men to support or oppose political measures, acquires importance. The peculiar nature of parliamentary debate contributes to render eminence in that province not so imperfect a test of political ability as it might appear to be. Recited

speeches can seldom show more than powers of reasoning
and imagination, which have little connexion with a capacity for affairs. But the unforeseen events of debate,
and the necessity of immediate answer in unpremeditated
language, afford scope for quickness, firmness, boldness,
wariness, presence of mind, and address in the management of men, which are among the qualities most essential
to a statesman. The most flourishing period of our parliamentary eloquence extends for about half a century, from
the maturity of Lord Chatham's genius to the death of
Mr. Fox. During the twenty years which succeeded, Mr.
Canning was sometimes the leader, and always the greatest
orator of the party who supported the administration:
among whom he was supported, but not rivalled, by able
men, against opponents who were not thought by him inconsiderable, of whom one, at least, was felt by every hearer,
and acknowledged in private by himself, to have always
forced his faculties into their very uttermost stretch.

Had he been a dry and meagre speaker, he would have
been universally allowed to be one of the greatest masters
of argument; but his hearers were so dazzled by the
splendour of his diction, that they did not perceive the
acuteness and the sometimes excessive refinement of his
reasoning; a consequence which, as it shows the injurious
influence of a seductive fault, can with the less justice be
overlooked in the estimate of his understanding. Ornament, it must be owned, when it only pleases or amuses,
without disposing the audience to adopt the sentiments of
the speaker, is an offence against the first law of public
speaking, of which it obstructs instead of promoting the
only reasonable purpose. But eloquence is a widely extended art, comprehending many sorts of excellence, in
some of which, ornamented diction is more liberally em-

ployed than in others, and in none of which the highest
rank can be attained without an extraordinary combination
of mental powers.   Among our own orators Mr. Canning
seems to be the best model of the adorned style.   The
splendid and sublime descriptions of Mr. Burke, his comprehensive and profound views of general principle, though
they must ever delight and instruct the readers, must be
owned to have been digressions which diverted the minds
of the hearers from the object on which the speaker ought
to have kept them steadily fixed.   Sheridan, a man of
admirable sense, and matchless wit, laboured to follow
Burke into the foreign regions of feeling and grandeur,
where the specimens preserved of his most celebrated
speeches show too much of the exaggeration and excess to
which those are peculiarly liable who seek by art and effort
what nature has denied.   By the constant part which Mr.
Canning took in debate, he was called upon to show a
knowledge which Sheridan did not possess, and a readiness
which that accomplished man had no such means of
strengthening and displaying.   In some qualities of style
Mr. Canning surpassed Mr. Pitt.   His diction was more
various, sometimes more simple, more idiomatical even in
its more elevated parts.   It sparkled with imagery, and was
brightened by illustration, in both of which Mr. Pitt for
so great an orator was defective.

  Mr. Canning possessed in a high degree the outward
advantages of an orator.   His expressive countenance
varied with the changes of his eloquence; his voice,
flexible and articulate, had as much compass as his mode
of speaking required.   In the calm part of his speeches,
his attitude and gesture might have been selected by a
painter to represent grace rising towards dignity.

  No English speaker used the keen and brilliant weapon

of wit so long, so often, or so effectively, as Mr. Canning. He gained more triumphs and incurred more enmity by it than any other. Those whose importance depends much on birth and fortune, are impatient of seeing their own artificial dignity, or that of their order, broken down by derision; and perhaps few men heartily forgive a successful jest against themselves, but those who are conscious of being unhurt by it. Mr. Canning often used this talent imprudently. In sudden flashes of wit, and in the playful description of men or things, he was often distinguished by that natural felicity which is the charm of pleasantry; to which the air of art and labour is more fatal than to any other talent. Sheridan was sometimes betrayed, by an imitation of the dialogue of his master, Congreve, into a sort of laboured and finished jesting, so balanced and expanded, as sometimes to vie in tautology and monotony with the once applauded triads of Johnson, and which, even in its most happy passages, is more sure of commanding serious admiration than hearty laugher. It cannot be denied that Mr. Canning's taste was, in this respect, somewhat influenced by the example of his early friend.

There are some of his speeches which deserve notice, as evincing powers which he did not ordinarily exert. At the beginning of the discussion, in 1811, on the resumption of cash payments by the bank of England, he was so little acquainted with the subject, as to be a stranger to its elementary terms. He so profited, however, by the friendly conversation of a master of the science, that his two speeches on that question were numbered among his most successful exertions. In them his exposition was simple and clear. His fancy was content with supplying illustration, and even his wit was confined to exposing to ridicule what he proved to be absurd.

Nothing could better prove the imperfect education of English statesmen at that time, and the capacity of Mr. Canning to master subjects the least agreeable to his pursuits and inclinations.

On the vote of thanks to the Marquis of Hastings, he related the events of the Indian war with a clearness, order, and rapidity, which gave occasion to his speech being called, in the debate, the most beautiful model of spoken history. In his speeches during the session in which he was appointed governor-general of India, the thought that he was about to leave his country, and was bidding farewell to the assembly which was the scene of his fame, seemed to have softened his asperities as well as chastened his diction, with an increase of uninterrupted power over his audience, which showed how very little more restraint on temper and fancy was wanting to enlarge and prolong his ascendant as a speaker, and to teach the public a more just conception of the virtues for which he was, with so much justice, beloved. Into the few unseemly expressions, which would have subjected a man of less known humanity to more serious imputation, he was seduced by the poignancy, or sometimes by the quaintness of phrases, which, on that account also, were more circulated and more resented.

The exuberance of fancy and wit lessened the gravity of his general manner, and perhaps also indisposed the audience to feel his earnestness where it clearly showed itself. In that important quality he was inferior to Mr. Pitt,

> " Deep on whose front engraven,
> Deliberation sat, and public care;"

and not less inferior to Mr. Fox, whose fervid eloquence flowed from the love of his country, the scorn of baseness, and the hatred of cruelty, which were the ruling passions of his nature. On the whole, it may be observed, that the range of Mr. Canning's powers as an orator was wider than that in which he usually exerted them. When mere statement only was allowable, no man of his age was more simple. When infirm health compelled him to be brief, no speaker could compress his matter with so little sacrifice of clearness, ease, and elegance. In his speech on colonial reformation in 1823, he seemed to have brought down the philosophical principles and the moral sentiments of Mr. Burke, to that precise level where they could be happily blended with a grave and dignified speech, intended as an introduction to a new system of legislation. As his oratorical faults were those of youthful genius, the progress of age seemed to purify his eloquence, and every year appeared to remove some speck which hid, or, at least, dimmed a beauty. He daily rose to larger views, and made, perhaps, as near approaches to philosophical principles as the great difference between the objects of the philosopher, and those, of the orator will commonly allow.

When the memorials of his own time, the composition of which he is said never to have interrupted in his busiest moments, are made known to the public, his abilities as a writer may be better estimated. His only known writings in prose are State Papers, which, when considered as the composition of a minister for foreign affairs, in one of the most extraordinary periods of European history, are undoubtedly of no small importance. Such of these papers as were intended to be a direct appeal to the judgment of mankind, combine so much precision, with such uniform circumspection and dignity, that they must ever be studied as models of that very difficult species of composition. His Instructions to

Ministers Abroad on occasions both perplexing and momentous will be found to exhibit a rare union of comprehensive and elevated views, with singular ingenuity in devising means of execution; on which last faculty he sometimes relied perhaps more confidently than the short and dim foresight of man will warrant. " Great affairs," says Lord Bacon, " are commonly too coarse and stubborn to be worked upon by the fine edges and points of wit*." His papers in negotiation were occasionally somewhat too controversial in their tone. They are not near enough to the manner of an amicable conversation about a disputed point of business, in which a negotiator does not so much draw out his argument, as hint his own object, and sound the intention of his opponent. He sometimes seems to pursue triumph more than advantage, and not enough to remember that to leave the opposite party satisfied with what he has got, and in good humour with himself, is not one of the least proofs of a negotiator's skill. Where the papers were intended ultimately to reach the public through parliament, it might be prudent to regard chiefly the final object; and when this excuse was wanting, much must be pardoned to the controversial habits of a parliamentary life. It is hard for a debater to be a negotiator. The faculty of guiding public assemblies is very remote from the art of dealing with individuals.

Mr. Canning's power of writing verse may rather be classed with his accomplishments, than numbered among his high and noble faculties. It would have been a distinction for an inferior man. His verses were far above those of Cicero, of Burke, and of Bacon. The taste

---

* It may be proper to remind the reader, that here the word " wit" is used in its ancient sense.

prevalent in his youth led him to more relish for sententious declaimers in verse than is shared by lovers of the
more true poetry of imagination and sensibility. In some
respects his poetical compositions were also influenced by
his early intercourse with Mr. Sheridan, though he was
restrained by his more familiar contemplation of classical
models from the glittering conceits of that extraordinary
man. Something of an artificial and composite diction is
discernible in the English poems of those who have acquired
reputation by Latin verse, more especially since the pursuit
of rigid purity has required so timid an imitation as not
only to confine itself to the words, but to adopt none but
the phrases of ancient poets; an effect of which Gray must
be allowed to furnish an example.

Absolute silence about Mr. Canning's writings as a
political satirist, which were for their hour so popular,
might be imputed to undue timidity. In that character
he yielded to General Fitzpatrick in arch stateliness and
poignant raillery; to Mr. Moore in the gay prodigality with
which he squanders his countless stores of wit; and to his
own friend Mr. Frere in the richness of a native vein of
original and fantastic drollery. In that ungenial province,
where the brightest of the hasty laurels are apt very soon
to fade, and where Dryden only boasts immortal lays, it
is perhaps his best praise, that there is no writing of his,
which a man of honour might not avow as soon as the
first heat of contest was past.

In some of the amusements or tasks of his boyhood
there are passages which, without much help from fancy,
might appear to contain allusions to his greatest measures
of policy, as well as to the tenor of his life, and to the
melancholy splendor which surrounded his death. In the

concluding line of the first English verses written by him at Eton, he expressed a wish, which has been singularly realised, that he might

" Live in a blaze, and in a blaze expire."

It is at least a striking coincidence, that the statesman, whose dying measure was to mature an alliance for the deliverance of Greece, should, when a boy, have written English verses on the slavery of that country; and that in his prize poem at Oxford, on the Pilgrimage to Mecca, a composition as much applauded as a modern Latin poem can aspire to be, he should have as bitterly deplored the lot of other renowned countries, now groaning under the same barbarous yoke.

Nunc Satrapæ imperio et sævo subdita Turcæ *.

To conclude:—he was a man of fine and brilliant genius, of warm affections, of high and generous spirit; a statesman, who, at home, converted most of his opponents into warm supporters; who, abroad, was the sole hope and trust of all who sought an orderly and legal liberty; and who was cut off in the midst of vigorous and splendid measures, which, if executed by himself, or with his own spirit, promised to place his name in the first class of rulers, among the founders of lasting peace, and the guardians of human improvement.

* Iter. ad Meccam, Oxford, 1789.

LIFE'S DAY.

BY W. JERDAN.

My friends of the morning are gone!
They have fall'n away, one after one;
  My friends of the morning of life!
When the distant mists roll'd off before us,
And the sun in his splendour shone o'er us,
And bliss sped but more bliss to restore us:
  All are gone with the morning of life!

My loves of the noontide are fled;
My soul's sole worshipp'd idol is dead;
  And the warmth of the noontide is cold!
When each gay passion brighten'd the eye,
And the deep only love heaved its sigh,
And the heart gush'd in full tides of joy:
  All are fled, all for ever are cold.

My calm of the evening is past;
Like the morn and the noon perish'd fast;
  Of feelings the still, dreamy end:
And the last ray of sunshine's faint rose,
Stain'd, but cheer'd not, the shades of repose—
'Tis in heav'n, not in earth, that it glows,
  As dull evening sinks down to the end.

And the night's darkness clips me around,
Close-girdling, enthralling, profound,
  The dreary descent to the tomb:
Where the morn's tints shall all be forgot,
Where the noon's heat shall penetrate not,
Where the eve's gather'd harvest shall rot,—
  Untroubled the rest of the tomb.

DESCRIPTION OF THE ENGRAVING ENTITLED A SCENE AT ABBOTSFORD.

BY THE AUTHOR OF WAVERLEY.

THE general idea of this spirited representation of animals and ancient armour is taken from a small apartment, at Abbotsford, near Melrose; which, from the peculiar tastes of the owner, as an admirer of animals and a collector of antiquities, often exhibits similar scenes.

The large dog, which forms the principal figure in the group, is the portrait of a very fine animal of the rare species called the deer, or sometimes the wolf, greyhound. The race was carefully preserved by the late MacDonnell of Glengarry, whose zeal for preserving the sports and manners of the ancient Highlanders, will be long remembered amidst his native mountains. In order to prevent that degeneracy which always attends breeding animals *in-and-in*, as it is expressed by agriculturists, Glengarry was in the habit of crossing the breed of the highland greyhound, with the blood-hound from Cuba, and the Spanish sheep-dog; renowned for its size, strength, and courage. Maida, which was the name of the dog in question, was of this last breed, his sire being a dog from the Pyrenees, of the largest size, and his dam, a very fine highland greyhound. While in his prime, he was perhaps as perfect a beauty of his kind as ever was seen; and from his size, aspect, and symmetry of form, recalled to mind the noble dogs which Scneiders has represented in close conflict with the bear or

Painted by Edwin Landseer, A.R.A.

Engraved by C. Westwood.

SCENE AT ABBOTSFORD.

Pub.ᵈ for the Proprietor by Hurst, Chance, & C.ᵒ St Paul's Churchyard, & R. Jennings, 2, Poultry.

Printed by M.ᶜ Queen

wolf, and not less of the alans whom Chaucer has introduced around the car of the king of Thrace:

> " ———————— grete as any steer,
> To hunten at the lion or the bear."

After having been distinguished in several deer chases,
Maida was, as an especial token of regard, presented by
Glengarry to Sir Walter Scott, with whom he lived many
years, and whom he seldom quitted. As Maida always
attended his master when travelling, he was, when in a
strange town, usually surrounded by a crowd of amateurs,
whose curiosity he indulged with great patience until it
began to be troublesome, when a single short bark gave
warning that he must be urged no further. Perhaps, however, the most remarkable proof of his peculiar size was,
that persons accustomed to *tracking*, which is still common
in Ettrick Forest, used to mistake the marks of his feet for
the traces of some wild animal escaped from a caravan, not
supposing it possible that they could have been imprinted
by the paws of a dog.

The colour of this splendid specimen of the Ossianic
dog, was black and white, regularly and beautifully marked.
His hair was rough and shaggy on the ridge of the neck,
which he could raise, when excited, like a lion's mane.

In his habits, Maida was attached and faithful; much
under his master's command, but an excellent watch-dog,
and very dangerous to suspected persons at suspicious
hours: on all other occasions he was gentle both to men
and animals, until he became aged, when his temper was
more capricious. The picture was done when he was in
the last stage of canine old age, which probably was the
sooner brought on by hard exercise and fatigue; for it was
his delight to go out with the ordinary greyhounds of the

low country, and, notwithstanding his size and weight, he could turn and sometimes take a hare. He was as sagacious as he was high-spirited and beautiful, and had some odd habits peculiar to himself. One of the most whimsical was a peculiar aversion to artists of every description. His noble appearance had occasioned his being repeatedly drawn or painted, until, not liking the constraint which attended this operation, he never could endure to see a pencil and paper produced without making an effort to escape, and giving marked signs of displeasure if attempts were used to compel him to remain.

When Mr. Landseer saw Maida, he was in the last stage of weakness and debility, as the artist has admirably expressed in his fading eye and extenuated limbs. He died about six weeks afterwards, and lies buried at the gate which he long watched, under a stone bearing the following inscription, which, to the astonishment of all who knew the author, contains only *one* sin against prosody, as the lines themselves will testify. They are placed round a figure of the dog in stone, cut by Mr. John Smith, of Melrose, whose natural talents might have distinguished him had he been regularly educated to the art.

> Maida, tu marmorea dormis sub imagine Maidæ
> Ad januam domini.   Sit tibi terra levis!

The armour and military weapons are characteristic of the antiquarian humour of the owner of the mansion, who, as Burns describes a similar collection,

> " —— has a fouth of auld nick-nackets,
> Rusty airn caps and jingling jackets,
> Would haud the Lothians three in tackets,
>   A twal'month good;
> And parritch-pots and auld saut-backets,
>   Before the flood."

The hawks are the gratuitous donation of Mr. Landseer, whose imagination conferred them on a scene where he judged they would be appropriate; as that of the artist liberally added a flock of sheep to attend the shepherdess in the Vicar of Wakefield's family picture.

The other dog represented in the picture is a deerhound, the property of the artist, and given to him by the Duke of Athol.

It only remains to be added, that the painting, which, as a piece of art, has attracted much and deserved praise, was the property of the Duke of Bedford, and presented by his Grace to the Right Honourable William Adam, Lord Chief Commissioner of the Jury Court in Scotland, whose property it now is. In the principal figure especially, it would be difficult to point out a finer exemplification of age and its consequences acting upon an animal of such beauty and strength. It would afford excellent hints for a painting of Argus at the gate of Ulysses, which was probably an animal of the same appearance and habits.

TO A CRITIC

WHO QUOTED AN ISOLATED PASSAGE, AND THEN DECLARED IT UNINTELLIGIBLE.

Most candid critic, what if I,
By way of joke, pluck out your eye,
And holding up the fragment, cry,
" Ha, ha! that men such fools should be!
Behold this shapeless mass!—and he,
Who own'd it, dreamt that it could see!"
The joke were mighty analytic—
But should you like it, candid critic?

S. T. COLERIDGE.

THE BROKEN CHAIN.

BY MRS. HEMANS.

Lift not the festal mask !
SCOTT.

I AM free!   I have burst through my heavy chain,
The life of young eagles is mine again!
I may cleave with my bark the glad sounding sea,
I may rove where the wind roves—my path is free!

The streams dash in joy down the tameless hill,
The birds pierce the depths of the skies at will;
The arrow goes forth with the singing breeze—
And is not my spirit as one of these?

Oh! the glad earth, with its wealth of flowers,
And the voices that ring through its forest-bowers,
And the laughing glance of the founts that shine,
Lighting its valleys!—all, all are mine!

I may urge through the desert my foaming steed,
The wings of the morning shall lend him speed
I may meet the storm in its rushing glee,
Its blasts and its lightnings are not more free!

Captive! and hast thou then riven thy chain?
Art thou free in the wilderness, free on the main?
Yes! *these* thy spirit may proudly soar,
But must thou not mingle with crowds once more?

The bird, when he pineth, may cease his song,
Till the hour when his heart shall again be strong;
But thou—wilt thou turn in thy woe aside,
And weep midst thy brethren?—no, not for pride!

May the fiery word from thy lip find way,
When the thought burning in thee would rush to day?—
May the love or the grief of thy haunted breast,
Look forth from thy features, the banquet's guest?—

No! with the shaft in thy bosom borne,
Thou must hide the wound from the eye of scorn,
Thou must fold the mantle that none may see,
And mask thee with laughter, and say thou art free.

Free!—thou art bound, till thy race is run,
By the might of all on the soul of one!
On thy heart, on thy lip, must the fetter be—
Dreamer, fond dreamer! oh! who is free?

IMPROMPTU,

ON THE ASSERTION OF A LADY, THAT IN HER DRAWING OF
VENUS, THE HAIR OF THE GODDESS WAS ARRANGED SO AS TO
CONCEAL A PORTION OF HER FIGURE, WITHOUT DISOBEYING
THE LAWS OF GRAVITY.

BY M. R.

YOUR Venus most surely deserveth applause,
    For your Zephyrs so curiously waft her,
That her tresses, though govern'd by *gravity's* laws,
    Excite irresistible *laughter!*

TO ————.

BY F. M. REYNOLDS.

THE day from me pass'd,
  I was buried in night;
To earth I was cast
  In the pride of my might.

I was struck by the shaft
  Of anguish and care;
And in bitterness quaff'd
  The dregs of despair.

My energies dropt,
  And I lived to be then
Contemn'd, and o'ertopt,
  By the meanest of men.

Yes, sunk, prostrated,
  By the depth of my wo,
I humbled my head
  The vilest below.

And then, as the bran
  That is scatter'd to rot,
I was valued by man,
  And by heaven forgot.

Yet *thou*, who might'st vie
  With an angel above,
Could'st deign to reply
  Even *then* to my love!

O! e'en if I were
  Immortal to be,
That kindness could ne'er
  Be forgotten by me!

By the light of thy brow,
  By the blush of thy cheek,
I *feel* for thee now
  Even more than I speak

By the earth and the air,
  By the heavens and sea,
For ever, I swear,
  I 'll be faithful to thee!

TO A PEARL.

BY LORD PORCHESTER.

I HAVE not seen thee shine in crowded hall
On gala night, 'mid gorgeous festival,
But thou wert to the southern stranger given
By the lone stream beneath a stormy heaven.
And, lady, when I took it from thy hand,
I deem'd there breathed no fairer in the land;
And thought when last I heard thee speak, no mind
More pure was e'er in mortal mould enshrined.
At times athwart thy calm and passive brow,
A rich expression came, a sunny glow,
That well might seem engender'd by the sky,
That canopies the maids of Italy.
It told that young Romance, a lingering guest,
Was still the inmate of thy chasten'd breast;
That fond illusive mood, which makes us still
Forget, in promised pleasure, present ill;
That makes me now, though years have roll'd away,
Cherish the mem'ry of that distant day,
And prize this relic of our friendship, far
Beyond the fabled gems of Istakhar.

A LEGEND OF KILLARNEY.

BY THOMAS HAYNES BAYLY.

CHAPTER I.

Exhausted by the fatigue of a long journey in a hot September day, we sat at the window of the Kenmare Arms, languidly looking into the high-street of Killarney, and scarcely noticing the groups of idlers who passed before us. Never did weary traveller rest in more comfortable quarters, and never did he obtain good fare and civility on more reasonable terms.

"Well," said I to our host, as he entered, "what success? Have you secured a good boat's crew for the morning?"

"Yes, sir," replied the landlord, (whose reply, had he been an Irishman, I should not have ventured to put on paper, as I abhor an Englishman's caricature of the brogue, while I adore the animated sketches of a Morgan or an Edgeworth.) "Yes, sir; the very best cockswain, four good rowers, and above all, Serjeant Spillane, whose bugle charms every stranger that comes amongst us."

"That's well," said I; "let all be in readiness early in the morning; fishing-tackle to catch salmon, a gun to rouse the echoes, and plenty of provisions for the crew."

"Certainly, sir," said the host, who still seemed inclined to linger. "*You* have been fortunate, for there is not a boat now disengaged. There is a young gentleman below, sir, who seems very anxious to go on the lake to-morrow; and I believe he 'll be obliged to stay at home."

" We have been fortunate indeed, then."

" Yes, sir. But, as I was saying to the young lad, (a college lad I take it from England,) if, now, any one who has a boat would let you join him——"

" Well," said I, laughing, " I see your drift; what is your young friend like?"

" Oh! quite a gentleman! pale, and thin, and very genteel."

After a moment's consultation with my companion, it was decided that we could not be so unsociable as to refuse accommodation to a young fellow-countryman, wandering, like ourselves, in search of the picturesque; and, moreover, pale, thin, and very genteel. We therefore desired the land-lord to inform the young man, that we should be happy if he would join our party.

The next morning was as beautiful and as bright as any that ever dawned upon a tourist; and without those too frequent accompaniments to a party of pleasure, um-brellas, cloaks, and changes of *hose*, we hastened to Ross Castle, the place of embarkation, not a little anxious to see our companion.

He was, indeed, pale and thin, and thoroughly what I believe the ladies call *interesting*. He blushed as he bowed to us, and he seemed reserved, but yet there was no awkwardness, no *mauvaise honte* in his manner.

We spoke to him at first frequently, and he always answered with politeness, but it was merely an answer that he uttered; and, as he never volunteered an observa-tion, we soon relapsed into silence: indeed, I could not help thinking, as he turned from me, and leant over the side of the boat, gazing on the deep clear water, that there was a something in the curl of his lip which seemed to say, ' how can you tease me with common-place remarks amid such scenes as these!'

I perceived that the boatmen thought him very stupid, and I confess I began to be of their opinion, when I saw him recline for hours silently looking on the water, the sky, or the holly and arbutus trees that crowned the rocks.

At length, after passing up the romantic narrow stream that unites the upper and lower lakes, we approached the Eagle's Nest, and Spillane blew a loud blast on his bugle.

The few wild notes were beginning to die away, when, far off upon the mountain, those notes were repeated!—and again! and again! and again!—far, far away, as if in some deep unseen recesses, those few wild notes were repeated more faintly, until all was again silent.

One of the boatmen began to speak, but our pale companion, who was standing with distended eyes and lips apart, seized him by the arm and murmured ' *silence,*' in a deep agitated voice; nor did he relax his hold, and change his posture until the last faint echo had long been hushed. He then passed his hand hastily over his eyes, threw himself into his old place in the boat, and relapsed into his former stupid-looking attitude. Whenever we paused to catch a fine view of the lakes, or to listen to one of the echoes, he was all animation; but when the boatmen told us to look at one rock because it resembled a man-of-war, or at another, because it was like a cannon, he did not deign to turn his head towards these wonders.

We landed at Glenaa Island, where we dined; but our pale companion was invisible during the repast; he seemed to prefer rambling by himself; and when we hailed him, that we might re-embark, he hastily concealed a little book and a pencil, and once more sat silent by my side.

Towards evening, as we were slowly coasting the Turk lake, the cockswain pointed out various fantastically shaped rocks, designating one as O'Dognohoe's Eagle, another as O'Dognohoe's Cloisters, another as O'Dognohoe's Wine Cellar.

" This O'Dognohoe seems to have been a person of importance here," said I; "tell me who he was, or show him to me."

" We shall not see him, sir, to-night, it's to be hoped," said the oldest boatman of the crew, with that nationally characteristic expression, which, as I said before, I dare not imitate. He informed me that O'Dognohoe had, in his time, been a chieftain of gigantic stature, who performed all sorts of wonderful feats. That his shade still haunted the lakes, and regularly paid them a visit once in seven years, walking on the water, dressed in white with a big three-cocked hat. He himself had been the last living person favoured with a glimpse of the spirit, which event happened just fourteen years before.

Our pale companion was now listening intently. "Fourteen years!" he exclaimed, " and he visits the lake every seventh year; he has been here once since you met him, and we have a chance of meeting him to-night!"

The suggestion of this possibility seemed by no means to gratify the old man, who told us that whoever had the luck to meet O'Dognohoe was sure to meet mischance afterwards.

" And," said I, " can no one tell me more of O'Dognohoe? Had he no mistress? Is there no love story connected with these beautiful lakes?"

The old boatman had no story for me, and though he dwelt much upon the certain fact of his having seen this same O'Dognohoe, the meeting seemed to have taken place to little purpose.

" What," cried the pale lad, " have you no legends? For shame!—there ought to be—there *must* be a legend connected with every lovely bay, every green island, every bright waterfall that we have passed this morning; the very echoes prattle of romance! who can listen to those unearthly responses, without imagining that he hears the revelry or the wailings of the guardian spirits of the mountain and the lake?"

" True," I replied; " yet these fellows can only talk of O'Dognohoe, without even giving us his history! I shall be sorry to go hence without hearing one legend of Killarney."

Our pale companion blushed as he replied, " If you can be content with an Englishman's method of telling an Irish tale, *I* will venture to give you one."

CHAPTER II.

There was *once upon a time,* near the western coast of Ireland, a romantic valley inhabited by a few peasants, whose rude cabins were surrounded by the most luxuriant trees, and sheltered by mountains rising almost perpendicularly on every side. Ireland has still many beautiful green vales, but there is not one so deeply, so securely nestled among the hills, as the one, of which I speak. Add the depth of the deepest of these lakes to the height of the loftiest mountain that towers above us, and you may *then,* form some idea of the deep seclusion of this forgotten valley.

Norah was the prettiest girl in the little village. She was the pride of her old father and mother, and the admiration of every youth who beheld her. The cottage of her parents was the neatest in the neighbourhood: Norah knew how to make the homeliest chamber look cheerful, and the honeysuckle round the casement was taught by her hand to twine more gracefully than elsewhere.

There was but one spring of water in this valley; it was a little well of the brightest and clearest water ever seen, which bubbled up from the golden sand, and then lay calmly sleeping in a basin of the whitest marble. From this basin, there did not appear to be any outlet; the water ran into it incessantly, but no one could detect that any part of it escaped again! It was a Fairy well!

In those days there were Fairies! so says the legend, and so says Crofton Croker, that inimitable historian of the *little people* of Ireland in the olden time: ours is not a story involving in its detail national habits and characteristics; on such ground who would dare to compete with HIM? Not I.

To return to the well: it was, as I said before, a Fairy well, and was held in great veneration by the inhabitants of the valley.

There was a tradition concerning it which had time out of mind been handed down from parent to child. It was covered with a huge stone, which, though apparently very heavy, could be removed with ease by the hand of the most delicate female; and it was said to be the will of the Fairy who presided over it, that all the young girls of the village should go thither every evening after sunset, remove the stone, and take from the marble basin as much water as would be sufficient for the use of each family during the ensuing day; above all, it was understood to be the Fairy's strict injunction that each young maiden, when she had filled her pitcher, should carefully replace the stone: if at any time this, were to be neglected, the careless maiden would bring ruin on herself, and all the inhabitants of the valley; for if the morning sun ever shone upon the water, inevitable destruction would follow.

Often did Norah trip lightly to the well with her pitcher in her hand, singing the wild melodies of her country, with her beautiful hair decorated with the bright red berries of the mountain-ash, or the ripe fruit of the arbutus tree, and leaning over the bubbling spring, fill her pitcher, carefully replace the stone, and return to her parents without one sad thought to drive away sleep from her pillow.

This, could not last for ever: Norah was formed to be beloved, and soon a stranger youth came to the valley,—a soldier—one who had seen the world. He was clad in armour, and he talked of brighter scenes:—ah! could there be a brighter scene than that lone valley? He dazzled the poor girl's eye, and he won her heart; and when she went at sunset to fetch water from the fairy well, Coolin was always at her side.

Her old parents could not approve of such an attachment. The young soldier's stories of camps and courts possessed no charms for them, and when they saw that Norah loved to listen to him, they reproved their child for the first time in their lives, and forbad her in future to meet the stranger. She wept, but she promised to obey them, and, that she might avoid a meeting with her lover, she went that evening to the well by a different path to that, which she had been accustomed to take.

She removed the stone, and having filled the pitcher, she sat down by the side of the well and wept bitterly. She heeded not the hour: twilight was fast fading into the darkness of night, and the bright stars which studded the heavens directly over her head, were reflected in the crystal fountain at her feet.

Her lover stood before her.

"Oh! come not here," she cried, "come not here. I have promised not to meet you: had I returned home when my task was done, we never should have met! I have been disobedient; oh! why did I ever see you? you have taught me how to weep!"

"Say not so, dearest Norah," replied the young soldier; "come with me."

"Never! never!" she emphatically exclaimed, as she hastily arose, and advanced from the well. "I, who never broke my word, have broken it to-night! I said I would not meet you, and we have met." She uttered this, in an agony of tears, walking wildly forwards, whilst Coolin, with her hand clasped in both of his, walked by her side endeavouring to pacify her.

"Your fault, if it be one," said he, kindly, "was involuntary: your parents will forgive you, and when they know how tenderly I love you, they will no longer reject me as their son. You say you cannot leave them; well, well; I perhaps may stay here, may labour for them and for you. What is there I would not resign for my Norah? You are near your home, give me one smile; and now, dearest, good night."

Norah did smile upon him, and softly opening the wicket, she stole to her own chamber, and soon fell asleep,

T

full of fond thoughts of the possibility of her parents' sanction to her lover's suit.

She slept soundly for several hours.—

At last, awaking with a wild scream she started from her bed. "The well! the well!" she cried: "I neglected to replace the stone! It cannot yet be morning.—No—no—no, the gray dawn is just appearing: I will run, I shall be in time."

As she flew along the well-known path, the tops of the eastern hills were red with the near approach of sunrise. Is that the first sunbeam that gilds yonder mountain? No! it cannot be—she will yet be in time!

Norah had now reached a spot from whence, looking downwards, she could see the well, at the distance of a few hundred yards. She stood like a statue; her eyes were fixed; one hand grasped her forehead, with the other she pointed forwards. So suddenly had amazement arrested her flight, that her attitude retained the appearance of motion: she might have passed for the statue of a girl running, but she was motionless. The unclouded morning sun was shining brightly on the spot: the spring, once so gentle, was now sending forth a foaming torrent, which was rapidly inundating the valley. Already the alarmed villagers were rushing from their cabins, but Norah did not move: her hand was still pointed towards the spot, but she appeared unconscious of danger.

Still the foaming torrent poured forth, and the water approached the spot where she stood: Coolin, who had been seeking her everywhere, now ran towards her: his footstep roused her, and, crying, "My parents! save them!" she fell at his feet.

He bore her in his arms up a hill which was near them:

still the torrent raged behind them, the vast flood became wider and deeper.

When they reached the summit of the hill, it appeared to be a wooded island; water surrounded them on every side, and their resting-place became gradually smaller and smaller.

Many other green islands were to be seen, some less extensive than that on which they had found a temporary security; and these gradually grew smaller and smaller, and vanished one by one.

"Oh! that we were on the summit of yon mountain," said Coolin; and kissing Norah's pale cheek, he cried, "Is there no hope? my poor girl, my own dear love."

"My parents!—my parents!" exclaimed Norah, "where are they?—Oh! they have perished, the victims of their only child's disobedience!"

Clasped in each other's arms the lovers awaited their doom. The waters still rose higher and higher—the island became indistinct—it was a speck—it was gone!

The cause of the calamity having expiated her error, the wrath of the Fairy was appeased. The waters rose no more; but the beautiful valley of the Fairy well now lies buried under the clear waters of the LAKE OF KILLARNEY.

Our companion had warmed with his subject; he was no longer pale, and so well had we performed our parts as listeners, and so evident was the interest we had felt in the tale, that a mutual good understanding was at once established between us. The youth had proved himself not to be the stupid nonentity we had supposed him; and he, having observed our fixed attention, condescended to believe that *we* were not the mere feasting, idle *party-of-pleasurists* he had thought us.

We at last became quite sociable, nay, almost confidential: as we proceeded homewards, he drew from his pocket the little book which he had before taken such pains to conceal; though diffident in the glare of noonday, he was self-possessed in the twilight; and when I inquired whether the scenery had inspired him, he told us he had only been invoking the fairies.

" This little book is full of rhymes," said he; " they are not worth showing." To avoid further solicitation, however, he read us the following stanzas:

Oh! where do fairies hide their heads
   When snow lies on the hills;
When frost has chill'd their mossy beds,
   And crystalized their rills?—
Beneath the moon they cannot trip
   In circles o'er the plain,
And draughts of dew they cannot sip
   Till green leaves come again.

Perhaps in small blue diving bells
   They plunge beneath the waves,
Inhabiting the wreathed shells
   That lie in coral caves.
Perhaps in red Vesuvius
   Carousal they maintain,
And cheer their little spirits thus
   Till green leaves come again.

When they return, then will be mirth
   And music in the air,
And mystic rings upon the earth,
   And mischief every where!
The maids, to keep the elves aloof,
   Will bar the doors in vain;
No key-hole will be fairy proof
   When green leaves come again.

That night we parted with our companion. He was to rise early the following morning to proceed in search of fresh beauties, and we were to return to the city of Cork. I never part with one who has accidentally been my companion in a pleasant excursion without a melancholy feeling: we have been by chance shuffled together in the pack of human beings *once* in our lives, and the chances of the game are much against our ever finding ourselves dealt face to face upon the same board again; I therefore shook hands with him with regret, and never expected to see him more.

My sensibility, however, was thrown away; six months after, I discovered him leisurely taking a slice of *the joint* at the Athenæum club, and at his elbow was a *cruet* containing half a pint of sherry. He studies law at Gray's-inn, writes for periodicals, patronises poet's corner, and is to be seen almost daily at the Athenæum at six o'clock, occupying the table to the left of the entrance door.

EPIGRAMS.

BY S. T. COLERIDGE.

YOUR poem must *eternal* be,
　　Dear sir!—it cannot fail—
For 'tis incomprehensible,
　　And wants both *head* and *tail*.

SWANS sing before they die—'twere no bad thing
Did certain persons *die* before they sing.

BURNHAM-BEECHES.

BY HENRY LUTTRELL.

Near the village of Burnham in Buckinghamshire, there is a wood called Burnham-Beeches, now the property of Lord Grenville, and adjoining his seat at Dropmore. Though of no great extent, and commanding no views beyond its own limits, it is well worth visiting by those who have any pleasure in woodland scenery. From Salt-Hill, Maidenhead, Windsor, or Beaconsfield, it is within an easy ride or drive, which whoever is disposed to take will have no reason for regret or disappointment.

Beeches of luxuriant growth, and of every size and shape, are here spread over unequal ground, and, intermixed with under-wood and fern in every direction, form the most striking combinations that a painter could desire.

This picturesque and beautiful spot, though at so short a distance from London, and in the near neighbourhood of so many remarkable places, is perhaps as little known to tourists and travellers in general as any forest in the interior of Africa. Gray, the poet (who, in his youth, resided for some time with his uncle in the village of Burnham), thus speaks of it in a letter to Horace Walpole, written in the year 1737, nearly a century ago: " I have," he says, " at the distance of half a mile, through " a green lane, a forest (the vulgar call it a common) all my own, at least " as good as so, for I spy no human being in it but myself. It is a little " chaos of mountains and precipices; mountains, it is true, that do not " ascend much above the clouds, nor are the declivities quite so amazing " as Dover-Cliffs, but just such hills as people who love their necks as " well as I do may venture to climb, and crags that give the eye as much " pleasure as if they were more dangerous. Both vale and hill are covered " with most venerable beeches, and other reverend vegetables."

It may be doubted if, at the present date, their "ancient solitary reign" is more frequently disturbed than when Gray thus appears to have monopolized it. Yet are they now, as they were then, objects of great curiosity and interest; as any one must feel, who, at the dawn or the close of a bright sunny day, should be tempted to wander among them.

The author of the following poetical trifle professes nothing but to have exhausted every rhyme to his subject that the language affords, and not to have exaggerated the beauty of the place he has attempted to describe.

I.

A BARD, dear Muse, unapt to sing,
    Your friendly aid beseeches.
Help me to touch the lyric string,
    In praise of Burnham-beeches.

II.

What, though my tributary lines
    Be less like Pope's than Creech's?[1]
The theme, if not the poet, shines,
    So bright are Burnham-beeches.

III.

O'er many a dell and upland walk,
    Their sylvan beauty reaches.
Of Birnam-wood let Scotland talk,[2]
    While we've our Burnham-beeches.

IV.

Oft do I linger, oft return,
    (Say, who my taste impeaches?)
Where holly, juniper, and fern,
    Spring up round Burnham-beeches.

---

[1] Pope himself has more than hinted at the difference.

    Plain truth, dear Murray, needs no flowers of speech;
    So take it in the very words of Creech.

[2] " Birnam-Wood."
        See MACBETH.

V.

Though, deep embower'd their shades among,
  The owl at midnight screeches,
Birds of far merrier, sweeter song,
  Enliven Burnham-beeches.

VI.

If "sermons be in stones," I'll bet[3]
  Our vicar, when he preaches,
He'd find it easier far to get
  A hint from Burnham-beeches.

VII.

Their glossy rind here winter stains,
  Here the hot solstice bleaches.
Bow, stubborn oaks!—Bow, graceful planes!
  Ye match not Burnham-beeches.

VIII.

Gardens may boast a tempting show
  Of nectarines, grapes, and peaches,
But daintiest truffles lurk below
  The boughs of Burnham-beeches.

IX.

Poets and painters, hither hie.
  Here ample room for each is
With pencil and with pen to try
  His hand at Burnham-beeches.

X.

When monks, by holy Church well schooled,
  Were lawyers, statesmen, leeches,
Cured souls and bodies, judged or ruled,
  Then flourished Burnham-beeches,

---

3 "Sermons in stones, and good in every thing."
SHAKSP.—AS YOU LIKE IT.

XI.

Skirting the convent's walls of yore,
As yonder ruin teaches. [4]
But shaven crown and cowl no more
Shall darken Burnham-beeches.

XII.

Here bards have mused—here lovers true [5]
Have dealt in softest speeches,
While suns declined, and, parting, threw
Their gold o'er Burnham-beeches.

XIII.

O ne'er may woodman's axe resound,
Nor tempest, making breaches
In the sweet shade that cools the ground
Beneath our Burnham-beeches!

XIV.

Hold!—Though I'd fain be jingling on,
My power no further reaches.
Again that rhyme?—Enough—I've done. [6]
Farewell to Burnham-beeches!

4 Of Burnham-Abbey.

5 Gray describes himself, in the letter before quoted, as seated at the foot of one of these trees, and "growing to the trunk for a whole morning." Among them he probably found the original of

"yonder nodding beech,
Which wreathes its old fantastic roots so high."

In the village of Stoke-Pogis, there is a churchyard which is supposed to have suggested to him the plan and the title of his celebrated Elegy. That village is at no great distance from Burnham.

6 It occurs before, in the third stanza.

THE GARDEN OF BOCCACIO.

BY S. T. COLERIDGE.

Of late, in one of those most weary hours,
When life seems emptied of all genial powers,
A dreary mood, which he who ne'er has known
May bless his happy lot, I sate alone;
And, from the numbing spell to win relief,
Call'd on the PAST for thought of glee or grief.
In vain! bereft alike of grief and glee,
I sate and cow'r'd o'er my own vacancy!
And as I watch'd the dull continuous ache,
Which, all else slumb'ring, seem'd alone to wake;
O Friend! long wont to notice yet conceal,
And soothe by silence what words cannot heal,
I but half saw that quiet hand of thine
Place on my desk this exquisite design,
Boccacio's Garden and its faery,
The love, the joyaunce, and the gallantry!
An IDYLL, with Boccacio's spirit warm,
Framed in the silent poesy of form.

Like flocks adown a newly-bathed steep
    Emerging from a mist: or like a stream
Of music soft that not dispels the sleep,
    But casts in happier moulds the slumberer's dream,
Gazed by an idle eye with silent might
The picture stole upon my inward sight.
A tremulous warmth crept gradual o'er my chest,
As though an infant's finger touch'd my breast.
And one by one (I know not whence) were brought
All spirits of power that most had stirr'd my thought

Drawn by T. Stothard.

Engraved by F. Englehart.

GARDEN OF BOCCACIO.

Printed by M°. Queen.

Published for the Proprietor, by Hurst, Chance, & C°. S.¹ Pauls Churchyard, and R. Jennings, Poultry.

In selfless boyhood, on a new world tost
Of wonder, and in its own fancies lost;
Or charm'd my youth, that, kindled from above,
Loved ere it loved, and sought a form for love;
Or lent a lustre to the earnest scan
Of manhood, musing what and whence is man!
Wild strain of Scalds, that in the sea-worn caves
Rehearsed their war-spell to the winds and waves;
Or fateful hymn of those prophetic maids,
That call'd on Hertha in deep forest glades;
Or minstrel lay, that cheer'd the baron's feast;
Or rhyme of city pomp, of monk and priest,
Judge, mayor, and many a guild in long array,
To high-church pacing on the great saint's day.
And many a verse which to myself I sang,
That woke the tear yet stole away the pang,
Of hopes which in lamenting I renew'd.
And last, a matron now, of sober mien
Yet radiant still and with no earthly sheen,
Whom as a faery child my childhood woo'd
Even in my dawn of thought—PHILOSOPHY.
Though then unconscious of herself, pardie,
She bore no other name than POESY;
And, like a gift from heaven, in lifeful glee,
That had but newly left a mother's knee,
Prattled and play'd with bird and flower, and stone,
As if with elfin playfellows well known,
And life reveal'd to innocence alone.

Thanks, gentle artist! now I can descry
Thy fair creation with a mastering eye.
And *all* awake!   And now in fix'd gaze stand,
Now wander through the Eden of thy hand;

Praise the green arches, on the fountain clear
See fragment shadows of the crossing deer,
And with that serviceable nymph I stoop
The crystal from its restless pool to scoop.
I see no longer!   I myself am there,
Sit on the ground-sward, and the banquet share.
'Tis I, that sweep that lute's love-echoing strings,
And gaze upon the maid who gazing sings:
Or pause and listen to the tinkling bells
From the high tower, and think that there she dwells.
With old Boccacio's soul I stand possest,
And breathe an air like life, that swells my chest.

The brightness of the world, O thou once free,
And always fair, rare land of courtesy!
O, Florence! with the Tuscan fields and hills,
And famous Arno fed with all their rills;
Thou brightest star of star-bright Italy!
Rich, ornate, populous, all treasures thine,
The golden corn, the olive, and the vine.
Fair cities, gallant mansions, castles old,
And forests, where beside his leafy hold
The sullen boar hath heard the distant horn,
And whets his tusks against the gnarled thorn;
Palladian palace with its storied halls;
Fountains, where LOVE lies listening to their falls;
Gardens, where flings the bridge its airy span,
And Nature makes her happy home with man;
Where many a gorgeous flower is duly fed
With its own rill, on its own spangled bed,
And wreathes the marble urn, or leans its head,
A mimic mourner, that with veil withdrawn
Weeps liquid gems, the presents of the dawn,

Thine all delights, and every muse is thine:
And more than all, the embrace and intertwine
Of all with all in gay and twinkling dance!
Mid gods of Greece and warriors of romance,
See! BOCCACE sits, unfolding on his knees
The new-found roll of old Mæonides;[1]
But from his mantle's fold, and near the heart,
Peers Ovid's HOLY BOOK of Love's sweet Smart![2]

O all-enjoying and all-blending sage,
Long be it mine to con thy mazy page,
Where, half conceal'd, the eye of fancy views
Fauns, nymphs, and winged saints, all gracious to thy muse!

Still in thy garden let me watch their pranks,
And see in Dian's vest between the ranks
Of the trim vines, some maid that half believes
The *vestal* fires, of which her lover grieves,
With that sly satyr peeping through the leaves!

[1] Boccacio claimed for himself the glory of having first introduced the works of Homer to his countrymen.

[2] I know few more striking or more interesting proofs of the overwhelming influence which the study of the Greek and Roman classics exercised on the judgments, feelings, and imaginations of the literati of Europe at the commencement of the restoration of literature, than the passage in the Filocopo of Boccacio: where the sage instructor, Racheo, as soon as the young prince and the beautiful girl Biancofiore had learned their letters, sets them to study the *Holy Book*, Ovid's ART OF LOVE. "Incominciò Racheo a mettere il suo officio in esecuzione con intera sollecitudine. E loro, in breve tempo, insegnato a conoscer le lettere, *fece leggere il santo libro d'Ovvidio, nel quale il sommo poeta mostra, come i santi fuochi di Venere si debbano ne freddi cuori accendere*."

THE OLD GENTLEMAN.

For days, for weeks, for months, for years, did I labour and toil in the pursuit of one bewildering, engrossing, overwhelming object. Sleep was a stranger to my eyelids; and night after night was passed in undivided, unmitigated application to the studies, by which I hoped (vainly, indeed) to attain the much desired end; yet all through this long and painful period of my existence, I trembled lest those who were my most intimate friends, and from whom, except upon this point, I had no concealment, should discover, by some incautious word, or some unguarded expression, the tendency of my pursuits, or the character of my research.

That I had permitted the desire with which my heart was torn, and my mind disturbed, to obtain such complete dominion over every thought, every wish, every feeling, seems, at *this* period of my life, wholly unaccountable; and I recur to the sufferings I endured in concealing its existence, with a sensation of torture little less acute than that, by which I was oppressed during the existence of the passion itself.

It was in the midst of this infatuation, that one evening in summer, when every body was out of town, and not more than eight hundred thousand nobodies were left in it, I had been endeavouring to walk off a little of my anxiety by a tour of the outer circle in the Regent's Park, and, hearing a footstep close behind me, turned round, and beheld a venerable looking old gentleman, dressed entirely in green, with a green cravat tied round his neck, and wearing a low-crowned hat upon his head, from under which, his silver hair flowed loosely over his shoulders. He seemed to have his eyes fixed on me when for a moment I looked round at him; and he slackened his pace (however much he had previously quickened it to reach his then position relative to me), so as to keep nearly at the same distance from me, as he was, when I first noticed him.

Nothing is more worrying to a man, or to one so strangely excited as I *then* was, more irritating, than the constant *pat pat* of footsteps following him. After I had proceeded at my usual pace for about ten minutes, and still found the old gentleman behind me, I reduced my rate of going, in order to allow my annoyance to pass me. Not he; *he* equally reduced *his* rate of going. Thus vexed, and putting faith in inferior age and superior strength, I proceeded more rapidly; still the old gentleman was close upon me; until before I reached the gates of Park-crescent, leading to Portland-place, I had almost broken into a canter, with as little success as attended my other evolutions. I therefore resumed my original step, and thinking to effect by stratagem what force could not accomplish, I turned abruptly out of Portland-place into Duchess-street—the old gentleman was at my heels: I passed the chapel into Portland-street—for a moment I lost sight of him; but before I had reached the corner of Margaret-street, there he was again.

At that time I occupied lodgings in the house of two maiden sisters in Great Marlborough-street, and considering that the police-office in that neighbourhood would render me any aid I might require to rid myself of my new acquaintance, should he prove troublesome, I determined to run for my own port at all events.

I crossed Oxford-street, and, in order to give myself another chance of escape, darted down Blenheim-steps and along the street of that name; but the old man's descent was as rapid as mine; and happening, as I passed the museum and dissecting rooms of the eminent anatomist Brooks, to turn my head, my surprise was more than ever excited by seeing my venerable friend actually dancing in a state of ecstacy along the side of the dead wall which encloses so many subjects for contemplation. At this moment I resolved to stop and accost him rather than make the door-way of my own residence the arena of a discussion.

"Sir," said I, turning short round, "you will forgive my addressing you, but it is impossible for me to affect ignorance that I am, for some reason, the object of your pursuit. I am near home; if you have any communication to make, or desire any information from *me*, I would beg you to speak now."

"You are perfectly right, sir," said the old gentleman, "I *do* wish to speak to you; and you, although perhaps not at this moment aware of it, are equally desirous of speaking to *me*. You are now going into your lodgings in Marlborough-street, and so soon as you shall have divested yourself of your coat, and enveloped yourself in that blue silk gown which you ordinarily wear, and have taken off your boots and put your feet into those morocco slippers which were made for you last March by Meyer and Miller, you purpose drinking some of the claret which you bought last Christmas of Henderson and Son, of Davies-street, Berkley-square, first mixing it with water; and immediately after you will apply yourself to the useless and unprofitable studies which have occupied you during the last five or six years."

" Sir," said I, trembling at what I heard, " how, or by what means, you have become possessed of these particulars I ——"

" No matter," interrupted my friend: " if you are disposed to indulge me with your society for an hour or so, and bestow upon me a bottle of the wine in question, I will explain myself. There, sir," continued he, " you need not hesitate; I see you have already made up your mind to offer me the rights of hospitality; and since I know the old ladies of your house are advocates for early hours and quiet visitors, I will conform in all respects to their wishes and your convenience."

Most true indeed was it that I had determined *coute qui coute* to give my new old friend an invitation and a bottle of wine; and before he had concluded his observations we were at the door of my house, and in a few minutes more, although my servant was absent without leave, we were seated at a table on which forthwith were placed the desired refreshments.

My friend, who continued to evince the most perfect knowledge of all my private concerns, and all my most intimate connexions, became evidently exhilarated by the claret; and in the course of one of the most agreeable conversations in which I had ever participated, he related

U

numerous anecdotes of the highest personages in the country, with all of whom he seemed perfectly intimate. He told me he was a constant attendant at every fashionable party of the season; in the dull time of the year the theatres amused him; in term the law-courts occupied his attention; and in summer, as, he said, I might have seen, his pleasures lay in the rural parts of the metropolis and its suburbs; he was at that time of the year always to be found in one of the parks or in Kensington-gardens. But his manner of telling his stories afforded internal evidence of their accuracy, and was so captivating, that I thought him without exception the pleasantest old gentleman I had ever encountered.

It was now getting dark, the windows of my drawing-room were open, the sashes up, and the watchman's cry of " past ten o'clock" was the first announcement to me of the rapid flight of Time in the agreeable society of my friend.

" I must be going," said he; " I must just look in at Brooks's."

" What, sir," said I, recollecting his grotesque dance under the wall in Blenheim-street, " over the way?"

" No," replied he, " in St. James's-street."

" Have another bottle of claret," said I, " and a devil—"

At this word my friend appeared seriously angry, and I heard him mutter the word " cannibalism." It was then quite dark, and, as I looked at his face, I could discern no features, but only two brilliant orbs of bright fire glittering like stars; those were his eyes, the light from which was reflected on his high cheek-bones and the sides of his nose, leaving all the rest of his face nearly black. It was then I first heard a thumping against the back of his chair, like a gentleman " switching his cane;"—I began to wish he would go.

" Sir," said the old gentleman, " any disguise with me is useless; I must take my leave; but you must not imagine that this visit was unpremeditated, or that our meeting was accidental: you last night, perhaps unconsciously, invoked my aid in the pursuit to which you have so long devoted yourself. The desire of your heart is known to me; and I know that the instant I leave you, you will return to your fascinating study, vainly to seek that, which you so constantly languish to possess."

" I desire"—I was going to say, " nothing;"—but the pale fire of his dreadful eyes turned suddenly to a blood-red colour, and glistened even more brightly than before, while the thumping against the back of his chair was louder than ever.

" You desire, young gentleman," said my visitor, " to know the thoughts of others, and thirst after the power of foreseeing events that are to happen: do you not?"

" I confess, sir," said I, convinced, by the question and by what had already passed, that *he*, whoever he was, himself possessed the faculty he spoke of—" I confess, that for such a power I have prayed, and studied, and laboured, and——"

" ——You shall possess it," interrupted my friend. " Who *I* am, or what, matters little: the power you seek is wholly in *my* gift. You last night, as I have just said, invoked me;—you shall have it, upon two conditions."

" Name them, sir," said I.

" The first is, that however well you know what is to

happen to others, you must remain in ignorance about yourself, except when connected with them."

" To that," said I, " I will readily agree."

" The other is, that whatever may be the conduct you adopt in consequence of possessing the power of knowing the thoughts of others, you are never to reveal the fact that you actually *do* possess such a power: the moment you admit yourself master of this supernatural faculty, you lose it."

" Agreed, sir," said I; " but are these all the conditions?"

" All," said my friend. " To-morrow morning, when you awake, the power will be your own; and so, sir, I wish you a very good night."

" But, sir," said I, anxious to be better assured of the speedy fulfilment of the wish of my heart (for such indeed it was), " may I have the honour of knowing your name and address?"

" Ha, ha, ha!" said the old gentleman: "*my* name and address—Ha, ha, ha!—my name is pretty familiar to you, young gentleman; and as for my address, I dare say you will find your way to me, some day or another, and so once more good night."

Saying which, he descended the stairs and quitted the house, leaving me to surmise who my extraordinary visitor could be;—I never *knew;* but I recollect, that after he was gone, I heard one of the old ladies scolding a servant-girl for wasting so many matches in lighting the candles, and making such a terrible smell of brimstone in the house.

I was now all anxiety to get to bed, not because I was sleepy, but because it seemed to me as if going to bed would bring me nearer to the time of getting up, when I should be master of the miraculous power which had been promised me: I rang the bell—my servant was still out—it was unusual for him to be absent at so late an hour. I waited until the clock struck eleven, but he came not; and resolving to reprimand him in the morning, I retired to rest.

Contrary to my expectation, and, as it seemed to me, to the ordinary course of nature, considering the excitement under which I was labouring, I had scarcely laid my head on my pillow before I dropped into a profound slumber, from which I was only aroused by my servant's entrance to my room. The instant I awoke I sat up in bed, and began to reflect on what had passed, and for a moment to doubt whether it had not been all a dream. However, it was daylight; the period had arrived when the proof of my newly acquired power might be made.

" Barton," said I to my man, " why were you not at home last night?"

" I had to wait, sir, nearly three hours," he replied, " for an answer to the letter which you sent to Major Sheringham."

" That is not true," said I; and to my infinite surprise, I appeared to *recollect* a series of occurrences, of which I never had previously heard, and could have known nothing: " you went to see your sweetheart, Betsy Collyer, at Camberwell, and took her to a tea-garden, and gave her cakes and cider, and saw her home again: you mean to do exactly the same thing on Sunday; and to-morrow you mean to ask me for your quarter's wages, although not due till Monday, in order to buy her a new shawl."

The man stood aghast: it was all true. I was quite as much surprised as the man.

" Sir," said Barton, who had served me for seven years
without having once before been found fault with, " I see
you think me unworthy your confidence; you could not
have known this, if you had not watched, and followed, and
overheard me and my sweetheart: my character will get
me through the world without being looked after: I can
stay with you no longer; you will please, sir, to provide
yourself with another servant."

" But, Barton," said I, " I did not follow or watch you;
I——"

" I beg your pardon, sir," he replied, " it is not for *me*
to contradict; but, you'll forgive me, sir, I would rather
go—I *must* go."

At this moment I was on the very point of easing his
mind, and retaining my faithful servant by a disclosure of
my power, but it was yet too new to be parted with;
so I affected an anger I did not feel, and told him he
might go where he pleased. I had, however, ascertained
that the old gentleman had not deceived me in his promises; and elated with the possession of my extraordinary
faculty, I hurried the operation of dressing, and before I
had concluded it, my ardent friend Sheringham was announced; he was waiting in the breakfast-room; at the
same moment a note from the lovely Fanny Hayward was
delivered to me—from the divine girl who, in the midst
of all my scientific abstraction, could " chain my worldly
feelings for a moment."

" Sheringham, my dear fellow," said I, as I advanced
to welcome him, " what makes you so early a visitor this
morning?"

" An anxiety," replied Sheringham, " to tell you that
my uncle, whose interest I endeavoured to procure for you,

in regard to the appointment for which you expressed a desire, has been compelled to recommend a relation of the Marquess; this gives me real pain, but I thought it would be best to put you out of suspense as soon as possible."

"Major Sheringham," said I, drawing myself up coldly, "if this matter concern you so deeply, as you seem to imply that it does, might I ask why you so readily agreed to your uncle's proposition, or chimed in with his suggestion, to bestow the appointment on this relation of the Marquess, in order that *you* might, in return for it, obtain the promotion for which you are so anxious?"

"My dear fellow," said Sheringham, evidently confused, "I—I—never chimed in; my uncle certainly pointed out the possibility to which you allude, but *that*, was merely contingent upon what he could not refuse to do."

"Sheringham," said I, "your uncle has already secured for you the promotion, and you will be gazetted for the lieutenant-colonelcy of your regiment on Tuesday. I am not to be told that you called at the horse-guards, in your way to your uncle's yesterday, to ascertain the correctness of the report of the vacancy which you had received from your friend Macgregor; or that *you*, elated by the prospect before you, were the person, in fact, to suggest the arrangement which has been made, and promise your uncle to ' smooth me over' for the present."

"Sir," said Sheringham, "where you picked up this intelligence I know not; but I must say, that such mistrust, after years of undivided intimacy, is not becoming, or consistent with the character which I hitherto supposed you to possess. When by sinister means the man we look upon as a friend descends to be a spy upon our actions, confidence is at an end, and the sooner our intercourse ceases

the better. Without some such conduct, how could you
become possessed of the details upon which you have
grounded your opinion of my conduct?"

"I——" and here again was a temptation to confess and
fall; but I had not the courage to do it. "Suffice it, Major
Sheringham, to say, I knew it; and, moreover, I know, that
when you leave me, your present irritation will prompt
you to go to your uncle and check the disposition he feels
at this moment to serve me."

"This is too much, sir," said Sheringham; "this must
be our last interview, unless indeed your unguarded conduct towards me, and your intemperate language concerning me, may render one more meeting necessary; and so,
sir, here ends our acquaintance."

Saying which, Sheringham, whose friendship even to
my enlightened eye was nearly as sincere as any other
man's, quitted my room, fully convinced of my meanness
and unworthiness: my heart sank within me when I heard
the door close upon him for the last time. I now possessed
the power I had so long desired, and in less than an hour
had lost a valued friend and a faithful servant. Nevertheless, Barton *had* told me a falsehood, and Sheringham
was gazetted on the Tuesday night.

I proceeded to open Fanny Hayward's note; it contained an invitation to dinner with her mother, and a
request that I would accompany them to the opera, it
being the last night of the last extra subscription. I admired Fanny—nay, I almost loved her; and when I gazed
on her with rapture, I traced in the mild and languishing
expression of her soft blue eye, approbation of my suit,
and pleasure in my praise. I took up my pen to answer
her *billet*, and intuitively and instinctively wrote as follows:

"Dear Miss Hayward,

"I should have much pleasure in accepting your kind invitation for this evening, if it were given in the spirit of sincerity, which has hitherto characterized your conduct; but you must be aware that the plan of going to the opera to-night was started, not because you happen to have a box, but because you expect to meet Sir Henry Witherington, with whom you were so much pleased at Lady G.'s on Thursday, and to whom you consigned the custody of your fan, on condition that he *personally* returned it in safety at the opera to-night; as I have no desire to be the foil of any thing in itself so intrinsically brilliant as your newly discovered baronet, I must decline your proposal.

"Your mother's kindness in sanctioning the invitation would have been more deeply felt, if I did not know that the old lady greatly approves of your new acquaintance, and suggested to you the necessity of having me to play propriety during the evening, call up her carriage, and hand her to it, while Sir Henry was making the *aimable* to you, and escorting *you*, in our footsteps. Tell Mrs. Hayward that, however much she and you may enjoy the joke, I have no desire to be admitted as a ' safe man,' and that I suggest her offering her *cotelette* to Sir Henry as well as her company. With *sympathetic* regards,

Believe me, dear Miss Hayward,

yours, ————."

This note I immediately despatched, overjoyed that the power I possessed enabled me to penetrate the flimsy mask with which Mrs. Hayward had endeavoured to disguise her real views and intentions, and had scarcely finished breakfast before Mr. Fitman, my tailor, was ushered in, in company with a coat of the prevailing colour, and the most fashionable cut: in less than five minutes it was on, and the collar, the cuffs, the sleeves, and the skirts, became at once the objects of the author's admiration.

" Him is quite perfect, I declare," said the tailor, who, of course, was a foreigner.

After his high eulogium upon the cloth, I told him that it was not what he represented, and actually detailed the place at which he had bought it, and the name of the shopkeeper who had sold it: this irritated the tailor, who became extremely insolent, and our interview ended with my kicking him down stairs, from the bottom of which, he proceeded to the police-office, in my own street, and procured a warrant for the assault, by which I was compelled to appear before the magistrates on the following day, knowing, before I went, the whole course the case would take, and the decision they would make, in precisely the terms which they subsequently adopted.

Still, however, I stood alone in power, unless indeed my old friend in green did actually share the talent I possessed; and not being able to make up my mind to put an end to the enjoyment of an object I had so long laboured to attain, I contented myself with resolving to be more cautious in future, and less freely or frequently exhibit my mysterious quality.

After the little disagreeable adventure I have just re-counted, I thought perhaps I had better proceed to the Temple, and consult my lawyer, who, as well as being professionally concerned for me, had been for a long time my intimate acquaintance. I knew what the decision of the justices would be, but I thought the attendance of a legal adviser would make the affair more respectable in the eyes of the public, and I accordingly bent my steps city-wise.

When I reached the Temple, my worthy Maxwell was at home; as usual his greetings were the warmest, his expressions the kindest. I explained my case, to which he listened attentively, and promised his assistance, but in a moment I perceived that, however bland and amiable his conduct to me might appear, he had several times during the preceding spring told his wife that he believed I was mad. In corroboration of which, I recollected that she had on the occasion of my last three or four visits placed herself at the greatest possible distance from me, in the drawing-room, and had always rung the bell, to have her children taken away the moment I entered.

In pursuance of my cautious resolution, however, I took no notice of this; but when I spoke of the length of time which had elapsed since I had seen Mrs. Maxwell, I found out, from what was passing in her husband's mind, that she had determined never to be at home when I called, or ever dine in her own house if I was invited. Maxwell, however, promised to be with me in the morning, in time to attend the magistrates, and I knew he meant to keep his promise; so far I was easy about that affair, and made several calls on different acquaintances, few of whom were at home—some were—but as I set down the exclusion which I found so general as the result of the wild abstracted manner consequent upon my abstruse studies, and my heart-wearing anxiety, I determined now to become the gayest, most agreeable person possible, and, profiting by experience, keep all my wisdom to myself.

I went into the water-colour exhibition at Charing-cross; there I heard two artists complimenting each other, while their hearts were bursting with mutual envy. There too, I found a mild, modest-looking lady, listening to the bewitching nothings of her husband's particular friend; and I knew, as I saw her frown and abruptly turn away from him with every appearance of real indignation, that she had at that very moment mentally resolved to elope with him the following night. In Harding's shop I found authors congregated to "laugh the sultry hours away," each watching to catch his neighbour's weak point, and make it subject matter of mirth in his evening's conversation. I saw a viscount help his father out of his carriage with every mark of duty and veneration, and knew that he was actually languishing for the earldom, and estates of the venerable parent of whose health he was apparently taking so much care. At Howell and James's I saw more than I could tell, if I had ten times the space afforded me that I have, and I concluded my tour by dropping in at the National Gallery, where the ladies and gentlemen seemed to prefer nature to art, and were actively employed in looking at the pictures, and thinking of themselves.

Oh! it was a strange time then, when every man's heart was open to me, and I could sit and see and hear all that was going on, and know the workings of the inmost feelings of my associates: however, I must not detain the reader with reflections.

On this memorable first day of my potency, I proceeded after dinner to the opera, to satisfy myself of the justness of my accusation against Fanny. I looked up to their box, and immediately behind my once single-minded girl, sat Sir Henry Witherington himself, actually playing with the identical fan, of which I had instinctively and intuitively written without ever having seen it before. There was an ease and confidence about the fellow, and he was so graceful and good-looking, and Fanny gazed at him so long and so frequently, that I could bear it no more, and thinking that after our long intimacy my letter of the morning might have gone for nothing, I proceeded to their box, determined to rally. Of Sir Henry's thoughts about me, I was utterly ignorant, for he did not even know my name, so that I could have shared none of his consideration. I was aware, however, that the mother was downright angry, and Fanny just so much piqued as to make our reconciliation a work of interest and amusement.

I certainly did not perfectly appreciate Mrs. Hayward's feelings towards me, for when as usual I entered her curtained territory, her glance was instantly averted from *me* to Fanny, who looked grave, and I found was seriously annoyed at my appearance: however, I knew I had influence, and with my commanding power I resolved to remain. After a pause, during which Sir Henry eyed me, and the ladies alternately, he inquired of Mrs. Hayward if I were a friend of hers.

"Assuredly not, Sir Henry," said Mrs. Hayward. "I *did* know the person, but his conduct renders it impossible that our acquaintance should continue."

Fanny's heart began to melt; *she* would have caught me by the hand, and bid me stay. I relied on this, and moved not.

"Pray, madam," said Sir Henry, "is this person's presence here disagreeable to you?"

"Particularly so, Sir Henry," said the old lady, with all the malice of offended dignity.

"Then, sir," said Sir Henry, " you must leave the box."

"Must I, indeed, sir?" said I, becoming in turn much more angry than the old lady.

"Pray! pray!" said Fanny.

"Be quiet, child," said her obdurate mother.

"Yes, sir," said Sir Henry, "must! and if this direction is not speedily obeyed, the boxkeeper shall be called to remove you."

"Sir Henry Witherington," said I, "the society you are in, seals my lips and binds my hands. I *will* leave the box, on condition that for one moment only, you will accompany me."

"Certainly, sir," said Sir Henry, and in an instant we were both in the passage.

I drew a card from my case, and putting it into his hand, said, "Sir Henry Witherington, your uncalled for interference of to-night must be explained; here is the card of one who has no other feeling for your insolence but that of the most ineffable contempt." Saying which, I walked out of the Opera-house, and he rejoined the ladies, who were in a state of serious agitation—Fanny on *my* account, and her mother on account of her.

This affair ended, I returned once more to bed, and once more fell into a deep slumber, from which I was aroused by Barton, who informed me that Colonel MacManton was waiting to speak a few words to me in the drawing-room.

Of course I knew the object of *his* visit; he came to invite me to Chalk Farm, where, probably, he had already ordered pistols for two, and breakfast for four; and I hastened down stairs, rather anxious than otherwise to exhibit my person in the field of honour, that I might at once become the friend of the brave, and the idol of the fair.

I entered the drawing-room, and found my visitor waiting.

" Sir," said the colonel, " I imagine, after what past last night between you and my friend, Sir Henry Witherington, I need hardly announce the object of my visit. I will not offend you by mentioning the alternative of a meeting, but merely request you to refer me to some friend of yours, with whom I may make the necessary arrangements as speedily as possible."

" Sir," replied I, speaking, as it were, not of myself, " I must decline a meeting with Sir Henry Witherington; and I tell you in the outset of the business, that no power will induce me to lend myself to any arrangement which may lead to one."

" This is a most extraordinary resolution, sir," said the colonel. " I can assure you, although I have stated the matter as delicately as I could, that Sir Henry will accept of no apology; nor indeed could I permit him to do so, even if he were so inclined."

" You have had my answer, sir," said I: " I refuse his challenge."

" Perhaps," inquired the colonel, " you will be good enough to state your reason?"

" Precisely this, sir," I replied. " Our quarrel and rencontre of last night arose out of the perverseness of an old lady, and the inconsiderateness of a young one: they both regret the circumstance as much as I do; and Sir Henry himself, in thus calling me to account, is obeying the dictates of fashion rather than those of feeling."

" But that, sir," said the colonel, " is Sir Henry's affair. I must endeavour to extract some better reason than this."

" Well then, sir," I rejoined, " if Sir Henry meets me he will fall—it must be so—and I will not consent to imbrue my hands in the blood of a fellow-creature in such a cause."

" Is *that* your only motive, sir, for declining his invitation?" exclaimed the gallant colonel, somewhat sneeringly.

" It is."

" Then, sir, it becomes me to state, in distinct terms, that Sir Henry Witherington must in future consider you unworthy to fill the station of a gentleman in society; and that he will, on the first opportunity, exercise the only means, left him under the circumstances, of satisfying his offended honour, by inflicting personal chastisement upon you wherever he meets you."

Saying which, the colonel, believing me in his heart to be the arrantest coward alive, took his leave; but however annoyed I felt at the worldly consequences of this affair, I gloried in my privilege of prescience, which had informed me of the certain result of our hostile interview. I then prepared myself to receive my lawyer, and attend the magistrates:—that affair was soon settled—the tailor entered into sureties to indict me at the sessions, and I knew that the worshipful personages on the bench calculated on no slight degree of punishment, as the reward of my correction of Fitman's insolence.

The story of Sir Henry's challenge soon got wind. Those who had been my warmest friends saw something extremely agreeable on the other side of the way, if they met me walking; and remarks neither kind nor gentle assailed my ears as I passed the open windows of the club-houses in St. James's-street. Although I yet had not had the ill-fortune to meet my furious antagonist, I did not know how long it might be before he would return to town, I therefore decided upon quitting it; and driven, as it were, out of society, fixed my abode in one of the prettiest villages in the kingdom, between forty and fifty miles from the metropolis.

How sweet and refreshing were the breezes which swept across that fertile valley, stretching to the feet of the lofty South Downs—what an expanse of view—what brightness and clearness of atmosphere—what serenity—what calm—what comfort! Here was I, domesticated with an amiable family, whose hearts I could read, and whose minds were open to me:—they esteemed, they loved me—When others would oppress and hunt me from the world, their humble home was at my disposal.

My friends had been married many years, and one only daughter was their care and pride. She was fresh and beautiful as a May morning, and her bright eyes sparkled with pleasure as she welcomed me to the cottage; and then, I knew, what years before I had so much desired to know, but never yet believed, that she loved me. " This effect of my knowledge repays me for all that is past," said I; " now shall I be truly happy."

I soon discovered, however, that although Mary's early affection for me (for we had been much together in our younger days) still reigned and ruled in her heart, that I had a rival, a rival favoured by her parents, for the common and obvious reason, that he was rich; but the moment I saw him, I read his character, and saw the latent workings of his mind—I knew him for a villain.

The unaffected kindness of Mary for her old playmate, and the endearing good-nature with which she gathered me the sweetest flowers from her *own* garden; the evident pleasure with which she recurred to days long past, and the marked interest with which she listened to my plans

for the future, soon aroused in her avowed lover's breast
hatred for *me* and jealousy of *her ;* and although to herself
and the family his manner remained unchanged, I, who
could fathom depths beyond the ken of other mortals,
watched with dreadful anxiety the progress of his passion;
the terrible workings of rage, and doubt, and disappointment, in his mind. Mary saw nothing of this; and considering her marriage with him a settled and fixed event,
gave him her society with the unreserved confidence of
an affianced bride. And although *I* knew that she would
gladly have left his arm to stroll through the meadows
and the groves with me; that, which she considered her
duty to her parents, and to her future husband, led her
to devote a great proportion of her time to him. Still
he was not to be satisfied with what, he could not but
feel, was a divided affection; and gradually the love he
once bore her, began to curdle on his heart, until it turned,
as I at once foresaw, to deadly hate; and the predominant
passion of his soul was revenge on me, and on the ill-fated
innocent girl for whom he once would have died.

At length the horrid spectacle presented itself to my all-
searching and all-seeing eye of two " minds o'erthrown."
Mary, as the period fixed for their marriage approached,
sickened at the coming event; and too sincere, too in-
artificial for concealment, owned to me the dread she felt
of marrying the lover accepted by her parents: — there she
paused, but I knew the rest; and pressing her to my
heart, received from her rosy lips the soft kiss of affection
and acceptance. She had resolved to fly with me from
the home of her parents, rather than fulfil the promise
they had made. My prescribed ignorance of my own fate,
and of my own affairs, hindered my knowing that her in-

tended husband had overheard this confession. We had fixed the hour for flight the evening following that, on which she owned her love, and preceding the day intended for his marriage. The blow was too powerful for him to resist: rage, jealousy, disappointment, and vengeance, occupied his whole mind; and the moment that my individual and particular conduct was disconnected from his proceedings, I discovered his desperate intention towards my poor Mary.

That evening—the next she would be mine—that evening we had agreed that Mary should take her usual walk with her lover; and although he had appeared gloomy during the day, I had detected nothing in his thoughts which could justly alarm me; but when the evening closed in, and he by appointment came to fetch her for their ramble, then my power enabled me to foresee the train of circumstances which were to follow. The weapon was concealed in one of his pockets which was to give his victim her deathblow; its companion, which was to rid *him* of life, rested in the other. The course of his thoughts, of his intentions, was before me: the spot where he intended to commit the double murder evident to my sight. As she was quitting the garden to meet him, I rushed after her; I entreated, I implored her not to stir. I foretold a storm—I suggested a thousand probable ills which might befall her if she went; but she told me that she had promised to meet Charles, and go she must: it was for the last time, she said—she must go. Was I jealous of her?

"No, no, my sweet girl!" said I: "your life, dearer to me than my own, depends upon your compliance with my desire, that you will stay."

"My life?" said Mary.

"Yes, beloved of my heart!" exclaimed I: "your cruel lover would be your murderer!"

"Charles murder me!" said she, half wild, and quite incredulous: "you are mad."

"No, no; *I know it*," said I, still holding her.

"This is the height of folly," replied Mary, calmly: "pray let me go—I have promised—it will lull suspicions—am I not yours?"

"Yes, yes, and go you shall not."

"Tell me how you have gained this information," said she, "and I will attend to it."

"If you go, you perish!" said I. "Stay, and the rage which this desperate madman now would vent on *you* will turn upon himself."

"What a thought!" said the half-distracted girl. "I'll go this instant!"

"No, no, my beloved! What shall I say to hinder you?"

"Tell me how or by what means you have attained this knowledge, and, I repeat, I will stay."

I had the power to save her; by confessing it, I should preserve her, but I should lose my envied faculty, the object of my life—was there a moment to doubt?

"Mary," said I, "I have a supernatural knowledge of events—I surrender it—stay!"

At that instant the report of a pistol near the place of appointment roused our attention from ourselves; and running to the place whence the noise proceeded, we found the unhappy victim of jealousy stone dead, and weltering in his blood: the pistol intended to take my Mary's life was yet clenched in his cold hand.

From this moment my power was gone, and I began

again to see the world as my fellow-creatures do. Mary became my wife with the consent of her parents; and as I was returning from church, I saw, amongst the crowd before the village inn, my old friend in green, who accosted me with great good-nature, and congratulated me upon my enviable situation.

" Sir," said I, " I thank you; and I thank you for having, by some means inexplicable by me, gratified the ruling passion of my heart. In the ignorance of my nature, I desired to possess a power incompatible with the finite character of the human mind. I have now learnt by experience that a limit is set to human knowledge for the happiness of man; and in future I shall be perfectly satisfied with the blessings which a wise and good Providence has afforded us, without daring to presume upon the bounty by which we are placed so pre-eminently above all other living creatures."

" A very moral and proper observation," said my friend, evidently displeased with my moralizing.

" Where ignorance is bliss, 'tis folly to be wise."

Saying which, he turned upon his heel, and was lost among the throng.

I have several times since seen the old gentleman walking about London, looking as hale and as hearty as ever, but I have always avoided him; and although I have reason to believe he has seen *me*, more than once; by a sort of tacit consent we never acknowledge each other.

I returned to my home, blest with an affectionate wife; hoping for the best, profiting by the past, enjoying the present, and putting our trust in GOD for the future.

THE ALTERED RIVER.

Thou lovely river, thou art now
    As fair as fair can be,
Pale flowers wreathe upon thy brow,
    The rose bends over thee.
Only the morning sun hath leave
    To turn thy waves to light,
Cool shade the willow branches weave
    When noon becomes too bright.
The lilies are the only boats
    Upon thy diamond plain,
The swan alone in silence floats
    Around thy charm'd domain.
The moss bank's fresh embroiderie,
    With fairy favours starr'd,
Seems made the summer haunt to be
    Of melancholy bard.
Fair as thou art, thou wilt be food
    For many a thought of pain;
For who can gaze upon thy flood,
    Nor wish it to remain
The same pure and unsullied thing
    Where heaven's face is as clear
Mirror'd in thy blue wandering
    As heaven's face can be here.
Flowers fling their sweet bonds on thy breast,
    The willows woo thy stay,
In vain,—thy waters may not rest,
    Their course must be away.
In yon wide world, what wilt thou find?
    What all find—toil and care:

Your flowers you have left behind
    Far other weight to bear.
The heavy bridge confines your stream,
    Through which the barges toil,
Smoke has shut out the sun's glad beam,
    Thy waves have caught the soil.
On—on—though weariness it be,
    By shoal and barrier cross'd,
Till thou hast reach'd the mighty sea,
    And there art wholly lost.
Bend thou, young poet, o'er the stream—
    Such fate will be thine own;
Thy lute's hope is a morning dream,
    And when have dreams not flown?

L. E. L.

EPIGRAM.

BY S. T. COLERIDGE.

I.

I ASK'D my fair, one happy day,
What I should call her in my lay,
By what sweet name from Rome, or Greece,
Neæra, Laura, Daphne, Chloris,
Carina, Lalage, or Doris,
Dorimene, or Lucrece?

II.

—" Ah," replied my gentle fair;
" Dear one, what are names but air?—
Choose thou whatever suits the line;
Call me Laura, call me Chloris,
Call me Lalage, or Doris,
Only—only—call me *thine!*"

LINES

WRITTEN IN THE ALBUM OF ELLIOT CRESSON OF
PHILADELPHIA.

BY THE AUTHOR OF LORENZO DE' MEDICI.

From distant climes the stranger came
With friendly view and social aim,
The various tribes of earth to scan
As friend to friend—as man to man.

No glittering stones the stranger brought;
No arts profess'd, no wealth he sought;
His every wish one view confined,
The interchange of mind with mind.

What he the richest prize would deem,
Was friendship, kindness, and esteem;
What he could in return impart—
The same warm feelings of the heart.

Not his with selfish views alone
To trace his course from zone to zone;
His hope—to stretch affection's chain
From land to land—from main to main,

The various powers and virtues tell
In human heads and hearts that dwell;
In bonds of love, the race to bind,
And make one people of mankind.

THE VICTIM BRIDE.

BY W. H. HARRISON.

> " Your father hath consented
> That you shall be my wife; your dowry 'greed on;
> And, will you, nill you, I will marry you."—SHAKSPEARE.

I.

I saw her in her summer bow'r, and oh! upon my sight
Methought there never beam'd a form more beautiful and
    bright!
So young, so fair, she seem'd as one of those aërial things
That live but in the poet's high and wild imaginings;
Or like those forms we meet in dreams from which we
    wake, and weep
That earth hath no creation like the figments of our sleep.

II.

Her parent—loved he not his child above all earthly things?
As traders love the merchandise from which their profit
    springs;
Old age came by, with tott'ring step, and, for the sordid gold
With which the dotard urged his suit, the maiden's peace
    was sold.
And thus (for oh! her sire's stern heart was steel'd against
    her pray'r)
The hand he ne'er had gain'd from love, he won from her
    despair.

III.

I saw them through the churchyard pass, but such a
    nuptial train
I would not for the wealth of worlds should greet my sight
    again.
The bridemaids, each as beautiful as Eve in Eden's bow'rs,
Shed bitter tears upon the path they should have strewn
    with flow'rs.

Who had not deem'd that white-robed band the funeral
    array,
Of one an early doom had call'd from life's gay scene away?

IV.

The priest beheld the bridal group before the altar stand,
And sigh'd as he drew forth his book with slow reluctant
    hand:
He saw the bride's flow'r wreathed hair, and mark'd her
    streaming eyes,
And deem'd it less a christian rite than a pagan sacrifice:
And when he call'd on Abraham's God to bless the wedded
    pair,
It seem'd a very mockery to breathe so vain a pray'r.

V.

I saw the palsied bridegroom too, in youth's gay ensigns drest;
A shroud were fitter garment far for him than bridal vest;
I mark'd him when the ring was claim'd, 'twas hard to
    loose his hold,
He held it with a miser's clutch—it was his darling gold.
His shrivell'd hand was wet with tears she pour'd, alas! in
    vain,
And it trembled like an autumn leaf beneath the beating rain.

VI.

I've seen her since that fatal morn—her golden fetters rest
As e'en the weight of incubus, upon her aching breast.
And when the victor, Death, shall come to deal the welcome
    blow,
He will not find one rose to swell the wreath that decks his
    brow;
For oh! her cheek is blanch'd by grief which time may not
    assuage,——
Thus early Beauty sheds her bloom on the wintry breast
    of Age.

CLORINDA:

OR,

THE NECKLACE OF PEARL.

THE TALE OF A BYSTANDER.

I HAVE all my life been reckoned a very odd fellow by those who know me, and I am now about to extend that reputation amongst those who do not, by giving to the world a story of which I am neither the author nor the hero, and which, consequently, can give me no claim on the favour of the reader, either on the score of invention exerted or sympathy excited. So far from being able to preface the events I am about to record with the old classical *pars magna fui* boast, I must own at once, that the extent of my concern in them arose from the interest I felt in the fate of a young and valued friend of mine; and whilst the task I, for his sake, imposed on myself, of watching the progress of his feelings, brought me constantly into the society of one who was acknowledged, by all who knew her, as the most fascinating woman of her day, yet it was only reflected back through the influence produced on that friend that I felt the power of her attractions.

To account for a man, still on the right side of forty, confessing to so culpable a degree of indifference, I must premise one other word about myself, the nature of which will at once exempt me from any imputation of vanity in obtruding it upon my reader. The fact is, my personal appearance is, unfortunately, ordinary. It is not disgusting, but it is what is perhaps as unlucky for producing a favourable impression upon the fair sex, insipid and common-place to the last degree. It is not that it expresses any evil passions, but that it will not express any thing. It is no index to the mind. It is like the dial of a watch without the hands: though all the working of the springs goes on within, its broad unmeaning surface shows no sympathy with the internal action. It was once said by a very ugly man, that there was but half an hour between him and the handsomest. Probably it may have been so, but I have never found it; or, at least, this half hour is like that which a late and lazy man is said to lose in the morning, and to be the rest of the day running after. It is a start which I lost at my birth, and have been half a life endeavouring to recover; for I by no means gave it up without a struggle. My dress was always particularly studied: perhaps the care I took of this may have arisen merely from the fact that, during the daily penance which, in imitation of my companions, I felt bound to perform before my looking-glass, I preferred to direct my attention to any thing else that was there reflected, rather than to my face. I was by no means fool enough to be vain: but if I had originally been sufficiently deluded to indulge in any such weakness, a little intercourse with the world must have undeceived any one who was not a positive idiot; for though I was a younger brother, with only five thousand pounds in the world, the most cautious of mothers never objected to my dancing ever so often with any of her daughters, and the most jealous and watchful of husbands sauntered unconcernedly to the other side of the room, if it were only to me that his wife was talking.

It may be imagined that the attractions of such a state of existence were not so irresistible as to make me, under any circumstances, object to change it, and therefore I eagerly adopted the alternative proposed to me by my maternal uncle, who is a "trusty and well-beloved counsellor" of his sovereign, when, upon turning me out of one of his boroughs, of which I had long been the *locum tenens*, he suggested, at the same time as the Chiltern Hundreds, another place in one of our Mediterranean colonies, of which, if the duties were not better defined, the tenure was more durable, and the emoluments more certain.

It was from this time that I date my intimacy with Alfred Mowbray. I had of course frequently seen him previously in the common intercourse of the world, for he was at that time five-and-twenty, and since the period of his leaving the university he had been every where. But endless as are the changes of London society, where people get accidentally shaken together like the patterns of the kaleidoscope, perhaps, like them, never to meet again, it is chance, not inclination, which determines the degree of one's acquaintance even with those moving in the same circle as ourselves, and sometimes for a whole season I may only once have heard, at the other end of the table, the animated tones or the joyous laugh of Alfred Mowbray. Still, though knowing him so little, I always felt inclined to like him, by no means a common feeling on the part of a slight acquaintance towards one whom the world seems inclined to elevate beyond any thing duly ascertained of his deserts. As I knew him better, I found that the non-existence towards him of that feeling of jealousy which another in his situation would have excited, arose principally from an utter absence of affectation on his part, amounting almost to an apparent unconsciousness of his own success and popularity.

Such a position, enjoyed with such a character, was almost too enviable a lot to last; and the drawback upon it in his case was, that the activity of his mind, and the vivacity of his feelings, had already over-excited a physical constitution which, whatever delusive appearances of health and vigour it might boast, had an hereditary tendency to disease and premature decay.

As the only surviving child of Lord and Lady Mowbray, it may well be imagined that the first doubtful symptoms of such a description were anxiously watched by his parents; and though he himself would not admit that there was the slightest necessity for care, yet, in compliance with their earnest entreaties, he consented to avail himself of the opportunity of my impending departure, to accompany me to the shores of the Mediterranean, and pass the winter in a milder climate; and as the duties of my new office were not so urgent as to require a hurried journey, we agreed to linger together as long as we could.

A few days previous to our departure, I received an invitation to dine in Portman-square with Lord and Lady Mowbray. I remember, at the time I wished to have sent an excuse: Portman-square was to me an unknown land, and six a heathenish hour; but Alfred wished it, and I went. Lord and Lady Mowbray had lived much out of the world, and I had never seen either of them. Of Lord Mowbray, who is since dead, I have little recollection, except that he was a remarkably silent man, and that, during the few sentences he did address to me, I could not keep my eyes off his bald head, which was plentifully plastered with powder, and curiously intersected with the marks of the comb. But how shall I describe the impression Lady Mowbray left on my mind? She was an elderly woman, with an old-fashioned air, whom I had always heard reckoned a bore, from being little versed in the ordinary topics of conversation, and peculiarly precise upon those to which she had devoted her attention:—but how different does such a person appear when the subject on which she speaks comes warm from the heart! She was talking to me of her only son, from whom she was about to suffer a distant and anxious separation, and at the time I thought her quite eloquent. I was much, I own, surprised at the tone of unrestrained confidence with which a woman habitually so reserved addressed a stranger, but one whom she would no longer consider such, as being the person who was thenceforward to supply her own place about her son.

"There is one subject," she said, "on which you will naturally laugh at an old woman's opinion; and yet, my dear Mr. ——" I was just going to let out my own name, which I did and do mean to conceal. But I need neither confess that, nor repeat her precise words, the purport of which was, that, from a constant study of her son's character, she felt convinced that his passions were liable to much stronger excitement, and might consequently exercise a much more dangerous influence upon his conduct than one would have been led to expect from any thing that had been remarked under any of those transient attachments to which, in common with all other

young men of his age, he had been subject. "I had
once," she said, "more tranquil expectations for him"—
at the same time slightly directing my attention to a
pretty pale-looking girl at the piano-forte, whose timid
and stolen glances at Alfred I had remarked during dinner, and who, I afterwards found, was a rich ward of Lord
Mowbray's, the accession of whose fortune would have
been highly serviceable in paying off the incumbrances
on the family estates. "But," added Lady Mowbray, "I
have perhaps said too much on these subjects: there may
be dangers from which it may be in your power to guard
him, though I am well aware that much which it is
natural for a mother to wish, it is not easy for a friend
to execute."

I think I need not say any thing farther of the preparations for our departure, nor, indeed, of any of the early part
of our journey, which would not be at all interesting in
recital, though it was so much so to ourselves at the time,
as to induce us to linger on till we had postponed our passage of the Simplon far beyond the period at which it is
usually recommended to travellers to effect it. Accordingly, upon our arrival at Brigg, we had of course to
encounter the usual hospitable attempts to detain us, by
magnifying the dangers of the present moment. Amongst
other things, we were told that no tidings had been heard
of an Italian nobleman, whose impatience had induced
him to hurry his own departure, the day before, in his
carrettella, leaving his suite to follow, in his cumbrous
berline, and that the servants were determined not to
start till some intelligence was heard of his safe arrival,
for which we were advised to wait. But, as out of the
incessant chattering of some Italian women of the party,

we extracted the fact that a lady and infant, about whose safety they appeared most anxious, had braved the danger with the Marchese, this, joined to the fear, at that season not unreasonable, that the delay might be long, or the passage completely stopped, determined us to proceed at once.

We therefore started many hours before daybreak, to avoid the probability of encountering a *tourmente* on the top, to which one is most subject in the afternoon. It had been snowing all the day before, but was now a clear frosty moonlight night. After a bad attempt at a joke or two at starting, we both remained perfectly silent. The scene was altogether too novel for sleep, and yet there was something in the swinging see-saw motion of the carriage, as it slowly moved through the silent snow, which promoted, if not sleep, that equally unprofitable wandering of the thoughts, when one delights to connect, as in a dream, the most dissimilar images by the most whimsical links. I looked on the round masses of snow as they shone in the moonbeam, and thought of Lord Mowbray's powdered head; thence arose on my recollection Lady Mowbray, and her lecture on love, and her fear of its influence on her son. I then stole a glance at the handsome profile of my friend, and thought how lucky it was that I could not compare it with my own.

From the depth of the newly fallen snow, the ascent occupied much longer than had been anticipated; and one of the galleries having been choked up, delayed us some hours till a fresh passage could be cut. As we advanced, the symptoms of our having chosen an unlucky moment for the undertaking increased. The guides were

Y

evidently taking additional precautions to guard themselves against the coming storm; and the two or three
straggling mountaineers whom we met hurrying downwards, screamed out, as they passed, cries which seemed
those of warning, though their import was unintelligible,
as the rush of the wind stifled the half-uttered sound,
whilst it triumphantly bore it far away on its wings.

At length, some time after sunrise, the indefatigable
exertions of both man and beast no longer availed any
thing against the power of the storm, and the carriage
sunk on its side, bedded in the snow. Disregarding the
entreaties of our guides, we determined to try our powers
as pedestrians. For some time all our efforts only sufficed to prevent our being blown over; but a comparative
calm having enabled us to gain the shelter of a snowbank
to windward, we proceeded somewhat more easily, though
the denseness of the cloud in which we were enveloped,
prevented us from seeing, till close upon their brink, any
of the precipices by which we were surrounded. Unable
to distinguish anything through the impenetrable mist
which was whirling in ever-varying masses around us,
we still fancied that the sound of human voices in distress,
as of another party in advance, were borne down on the
blast. To this state of indistinctness and doubt succeeded one of those extraordinary gleams by which the
worst weather is, at that great height, momentarily
chequered, when the clouds, swept along by the eddy,
dive suddenly downwards into the valleys below. The
sun shone for an instant around us, and we beheld, within
a few paces, the figure of a woman with an infant in her
arms, leaning against one of the gigantic crosses which

mark the road, and which was half buried in the snow-bank which sheltered us.

I had lived all my life in the land of beauty; I had seen all its boasted fair ones in their happiest hours of pride and of conquest; but neither before nor since can I recall any impression at all to compare with that caused by the loveliness of her, I thus unexpectedly met in this extraordinary scene. Let no one impugn the impartiality of this opinion as to the personal appearance of her I then saw for the first time. Often as I afterwards encountered her, this is the testimony of one who never was, who never aspired to be, her lover. With the experience I then had of the world, I could not, even if we had been in that desert alone, have blinded myself to the folly and hopelessness of such a feeling on my part: what must it then have been when by my side stood Alfred Mowbray?

She did not notice our approach till we had advanced close to her, so completely did she seem absorbed in the care of the infant in her arms, which she had enveloped in all the protections against the cold which had evidently been designed for herself. Her own consequent exposure to the weather was painful to witness. Her plain black dress, the common morning costume of the country, would have left one in doubt as to her rank, had she not at the moment removed a handkerchief from her throat, to bind it round the rest with which she had already enveloped her child, and thereby given me a glimpse of the most splendid pearl necklace I had ever beheld. There was something singular in wearing such an ornament at such a time, which made me remark it the more, and I mentioned it afterwards to Alfred: but his attention had been better employed, and he had not noticed it. Upon

Alfred's anxious offer of assistance, she raised the most
beautiful black eyes I had ever beheld; and answered in
a voice, the tones of which, even in that snowy wilderness,

> " Came o'er my ear like the sweet south
> That breathes upon a bank of violets."

The most obvious mode of making ourselves useful
was evidently to procure some of those fur-wraps and
protections with which an Englishman's carriage is always
abundantly provided; and, leaving the lady in my charge,
Alfred accordingly descended rapidly towards the spot
where we had left our carriage. The gleam had now so
far extended as to enable me to perceive a group of can-
tonniers engaged in endeavouring to raise a half-buried
carriage, which I guessed at once to be the carrettella
we had been told had started the day before, from
Brigg. I marked at once a tall figure in a military cloak,
who appeared superintending the labour of extracting
the vehicle from the snow. He turned suddenly round,
and then descending immediately to the spot where the
lady and I were standing, she began to explain to him,
with, as it appeared to me, nervous anxiety as to how
he would receive the communication, that I, and another traveller, who were also ascending the mountain, had
offered every assistance in our power. Upon which, he
thanked me courteously enough in French, adding, at the
same time, a few words to her in Italian, which did not
seem to relate to me; though I could not collect their
purport precisely, having at that time much less colloquial
knowledge of that language than I soon afterwards acquired. The tone in which he addressed her was, however,
harsh; so much so, that I at once thought that none but

a husband, and that not a very contented one, could so address such a creature. He then took a hasty survey of my appearance, which seemed to satisfy him; for he entered into conversation, detailing the difficulties of the passage, and explaining the various accidents which had obliged them to seek shelter for many hours in one of the refuges. Alfred at this time returning loaded with cloaks and *douillettes,* my new acquaintance stopped in the midst of his detail, and the impression that the appearance of my young friend made upon him at first sight, did not, for some reason, seem so satisfactory as that, he had derived from mine. Whilst he was watching the air of interest with which Alfred offered to shroud the delicate form of the lady in some of the wrappers brought for that purpose, I marked the countenance of the husband (as I had already settled him to be), and was at a loss to account for the unpleasant expression which was then evident. I have since been disposed to attribute to some species of instinct, which must have led him to anticipate the future, the extraordinary degree of dislike he thus prematurely manifested.

The weather having somewhat mitigated, we determined to attempt to proceed. The lady, leaning on the arm of her husband, and still carrying the infant in her own, found her strength unequal to bear even her own weight many steps towards the carriage. Alfred offered to relieve her of her interesting burden. From most people such a proposal would have sounded ridiculously, and certainly, of all offices, I should have thought him least fitted for that of a nurse; but he never did anything in his life awkwardly, and upon this occasion he must have been inspired by the look with which she thanked him, as she transferred her charge to his care. From the time of consigning our new acquaintance to their carriage, and resuming our journey, nothing particular occurred: after difficulties of a tedious but not dangerous nature, we at length arrived at the inn of the Simplon.

Alfred had for the last few hours been suffering from an inflammatory attack, arising from cold caught during our exposure to the storm; and the next morning his fever was so high as to render the continuance of our journey that day out of the question. I found that our Italian friends were also detained, and should have availed myself of that opportunity to endeavour to improve my acquaintance with them, but I heard that the lady was entirely engrossed with the care of her child, whose dangerous illness caused their stay, and the husband evidently avoided me. I was therefore, in the absence of all occupation which could prevent its reaching me, obliged to overhear much of the gossip of their servants, who had arrived some hours after us, from which I gathered that it was the family of the Marchese di Montalto, a noble Genoese, who had been for some time on a visit to some of the Marchesa's relations in Venice: that she had been very anxious not to attempt the passage of the Alps at this late season with so very young an infant, which had been delicate from its birth; but that he had been urgent not to risk missing the carnival at Genoa, for which he had particular reasons for wishing to return. Of course I was unable at the time to understand many comments which they made in a foreign language, and which only reached me at intervals in a disjointed manner; but I collected enough to convince me that the Marchese di Montalto's was not a happy marriage, and that the establishment were, without any exception, warm partisans of the lady, who seemed universally beloved by them.

The next morning, my friend being sufficiently recovered to proceed, we were anxious, before starting, to take leave of our fellow-travellers; but were much shocked at learning that the poor little child, the object as it appeared of the undivided affection of its doting mother, had died in the night. This was, of course, not the moment to attempt to intrude, and we therefore hurried our departure.

A considerable interval elapsed before we again saw those we left behind us, during which interval it was evident to me that the meeting on the mountain had made a stronger impression upon Alfred than so transient an incident could have been expected to produce. It was not a subject on which he was directly communicative; but often when he again spoke, after any of those protracted pauses in conversation to which all companions on a long journey must be subject, I could trace, more or less distinctly, where his thoughts had been wandering the while.

After we had been some days settled in Genoa, we determined, in the absence of all other acquaintance, to avail ourselves of a letter of introduction to a house that was open every evening, ostensibly for society, but in point of fact for play. Knowing nobody, we were, of course, driven to the gambling table for our resource. I played cautiously, and left off much as I had begun; but Alfred, who entered into it with much more eagerness, was a loser of two hundred double Napoleons; an unusual circumstance for him, as he never was accustomed to play deeply, or indeed at all, if he could help it.

The next morning, as we were strolling through the

street of palaces, we met our Alpine acquaintance, the
Marchese di Montalto. He hastened to recognise us;
but his manner was completely changed towards both.
He now seemed to consider me but as an appendage to my
friend; and instead of manifesting towards Alfred that ill-
concealed dislike which I had observed upon the mountain, he overwhelmed him with civilities; invited us both
to his villa, from which, he said, he had only just that
morning come in for a few hours: added, how glad the
Marchesa would be to renew her acquaintance with a person of whose attention she retained a grateful remembrance, though the melancholy event which had immediately succeeded, and which still affected her spirits,
would prevent any direct allusion being made to our
previous meeting. I was surprised that the too evident
eagerness with which Alfred accepted the proposal did
not check the cordiality with which it was repeated; but
the Marchese seemed an altered man, and no drawback
therefore appearing to the pleasure which we anticipated
from our visit to the villa, we readily adjourned thither
on the morrow.

It was one of those delicious retreats with which the
neighbourhood of Genoa abounds, from without whose
fairy limits are banished all that, by recalling the changes
of the seasons, might remind one of the instability of
present enjoyments. Alike unknown here, those habitual
accompaniments of our northern solitudes, the rustling
shower of the falling leaves, that emblem of hopes that bloom
but to fade; and the obtrusive moaning of the blast, which
sounds as the key-note of cares that will be heard. Here,
on the contrary, even at that season which the calendar
calls winter, the blooming exotic and the triumphant
evergreen revel in their beauty and their fragrance even

to the margin of the ocean, whose sunny ripple rises but to meet them. Such a scene, so rich in the luxuriance of all nature's choicest productions, is peculiarly calculated to ripen and to foster the illusions of the imagination, or the excitement of the feelings; and such, I soon perceived, was the effect it produced on Alfred.

I say that I plainly perceived the existence of attractive sympathy between my friend and our fair hostess; but if asked to cite the first proofs, or to detail the progress, I then find the peculiar difficulty of the position in which I stand towards my reader. Were I the author of a fictitious tale, creating characters and inventing incidents, I could then move my puppets at my pleasure, could open with the point of my pen the inmost recesses of the heart, could expose on this page, to the most transient glance of the curious, thoughts which scarce were formed, and words which never were muttered; could make the most frivolous, or unfeeling, the fancied confidant of imaginary confessions, from the first hinted feelings of unacknowledged attachment, to the last lingering struggles of resistance to triumphant passion. But no such fairy fields are open for me to sport in: I have imposed upon myself the dry task of recording one or two events of which I was an eye-witness, and in placing before my readers the actual actors in those scenes, I can, of course, only guess at the nature of those feelings which led to them, and which the parties themselves could as little trace to their origin, as limit in their influence; but of which the peculiar character was to elude the observation of a third person.

True, in England, I have often seen flirtations which the lady has appeared proud to exhibit as the boast of the

ball-room, and the gentleman been pleased to hear re-
echoed as the jest of the club : but such was not the nature
of the attachment which unhappily subsisted between
Alfred Mowbray and the unfortunate Clorinda de Montalto.

During the period of which I am speaking, the most
unrestrained confidence was shown by him towards me
in all that related to his former life or his family concerns; but never did one single word pass his lips which
could be construed into an acknowledgment, nay, even to
a hint, that Madame di Montalto was other to him than
a common acquaintance. If, on her part, I attempted to
mark the progress of awakened interest, it was in no common-place appearance of *empressement*, no outward eagerness of manner, that I could trace its existence: my experienced eye sought its symptoms the rather in an unconscious absence, when addressed by him, of that natural
ease which distinguished her general deportment; a forced
and hurried acquiesence in his praise when absent; and,
when present, sometimes even a capricious avoidance of
his casual affinity, which, by the uninitiated, might for
the moment be mistaken for aversion.

In the meantime, I of course became acquainted with
much of the family history of the Montaltos. Clorinda's
father had, I found, as an officer in the French service,
distinguished himself much in some of the Italian campaigns, and having been killed at the moment of victory,
in one of Napoleon Buonaparte's last actions in that penin-
sula, his infant child was adopted as the protegée of the
Empress Josephine, and it was under the auspices of that
amiable and kind-hearted woman that much of her early
education was conducted. In the extraordinary vicissi-

tude of fortune of which Josephine was the victim, her
young favourite of course participated, though then much
too young to feel the extent of the change, when, after
having been the spoilt inmate of the most powerful court
in the world, she was restored to her native home with
only one solitary token of its splendour, that necklace of
matchless pearl which I had remarked the first time I
saw her. This had been a favourite ornament of her
royal mistress; and when the infant Clorinda had first
been received into the arms of Josephine, her little hands
unconsciously clinging fast to this string of pearls, and
appearing anxious to appropriate that of whose con-
ventional value she had as yet of course no idea, it had
immediately been transferred to the neck of the child by
its whimsically generous owner; with this injunction, that
she should never be seen without it till that eventful moment should arrive when "*qui l'emporte, le porte,*" or, as
it might be freely translated, "till he who wins it, wears
it;" meaning, probably, that she hoped that the recollection of her would always be present to the grateful
mind of her young protegée, to be superseded only by
that one great passion in a woman's life, which, she well
knew, sooner or later, is paramount to all.

When that caprice of fate of which Josephine was but
the first victim, had likewise involved all who had either
partaken in her elevation or promoted her downfal, the
deplorable change which this produced in the circumstances of most of Clorinda's relations, who had almost
all been employed in the French service, would, in spite
of her then budding beauties, have made the convent the
only resource for a person of her family and destitute
state, had not those, in whose charge she then was, fore-

seeing the impending crisis, with an eagerness which does their prudence credit, accepted, on her part, the proposals of the Marchese di Montalto, a noble Genoese. Montalto was young, highly connected, and supposed wealthy; what more could they desire? Whether his was a character which was likely to make their young charge happy, was an inquiry which, even in calmer moments, and with more time for deliberation, Italian guardians would have had the plea of custom for disregarding: but they foresaw the coming storm which was to involve them all in ruin, and therefore hurried the preparations for the marriage. The fact was, the game was a desperate one on both sides; and it was not the first time that Montalto, who was a professed gambler, had miscalculated the chances. He had, indeed, just then withdrawn, in disgrace, from the French service, on account of some discreditable transactions at play, and he thought that, through the connexion he was then forming, the influence possessed by his wife's relations would shield him from the consequences of any impending exposure. But the magnitude of the political changes which followed his marriage made his insignificance sufficient protection, and he found himself embarrassed with the charge of a beautiful but pennyless wife. It would be injustice to human nature to suppose him, or any one in his situation, insensible to her charms; indeed, an inconvenient, but an undeniable, proof that he was not so, might be found in the uncontrollable fits of jealousy to which he was sometimes subject, principally after the vicissitudes of the gambling table had too severely tried a temper which was originally none of the best. The passion for play, which never diminishes, had very much increased since his marriage:

he now seemed to look upon its produce as a principal source of income; he sought its favoured haunts in the German watering-places in the summer; and the varied attractions of the villa, which we were then enjoying, had, in fact, but one real object—temptation to play, on the part of the visitors.

It required but little penetration to discover, that it was to our visit to the gambling-table of the evening before, that we owed our invitation to the villa; and that the alteration of Montalto's manners towards Alfred arose from his expectation that he would be valuable as a dupe. Alfred seemed so far to acquiesce in this expectation that he played occasionally, and when he did so, certainly sufficiently ill to justify the anticipation of profit on the part of Montalto. But though careless of his money to a degree that must have contented even his host, my friend was not so prodigal of the precious moments thus wasted; and, accordingly, his visits to the faro-table became more and more rare, his walks on the terrace more protracted, and his habit of lingering in the private apartments of Clorinda more inveterate. To a person of Alfred's character, so easy a transfer of himself must have indeed been irresistible, when he could at once escape from the degrading familiarity, constant noise, and frequent wrangling, of professed gamesters, and could, under the same roof, shelter himself in so perfect a fairy retreat as was the boudoir of Clorinda. The invitations which I occasionally received to visit it, and of which I, of course, had tact enough not too often to avail myself, had enabled me to judge how congenial a spot it was for so perfect a mistress of the powers of fascination to exert her influence over one to whom her whole soul seemed devoted.

Opening upon the terrace, which overhung the sea, but sheltered with luxuriant shrubs of the sweetest fragrance, the outward charms which it derived from natural position had been enhanced by every effort of art to vary its internal resources. That Clorinda had here passed many solitary hours, might be inferred from its containing a choice and varied collection of the best works in almost all modern languages. If on the shelves were to be found a somewhat striking preponderance of those authors who have treated with favourable indulgence the illusions of the heart, there were not, however, wanting a judicious selection of those by whom right has been most powerfully enforced through the medium of reasoning. She was a passionate admirer of many of our northern poets, and was one of the few foreigners I ever knew who understood English so thoroughly as to do justice to the different merits of our standard writers, from Shakspeare down to Byron.

I never was told that Madame di Montalto had any pretensions to the character of an improvisatrice; yet, when she has been excited, I have heard, even in mixed companies, the full flow of her brilliant imagination, combined with the musical tones of her voice, and the sonorous cadence of her native tongue, have all the effect of poetical inspiration. But the native spring of such a talent rises even more from the heart than the brain; and if sometimes its spontaneous stream thus burst forth upon the flat and deadening surface of general society, what its power must have been at the fountain-head, and over him on whom were concentrated all the energies of its sources, I can only guess, but Alfred at this time knew and felt.

I have mostly confined what I have said of the cha-

racter of Clorinda to the outward attractions of person
and of manner, because at this time I knew little else of
it; but coupling what came even within the sphere of my
observation with what I had heard of her previous conduct, it was evident to me that her acquaintance with
Alfred formed a new era in her existence. Married by
her relations, as a matter of course, to a man whom she
had previously hardly seen, and whom it was impossible
she could ever love, she had never been inclined to adopt
the organized system of gallantry peculiar to her country;
and if she ever violated her conjugal duties, it would not
be under the strange sanction of objectionable custom,
but rather under some overpowering impulse strong
enough to set at defiance the forms of society. During
the months which preceded and followed the birth of her
child, she was described to me as having been amply and
innocently occupied first in the anticipation, and then in
the exercise, of her maternal duties; unfortunately for
both of them, the moment that bereaved her of this best
of feminine resources was the date of the commencement
of her acquaintance with Alfred Mowbray.

Perhaps it was not to be expected that one whose soft
nature seemed as peculiarly calculated to feel the influence
of love, as her personal attractions were to excite that
passion in others, should long be insensible to the devoted
attachment of such a person as Alfred. All I know is,
that even I, acting as I was the part of an observant by-
stander, whose very nature is to criticise and condemn,
could only feel provoked with myself that I was not more
provoked with them.

In the evident disgust taken by Montalto at the recent
conduct of Alfred, it might have been difficult to decide

which was the predominant feeling, annoyance that his
time should be thus employed, or disappointment that he
was not otherwise engaged; but it is probable that the
violent ebullitions of temper to which he was frequently
subject, were caused partly by the yearnings of a disappointed gamester, partly by the jealous rankling of an
unloved husband. Be this as it may, the failure, on his
part, of the attempt to inveigle Alfred into the mazes of
play, joined, no doubt, to the desire he now felt to interrupt the growing intimacy between him and Clorinda,
determined Montalto to break up the reunion at the villa,
and return to Genoa, where the separation between his
wife and Alfred might, if he chose, be complete, and the
indulgence, on his part, of his favourite passion much
more unlimited. As the approach of the carnival afforded
a plausible pretext for proposing this, we were all obliged
to submit, with more or less good grace in proportion as
we were interested in the continuance of things as they
were. Upon the return to Genoa, the first step taken by
Montalto to interrupt the intercourse between his wife and
Mowbray, was to give orders that the latter should not be
admitted within the walls of his palazzo. How this was
evaded by those who were most interested, I can only
guess; but I have reason to believe that the attempt to
separate them was not successful.

The first half of the carnival passed over without any
important event occurring, or, at least, coming within my
cognizance, but the last few days made unwelcome amends
for the previous calm. It was on the first of the series of
veglionis, or masked balls, which are given towards the
conclusion of the carnival, that, during the early part of
the evening, having no particular interest of my own to

attend to, I had been distracted with the variety of gay and motley groupes which surrounded me; but latterly my attention had become riveted on two figures who seemed to wander about unconscious of any other pleasure to be derived from the scene around them, than the opportunity it afforded them of being together. It was not difficult for me to guess, from the peculiar colour of the domino, which I had seen him select, that the man was no other than Alfred; and though the rich fancy dress of the lady was calculated rather to conceal the figure, and mislead as to the identity, of her who wore it, I still felt assured that his companion could be no other than Clorinda. After a while I lost them in the crowd, and having in vain for some time endeavoured to catch another glimpse of them, I left the ball with that vague feeling of disapprobation so common to the uninterested, cold-blooded spectator of an imprudence, sagely shaking my head as I went, in answer to my self-inquiry, "Where will this end?"

Feeling altogether too dissatisfied to think of bed as a resource, I went from thence to the cassino, or gambling-house, where they were still playing; on the threshold of which I met Montalto, who rushed by me, apparently much agitated. Upon inquiring of those whom he had just left, I found, that for some time his usual caution, and consequently his good fortune, had forsaken him; that he had been losing very considerably; and that this very night it was supposed that he had lost more than he was worth in the world.

This detail, differently coloured in proportion as the narrators had more or less shared in the spoil, was hardly finished when Montalto again rushed in, and, to my surprise, throwing upon the table the beautiful pearl necklace which I had never seen his wife without, offered to stake it for certainly less than it was worth, but apparently for more than those around him chose to risk against it.

I could only guess, that Madame di Montalto having assumed the dress she wore for the purpose of disguise, had, for the first time, omitted to wear an ornament by which she would at once have been identified; that Montalto, returning home in despair, had found her still absent, and that accidentally laying his hands upon the necklace, the thought had suddenly occurred to him of appropriating it, and thereby recovering his former losses.

His sudden return, his frantic manner, and the strange nature of the stake he proposed, had collected round the table, from every corner, all those who had retired either to count their gains or to brood over their misfortunes; but in vain he indignantly appealed to them against the cowardice of refusing to give him a chance of recovering his losses, when they knew, too, that, at the price at which he was offering that which he held in his hand, he was staking at least two, to one. Some professed not to understand trinkets, some would have been happy to accommodate him if it had been any thing in reason; but common prudence forbad their hazarding so immense a stake at once.

"Then take it piecemeal, if it must be so," exclaimed Montalto, "for I will have it out of some of you if I play bead by bead, and count them here till doomsday!"

As he thus vociferated, he was preparing to snap the string, and scatter around all that it confined together, when, from without the crowd, a voice was heard—

"Play—I accept the stake—the game is mine:" and

from behind those who at the sound of his voice opened a passage for him, appeared the figure of Alfred, still in the domino in which I had seen him at the ball.

Montalto shrank and turned pale at the sight of him, and attempted to draw back, muttering something about the stake being too large for which to trust a stranger. I seized the opportunity which this pause occasioned, to advance towards Alfred, and remonstrate with him on the folly of his proceeding. He only answered, "Were the fate of every oak in Mowbray Park to depend on this throw, I would risk them all for the chance of regaining from him that which he now holds in his hand."

Any difficulty as to the stake being obviated by the bank making itself answerable for Mowbray, our suspense was not of long duration—they played, and Montalto lost.

I, who had seen his former state of excitement upon much less provocation, was prepared for some unaccountable burst of passion at this, on every account, most severe blow of all: but, by a wonderful effort, he seemed to control himself; and, as he handed the necklace to Alfred, he only said, in an under tone, which hardly betrayed any inward emotion—

"You Englishmen, Mr. Mowbray, carry all before you: you have been, I perceive by your dress, amusing yourself at the ball. The colour of your domino does credit to your taste—it is beautiful, but singular."

Looking all the while steadily at the dress of Alfred, as if to avoid his eye, with a formal bow to him, and a passing acknowledgment of the rest of the company, he then slowly left the room.

The next morning, an English government courier

z 2

passed through Genoa on his way to ———, and brought
a long arrear of letters from home, both for Mowbray
and myself. The purport of mine was only what I might
have long expected: that it was thought I had delayed
long enough reaching my destination, and entering upon
the duties of my new office; and it was recommended that
I should take my passage on board the ——— frigate,
which was expected to touch at Genoa, and which I too
well knew had arrived in the roads the day before. This
was disagreeable enough, though it would have puzzled
me to give any reason why Genoa was a peculiarly desirable residence for me; but yet one hates to be ordered
to quit any place. Alfred's correspondence, however,
involved considerations of a more serious nature. One
letter in particular from his mother, mentioning Lord
Mowbray's declining state of health, stated, that as he
felt his end approaching, he became more than ever
solicitous about his son's marriage with that rich ward of
his whom I had seen in Portman-square. Lady Mowbray also added a hint on her own part, " that she feared
the young lady retained a stronger recollection of Alfred
than was consistent with her peace of mind:" she concluded, " with my best regards ɔ Mr. ———, who I hope
has not been unmindful of aɪ l woman's wishes—he
will know to what I allude."

Now, though the united e orts of a hundred friends,
acting at the instigation of as many old women, would
probably not have succeeded in at all interrupting the
course of Alfred's passion for Madame di Montalto; yet
now that I could foresee from it nothing but mischief
and misery, I reproached myself with never having at
any earlier period of the affair attempted to remonstrate

with him upon its inevitable tendency: for Clorinda was
not one of those to whom an intrigue could be the amusement of an hour, who could show themselves equally
expert in its conduct, and careless at its termination.
How different the nature of her feelings on the subject I
had that very day an opportunity of judging; for finding
that my presence at home was a restraint upon Alfred,
who was much perplexed how to answer the letters from
England, I strolled out, intending to call on the Marchesa. I was readily admitted, as Montalto had never
thought of extending to me the embargo he had laid
against the admission of my friend.

I found Clorinda occupied in folding up a small paper
packet.

" I was about," she said, after some hesitation, " to
send this to your friend Mr. Mowbray"—she now never
pronounced his name without evident agitation—" as it
is of value, and I am particularly anxious he should
receive it safe, which might otherwise be doubtful, perhaps you would take charge of it?"

After some indifferent conversation, which perhaps
she thought was conducted with effort on my part, she
inquired—" Mr. Mowbray is not with you? he is well?
is engaged?"—I informed her that he was engaged with
letters from England.

I always remarked that the mention of any communication from England caused her uneasiness, as reminding
her of the frail nature of the ties that bound him to her,
compared with the demand which, sooner or later, his
country would make upon him.

" These letters are of consequence?" she anxiously
inquired.

" They relate to family matters," I replied. " His
father is in a declining state of health, and before he
dies, wishes to see Alfred well married."

I cannot say what it was at the moment which induced me to give vent to such a gratuitous piece of
barbarity; for I knew at the time that there was not a
chance that Alfred would accede to the barter of himself
which had been proposed to him. But as the words
passed my lips, Clorinda dropped the packet she had
been holding in her hands, and I then saw that it contained the pearl necklace, which Alfred had probably
immediately restored to her, and which she, refusing to
accept from him, was now returning : the occupation of
recovering and refolding it enabled her to conceal any
further mark of agitation. She held in her hand a note
which the parcel had contained, seeming to hesitate an
instant whether she would now send it; but half muttering to herself, " No, I will not change in any thing," she
consigned the parcel to my hands, showing evidently by
her manner that she wished me to shorten my visit.

I have reason to believe that the precautions which
were taken, prevented her and Alfred from again meeting previous to the veglione of the subsequent evening. This was to be the last night of my stay in Genoa,
as the frigate was to sail the next day; and having consequently many things to arrange previous to my departure, I did not accompany Alfred as usual to the ball,
but went out first, settling to meet him there.

I had wandered till I was weary, bewildered with the
maze of masks, and deafened with the discordant shrieks
of merry voices; and, escaping from the glare of lamps,
had retired, in a contemplative mood, under the shade of

a portico, from which I looked alone on those external objects, on which the milder light of the moon exercised its tranquillizing influence. I had been there some little time, when I saw approaching the same rich fancy dress, and the singular coloured domino, which I had remarked together at the preceding ball. They had evidently purposely escaped the crowd, and I was so situated that I could not pass them without an interruption, nor could I remain where I was without the chance, at least, of overhearing what they said. Feeling assured that any unintentional confidence would only meet a friendly ear, I preferred, as the least evil of the two, remaining where I was concealed, in the shade of the portico. The lady appeared fondly clinging to the arm of her companion, whom she was addressing in a voice of entreaty. I could only at first catch parts of disjointed sentences, but her tones were plaintive, and she seemed referring to the subject of the English letters I had mentioned to her the day before. She dwelt on their recent vows—she enumerated their mutual protestations; asking what love could vie with hers, who for his sake would have —— or (I thought she softly murmured) *had* sacrificed all.

At this I could perceive that her companion's arm trembled with emotion; yet, to my surprise, he answered nothing. This unaccountable silence seemed to alarm her; and, in an earnest manner and a louder tone, every word of which reached my ear, she added—

" For God's sake, Alfred, speak! this suspense is worse than anything. Rather let me know at once that you despise and hate me."

" Know it then, and curse the knowledge!" was the answer of him thus addressed; whilst with one hand he tore off the mask, and with the other dragging Clorinda out of the shade of the portico, the light of the moon fell full upon the infuriated countenance of Montalto. " Know 'tis I who hate—I who abhor, despise, and trample on you!"

A blow was struck—I saw it—I heard it. Never shall I forget the sound; for if there is a sound that curdles the blood but to imagine, it is that of a furious blow struck against a woman. His victim fell to the ground, and his foot was raised to execute the last part of his threat, when I sprang from my concealment, and seized him by the throat. It was a grasp from which it required the efforts of four of his myrmidons, posted on purpose, to extricate him. I have never seen him since, but I am much mistaken if he will not carry to his grave the marks of that gripe. What happened afterwards I know not. I was conveyed by the slaves who seized me direct to the police, and accused of what all Italian governments consider the greatest offence, the excitement of a disturbance. The authorities, proceeding upon their usual principle of avoiding if possible the scandal of publicity rather than inflicting punishment for the sake of example, and finding by my passport that I was to sail the next day in the ———— frigate, had me conveyed on board that vessel in a government boat, without allowing me any further communication with any of the parties. It was only by accident that I heard that Alfred Mowbray, who had been by a stratagem of Montalto's successfully kept out of the way of the scene of the preceding evening, was also ordered directly to quit the Sardinian states. What was the melancholy fate of the unfortunate Clorinda I had then no means of ascertaining.

Painted by F. P. Stephanoff.   Engraved by Chas. Heath.

CLORINDA, OR THE NECKLACE OF PEARL.

Printed by McQueen.

Published for the Proprietor by Hurst, Chance, & Co. St. Pauls Churchyard, and R. Jennings, 2, Poultry.

With the tranquil inaction of the voyage came many reflections, which might have occurred to any one less occupied in the concerns of others, even during the progress of events in which, after all, I had no individual interest. I now sagely thought on the constant risk that attends, and the certain punishment that awaits, the course of unhallowed love, even under those circumstances which seem to render its indulgence most venial, and in that country where its career is least checked; but, after having made the somewhat tardy sacrifice of these acknowledgments at the shrine of injured morality, I could not divest myself of a feeling of unceasing interest as to the fate of those who had most offended against her laws; and ever as I lay between sleeping and waking in my cot, the moonlight scene in the portico would constantly recur. The convulsive shudder given by Clorinda when she perceived whom she had been addressing with such misplaced confidence—the sight, and, worse still, the *sound* of the blow which instantaneously followed—all recurred to my fancy, till I roused myself with the involuntary effort I unconsciously made again to rush forward to the rescue of the fallen fair one.

Arrived at my destination, I longed impatiently for further information as to those I had left behind; but I knew not how to proceed to obtain it. Of Alfred, as I before stated, I only accidentally heard, that he had been obliged to quit Genoa, but continued ignorant of the direction he had taken; I had therefore only to hope that, as he knew where I was to be found, he would volunteer a letter to me. Months passed, however, without my being gratified. Those who know any thing of the quarantine laws are aware how uncertain and difficult they make communications even by letter to all places under their control; and as I was so situated, I attributed to this, rather than to any carelessness on the part of Alfred, the absence of any intelligence from him.

The seasons had revolved, when, circumstances requiring my presence in England, I readily obtained leave of absence for some months, and embarked for Naples. The weary voyage being at length past, and, worse still, the tedium of the lazaretto also, I quartered myself at the hotel of the Gran' Bretagna, on the Chiaja, anticipating a better night's repose than I had been able to obtain either on shipboard or in the confined and crowded lazaretto. But in this I was disappointed. I had one half of a long suite of apartments, and next to my bedroom, and separated only by a single door, was that of an invalid, whose almost incessant attacks of the worst kind of cough were so painfully audible through the thin partition, and the increasing debility, which was apparent in his struggles during each fit, made me so completely aware of the disease under which he was suffering, that in vain I attempted to close my eyes to sleep.

" Why," thought I, " am I for ever placed in a situation to suffer as much from the misfortunes of others as if they were my own?"

In the morning I sent for the book containing the names of the inmates of the hotel. Almost the first that met my eye were those of Lord and Lady Mowbray. It at once occurred to me that Lord Mowbray could only be Alfred, as the last account I had heard of him whom I had known as Lord Mowbray, made his death much more probable than that he should have undertaken such a journey. Who Lady Mowbray might be, I had for a

moment vague ideas and fancies, till, looking for the
number of their apartment, I saw that it was next to the
one that marked my own; and the painful conviction at
once came across me that he, of whose illness I had through
the night suffered such painful proofs, could only be my
friend. I was confirmed in this by the waiter, who, on
my pointing out the name, described them as " Un
giovane malato colla sua madre." Unwilling to risk the
effects of a surprise, I sent my name in, meaning that it
should be given to Lady Mowbray; but it was carried
direct to Alfred, as his mother had retired to repose after
many a night's watchful attendance: for though I thought
that no sound in the next room had escaped me, I had
not been conscious that there had been one, with noiseless
step and prudent silence, administering to all the wants
of the invalid.

The conveyance of my name to Alfred produced an
instant request to see me. I found him so sadly altered,
that, but for the smile of welcome which lighted up his
features for a moment with their former expression, as
he received me, I doubt whether I could have recognised
him.

" This is what I most wished," he said; " and as you
see I must not speak much, I will proceed at once to what
I have to say. There is one subject which I cannot con-
fide to her, who, in every other respect, will faithfully
execute my last wishes—my mother knows nothing of
Clorinda!"

The effort he made to pronounce that name caused
him to pause a moment. I would willingly have requested him to believe, that it was, as yet, unnecessary
for him to give any directions as to his final wishes; but,

looking at him again, I could not conscientiously say that I thought they ought to be delayed.

" You," he added, " who best know how, in happier moments, and even to one of congenial disposition, I shunned all communication of what passed at Genoa, will not suspect that, at this awful hour, I am about to palliate the impropriety of my conduct; but, as necessity forces me to speak to you about it, thus much I must say, that it was no light temptation to which I yielded. I have felt the difference between the ephemeral fancies of my earlier days, and this one only passion of my exist- ence. Let others talk of the power of first love; the very name tells at once a hasty beginning, a comparative suc- cession, and consequent oblivion. No! I have felt the power, have fallen the victim, of that which, had my life been spared till age had withered feeling, had still ever been my last love !"

After a pause, he continued, " I have never heard of Clorinda since that night. Upon my return to Italy with my mother, I was already too ill to make any personal inquiries; and to whom could I trust the delicate task, when I had never confided to any one, even to you, the interest I felt about her? You will remember these," he said, drawing from his breast the string of pearls I had so often seen: " I feel my strength unequal to the task of explaining why I am so anxious that, upon my death, this should be by you restored to her. This note could tell"— producing at the same time, as I thought, the same note which had once before been trusted to my hands: " but no," he added; " there are words which no mortal eye but mine must ever see." He then pressed it fervently to his lips, and stretching forth his emaciated hand towards the fire, near which his couch was, dropped it into the flames.

"Why I wish, it signifies not; it will be enough for you, that your friend could, at such a moment, attach such importance to it, for you to endeavour to do what he could so desire."

He lived many days, and I saw him again; but had no farther communication with him on this subject: and I had begun to hope that, at the instigation of his excellent mother, his thoughts had altogether taken another turn; but I was soon taught to know that this had never been the case.

It was on the morning of the day which terminated his existence, in one of the struggles of approaching dissolution, that his hand was suddenly withdrawn from his breast, against which it had been constantly pressed, as I thought, from pain, and I marked, that it had there grasped a small locket of hair, which, as telling no tale to any other eye but his, he had preserved till the last, trusting that it could compromise no one, even when its discovery should be the consequence of his being no longer able to guard his own secret.

I followed my friend to the grave; and then set forward to endeavour to execute his wishes.

The journey was a melancholy one. External objects had no power to drive from my recollection the untimely fate of my young friend. But a few months since, and who would not have gladly exchanged lots with Alfred Mowbray? and of all the varied advantages he then could boast, youth, wealth, brilliant talents, fine feelings, what had they availed him? The warmth of his feelings had been the source of his misery; the captivation of his talents had but assisted to mislead and delude her who had been his victim; his youth had served but to feed disease; his wealth, to buy a stranger grave. And how sudden had been the reverse of all his hopes, bearing date even from that very time when all seemed most favourable to his wishes! On the morning on which we together quitted the gambling-table at Genoa, he with the newly-won pearls in his hand, I now remember he said nothing: his deportment was tranquil; but I never saw such an expression of conscious happiness as lighted up his countenance. The softer pleasures of the earlier part of the evening, allowing him to dwell on their promised repetition, had been enhanced by the peculiar nature of the triumph he had just obtained over him, whom he could not but hate: and yet, even at that moment, when all his wishes seemed gratified and the fondest anticipations for the future justly his, he had gazed his last on her he loved.

Arrived at Genoa, I made anxious inquiries at the palace of the Montaltos, and heard, in the first place, intelligence which did not much surprise me, that Montalto had been detected in some unfair dealings at play, had been consequently banished, and his property seized. But no previous fears I had entertained as to what might be the fate of the unfortunate Clorinda, at all prepared me for the shock I received, upon hearing that she was an inmate of the hospital of St. ——, a receptacle for the insane; her intellects having been decidedly, and, it was feared, incurably deranged, since the fatal night of the last masked ball.

I prepared for my visit with that vague horror felt by all on entering for the first time an establishment of the kind, when they have only read of those horrors to which some are subject. In this respect my expectations were fortunately not realized: it was a well-regulated establishment, being under the superintendence of sisters of a religious order. But the feelings excited by the scene I was about to undergo needed no external aggravation of circumstance. What availed it that I heard not the sound of the lash, or the cry of its victim? the sight of that key was enough for me, which gave the very ordinary-looking female who bore it, absolute control over the most gifted being I had ever beheld; and that such a creature should, even in her moments of consciousness, be subject to the caprice of those who could draw no distinction between the inspirations of her genius and the ravings of insanity!

As the attendant prepared to apply the key to the door, she turned to me and said, "You need not expect to be much shocked at her appearance, sir; she gives us little trouble, poor lady; she behaves very properly, and is very careful about her person, herself." Had I been told that I should have seen her chained, and in straw, I could not have felt a greater sinking of the spirits than at this familiar and degrading mention on the part of a menial, of her whose every movement was grace, and whose appearance was a model for imitation.

The first glance I had of Clorinda contributed to calm me. She did not appear so much altered as I had expected. Her dress was of a nature calculated to conceal the ravages which sorrow and disease had made in her well-proportioned figure; her long black hair, it is true, unconfined, hung down its whole length behind; but from off her beautiful brow it was, as formerly, drawn back, and simply parted: her eyes were bent downwards;

and she sat crouched in a corner, shivering with cold;
and from the manner in which she was intently gazing
on her own folded arms, it seemed as if she thought she
was still, as when we first saw her, nursing her child upon
the mountain.

"This," said the woman, "is the best fit to see her in;
she has other illusions less tranquil, and, I fear, less innocent." I thought that it would be well to endeavour to
discover if she would recognise me, by repeating the offer
made at the period to which her recollection seemed to
tend: "Can I be of any assistance to you, madam?" It
was the first external impulse her thoughts had received
for some time. At the sound of my voice she started up,
raised one hand to her brain, as if she there felt the impression of the sound, and then pushing me on one side,
grasped at vacancy beyond, saying, with a wild laugh,
which seemed the very antidote to gaiety, "Oh! so you
are come again, and without your English bride!"

From this time forward I cannot repeat—I do not like
to remember—what she said. She uttered every thought
aloud: some were piteous to hear; few were extravagant,
except in their unconscious avowal; yet though there was
not one which the most delicate-minded might not have
cherished in the secret recesses of thought, still, who
could bear that all their wandering imaginations, their
involuntary fancies, should witness against them, em-
bodied in words!

She spoke much, as if to Alfred, in ardent, impassioned
terms. I, who well remembered, whilst her sovereign
reason still held its seat, how sensitively nervous she used
to be, lest any symptoms of her preference should appear in public, could not bear the situation in which I

was placed. It seemed to me as if, by participating in this involuntary confidence, I was taking an unworthy advantage of her infirmity, and committing a sort of treachery to my friend, who, to the last, had kept his own secret. I therefore seized the first opportunity of a comparative pause in her ravings, to produce before her the object of my mission, the necklace of pearl.

The moment I silently placed it in her hands, she seemed to divine its import, exclaiming, "Dead—I know it—I saw it! He has been here, but now he's gone, for they've shrouded him in the snow, with my poor child!" One solitary tear dropped upon its rival pearls—I watched long and anxiously for a second—I should have hailed it as the symptom of returning consciousness, but it never came. Instead, her eyes gradually fixed on the necklace in a vacant, unmeaning, immovable stare. I often tried in vain to rouse her by words—they had no effect. I at length sought to awaken her attention by a change of external objects—I took my leave—she still stood in unconscious silence—I opened the door, and paused upon its threshold—still the same senseless stare—the door was closed, and again opened—still not the slightest symptom of a change—the case seemed hopeless—at last the key was turned—I never saw her more!

THE KING AND THE MINSTREL OF ELY.

FROM THE NORMAN-FRENCH*.

BY J. G. LOCKHART.

LORDINGS list a little space,
And I'll well repay your grace:
For of a Minstrel ye shall hear
That sought adventures far and near.
Not far from London, on a day,
As through the fields he took his way,
He met the King and his menée.
Around his neck his tabour hung,
Stamped with gold, and richly strung:
" For love now (quoth the King) me tell
Who art thou, Master Minestrel?"—
And he replies, withouten dread,
" My master's man, sir King, indeed."—
" And who, sir, may this master be?"—
" In faith, my mistress masters me."—
" And who thy mistress?"—" By my word
The goodly dame that is my lord."—
" What name, I pray thee, dost thou bear?"—
" The same that was my sire's whilere."—
" What name, then, had this sire of thine?"—
" The same, an't please ye, that's now mine."—
" Whence comest thou, merry Minstrel?"—" Thence."
" And whither may'st be passing?"—" Hence."—

* Recently printed by the Roxburghe Club.

" Speak plainly, man: whence comest thou?"—
" Why from our own good town, I trow."—
" Which town may that be, Master Quirk?"—
" The town about the minster-kirk."—
" What minster-kirk?—come, tell us freely."—
" The minster, sure, that stands in Ely."—
" And where stands Ely?"—" God us guide,
Where but by the water side!"—
" And how's this water call'd, I pray?"—
" Call'd! not at all, Sir; by my fay,
The water chooseth his own way,
And comes uncall'd both night and day."—
" All this we knew before, my friend."—
" Your wisdom, then, I can't commend:
To question, question like a barne,
When there was no need to learn."

   " So help me, Jesu! (quoth the King)
I'll ask thee yet one other thing.
Minstrel, wilt sell thy nag to me?"—
" More gladly, 'faith, than give it thee."—
" For how much shall I have the nag?"—
" For just the money I shall bag."—
" Is he a young one?"—" Well I wean
His chin hath yet no razor seen."—
" Speak truly—is he sharp of sight?"—
" Sharper, I think, by day than night."—
" Come, Minstrel, one plain truth declare:
Is't a good eater?"—" That I'll swear:
This gelding in a single day
Will eat more trusses, grass or hay,
Than you 'tween January and May."—

" And drinks he well?"—" Now, God us guard!
He 'll swill ye, by St. Leonard,
More water at a single draught
Than I in weeks, yea months, have quaff'd."—
" Is he a creature of good speed?"—
" A pretty question 's here, indeed;
Howe'er I spur, howe'er I thump,
The head keeps still afore the rump."—
" Now on thy conscience, draws he well?"—
" Good King, I scorn a lie to tell,
He ne'er was tried, for aught I know,
At either harquebuss or bow."—
" Nay, answer me—a truce to wit—
Is he an easy nag to sit?"—
" Conscience is conscience—I declare,
Less easy than an elbow-chair."—
" These answers (quoth the King) are folly:
Is the nag sound—completely, wholly?"—
" In truth, lord King, I must confess,
He hath small claim to holiness *,
Else monks and priests would dress him out
With trappings gay and fine, no doubt."—
" Tush! (quoth the Monarch) art thou raving?
I spake of staggers or the spavin."—
" Nay, (quoth the Minstrel) if he be
Afflicted with such malady,
He keeps his thumb thereon to me."—
" Knave (quoth the King) I value not
Thy ribald turns and quirks, a jot."—
" I 'd rather that thou did'st, by half,
For 'tis my trade to raise a laugh."—

* The quibble is on *sain* and *seint*.

" What art thou?"—" By our lord the pope,
No harm's in telling that, I hope:
I'm one of not a few whose trade
Is most to eat where least is paid;
As also, when a cup's in hand,
To sit more willingly than stand;
Especially if dinner's o'er,
For then one's heavier than before;
And to sport with dame or maid,
When the supper-table's laid—
Now, good my lord, I pray thee say,
What thinkest thou of a life so gay?"

  The King made answer: " By my troth,
To waste my thoughts I should be loth
On life and manners worthless both."

  " Sir King (quoth Minstrel, bending low),
Much to learn and much to know,
Sober life and solemn cheer,
What avail they mortals here?
It is as sound a proof of wit,
To gaily dance as gravely sit.
Be sad and still, as suits the wise,
'Tis cunning all in worldly eyes;
Be blithe, and gay, the envious race
Will pay your smile with,—*Babyface;*
But frown, and they'll exclaim, *What art
Can lighten guilt's uneasy heart?*
Be thou wealthy cavalier,
And eschew the tourney-spear,
Slander's tongue will not be dumb,
But hint thou art *A rotten plum.*
And if, upon the other hand,
Thou haunt high places in the land,

Heads as many shall be shaken,
And as dark suspicions taken.
Your courtly gallants, thus they speak,
Ride brave, and honest burghers break.—
If e'en the shoes upon thy feet
Be, as beseemeth, tight and neat,
They'll say: *I wis they pinch and smart,*
Much comfort to thy silly heart!
But if, perchance, they're old and wide,
One's ready on the other side
Who, with a grin of equal grace,
Shall whisper: *Blessing on his face,*
The kind good frere for charity,
That did his sandal shoon untie
And give to this poor passer-by!
If thou love the ladies dearly,
Praise and honour them sincerely,
Each ribald tongue is prompt to swear,
Yon rake betrays him by his air.
But if aloof thou 'rt seen to keep,
That will not set the fiend to sleep.—
If duly as the morn comes round,
In the confessional I 'm found,
Before the priest to speak my sin,
And pardon of the church to win,
One says, *Some prayers are starling-tricks,*
On such my hope I scarce would fix:
But if I pass the steeple by,
Another whispers, with a sigh,
Alas! to death some people jog,
As careless as my puppy-dog!
If sorrowing over follies past,
My soul I humble with a fast,

Says one, *What horror hath he done?*
Destroy'd a father? or a son?
Yet, if I never fast a whit,
This mends the matter ne'er a bit;
An open reprobate once more,
I'm *Curst of God, and clean given o'er!*
—O God! we live in such a time,
That keep us e'er so pure from crime,
We ne'er can hope to shelter'd be
From bold or coward calumny!"
  " Sir Minstrel, (quoth the King,) in sooth,
Jest when thou wilt, thou knowest the truth:
Here, hold thy hand, and take thy fee;
But ere thou go'st—one word with thee—
What art may keep a Royal Name
In uncalumniated fame?"—
  " Sir, (quoth the Minstrel,) thus say I,
Be nor too humble nor too high;
Too much of one thing, runs the saw,
Is good for nothing; make that law.
In Latin also down 'tis come,
Tenent beati medium."

Whoso this tale shall well perpend,
To him sound doctrine it may lend;
He, even he, God's truth may tell,
That doth wear the cap and bell.
And so unto an end I bring
The story of our lord the King,
And Ely's merry Minestrel.

EPIGRAM.

BY S. T. COLERIDGE.

Sly Belzebub took all occasions
To try Job's constancy, and patience.
He took his honour, took his health;
He took his children, took his wealth,
His servants, horses, oxen, cows,—
But cunning Satan did *not* take his spouse.

But heaven that brings out good from evil,
And loves to disappoint the devil,
Had predetermin'd to restore
Twofold all he had before;
His servants, horses, oxen, cows—
Shortsighted devil, *not* to take his spouse!

FINIS.

LONDON:
PRINTED BY THOMAS DAVISON, WHITEFRIARS.